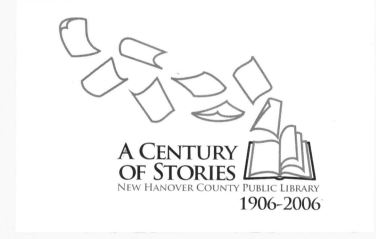

A CENTURY
OF STORIES
NEW HANOVER COUNTY PUBLIC LIBRARY
1906-2006

The
STOREKEEPER'S
DAUGHTER

**Center Point
Large Print**

**This Large Print Book carries the
Seal of Approval of N.A.V.H.**

The STOREKEEPER'S DAUGHTER

WANDA E. BRUNSTETTER

CENTER POINT PUBLISHING
THORNDIKE, MAINE

This Center Point Large Print edition
is published in the year 2006 by arrangement with
Barbour Publishing, Inc.

Scripture quotations are taken from
the King James Version of the Bible.

The text of this Large Print edition is unabridged. In other
aspects, this book may vary from the original edition. Printed in
Thailand. Set in 16-point Times New Roman type.

ISBN 1-58547-736-2

Library of Congress Cataloging-in-Publication Data

Brunstetter, Wanda E.
    The storekeeper's daughter / Wanda E. Brunstetter.--Center Point large print ed.
      p. cm.
    ISBN 1-58547-736-2 (lib. bdg. : alk. paper)
      1. Amish--Fiction. 2. Pennsylvania--Fiction. 3. Large type books. I. Title.

PS3602.R864S76 2006
813'.6--dc22

                                                                    2005028132

To Leeann and Birdie, my dear friends and critique partners. To Audrey, Marijane, Monk, and Melissa, who willingly shared their knowledge with me. Thank you all!

*Trust ye in the LORD for ever:
for in the LORD JEHOVAH is everlasting strength.*

ISAIAH 26:4

PROLOGUE

"Naomi, come! *Schnell*—quickly!"

Naomi hurriedly finished the job of diapering her two-month-old brother, pulled the crib rail up, and turned to face her younger sister. "What is it, Nancy? You look upset."

Nancy stood just inside the bedroom door, her green eyes wide and her lower lip trembling. "It's our *mamm,* Naomi. She's been hit by a car."

Naomi stood there a few seconds, staring at an odd-shaped crack in the wall and trying to let Nancy's words sink into her brain. Mama hit by a car? How could it be? Their mother couldn't have been in the road. Only moments ago, she had announced that she was going out to get the mail, and Naomi said she would change Zach's diaper. When they were done, they planned to meet in the garden to pick peas. The mailbox was at the end of the driveway, several feet off the main road. There was no way a car could hit Mama. Unless . . .

"Don't just stand there, Naomi!" Nancy shouted. "Mama needs you. We have to get her some help."

A chill crept up Naomi's spine, and she trembled. Mama had to be all right. She just had to be.

"Stay with the *boppli!*" Naomi ordered.

"No, Mary Ann's in the house, and he'll be okay.

I'm comin' with you."

With her heart pounding so hard she feared it might burst, Naomi dashed down the stairs and bolted out the front door.

As soon as she started down the graveled driveway, Naomi could see a red car parked along the shoulder of the road. An English man knelt on the ground next to a woman's body.

"Mama!" The single word tore from Naomi's throat as she dropped to her knees beside her dear mamm. Mama's eyes were shut, and her skin was as pale as goat's milk. There was a deep gash on the side of her head, and blood oozed from the open wound.

"I used my cell phone to call 9-1-1," the man announced. "An ambulance should be here soon."

Naomi looked up at the middle-aged man. Sympathy filled his dark eyes, and deep wrinkles etched his forehead. "What happened?" she rasped.

"I—was driving down the road, minding my own business, when I noticed an Amish woman at her mailbox. Never thought much of it until she dropped a letter to the ground. Then the wind picked up and blew the envelope into the road." He shook his head slowly as his eyes clouded with tears. "Sure didn't expect her to jump out after it. Not with my car coming."

Just then, Naomi noticed the letters strewn every which way along the roadside. Mama must have dropped the mail she had been holding when she was struck by the man's car.

"I'm so sorry." The man's voice shook with emotion. "I slammed on my brakes, but I couldn't get stopped in time."

Naomi squeezed her eyes shut and tried to think. How bad was Mama hurt? Should they try to move her up to the house? No, that wouldn't be a good idea. What if she had something broken? What if there were internal injuries?

"Is Mama gonna be all right?"

Naomi had forgotten her younger sister had followed her out the door. She glanced up at Nancy and swallowed hard. "I hope so. *Jah,* I surely do."

Sirens could be heard in the distance, and Naomi breathed a prayer of thanks. Once a doctor saw her, Mama would be okay. She had to be. Baby Zach needed her. They all needed Mama.

"Naomi?" Mama's eyes opened, and Naomi could see the depth of her mother's pain. "I need you to—" Her words faltered.

"Be still, Mama," Naomi instructed. "An ambulance is comin'. You're gonna be okay. Just rest for now."

Tears slipped out of Mama's eyes and trickled down her cheeks. "I—I need—to ask you a favor—just in case," she murmured.

"What is it, Mama? I'll do anything to help." Naomi took hold of her mother's hand, so cold and limp.

"If I don't make it—"

"Please, don't even say the words." Naomi's voice came out in a squeak. She couldn't bear to hear her mother acknowledge that she might not survive.

"That's right, Mama. You shouldn't try to talk right now," Nancy added tearfully.

"I must." Mama's imploring look made Naomi's heart beat even faster.

"If I should die, promise you'll take care of the *kinner*—especially the boppli."

"You're gonna be fine, Mama. See here, the ambulance has arrived now, and soon you'll be at the hospital." Panic edged Naomi's voice, and when she swallowed, the metallic taste of fear sprang into her mouth.

More tears splashed onto Mama's pale cheeks. "This is important, Daughter. Do I have your word?"

Naomi hardly knew what to say. She could continue to insist her mother was going to be all right, or she could tell Mama what she wanted to hear. Naomi decided the latter would be better. No use upsetting poor Mamm more than she already was. She would agree to her mother's request, only to make her feel better. However, Naomi felt certain she would never have to keep the promise. Her dear mama was going to be all right.

Naomi gently squeezed her mother's hand. "Jah, Mama, I promise."

CHAPTER 1

Naomi Fisher tiptoed out of the back room and headed to the front of her father's general store. She'd finally gotten Zach down for a nap and felt ready for a break.

"Since there aren't any customers at the moment, would it be all right if I ate my lunch now?" Naomi asked Papa, who was going over his ledger behind the counter near the front of the store.

"Jah, okay. Just don't be too long." He raked his fingers through the long, full beard covering his chin. "That new order of candles still needs to be put on the shelves."

Naomi's hand brushed against her father's arm as she reached under the counter for her lunch pail. "I know."

"Your mamm would've had those candles out already," he mumbled. "She'd never allow the shelves to get dusty, either."

Naomi flinched as though she'd been slapped. She enjoyed working at the store, but it was getting harder to help run the place. There was no way she could keep up with the chores she was responsible for at home and do everything Mama used to do, too. It wasn't fair for Papa to compare her with Mama, and she wished he would consider hiring a maid to help out. She squeezed the handle on her lunchbox. If only

Mama hadn't stepped into the road and been hit by a car. The bishop said it was God's will—"Sarah Fisher's time to die," he'd announced at her funeral.

Naomi wasn't so sure about that. How could Mama's death be God's will?

"I—I think I'll take my lunch outside if you've got no objections," she said, forcing her troubling thoughts aside.

Papa shook his head. "Schnell—quickly then, and eat your lunch before the baby wakes."

"I'm goin'." Naomi's sneakers padded across the hardwood floor. When she reached the front door, she turned around. "Papa, I'm not Mama, but I'm doin' the best I can."

His only response was a brief nod.

"I'll tend to the dusting and those candles as soon as I'm done eating."

"Jah, okay."

She hurried outside. Some fresh air and time alone would be ever so nice.

Naomi leaned against the porch railing and drew in a deep breath. Spring was her favorite time of the year, especially after it rained the way it had this morning. The air was invigorating and clean—like newly laundered clothes hung on the line to dry. Today the temperature was warm but mild, the grass was as green as fresh broccoli, and a chorus of birds sang a blissful tune from the maple tree nearby.

"It looks like you're takin' a little break. Is your *daed* inside?"

Naomi hadn't even noticed Rhoda Lapp heading her way. "I'm eating my lunch, and Papa's inside going over his books," she replied.

"I guess keepin' good records is part of running a store." Rhoda chuckled, and her pudgy cheeks turned slightly pink. "Them that works hard eats hearty, don't ya know?"

Naomi nodded and stepped aside so the middle-aged Amish woman could pass.

"You have a *gut* lunch now, ya hear?" Rhoda said before entering the store.

Naomi lowered herself to the top step and snapped open the lid of her metal lunch pail. Even a few minutes of solitude would be a welcome relief after her busy morning. She'd gotten up before dawn to start breakfast, milk the goats, feed the chickens, and then, with her ten-year-old sister Nancy's assistance, made lunches for everyone in the family.

This morning, when breakfast was over, the three older boys headed for the fields. Naomi saw the younger children off to school, and then she'd washed a load of clothes, bathed little Zach, and baked a couple loaves of bread. By the time Papa had the horse hitched to their buggy, Naomi and the baby were ready to accompany him to their store near the small town of Paradise. She'd spent the next several hours waiting on customers, stocking shelves, and trying to keep one-year-old Zach occupied and out of mischief.

Tears clogged Naomi's throat, and she nearly choked on the piece of bread she had put in her mouth.

Mama would have done many of those duties if she hadn't died on the way to the hospital. Mama would be holding Zach in her arms every night, humming softly and rocking him to sleep.

Naomi and her mother had always been close, and Naomi missed those times when they'd worked side by side, laughing, visiting, and enjoying the pleasure of just being together. Some days she still pined for Mama so much it hurt clear down to her toes.

A vision of her dear mamm popped into Naomi's mind, and she found comfort in memories of days gone by—a time when life seemed less complicated and happy. . . .

"Sit yourself down and rest awhile. You've been workin' hard all morning and need to take a break."

"In a minute, Mama. I want to put away these last few dishes." Naomi grabbed another plate from the stack on the cupboard.

"Let's have a cup of tea together," Mama said. "I'll pour while you finish up."

A few minutes later, Naomi took a seat at the kitchen table beside her mother. Mama looked more tired than Naomi felt, and the dark circles under her eyes were proof of that.

"Here you go." Mama handed Naomi a cup of tea. "It's mint . . . the kind I mostly drink these days. Hope you're okay with it."

"Sure, Mama. Mint's fine by me."

Naomi knew her mother had been plagued with

morning sickness ever since she'd become pregnant. She was in her fifth month but still fought waves of nausea. Mint tea helped some, although there were still times when Mama was forced to give up the meal she'd eaten.

Mama leaned over and brushed a strand of hair away from Naomi's face, where it had come loose from her bun. "I'm awful sorry you have to work hard and have so many extra chores now. If I were feelin' better, I'd do more myself, but this awful tiredness and stomach rollin' has really got me down."

Naomi touched her mother's hand. "It's okay."

"You sure?"

She nodded in reply.

"But a girl your age should be goin' to singings and other young people's functions, not doing double chores and waitin' on her old mamm."

Naomi fought to keep her emotions under control. She did wish there was time to do more fun things, but this was only temporary. Once Mama had the baby and regained her strength, everything would be as it once was. She'd be able to attend social functions with others her age, someday she would be courted, and then marriage would follow. Naomi could wait awhile. It wouldn't be so long.

The unmistakable *clip-clop, clip-clop* of a horse and buggy pulling into the store's parking lot brought Naomi back to the present. Caleb Hoffmeir, the young buggy maker, stepped down from his open carriage and waved. She lifted her hand in response.

As Caleb sauntered up the porch steps, his blue eyes twinkled; and when he smiled, the deep dimple in his right cheek was more pronounced. He flopped onto the step beside her. "It's a *wunderbaar* fine day, wouldn't you say?"

His face was inches from hers, and she could feel his warm breath against her cheek. Naomi shivered, despite the warmth of the sun's rays. "Jah, it is a wonderful day."

"Did ya hear there's gonna be a singin' out at Daniel Troyer's place this Sunday evening?"

Her heart clenched, but she merely shrugged in response. She was eighteen years old the last time she attended a singing.

Caleb lifted his straw hat, raked his fingers through his thick blond hair, and cleared his throat a couple times. "You—uh—think ya might be goin' to the singing, Naomi?"

She shook her head, feeling as though a heavy weight rested on her chest.

"Was is letz do?" he questioned.

Naomi sniffed deeply. "Nothin's wrong here, except I won't be goin' to no singing. Not this Sunday—and probably never."

Caleb raised his eyebrows. "Why not? You haven't been to one since long before your mamm died. Don't ya think it's about time?"

"Somebody's gotta feed the kinner and see that they're put to bed."

16

He grunted. "Can't your daed do that?"

"Papa's got other chores to do." Naomi squeezed her eyes shut and thought about the way her father used to be. He wasn't always cranky and out of sorts. He didn't shout orders or come across as overly critical. He used to be more easygoing and congenial. Everything had changed since Mama died—including Papa.

"Abraham could surely let you go to one little singing," Caleb persisted.

Naomi looked up at him, and Caleb leveled her with a look that went straight to her heart. Did he feel her pain? Did Caleb Hoffmeir have any idea how tired she was? She placed the lunch pail on the step and wrapped her hands around her knees, clutching the folds of the long green dress that touched her ankles.

Caleb gently touched her arm, and the tiny lines around his eyes deepened. "I was hopin' if you went to the singing, I could take you home afterwards."

Naomi's eyes filled with unwanted tears. She longed to go to singings and young people's gatherings. She yearned to have fun with others her age or take leisurely rides in someone's courting buggy. "Papa would never allow me to go."

Caleb stood. "I'll ask him."

"*Nee*—no! That's not a good idea."

"Why not?"

"Because it might make him mad. Papa's awful protective, and he believes my place is at home with him and the children."

"We'll see about that. If Abraham gives his permission for you to go to the singing, you'd better plan on a ride home in my courtin' buggy."

Courtin' buggy? Did Caleb actually believe they could start courting? It wasn't likely to happen because Naomi had so many responsibilities. Truth be told, Naomi felt confused whenever she was around Caleb. His good looks and caring attitude appealed to her. But if she couldn't go to singings and other young people's functions, it wasn't likely she'd ever be able to court.

"Maybe I should talk to Papa about this myself," she murmured.

Caleb shook his head. "I'd like to try if ya don't mind."

Naomi's heartbeat quickened. Did she dare hope her daed might give his consent? "Jah, okay. I'll be prayin'."

Caleb glanced over his shoulder. Naomi sat with her head bowed and her hands folded in her lap. She looked so beautiful there with the sun beating down on the white *kapp* perched on her head. The image of her oval face, golden brown hair, ebony eyes, and that cute upturned nose brought a smile to his face. He'd taken a liking to Naomi when they were kinner, but during their teen years, he'd been too shy to let her know. Now that he'd finally worked up the nerve, Caleb didn't know if they'd ever have the chance to court, what with Naomi being so busy with her family and all. He wasn't sure if Naomi returned his feelings, either, but he'd never know if they couldn't find a way to spend time alone.

He pulled the door open with a renewed sense of determination.

When Caleb stepped into the room, he spotted the tall, brawny storekeeper stocking shelves with bottles of kerosene. *"Gude mariye."*

Abraham nodded. "I'd say 'good morning' back, but it's nearly noontime."

Caleb felt a penetrating heat creep up the back of his neck and spread quickly to his face. "Guess you're right about that."

"How's your daed?" Abraham asked.

"He's gut."

"And your mamm?"

"Doin' well." Caleb rubbed his sweaty palms along the sides of his trousers.

"What can I do for you?" the storekeeper asked, moving toward the wooden counter near the front of his store.

Caleb prayed he would have the courage to ask the question uppermost on his mind. "I was wonderin'—"

"I just got in a shipment of straw hats," Abraham blurted out. "Looks like the one you're wearin' has seen better days."

Caleb touched the brim of the item in question. It was getting kind of ragged around the edges, but there were no large holes. He could probably get another year's wear out of the old hat if he had a mind to. "I—uh—am not lookin' to buy a new hat today." Caleb hoped his voice sounded more confident than he felt, because his initial presentation had dissolved like a block of ice on a hot summer day.

Abraham raised his bushy dark eyebrows and gave his brown beard a couple of tugs. "What are ya needin' then?"

"There's to be a singin' this Sunday night in Daniel Troyer's barn."

"What's that got to do with me?" Abraham yawned and leaned his elbows on the counter.

"It doesn't. I mean, it does in one way." Caleb shuffled his boots against the hardwood planks. He was botching things up and felt powerless to stop himself from acting like a self-conscious schoolboy. After all, he was a twenty-two-year-old man who built and repaired buggies for a living. Abraham Fisher probably thought he was *letz in der belskapp;* and truth be told, at this moment, Caleb felt like he was a little off in the head.

"Which is it, son?" the older man asked. "Does your bein' here have something to do with me or doesn't it?"

Caleb steadied himself against the front of the counter and leveled Abraham with a look he hoped would let the man know he meant business. "I'm wonderin' if Naomi can go to that singing."

Abraham's frown carved deep lines in his forehead. "Naomi's mamm died nearly a year ago, ya know."

Caleb nodded.

"Ever since the accident, it's been Naomi's job to

look after the kinner."

"I understand that, but—"

Abraham brushed his hand across the wooden counter, sending several pieces of paper sailing to the floor. "It ain't polite to interrupt a man when he's speakin'."

"I—I'm sorry," Caleb stammered. Things weren't going nearly as well as he'd hoped.

"As I was saying . . . Naomi's job is to take care of her brothers and sisters, and she also helps here at the store."

Caleb nodded once more.

"There's only so many hours in a day, and there ain't time enough for Naomi to be socializin'." Abraham's stern look set Caleb's teeth on edge. "You might have plans to court my daughter, but the truth is, she ain't right for you, even if she did have time for courtin'."

"Don't ya think that ought to be Naomi's decision?" Caleb clenched his fists, hoping the action would give him added courage.

"Anything that concerns one of my kinner is my business." Abraham leaned across the counter until his face was a few inches from Caleb's.

If Caleb hadn't known Amish were not supposed to engage in fighting, he would have feared Naomi's father was getting ready to punch him in the nose. But that was about as unlikely as a sow giving birth to a calf. If Abraham was capable of anything, it would probably involve talking with Caleb's father, which, in turn, could end up being a thorough tongue-lashing.

Pop had plenty of rules for Caleb and his brothers to follow. He often said as long as his children lived under his roof, he expected them to obey him and be well mannered.

Caleb figured he would have to watch his tongue with Abraham Fisher, but maybe it was time to take a stand. How could he expect Naomi to respect him if he wasn't willing to try for the right to court her?

"If Naomi started attending singings again, first thing ya know, she'd be wantin' to court," Abraham continued. "Then gettin' married would be her next goal. I'd be left with a passel of youngsters to raise by myself if I let that happen." Abraham made a sweeping gesture with his hand. "Who would mind the store if I was at home cookin', cleanin', and all?"

"Have you thought about getting married again or even hiring a *maad?*"

"Don't need no maid when I've got Naomi. And as far as me marryin' again, there ain't no one available in our community right now, except for a couple of women young enough to be my daughter." The man grunted. "Some men my age think nothin' of takin' a child bride, but not Abraham Fisher. I've got more dignity than that!"

Caleb opened his mouth to comment, but Naomi's father cut him off. "Enough's been said. Naomi's not goin' to that singing on Sunday." Abraham pointed to the door. "Now if you didn't come here to buy anything, you'd best be on your way."

All sorts of comebacks flitted through Caleb's mind,

but he remained silent. No use getting the man more riled. He would bide his time, and when the opportunity afforded itself, Caleb hoped to have the last word where the storekeeper's daughter was concerned.

CHAPTER 2

Naomi had just taken a bite from her apple when the screen door creaked open. She looked over her shoulder and saw Caleb exit the store. The scowl on his face told Naomi things probably hadn't gone well with Papa, and a sense of disappointment crept into her soul.

"He said no, didn't he?" Naomi whispered when Caleb slumped to the step beside her.

"Your daed is the most stubborn man I've ever met." He shrugged. "Of course, my pop's runnin' him a close second."

"Matthew says Papa's overprotective 'cause he cares." She blinked against the tears flooding her eyes. Truth be told, Naomi wasn't sure her father cared about her at all. If he did, then why had he been keeping it to himself? Not once in the last year had he said he loved her or appreciated all the work she did.

"I'm thinkin' your daed saying no to my request has more to do with his own selfish needs than it does with him carin'. Tell that to your oldest brother."

Naomi tossed what was left of her apple into the

lunch pail and slammed the lid shut. "Papa's not bein' selfish. He's hurting because Mama died."

Caleb crossed his arms. "That was a whole year ago, Naomi. Don't ya think it's time your daed got on with his life?"

"When Mama was alive, Papa used to be fun-loving and carefree. He'd joke around with the brothers and tease me and the sisters sometimes, too." Remembering how happy she used to be, Naomi fought to control her emotions. Things were all mixed up now that she was trying to fill her mother's shoes. Life had been much better before Naomi's mother got pregnant with Zach. It had come as a surprise to everyone in the family because Mama was forty-two years old and hadn't had any children since Mary Ann was born six years ago. All during her mother's pregnancy, she'd been sickly. Naomi's only consolation was her confidence that the dear woman was in heaven with Jesus, happy and healthy, no more cares of the world—cares Naomi now shouldered.

"Ain't ya got nothin' to say about all this?"

Caleb's question drew Naomi's thoughts aside, and she turned to look at him. "What's to be said? My daed won't let me go to the singin', I've gotta take care of my family, and I have a store to help run." She grabbed her lunch pail and stood. "I'd best be getting back to work before Papa comes lookin' for me."

Caleb scrambled to his feet and positioned himself between Naomi and the door. "There has to be some way we can make your daed listen to reason. I want to court you, Naomi."

She hung her head. "Maybe you should find someone else to court, 'cause it doesn't look like I'll ever be free. Leastways, not 'til all the kinner are old enough to fend for themselves."

Caleb lifted her chin with his thumb. "I care for you."

Naomi's throat constricted. She cared for Caleb, too, but what was the point in saying so when they couldn't court? Too many problems plagued her mind already. She didn't need one more. "You'd better find someone else." She pushed past him and hurried into the store.

Naomi found Papa kneeling on the floor, holding a sheet of paper, with several more lying next to his knee. He looked up, and a deep frown etched his forehead. "I'm glad you're back. I think I heard the baby fussin'."

She glanced at the door to the back room and tipped her head. She didn't hear anything. Not even a peep out of Zach. Naomi was tempted to mention that to Papa but thought better of it. "I'll go check on the boppli."

A few seconds later, Naomi stepped into the room used for storage. The baby's playpen, a rocking chair, and a small couch were also kept there. Sometimes, when there weren't many customers, Papa liked to lie down and take a nap, which was usually whenever Zach was sleeping.

Naomi liked those moments when she could be by herself. It gave her a chance to daydream about how she wished her life could be. If an English customer came into the store, she worried about her father scrutinizing everything she said or did. Naomi often wondered if Papa was afraid something an Englisher might say would cause her to become dissatisfied with their way of life and turn worldly.

She remembered the last time Virginia Meyers dropped by. Papa hovered around, acting like a mother hen protecting her young. Virginia, who liked to be called "Ginny," came into the store at least once a week, sometimes to buy rubber stamps, other times just to look around. Naomi and Ginny were about the same age and had struck up a friendship, although Naomi was careful not to let Papa know.

She stared at the playpen where her little brother lay sleeping. He looked so peaceful, lying on his side, curled into a fetal position. One hand rested against his rosy cheek, a lock of russet-colored hair lay across his forehead, and the tiny little birthmark behind his right ear seemed to be winking at Naomi. "Sleep well, little one, and enjoy your days of untroubled babyhood," Naomi whispered. "Soon you'll grow up and see life for what it really is—all work and no play."

Tears clouded Naomi's vision. *Oh, Lord, You know I love my family and want to keep my promise to Mama, but sometimes it's ever so hard.*

If there were someone to help on a regular basis, Naomi's burdens might be a bit lighter. Her maternal grandparents were both dead, and Papa's folks had moved to an Amish settlement in Indiana several years ago to be near their daughter Carolyn. They were both ailing now, so even if they had lived close, Grandma Fisher wouldn't be much help to Naomi. Many of the women in their community offered assistance after Mama died, but they had their own families to care for, and Naomi knew she couldn't continually rely on others. Looking after the family was her job, and even though she was exhausted, she would do it for as long as necessary.

Naomi swiped at the moisture on her cheeks. *Nobody understands how I feel.*

Naomi was twenty years old. She should be married and starting a family of her own by now. Her friends Grace and Phoebe had gotten married last fall. Naomi had been asked to be one of Phoebe's attendants, and it was a painful reminder that her chance at love and marriage might never come.

Drawing in a deep breath and forcing her pain aside, Naomi slipped quietly out of the room. Zach was obviously not ready to wake from his nap, and she had plenty of work to do. There was no more time for reflections.

Abraham Fisher glanced at his daughter when she entered the room. It was clear by her solemn expression that Naomi was unhappy. No doubt Caleb had told her what had been said in regard to the singing. He grabbed the broom and gave the floor a few brisk sweeps. Naomi didn't understand. No one did. Life held little joy for Abraham since Sarah died. Even though Zach's first birthday last Saturday had been a happy occasion, it was also a painful reminder that ten months ago the baby's mother had gone to heaven, leaving Abraham with a broken heart and eight kinner in his charge. He couldn't care for them alone, and he relied on Naomi's help.

Naomi strolled past him without a word. She reached under the counter, grabbed a dust rag, and started working on the shelves near the front of the store.

"Where's Zach?" he called to her.

"Still sleeping."

"Oh. I thought I heard him cryin'."

"Nope."

"Guess maybe I'm hearin' things in my old age."

"You're not old, Papa."

Abraham pushed the broom back and forth. "Forty-four's old enough. Don't get nearly as much done as I used to."

"Mama was a big help, wasn't she?" Naomi asked.

"Jah, she was. Your mamm loved workin' at the store. Since this place used to belong to her folks, she grew up helpin' here."

"Do you ever wish you were doing something other than working at the store six days a week?"

Naomi's question startled Abraham. Did she know what was on his mind? Had she guessed he wasn't happy running the store? Truth of the matter, he'd much prefer to be at home farming with his boys than stocking shelves all day or dealing with the curious English who often visited the store.

"Papa, did ya hear what I asked?"

He nodded and grabbed the dustpan he had leaned against the front of the counter. "Jah, I heard. Just thinkin'; that's all."

"Mind if I ask what you were thinking about?"

Abraham did mind. He didn't want to talk about an impossible dream. He was committed to running the store. It was the least he could do to preserve his late wife's memory. "Just remembering how things were when your mamm was alive."

Naomi didn't say anything. He figured she probably missed her mother as much as he missed his wife of twenty-five years. Their marriage had been good, and God had blessed their union with eight beautiful children. Things had gone fairly well until Sarah's life had been snuffed out like a candle in the breeze.

Wish it had been me God had taken, Abraham thought painfully. Truth was, he'd blamed himself for Sarah's death. If he hadn't closed the store that day last June and gone fishing with his friend, Jacob Weaver, his precious wife might still be alive. If he hadn't suggested Naomi stay home from the store and help her mamm in the garden, Sarah probably wouldn't have gone to the mailbox.

During the two months of Sarah's recuperation from Zach's birth, she hadn't worked at the store. Abraham had insisted she stay home and take it easy. Up until the fateful day of her death, someone else had always

29

gotten the mail. Sarah probably felt since Naomi was there to watch the baby and the younger ones, it would be fine for her to take a walk to the mailbox.

He thought about the way Jacob had helped him work through his grief as well as the guilt he felt. Yet, there were still moments when Abraham berated himself for going fishing, and he'd not gone again since Sarah died.

Didn't God care how much I loved that woman?

Abraham thought about Caleb Hoffmeir's suggestion that he find another wife. The young man hadn't been the first person to recommend he remarry. Several of his friends, including Jacob Weaver, had also made such a remark.

"There will always be a place in your heart for Sarah," Jacob said the other day, "but takin' another wife would be good for you as well as the children."

Abraham squeezed the broom handle. *No, I can't bring myself to marry a woman merely to look after my children. There has to be love, and I doubt I could ever care for anyone the way I cared for Sarah.* He swept the dirt into the dustpan and dumped it in the wastepaper basket. *As I told Caleb earlier, there ain't no available widows in the area right now, and I'm not about to court some young, single woman, the way I've seen others do.*

Feeling a sudden need for some fresh air, Abraham leaned the broom against the wall and grabbed his straw hat from the wooden peg by the front door. "I'm goin' out to run a couple errands," he announced. "Can ya manage okay by yourself for a while?"

Naomi nodded. "Sure, Papa. I'll be fine."

"See you soon then."

Caleb was halfway home before he remembered that he'd planned to stop by the bookstore in Paradise to see if the book he'd ordered on antique buggies had come in. Besides working on Amish buggies, Caleb had recently expanded his business to include building and restoring old carriages. It hadn't taken long for word to get out, and he'd already built some finely crafted buggies for folks as far away as the state of Oregon. Caleb made a fairly good living, and he'd even hired two of his younger brothers to help when things got busy. He knew he could easily support a wife and a family, and he wanted that wife to be Naomi Fisher.

"Maybe I should set my feelings for the store-keeper's daughter aside and find someone else to court like Naomi suggested," Caleb muttered. It made sense, but it wasn't what he wanted. He had been interested in Naomi for a long time. He remembered the exact moment he'd known she was the one he wanted to marry. . . .

"Somebody, come quick! There's a kitten stuck up there." Ten-year-old Naomi Fisher pointed to the maple tree in their schoolyard. Sure enough, there was a scraggly white cat perched on one of the branches, meowing for all it was worth.

"Ah, it's just a dumb cat, and if it climbed up there,

it can sure enough find its way back down," Aaron Landis said with a smirk.

Caleb was tempted to climb the tree and rescue the kitten, but recess was nearly over, and their teacher would be ringing the bell any second. Besides, Aaron was probably right about the kitten being able to come down on its own.

Naomi thrust out her chin. "If no one will help, then I'll do it myself." With that, she promptly climbed the tree, paying no heed to her long skirt.

Caleb stood mesmerized. She was as agile as any boy and not one bit afraid.

Across the branch Naomi scooted, until she had the kitten in her arms.

How's she gonna get back down? Caleb wondered.

Naomi slipped the cat inside her roomy apron pocket and shimmied to the ground. The girls all cheered when she landed safely with the animal in tow, but Caleb stared at Naomi with a feeling he couldn't explain.

When I'm old enough to get married, she's the one I'm gonna ask. Any man in his right mind would want a girl as brave as Naomi Fisher.

Steering his thoughts back to the present, Caleb had half a mind to turn his buggy around and return to Paradise. He could go to Byer's Bookstore and see if his book was there, and afterward he'd stop back at Fisher's General Store and try once more to reason with Abraham.

He glanced at the darkening sky. It looked like rain was heading their way, and his open buggy would offer little protection if there was a downpour. Besides, Caleb needed to get home. He had work waiting at the buggy shop, and Pop would no doubt have several chores he wanted done. It was probably for the best. Caleb was pretty sure Abraham Fisher wasn't going to change his mind, so if there were any chance for him and Naomi, he would have to be the one to make it happen.

Naomi was at the back of the store when she heard the bell above the front door jingle. Could Papa have returned so soon? She hurried up front and was greeted with an enthusiastic "Hi, there! What's new?" Ginny Meyers's green eyes shimmered as she gave her blond ponytail a flip with her fingers.

"I'm okay. And you?"

"Great, now that I'm away from our crowded restaurant for a while, but you look kind of down. Is everything all right?"

Naomi shrugged. "As all right as it's ever gonna be, I guess."

Ginny looked around the store. "Is your dad here?"

"No, he's out runnin' errands." Naomi motioned with her hand. "There's no one else in the store right now, either. Except me and Zach, who's asleep in his playpen in the back room."

"Sorry to hear the little fellow's taking a nap. He's such a cutie, and I love to watch him play."

Naomi nodded. "He is a sweetheart, even though he does get into things when I let him crawl around during the times there are no customers in the store."

"Is he walking yet?" Ginny asked.

"Nope. He turned one last Saturday, and we were all hopin' that would be the big day."

"Wish I could have been at his birthday party. Zach is always so friendly toward me." Ginny snickered. "I think the little guy would go with a total stranger if given the chance."

Naomi opened her mouth to reply, but Ginny cut her off. "Since nobody's here except you and me, you can bare your soul." The young English woman took hold of Naomi's arm and led her to the wooden stool behind the counter. "Take a load off your feet and tell Dr. Meyers your troubles."

Ginny moved to the other side of the counter and leaned her elbows on the wooden top. She always seemed so enthusiastic and sure of herself, completely opposite of Naomi. Ginny attended college in Lancaster part-time, and when she wasn't in school, she worked at her parents' restaurant. Even so, she seemed to find time for fun and recreation. Last week, she'd come by the store and invited Naomi to go to the movies. Of course, Naomi refused. She knew her people viewed going to shows as worldly and not something parents wanted their children to do. Still, many young people like Naomi who hadn't joined the church yet often went to shows. Naomi wished she were brave enough and had the time to sneak off with

Ginny, even for a little while.

"Don't sit there staring into thin air," Ginny said, snapping her fingers in front of Naomi's face. "Spill it!"

Naomi chewed on her lower lip. How much should she tell Ginny? Would the young woman understand the way she felt, her being English and all? "Well," she began hesitantly, "Caleb Hoffmeir was here earlier, and he wanted me to go to a singing this Sunday night."

"What'd you tell him?"

"I said I was sure my daed wouldn't allow it, but Caleb thought otherwise, so he was foolish enough to ask Papa outright."

"What'd your dad say?"

"He said no, as I figured he would."

Ginny clicked her tongue. "Why is it that parents think they can control their grown kids?" She drew in a deep breath, and when she released it, her bangs fluttered above her pale brows. "My mom and dad are bound and determined for me to take over their restaurant someday. That's why they insisted I go to college and take some business classes."

That made no sense to Naomi. She'd been helping at the store ever since she was a young girl, and she'd never had more than an eighth-grade education.

"I've got other plans, though," Ginny continued. "As soon as I get my degree, I'd like to buy my own health club. Instead of serving a bunch of tourists plates full of artery-clogging food, I'll be helping people stay fit and trim."

Naomi studied her English friend a few seconds. Not only was Ginny blessed with a pretty face but also a healthy, robust body. Ginny had told her that she worked out several times a week, and it showed.

Of course, Naomi reasoned, *I'm in good shape from all the chores I have to do here and at home. I don't need any fancy health club to make me strong.*

Ginny leaned across the counter. "You want to know what I think?"

Naomi shrugged her shoulders.

"I think you should stand up to your father and tell him you've got a life to live, which doesn't include baby-sitting his kids seven days a week or cooking and cleaning from sunup to sunset."

Naomi's cheeks burned hot as she considered that option. Papa would have a conniption fit if she ever talked to him that way. She'd been raised to be respectful of her elders, and even though she might not agree with everything her father said, she'd never speak to him in such a disrespectful tone. Besides, she had an obligation to fulfill.

"You won't get what you want out of life if you remain silent and keep doing what everyone else thinks you should." Ginny shook her finger. "Determine to stand up for yourself, and then just do it."

"I've a family to care for," Naomi mumbled. "So even if I could stand up to Papa, I wouldn't be able to get away."

Ginny reached over and patted Naomi's hand.

"Don't you think you deserve to do something fun for a change?"

Naomi blinked. Of course she deserved it, but it wasn't meant to be.

"I'm planning a camping trip sometime this summer with a couple of friends. I'd like it if you could figure out some way to go along," Ginny announced.

Going camping did sound like fun, and there was something about being with Ginny that intrigued Naomi. Maybe it was her friend's perky attitude and determined spirit. Or it could be just the idea of spending time with a worldly English woman that held so much appeal.

Naomi thought about how she and her siblings used to camp out by the creek behind their home when they were younger, but they hadn't done that in some time. Maybe when the weather turned warmer, she could talk Papa into letting them pitch their tent and sleep outside one Friday night. It wouldn't be as exciting as going camping with a bunch of English women, but at least it would be a reprieve from their normal, busy lives.

The bell above the door rang again, and two Amish women walked in. Ginny turned to go. "I've gotta run, but think about what I said. I'll get back to you when the camping trip is planned, and if there's any way you can go, let me know."

Naomi nodded as a ray of sunlight burst through the window she still needed to wash. "Jah, okay, I'll think on it."

CHAPTER 3

Jim Scott leaned over to kiss his wife. "I should be home by six, so if you have dinner ready by then, we can go shopping for baby things after we eat."

Linda looked up at him and frowned. "What for? We already bought a crib and set up a nursery in the spare bedroom, but we still have no baby."

"Not yet, but our lawyer's working on it."

With a look of defeat, she folded her arms. "We've heard that before. Max Brenner had a baby lined up for us twice, and both adoptions fell through. "

Linda's blue eyes filled with tears, and with a feeling of compassion, Jim stroked her soft cheek. "We need to be patient, honey. You believe in fate, don't you?"

She lifted her chin. "What's that got to do with anything?"

"When the time's right, we'll have our baby. Just wait and see."

Linda's gaze dropped to the kitchen floor.

Jim bent his head, entwined his fingers through the back of her soft, golden curls, and kissed her on the mouth. "See you after work."

She offered him a weak smile and reached up to tousle his hair. "You'd better stop and get a haircut on the way home. You're beginning to look like a shaggy bear."

He shrugged. "Aw, it doesn't look so bad yet."

"Have you looked in the mirror lately?"

He wiggled his eyebrows. "Yep, whenever I brush my teeth. And the other day, I noticed a couple of gray hairs poking through my dark tresses."

She studied him intently, until he broke out laughing. "I had you worried there, didn't I?"

Linda playfully squeezed his arm. "I wouldn't care if you turned prematurely gray—just don't lose these hunky biceps."

He kissed her again. "Don't worry; as long as I keep on painting, I'll have muscular arms."

Jim stepped out into the garage and opened the door of his work van. He knew Linda wanted him to stay, but if he didn't leave now, he'd be running late. Jim had owned Scott's Painting and Decorating for the past six years, and they'd been living in Puyallup, Washington, a year longer than that. Jim's business provided them with a good living, and he'd recently hired three new employees, which gave him a crew of six. He and Linda had everything now—a successful business, a nice home. The only thing they lacked was a child, and Linda wanted that more than anything.

With each passing day, Jim had watched her sink slowly into depression. They'd been married eight years, and she hadn't been able to conceive. At first, Linda believed there was something wrong with her; but after she and Jim both went to the doctor, it was determined he was the reason she couldn't get pregnant. He tried not to feel guilty about it, but Linda wanted a baby, and Jim couldn't give her one. Two years ago, they decided to adopt. They'd hired a lawyer who specialized in adoption cases, but so far everything had fallen through. Now they were in limbo again, waiting and wondering if it would ever happen.

As Jim backed out of the garage, he waved at Linda and mouthed the words, "I love you."

She lifted her hand in response and stepped into the house.

If only I could make her smile again. Suddenly, an idea popped into Jim's head. *Maybe I'll call Mom in Ohio this morning and see if she can find Linda an Amish quilt. She's wanted one for a long time, and it might make her feel a little better.*

Jim snapped on the radio. *On second thought, maybe I'll see about taking some vacation time so the two of us can go to Ohio for a visit. I'll take Linda on a tour of Amish country, and she can buy that quilt herself.* He smiled. *Besides, it'll be nice to see Mom and Dad again.*

Naomi scrubbed at the spot on the bathroom floor where Mary Ann had recently vomited. "Ick! I'd rather slop hogs than clean *kotze*."

She didn't see how her life could get any busier, but for the last several days, things had been even more hectic than usual. Her two younger sisters were both sick with the flu and had to stay home from school.

Since Naomi needed to care for them, she couldn't go to the store, which she knew did not set well with Papa.

Naomi didn't enjoy home chores nearly as well as the tasks she did at the store, but there was little she could do about it. Her brothers Matthew, Norman, and Jake had to work in the fields; and Samuel, the youngest boy, complained how unfair it was for his sisters to stay home when he had to go to school. To make things worse, Zach was cutting another tooth and fussed continually.

"I'm sorry I'm sick and my *kotze* didn't make it to the toilet."

"It's not your fault you got sick."

"But I should have been faster to the bathroom."

Naomi washed her hands at the sink, then turned to face her six-year-old sister. "Come here." She opened her arms.

Mary Ann snuggled into her embrace. "You aren't mad at me?"

She shook her head. "How could I be mad at someone as sweet as you?"

The little girl leaned her head against Naomi and sobbed. "I hate bein' *grank*. I'd rather be in school."

"It's never fun being sick, but soon it will go better." Naomi felt the child's forehead. "Your fever seems to be gone. That's a gut sign."

Mary Ann's dark eyes looked hopeful. "Sure hope so."

"Jah." Naomi gently tapped the little girl's shoulder.

"Now, back to bed with you."

"Okay." Mary Ann scampered out of the room.

Naomi sighed. *Maybe in another day or so, things will be back to normal.*

By Friday, Naomi felt frazzled and wondered if she, too, might be coming down with the flu. Every bone in her body ached, and she had a splitting headache. Of course, the headache might have been caused from listening to her younger sisters whine or from hearing the baby's incessant howling. Naomi's achy body could have been the result of doing so many extra chores. She'd had to change her sisters' sheets every morning since they'd taken sick, as the girls left them drenched in sweat after each night of feverish sleep. Then there were dishes to be done, cooking that included several batches of chicken soup, and the chores Nancy and Mary Ann normally did. When the children took their naps, Naomi longed to do the same, but she had to keep working. If she didn't, everything would pile up, and she'd have even more of a workload.

Since Naomi was home all day, her brothers decided they could come to the house whenever they felt like taking a break from their work in the fields. Those breaks always included a snack, which they thought Naomi should furnish.

Naomi popped two willow-bark capsules into her mouth and swallowed them with a gulp of cold water, hoping they might take care of her headache. "Air is what I need. Fresh, clean air to clear my head and calm my nerves."

The girls and baby Zach were sleeping, so if she hurried and cleaned up the kitchen, there might be time to take a walk to the creek, where she could rest and spend a few moments alone. The sound of gurgling water and the pleasure of sitting under the trees growing along the water's edge had always helped Naomi relax. She hadn't made a trip to the creek in many weeks, and she'd missed it.

Ten minutes later, with the kitchen cleaned and straightened, Naomi stepped out the back door. Free at last, if only for a short time.

Abraham wiped the sweat from his brow as he finished stocking another shelf with the kerosene lamps that had been delivered on Tuesday. It had been a long week, working at the store by himself. He'd had a steady stream of customers from the time he opened this morning, with barely a break so he could eat the lunch Naomi had fixed for him at dawn.

"Sure wish the girls hadn't come down with the flu," he grumbled. "I really could have used Naomi's help this week." Abraham knew his oldest daughter was needed more at home than at the store right now, but that didn't make his load any lighter. He hadn't been able to take a single nap these past few days. How could he, when he had to attend to business and there was no one to take over when he became tired? He'd been sleeping a lot since Sarah's passing.

Maybe it was because he felt so down and depressed.

He glanced at the clock on the wall across the room. It was two in the afternoon, and for the first time all day, he had no customers. This was the only chance he'd had to restock, which was why the lamps had been sitting in the back room for the last two days.

Abraham reached into the box for another lantern when the bell above the door jangled and in walked Virginia Meyers. She was not one of his favorite customers, as the sassy young woman seemed to have a bad attitude. She had a way of hanging around Naomi, bombarding her with a bunch of silly questions, and insinuating she should explore some of the things found in her English world. Virginia probably thought she was being discreet, but Abraham had overheard her speaking to his oldest daughter on more than one occasion.

"Is Naomi here?" Virginia asked as she sashayed across the room.

He shook his head. "She's been home most of the week, takin' care of her sisters. They're down with the flu."

Virginia pursed her lips. "That's too bad. Sure hope Naomi doesn't get the bug. She's got enough problems without taking sick."

Abraham reached around to rub the kinks in his lower back. "If you've got something to say, Virginia, please say it."

"Ginny. I prefer to be called Ginny."

44

"What kind of problems do ya think my daughter has?"

She shrugged her slim shoulders. "Naomi works hard. Seems to me you ought to cut her some slack."

Abraham frowned. "Some what?"

"Some slack. You know, give her a bit of space."

He raised his eyebrows.

"Let her do some fun things once in a while. Nobody should have to spend all their time doing chores and baby-sitting. Especially not a twenty-year-old woman who's never even been on a date."

He squinted. "How would ya know that? Has my daughter been whining about how unfair her daed is by makin' her work so hard?"

Virginia shook her head. "Naomi's too sweet to whine."

Abraham was tempted to tell the English woman she didn't know anything about his daughter, but he decided to change the subject instead. "What brings you to my store this afternoon? Shouldn't you be at school today? Naomi's mentioned you attend some fancy college in Lancaster."

"I'm done for the day, and I came by to see if you have any new rubber stamps. I'm doing a scrapbook of my Christmas vacation to Florida."

"Haven't had anything new since the last time you came askin' for stamps."

"I see."

"If there's nothin' else I can help ya with, I need to get back to settin' these lamps in place." He gestured

45

to the shelf where he'd already put four kerosene lanterns.

A ripple of strange-sounding music floated through the air, and Virginia reached into her pocket and retrieved a cell phone. She wrinkled her nose when she looked at the screen. "That's my dad calling. Guess I'd better head over to the restaurant and see what horrible things await me there. Tell Naomi I dropped by." Virginia marched out the door, not even bothering to answer the phone.

Abraham bent down and grabbed another lamp. "If that girl was mine, I'd wash her mouth out with a bar of soap!"

Naomi gathered the edge of her dress so it wouldn't get tangled in the tall grass and sprinted toward the creek. By the time she arrived, she was panting for breath but feeling more exhilarated than she had in a long time. She flopped onto the grass under a weeping willow tree, leaned her head against the trunk, and lifted her face to the warm sunshine. So many days Naomi used to spend here when she was a girl and life had been uncomplicated. She wished she could step back in time or make herself an only child so she wouldn't have any siblings to care for.

"No point wishin' for the impossible," Naomi mumbled as she slipped her shoes off and curled her bare toes, digging them into the dirt. "I'm supposed to be satisfied, no matter what my circumstances might be."

At their last preaching service, the bishop had

quoted a verse of scripture from the book of Philippians, and it reminded Naomi she should learn to be content. The apostle Paul had gone through great trials and persecutions, and he'd been able to say in chapter 4, verse 11: "For I have learned, in whatsoever state I am, therewith to be content."

Naomi sighed deeply and closed her eyes. *Heavenly Father, please give me rest for my weary soul and help me learn to be content.*

Naomi awoke with a start. She'd been dreaming about camping with Ginny and her English friends when a strange noise woke her. She tipped her head and listened, knowing she shouldn't have allowed herself the pleasure of drifting off. No telling how long she'd been down here at the creek. What if the kinner were awake and needed her? What if Papa had come home and discovered she wasn't in the house taking care of his sick children?

She clambered to her feet as the noise drew closer and louder. What was that strange sound?

She looked up. "Oh no! Bees!"

Naomi ducked, but it was too late. It seemed as if her head were encased in a dark cloud. One that moved and buzzed and stung like fire. She swatted at the enemy invaders as they pelted her body with their evil stingers, and she shrieked and rolled in the grass.

It seemed like an eternity before the swarm was gone. When she was sure they had disappeared, Naomi crawled to the edge of the creek. She grabbed a handful of dirt, scooped some water into her hands, mixed it thoroughly, and patted mud all over the stingers. Her face felt like it was twice its normal size, and her arms ached where the buzzing insects had made their mark. *If Caleb could see the way I look now, he would surely change his mind about wanting to court me.*

"I need to get back to the house and fix a real poultice," Naomi muttered. She'd never had an allergic reaction to a bee sting, but then she'd never had so many all at once. Even if she wasn't allergic, she had a homeopathic remedy that should help the swelling go down and take away some of the pain.

Naomi took off on a run. Beside the fact that the stingers hurt something awful, it had begun to rain. By the time she reached the back porch, raindrops pelted her body, while streaks of lightning and thunderous roars converged on the afternoon sky.

Naomi flung the door open and bounded into the kitchen. She screeched to a halt and stared at the floor. "*Was in der welt*—what in the world?" she gasped.

Mary Ann knelt in the middle of the room and looked up at Naomi with tears in her eyes. "Me and Nancy woke up and were hungry. We're feelin' better and wanted to make ginger cookies."

Streaks of flour dotted the little girl's face and pinned-up hair, which made the otherwise mahogany tresses look as though they were splattered with gray. The floor was littered with broken brown eggshells mixed with runny yellow yolks, and a sack of flour had been dumped in the middle of the mess.

Naomi's gaze traveled across the room where Nancy stood at the sink with a sponge in her hand. "What happened here?"

"Everything was goin' okay 'til Mary Ann dropped the carton of eggs," Nancy huffed. "I was haulin' the flour over to the cupboard and slipped." She lifted her chin. "The flour spilled and landed on Mary Ann's head, and it's all her fault."

Naomi groaned. Nancy was four years older than Mary Ann and usually managed fairly well in the kitchen. She also tended to be a bit bossy where the younger ones were concerned. *Why did I allow myself the luxury of falling asleep at the creek? For that matter, why did I go there in the first place? Now I'm paying the price for my desire to spend a little time alone.*

A piercing wail shattered the air, and she whirled around. It was Zach hollering from his playpen in the adjoining room.

"The boppli's awake," Mary Ann announced.

"Jah, I know the baby's awake, but I can't go to him now." Naomi lifted her arms, covered in mud. "I've been stung by a swarm of bees."

"Oh, Sister, you look so *elendich!*" Nancy cried. It was obvious she hadn't even noticed Naomi's condition until now.

Naomi nodded. "I'm sure I do look pitiful, but I feel even worse than I appear."

"Are you gonna help us bake ginger cookies?" Mary

Ann asked, scooping up a handful of eggshells.

"No." Naomi tried to keep her voice steady and calm. There was no point getting upset and yelling at her sisters. It wasn't as if they'd made the mess on purpose. "I need to tend these bee stings."

Naomi opened the cabinet door above the sink, grabbed a box of baking soda and her bottle of medicine. "I'm going upstairs to the bathroom. While I'm gone, one of you needs to clean this mess, and the other can get the baby before he tries to climb out of his playpen." She pointed toward the living room where Zach still screamed. "When I get back, I'll see about gettin' the little guy diapered and fed." Naomi hurried out of the kitchen.

Ten minutes later, she reentered the room, only this time her face and arms were covered with baking soda instead of mud. She stopped inside the door. The mess had been cleaned, and Zach was in his highchair eating a cracker; but her brothers Matthew, Norman, and Jake sat at the table, dripping wet.

"*Ach,* my! You're gettin' water everywhere!" Naomi shouted. "What are you three doin' in here anyways?"

"It's rainin' cats and dogs outside, and we sure couldn't keep on plowing the fields in this kind of weather," Matthew answered. His dark brown hair was plastered against his head like a soggy leaf, and his cheeks were as red as a raspberry. At the moment, he looked like a little boy rather than a twenty-two-year-old man.

"That's right; it's a real downpour out there,"

Norman agreed. "If it keeps up for long, we'll have us a flood, and that's for certain sure." He raked his fingers through his hair, almost the same color as Matthew's and just as wet. A spray of water splattered onto the table, and Norman grinned at Naomi, kind of sheepishlike.

"What happened to you, Sister? You look awful," Jake commented. The seventeen-year-old had recently celebrated his birthday; but soaked to the skin and with his hair in his face, he, too, looked like an overgrown child.

"I had a run-in with some bees." Naomi glanced at the clock above the refrigerator. It was half past four. Samuel should have been home from school by now. She ran to the back door and flung it open. No sign of her little brother—just pouring rain and jagged lightning.

She spun around to face her brothers. "One of you needs to go after Samuel. He'll catch his death of pneumonia if he walks home in this terrible weather. Besides, he could be hit by lightning."

"It wonders me so that you're such a worrywart. Why, a little rain won't kill the boy, and he's sure smart enough to stay out from under a tree if lightning were to strike." Matthew reached for a wad of napkins and swiped them across his forehead.

"Yeah, that's right." Jake's blond head bobbed up and down. "I can't begin to tell ya how many times I walked home from school in the rain when I was a boy."

Zach let out another ear-piercing yelp, and Naomi thought she was going to scream. Wasn't there a single person in her family who cared about anyone but himself?

She clapped her hands together and stomped one foot. "Now listen to me! One of you had better go after Samuel—now!"

Matthew blinked, then turned to face Norman. "Guess the boss means business, Brother. Get the buggy hitched, schnell!"

"Okay, I'm goin'." Norman pushed his chair away from the table. He sauntered past Naomi but halted when he got to the back door. "You'd better have supper started before Papa gets home. He won't like it if he shows up expectin' to eat and nothin's ready."

Naomi had taken as much as she could stand. She grabbed a wet sponge from the sink, took aim, and pitched it at her brother. It hit its mark, landing in the center of Norman's back.

He didn't seem the least bit affected but merely chuckled and marched out the door.

"Brothers!" Naomi hollered. She hurried over to Zach, scooped him into her arms, and headed upstairs.

Caleb couldn't believe how hard it was raining. When he left for town to get supplies a few hours ago, the weather had been warm and sunny. By the time he left Zook's Tool Shop, a noisy thunderstorm churned across the sky, dropping buckets of rain. He'd planned to stop by Fisher's General Store and see if he could catch Naomi alone, but now he thought it would be best to go straight home. Besides, judging from the time on his pocket watch, Abraham's store was probably closed.

Speaking softly to his four-year-old gelding, Caleb stood near the front of the buggy and stroked the horse's ear. "I don't like storms any better than you, but we need to be gettin' home."

The horse snorted and nuzzled Caleb's arm. He patted the animal's head and hopped into his open carriage.

"Sure wish I'd driven one of Pop's closed-in buggies today," Caleb mumbled. "By the time we get home, we'll both be near drowned." He pulled the brim of his straw hat down and leaned into the wind. From the way the rain pelted the ground, there might be some flash flooding in the area.

Caleb drove the horse and buggy as fast as he could. He'd only gone a short ways, when he came upon a gusher of muddy water running over the road and into a nearby field. Several cars had pulled onto the shoulder, obviously stalled.

"Guess there's some good in us Amish usin' *real* horsepower. At least my buggy's got no engine to peter out on me."

By the time Caleb reached the halfway point between the town of Paradise and his folks' farm, the floodwaters had become a hazard. He noticed a herd of horses owned by one of the English farmers who lived in the area. They stood up to their flanks in a lake of murky, brown water.

Caleb wondered if the pond at the back of his folks' farm might be flooded, too. If it was, Pop would need Caleb and his brothers to put the animals in the barn.

Moving on down the highway, Caleb spotted a closed-in buggy sitting on the shoulder of the road. He swiped his hand across his rain-drenched face and squinted. It looked like Abraham Fisher's horse and buggy. Was something wrong? Were the Fishers stranded? Maybe they'd had an accident.

Caleb guided his horse to the edge of the road and stopped behind the rig. He jumped down and sprinted around to the right side, where he knew the driver would be sitting. When he peered through the window, his heart lurched. Abraham Fisher was hunched over, his head leaning against the front of the buggy, but there was no sign of Naomi or her baby brother.

Caleb grasped the handle and opened the door. Abraham didn't budge, although he could see by the rise and fall of the man's shoulders that he was still breathing.

"Abraham, can ya hear me?" Caleb touched the storekeeper's shoulder. There was no response, so he shook the man's arm.

Naomi's father jerked upright. "Ach, my! What are ya doin', boy?"

"I thought you might be hurt or had broken down."

Abraham yawned. "I ain't hurt—just pulled over to take a little nap. With the rain comin' down so hard, it was gettin' difficult to see, and since I've been minding the store by myself most of the week, I was feelin' kind of tired."

"You've been at the store by yourself?" Caleb's mouth dropped open like a broken hinge. "But I came by on *Mondaag,* and Naomi was helping you."

Abraham grunted. "Jah, well, Monday was the only day I had my daughter's help. She's been home the rest of the week, takin' care of her sick sisters."

"Everything's okay with you then?"

The storekeeper frowned. "Why wouldn't it be?"

"Like I was sayin' . . . I saw your buggy pulled to the side of the road and figured I'd better stop and see if you were hurt or anything."

"Except for bein' tired, I'm right as rain." Abraham shook his head. "Sure hope this storm lets up soon. It's gonna cause a passel of trouble if the creeks and ponds should flood."

Caleb didn't bother to tell Abraham about the swamped farm he'd already seen. He figured it would be best if they both headed for home. He tapped the side of Abraham's door. "Guess I'll be on my way then. Glad you're not hurt." The only response was a muffled murmur.

When the door shut, Abraham took up the reins.

Caleb hurried to his own buggy, shaking his head. The storekeeper hadn't even said thanks.

CHAPTER 4

Naomi stood at the kitchen sink with a sponge in her hand. She needed to hurry. They'd soon be leaving for Sunday church at the Beechys' house.

At least the swelling from my bee stings has gone down, she mused. *I no longer look like a bumpy old horny toad. The floodwaters have gone down, too, and it's not raining. That's something to be thankful for on this Lord's Day.*

Naomi washed each dish in one container, then rinsed it in another. As she finished, the dishes were placed in the draining rack for Nancy to dry and put away. Every step was done with attention, adding up to a simple, unspoken task performed after each and every meal. Strangely enough, Naomi found this ritual comforting. It gave her time to think and sometimes pray.

"Baby Zach's hollerin'. Want me to get him out of the playpen?"

Nancy's question drew Naomi's thoughts aside, and she whirled around. There stood Zach, gripping the playpen rails with slobbery hands while tears streamed down his chubby cheeks.

"I'll tend the baby," Naomi told her sister. "All but two cups and three plates have been washed, so you can finish those and get them dried and put away.

Hopefully, we'll all be ready to go by the time Papa gets the horse and buggy hitched."

"Why can't I take care of the boppli while you finish the dishes?" Nancy asked with a lift of her chin.

Nibbling on the inside of her cheek, Naomi contemplated her sister's suggestion. Finishing the dishes would be much easier than trying to calm Zach, who probably had a dirty diaper. Even though she wasn't looking forward to changing it, she knew she could get the job done quicker than Nancy.

"I appreciate the offer," she said, "but I think it would be best if I get the baby."

A look of disappointment flashed across Nancy's face, but she slid over to the sink and grabbed the sponge without a word.

Naomi hated to be in charge of her younger siblings, always telling them what to do and sometimes handing out discipline when it became necessary. That was supposed to be a mother's job.

Naomi dried her hands on a terry cloth towel and went to get her baby brother. Zach quit crying the minute she picked him up, and after a quick check of his diaper, she was relieved to see there was no need for a change. How glad she would be when the boppli was potty trained and no longer needed to wear *windels*.

Zach squealed and kicked his hefty legs as she carried him across the room. Apparently, all the little guy wanted was to be out of his playpen.

Naomi hugged her little brother. "You're gettin' mighty spoiled, ya know that?"

"Guess that's because he's so *lieblich,*" Nancy put in.

"Jah, he's adorable all right." Naomi nuzzled the boy's cheek with her nose. "Adorable and spoiled rotten."

She took a seat in the rocking chair near the fireplace and rocked Zach as she sang a silly song she had made up. "Spoiled little baby, you're awfully cute. You're sure to grow up happy and loved to boot."

Zach giggled as she tugged gently on his soft earlobe.

Nancy placed another dish in the cupboard when the back door swung open. Papa entered the kitchen, followed by Samuel.

"A sly old fox was in the chicken coop last night," Samuel announced.

"How do ya know that?" Nancy asked.

"We found evidence of it . . . several dead chickens," their father said with a frown.

"Papa's gonna set a trap for the scoundrel," Samuel added excitedly.

"I hope you're plannin' to set it someplace where the kinner won't get hurt," Naomi said.

Papa moved toward the rocker, and his blue eyes narrowed. "Don't ya think I've got brains enough to know how to set a trap without taking the chance of one of my youngsters gettin' injured?"

Tears stung the back of Naomi's eyes, and she blinked to keep them from spilling over. "I—I meant no disrespect, Papa."

He fingered the tip of his beard. "Jah, well, your mamm never questioned my decisions when she was alive."

There he goes again—comparing me to Mama.

"Is everyone ready for church?" Papa asked, changing the subject.

"I think so," Naomi replied.

Papa studied Nancy. "Where's your head covering?"

She pointed to the back of a chair.

"Put it on now. Mary Ann's already in the buggy, and the older boys left a few minutes ago in Matthew's rig."

Nancy shut the cupboard door, grabbed her kapp off the chair, and scampered outside.

Papa glanced at Samuel, who had taken a seat at the kitchen table. "Get your lazy bones up and hightail it out to the buggy. If we don't hurry, we'll be late."

Samuel jumped up, grabbed his hat from a wall peg, and made a beeline for the door.

Papa turned to Naomi again. "If your mamm were here, the kinner would be ready for church on time—with their head coverings in place."

Naomi stood, positioning Zach against her hip. "Papa, why do you always compare me to Mama?"

He blinked as though surprised by her question. "I ain't comparin' you, and I don't appreciate your tone."

Feeling the need for comfort, Naomi hugged the baby. "I'm sorry, Papa."

He cleared his throat but said nothing in return. For a minute, Naomi thought she saw a look of tenderness cross her father's face, but it disappeared as fast as it had come.

Oh, please, Papa. Can't you just say, "I love you, Naomi, and I appreciate all you do?"

"You got the boppli ready to go?"

She nodded.

"Then let's be off."

Caleb paced back and forth along the side of Beechy's barn, where twenty buggies were already parked. He'd seen Mathew, Norman, and Jake Fisher arrive awhile ago, so he figured Naomi and the rest of the family wouldn't be far behind.

Caleb hadn't seen Naomi since he stopped by Fisher's General Store on Monday, so he'd had nearly a week to come up with a plan. He hoped to speak with Naomi about it today. If he could get her alone for a few minutes, that is.

"Hey, Caleb, how's it going?"

At the sound of Aaron Landis's deep voice, Caleb turned around. Aaron tipped his head and grinned.

"It's goin' okay. How 'bout with you?"

"Things are great with me and Katie." Aaron slapped Caleb on the back. "We just found out she's gonna have a baby in late November."

Caleb clasped his friend's hand. "Congratulations. I know you'll make a gut daed."

Aaron's smile widened, and his dark eyes twinkled in the sunlight. "Sure hope so. Katie and me want a whole houseful of kinner."

Caleb only nodded in reply.

"Well, I should go see how Katie's feelin' before we go inside for church. She's had the morning sickness real bad."

"Tell her I'm happy to hear your news," Caleb said, forcing a smile.

"Sure will." Aaron ambled off in the direction of the women gathered on the Beechys' front porch. No doubt about it—Aaron was one happy man.

I wonder if I'll ever have a wife or a boppli.

Naomi took a seat on a backless bench near the kitchen door. She wanted to be close to an exit in case Zach started to fuss. At the moment, the child was sitting quietly on her lap, but Naomi had a box of baby crackers tucked inside a wicker basket in case he got hungry. The basket also contained a stack of diapers, a change of clothes for the baby, and a bag of dried fruit for Nancy or Mary Ann if they became restless. Naomi knew the worship service would last a good three hours, and it was hard for the younger ones to sit so long.

She glanced across the room and noticed Caleb sitting on the men's side between his younger brothers, Andy and Marvin. He smiled, but she looked away. No use giving him hope she might care for him. If they couldn't court, Caleb should find someone else. Naomi didn't expect him to wait until she was free of her responsibilities to the family. Matthew was Caleb's age, so if he ever got over his shyness around women, he might find a suitable wife soon. Norman was nineteen and not far behind; but Jake, Nancy, Samuel, and Mary Ann still had several years before they could marry.

Naomi jerked her hand when Zach bit down on her thumb. *And then there's the boppli, who won't be ready for marriage for another eighteen years or so.*

Tears stung the backs of her eyes. *By then I'll be so old nobody will want to marry me.*

She reached into the basket and withdrew a cracker. At least Zach wouldn't be chomping on her thumb anymore.

Such a week this has been, she mused. First, her sisters had gotten sick and she'd stayed home from the store to care for them. Next, that horrible encounter with the bees. Then, Mary Ann and Nancy's egg and flour mess, followed by the brothers coming into the kitchen, dripping wet. *I don't know how Mama managed so well.*

Naomi's thoughts went to Papa. *Why must he always compare me to Mama? I try my hardest to please him, but nothin' ever seems to be good enough.*

A familiar lump lodged in her throat, and she swallowed against the constriction.

" 'I have learned, in whatsoever state I am, therewith to be content,' " Bishop Swartley quoted from the book of Philippians. Crippled with arthritis and in his eighties, the man could still preach and lead the people, even if he did often repeat the same verse of scripture.

Naomi closed her eyes. *Help me, Lord, for I'm still havin' trouble learning to be content.*

When church was over, Naomi stepped outside. As she stood on the front porch, Zach clung to her neck while he wrapped his legs around her waist. Naomi held him tightly and inhaled. The trees and grass were such a deep green, and everything smelled clean and new after the rain they'd had a few days ago. A group of children gathered to play in the yard, including her three younger siblings.

Naomi had only a few minutes to savor the peaceful scene, for it was time to help with the meal. She sighed and turned toward the door.

"Why don't you let me hold the little one awhile?" Anna Beechy spoke up from her rocking chair on the front porch.

With a grateful heart, Naomi handed Zach to the elderly woman. Anna smiled as she snuggled the boy. She had a special way with the kinner. After all, she'd raised ten of her own and now had twenty-five grandchildren. Naomi knew she was leaving her baby brother in capable hands, so she headed into the house and busied herself with pouring coffee and serving bowls of bean soup to the menfolk.

When the meal was over, the men meandered into the yard, breaking into groups so they could visit, play horseshoes, or relax under the shady maple trees.

Naomi shook her head when she noticed her dad already nodding off. He'd been doing that a lot since

Mama's passing, and it worried her some. Was Papa dealing with his depression by napping so much, or was he simply tired from not sleeping well at night?

Directing her focus back to the meal, she ushered her sisters to a table and took a seat on the bench between them. She'd just finished her bowl of soup when she looked out the window and noticed Emma Lapp across the yard, standing near one of the open buggies.

Naomi squinted. Was that Caleb Hoffmeir Emma was talking to? She squeezed her napkin into a tight ball and clenched her teeth. Was Caleb asking Emma to tonight's singing? Would he be taking her home in his courting buggy? A pang of jealousy stabbed Naomi's heart as she imagined the couple beginning to court.

Caleb's only doing what I told him to do, she reminded herself. *I really can't fault him for that.*

"Naomi, did ya hear what I said?"

"Huh?" Naomi forced her gaze away from Caleb and Emma, turning her attention to Mary Ann.

"I'm full now. Can I go play?" The child pointed to her empty plate.

Naomi nodded. "Jah, you ate well. Run along, but don't be gettin' into any trouble, ya hear?"

"I won't." Mary Ann scrambled off the bench and hurried outside.

Naomi glanced at Nancy. "You about done, too?"

Nancy crammed another piece of bread in her mouth and mumbled, "Am now."

"Okay, you can go."

Nancy bounded away, and Naomi scanned the yard once more. Caleb and Emma were gone.

Probably snuck off somewhere to be alone. She squeezed her eyes shut, hoping she wouldn't give in to the threatening tears.

When Naomi felt someone touch her shoulder, her eyes snapped open. Emma smiled and dropped to the bench beside her. "I've got a message for you. It's from Caleb," she whispered.

Naomi's mouth went dry, and she quickly reached for her glass of water.

Emma leaned closer. "He wants you to meet him at the pond behind the house."

"Is that what the two of you were talkin' about out there by Caleb's buggy?"

Emma's pale eyebrows furrowed. "Of course. What'd ya think we were talkin' about?"

"I—uh—never mind."

Emma adjusted her wire-rimmed glasses and stared at Naomi. "You didn't actually think—" She giggled. "I'm not romantically interested in Caleb, if that's what you were thinkin'."

"Well . . ."

"Go to him, Naomi."

Naomi shook her head. "I can't."

"Why not?"

"I've got to keep an eye on Mary Ann, Nancy, and Samuel, not to mention little Zach."

"The last time I saw your baby brother, he was

asleep on the Beechys' couch." Emma nodded toward the yard. "As far as the other kinner are concerned, I'll watch out for them while you're gone."

"You mean it?"

"Of course. Now be off with you."

Caleb hunkered near the edge of the water, watching a pair of mallard ducks float past. *Will Naomi show up? Did Emma deliver my message?*

A twig snapped, and Caleb turned his head. "You came."

Naomi smiled and he stood. "I can't stay long," she said breathlessly. "My daed might come lookin' for me if I'm gone too long."

Caleb motioned to a grassy spot beneath a white birch tree. "Should we have a seat?"

She shook her head. "The grass is still damp from that awful storm we had on Friday."

He shrugged. "Guess we'll have to stand then."

"What'd you want to talk to me about?"

"I'd sure like to court you, Naomi."

"You said that the other day, but you know it's not possible."

"Because your daed says no, or because you have too much work to do at home?"

"Both."

Caleb's stomach clenched, and he lifted Naomi's chin with his thumb. Her brown eyes were still as large and inviting as he remembered. A man could lose himself in them. "If Abraham had his way, you'd never have any fun. Probably never get married, either."

Naomi's eyes filled with tears, and her chin quivered. "That may be true, but I made a promise to Mama before she died, and I aim to keep it."

"I understand that, but I think we can still be together." He smiled. "I've come up with a plan, and I hope you'll give some consideration to it."

"What kind of plan?"

"You can still take care of your family while we see each other in secret."

"I can't. Papa might find out, and he'd be furious."

Caleb shrugged. "I'm not worried about that. We can meet at night, after your family has gone to bed."

Naomi shook her head. "I'm needed at home, Caleb. I thought I made that clear the other day."

"You won't even think about meetin' me in secret?"

Tears rolled down Naomi's cheeks, and she swiped them away. "I can't."

"But you would if your daed said it was all right?"

Her eyes widened. "Papa would never allow it. And even if he did, I'd still be too busy."

"Is that your final word?"

"It has to be."

He grunted. "Fine then. Don't blame me if you end up an old maid."

CHAPTER 5

The next few weeks seemed to drag by, even though Naomi had been plenty busy. Maybe that was the problem. There were too many chores to do. Last Friday had been the kinner's last day of school, which meant she would be taking the three youngest ones with her to the store until the end of August, when they returned to the one-room schoolhouse. Matthew said he'd be in charge of Samuel, who would be put to work in the fields. It was hard for a boy of eight to labor in the fields all day, but Naomi knew he would work well under Matthew's supervision.

As Naomi bent to grab another towel from the basket by her feet, she made a mental note to be sure and pack plenty of cookies to give her brothers in case Samuel or the others got hungry between breakfast and lunch. She planned to take some cookies to the store as well so the girls and Zach could have a snack. Even though having Nancy and Mary Ann along meant two more children Naomi had to watch, it was nice to know when the baby got fussy or needed to be fed, Nancy could help out. Also, both girls would have jobs to do at the store, like dusting, stocking lower shelves, and sweeping the floor.

Naomi's thoughts drifted to Caleb and the discussion they'd had when they met at Beechy's pond. Oh, how she wished they could court. She wouldn't blame Caleb if he found someone else and married straight away. "I sure can't expect him to wait for me," she mumbled.

"Help! Help!"

Naomi whirled around. Mary Ann clutched a basket of eggs as she circled the yard with Hildy the goose in hot pursuit.

"She's after the eggs!" the child shouted. "Get her away from me, please!"

"Calm down and stop running. She'll only keep chasin' if you don't."

Mary Ann's eyes were wide, and several strands of blond hair had come loose from the back of her head. Naomi could see her sister was struggling with the need to keep running, but the child screeched to a halt in front of Naomi's basket of clean clothes.

"Hand me the basket," Naomi instructed. "Then get behind my back and stand very still."

Mary Ann complied, crouching low and whimpering as she clung to the edge of Naomi's long dress.

Naomi bent down. She grabbed a wet towel, snapped it open, and smacked Hildy on the head. The goose let out a blaring squawk, spun around, and honked her way to the barn.

"That was close!" Mary Ann exclaimed. "I thought that old bird was gonna peck me to death."

Naomi knelt in front of her sister. "She didn't draw blood, did she?"

"I don't think so. Just scared me silly—that's all."

Naomi hugged Mary Ann and stood. "I'm going to ask Matthew or Norman to put that nasty critter down."

Mary Ann's eyes filled with tears. "You mean to kill Hildy?"

"That's the only way to keep her from chasin' folks, and it's become an everyday occurrence here of late."

"Please don't let her be killed. She don't mean to be bad."

"I know. We'll see what Papa has to say." Naomi handed her sister the basket of eggs. "Now hurry into the house and tell Nancy she needs to have Zach fed and diapered by the time I come inside."

Mary Ann grabbed the basket of eggs and scampered off.

At least one problem has been solved. Naomi hung the last towel on the line and turned when she heard a horse trot out of the barn. Norman led the gelding into the yard and proceeded to hitch him to the waiting buggy.

"What do you think you're doing?" she called.

"What's it look like? Papa asked me to hitch up a horse so he could leave for the store, and that's what I'm doin'."

She frowned. "You'd better think about choosing a different horse. This one's barely green broke."

Norman waved his hand. "Aw, Midnight will be fine. All he needs is the chance to prove himself."

Naomi shook her head, wondering if it was the horse that needed to prove himself or her nineteen-year-old

70

brother. She gathered the empty laundry basket and started across the yard. Without warning, the horse whinnied, reared up, and kicked his back hooves against the front of the buggy.

"I refuse to ride to the store with that horse!" she shouted.

"Whoa there! Steady, boy." Norman stepped in front of the gelding and reached for his harness.

"Look out! You might be the next thing he kicks."

"He'll settle down soon." Norman's face was cherry red, yet he continued to struggle with the boisterous animal. Midnight alternated between rearing up and kicking out his back feet. The buggy rocked back and forth.

Naomi covered her mouth to keep from screaming, which would rile the horse more. Things were getting out of control, and if Norman didn't do something soon, she feared the buggy would overturn.

"Let that horse loose!" Papa's voice shattered the air like a gunshot, and Norman quickly did as he was told.

He led the panicked horse back to the barn and returned a few minutes later with one of their gentle mares. "Guess Midnight wasn't quite ready yet," he mumbled.

"You think?" Papa shook his finger. "If you were a few years younger, I'd take you to the woodshed for a sound *bletsching*."

Norman hung his head. "Sorry, Papa. I didn't expect Midnight to act that way."

"Jah, well, use your brain next time." Papa turned to face Naomi. "You and the kinner 'bout ready to go?"

She nodded. "I'll run inside and see if Nancy's got Zach ready." She figured now probably wasn't the best time to tell Papa about Hildy.

Jim Scott heard his cell phone ringing in the distance, and he glanced around to see where it was. He usually kept it clipped to his belt, but he'd been on a ten-foot ladder and didn't want to take the chance of the phone coming loose and falling to the ground. That had happened several months ago, and since he hadn't been smart enough to buy insurance on the phone, it had cost him plenty to buy a new one. Today, he'd put the phone in a safe place. He just couldn't remember where.

"Your phone's on the lid of that paint bucket, and it's ringing like crazy," Ed called from across the yard. "Want me to get it for you?"

"Sure, if you don't mind."

Jim climbed down the ladder, and his feet had just touched the ground when his employee handed him the phone. "The guy says he's your lawyer."

"Thanks."

When Ed kept standing there with his hands in the pockets of his painter's overalls, Jim nodded and said, "You can finish up with the trim on those windows now."

"Oh, sure. Right." Ed sauntered off, and Jim turned his attention to the phone.

"Hello, Max. How are you?"

"I'm fine, and I have some news that I think will make your day."

"Really? What's up?"

"My friend, Carl Stevens, is a lawyer in Bel Air, Maryland. He called this morning and said a young woman came to his office the other day. She's a single mother and can no longer care for her one-year-old boy, so she's decided to put him up for adoption."

Jim's heart skipped a beat. Did he dare believe this baby might be theirs? Should he risk telling Linda and getting her hopes up, too?

"Jim, are you still there?"

"Yeah, Max. Just trying to digest this bit of news."

"Carl said he'd be meeting with the woman again in a few weeks and should be able to tie things up then. My question is, would you and Linda be interested in a child that old? I know you had wanted a newborn."

Jim blew out his breath and sank to the grass. "Whew! This is so sudden, and I'm not sure Linda would want an older child."

"One isn't that old," Max said with a chuckle. "He's still pretty much a baby in my book; and at his young age, it shouldn't be that difficult for the little guy to adjust to his new surroundings."

"What about a father? Is there one in the picture?" Jim asked.

"No. Carl said the woman severed ties with the baby's father, and he's married to someone else and living in another state. He's signed away all parental rights to the child."

"Hmm . . ."

"Talk it over with your wife tonight, and then give me a call with your decision."

Jim frowned. "I hate to get Linda all fired up about something that might not even happen. It's not a done deal with the mother yet, right?"

"Not quite."

"And you'll know something definite in two weeks?"

"I believe so."

"Then I think it would be best if I wait to tell Linda until we know for sure that the woman is actually going to give up her son."

"Sounds fair to me," Max said. "I'll get back to you as soon as I hear from Carl again."

"That'd be great. Thanks." As Jim hung up the phone, his mind swirled with mixed emotions. If the woman in Maryland decided to give them her child, they would have two reasons for making a trip to the East Coast—one to pick up their son and the other to visit his folks. He was sure it would be a vacation they would never forget.

Naomi grabbed a stack of invoices Papa had asked her to go over. She had to take this time to get caught up on paperwork. Summer was not far off. Then there would be carloads and busloads of tourists flocking to their place of business. Some would be coming in merely to gawk at the curious Plain folks who ran the general store. Others would drop in to purchase something made by one of the locals. Papa didn't care much for English tourists, but he said it was a free country, and it did help their business.

When the front door opened, Naomi looked up from her work, and her heart skipped a beat.

Caleb removed his straw hat and offered her a dimpled grin. "Gude mariye."

She slipped from behind the counter and moved toward him. "Good morning. What can I help ya with?"

He glanced around the room. "Are we alone?"

Naomi nodded. "For the moment. Papa's out back with the kinner. He could come inside at any moment, though."

Caleb shrugged. "I'll take my chances."

"What are you needing?" she asked, feeling a bit impatient.

"I'm sorry about last Sunday and sayin' I thought you were gonna end up an old maid. I didn't mean it, Naomi. I just spoke out of frustration."

She sniffed. "It's okay. I understand."

Caleb smiled. "Since this Sunday comin' is an off-week and there won't be any church, I'm plannin' to go fishing at Miller's pond. Want to join me there?"

Naomi released an exasperated groan and moved back to her wooden stool. "I can't. You know that."

Caleb leaned on the edge of the counter and studied her intently. "It's not fair, Naomi. A woman your age should be having fun, not babysittin' her brothers and sisters and be expected to slave away here as well as at home."

Naomi felt her defenses rise, and she stiffened. "For your information, Caleb Hoffmeir, I like workin' in this store."

"That may be, but you should still have a little fun now and then."

The back door creaked open, and Naomi jumped. "That's Papa and the kinner. Look as if you're buyin' something," she whispered.

Caleb grabbed a straw hat off the rack nearby and plunked it on the counter. "I'll take this one," he announced in a voice loud enough so Papa could hear. "My old hat's seen better days."

Naomi had just put Caleb's money inside the cash register when her father came sauntering up front. He held Zach in his arms and was followed by Naomi's younger sisters. He spotted Caleb right away and gave him a nod.

Caleb smiled in return and pointed to his new hat. "Last time I was here, you said I should buy a new one. Finally decided to take your advice."

"I'd say it's high time, too." Papa set the baby on the floor, and Zach crawled off toward a shelf full of wooden toys. "Watch your brother now," he said to Nancy.

Nancy and Mary Ann both knelt next to Zach, and Caleb turned his attention back to Naomi, giving her a quick wink.

She shook her head, hoping he would take the hint and leave. He just stood there gazing at her, however.

"Want me to dispose of your old hat?" she asked.

"Naw. Think I'll hang onto it awhile. I might decide to wear it for everyday and keep the new one just for good."

"Makes sense to me," Papa said.

Caleb grabbed the new hat off the counter, gave Naomi another wink, then headed out the front door. "See you around, Abraham," he called over his shoulder.

Papa's only response was a muffled grunt, and Naomi almost laughed out loud. Sometimes it amazed her the way a twenty-two-year-old man could act so big and smart one minute, and the next minute he was carrying on like a little boy.

As soon as Caleb pulled into his yard, he realized something was amiss. Timmy, one of their goats, had gotten out of his pen and was running around the yard, *baa*-ing like crazy.

"Get back in your pen, you stupid animal, and leave my buggy alone!"

Caleb jumped down from his rig as his dad whizzed past, brandishing a buggy whip and hollering like the barn was on fire.

"What's goin' on?" Caleb called.

"That stupid goat was in my buggy, and he chewed up the front seat." Pop jumped to one side as the goat whizzed past him and leaped onto a tree stump. He raised the buggy whip, but the critter took off before he could take aim. Timmy jumped onto the front porch, toppling a chair in the process. He raced back and forth two times, then ran down the other side and headed straight for Pop's buggy.

"Oh no, you don't!" he railed.

When Pop climbed in after him, Timmy hopped into the front seat and made a beeline for the back. Out the back side the goat went, tearing the canvas cover in the process.

Deciding to join the chase, Caleb sprinted after Timmy, with his dad right behind him. They cornered the goat near the barn, but when Caleb reached for him, the animal skirted away and took off again. Pop was on his heels, with the buggy whip swishing this way and that. Caleb ducked to avoid being hit, but it was too late.

Snap! The whip caught Caleb's left shoulder, and he winced. "Hey, it's Timmy you should be after, Pop, not me!"

His dad halted. "I hit you?"

Caleb nodded and reached up to rub the welt that had already formed on his shoulder.

"I'm sorry, Son. Sure didn't mean that to happen."

"I know you didn't do it on purpose," Caleb said, forcing a smile. He'd never admit it, but the welt stung like crazy.

Timmy made another pass, this time right between Caleb's legs. He leaned over and grabbed the goat's back legs, and the animal hollered like a stuck pig.

"It's off to the goat corral for you." Caleb lifted the squirming animal into his arms and trudged toward the pen. If this were any indication of how the rest of his day was going to be, he might as well take the afternoon off. Only trouble was, he had tons of work to do. Now, thanks to Timmy the goat, he'd have his daed's buggy to fix, as well.

"You'd better let your mamm take a look at that shoulder. Don't want to chance infection," Pop called as Caleb headed to his buggy shop.

Caleb shook his head and kept walking. "I'll be okay. It can't be any worse than the bletschings I used to get when I was a boy."

CHAPTER 6

As Caleb rolled out of bed the next morning, a stinging pain sliced through his left shoulder. He winced as he lifted one arm to slip on his cotton shirt. "Should have asked Mom to put some salve on it last night," he muttered as he stepped into his trousers.

A short time later, he found his mother in the kitchen, slicing an apple crumb pie. His younger sisters, Irma and Lettie, were busy setting the table for breakfast.

"How ya feelin' this morning?" Mom questioned. "Your daed never said a thing about the goat gettin' out and him hitting you with the buggy whip 'til we went to bed last night."

Caleb shrugged. "I'll live, and Pop didn't do it on purpose."

"Of course not." Mom pushed a wayward strand of grayish blond hair back into place and pulled out a chair. "Have yourself a seat, and I'll put some peroxide on that welt. No doubt it's hurtin' this morning."

Caleb's manly pride called for denial, but he knew he'd be miserable all day if he didn't get the pain to subside. Besides, as Pop had said yesterday, it could become infected if left untreated.

He undid his shirt and slipped it over his shoulder.

Irma, who was nine, let out a low whistle. "Ach, my! That sure looks elendich."

"Never mind how pitiful it looks," their mother scolded. "Run over to the cupboard and get some peroxide and salve."

Irma and Lettie both stood near Caleb, each of them peering at his wound as though they'd never seen anything like it before.

"Hurry and get the salve," Mom persisted as she gently washed the welt with a damp piece of cloth.

Irma trotted across the room and returned a few seconds later with both salve and peroxide.

The cold, stinging contact of the cleansing liquid caused Caleb to let out a little yelp.

"Sorry, but it's really red, and this should keep it from getting infected." Mom allowed it to dry a few minutes, then she slathered some healing salve on the area. "We should probably cover it with a bandage, but I don't think we've got one large enough."

Caleb slipped his shirt back in place. "That's okay. It'll be fine now. *Danki,* Mom."

Her dark eyes held a note of sympathy. "Haven't had to tend a wound on my oldest boy in ever so long. Still hurts me as much as it does you, ya know."

"That's what Pop always says when he gives me a bletsching," Lettie said, wrinkling her freckled nose.

Mom patted the young girl's arm. "It's true. Neither your daed nor I take any pleasure in doling out punishment."

"You punish us 'cause you love us—that's what Pop has told me many times," Irma interjected.

"And don't you ever forget it," Caleb said, giving his little sister a tickle under her chin.

She giggled and scampered away from the table.

Caleb had just poured himself a cup of coffee when his two younger brothers, Andy and Marvin, entered the room, each carrying an armload of firewood for the cookstove. Mom hadn't begun using the gas stove yet, as she said she much preferred wood and wouldn't use propane until the summer days became too warm.

"Say, Caleb, Bishop Swartley's outside waitin' to see you," Andy announced.

"Why didn't you invite the man in for a cup of coffee or to join us for breakfast?" Mom asked.

Marvin gave Mom a look that resembled a young boy rather than a nineteen-year-old man. "I did ask, but he says he's in a hurry and needs to speak to the buggy maker."

Caleb pushed his chair away from the table. Even though Andy and Marvin worked part-time in his shop, many of their customers wished to speak with Caleb instead of his brothers who didn't know a lot about the business yet. "Keep a plate of breakfast warm for me, Mom," he said on his way out the door.

Caleb found Andrew Swartley standing beside his buggy with one eye squinted, his nose crinkled, and lips set in a thin line. The straw hat on the man's gray head sat at an odd angle, nearly covering his other eye.

"What can I do for you, Bishop Swartley?" Caleb asked as he strode alongside the elderly man.

"Got a little problem with my buggy wheel." The bishop motioned to the left side of his rig. "It wobbles something fierce."

Caleb squatted down beside the wheel. "Looks like you're missing a couple spokes, and the wheel is bent besides. What happened?"

The bishop cleared his throat a few times and dragged the toe of his black boot in the dirt, much like a young boy might do when he was caught doing something wrong. "Well, it's like this. . . . Me and Mose Kauffman were havin' ourselves a little race the other day, and I kinda ran off the road and hit a tree."

Caleb nearly choked on the laughter bubbling in his throat. He knew a lot of the younger Amish men raced their buggies against one another, but the bishop was eighty-two years old, for goodness sake. He ought to have better sense.

Fighting for control so as not to appear disrespectful, Caleb clenched his teeth.

"Think you might be able to fix it while's I wait?" the bishop asked.

"I suppose I could. Since Pop and my brothers finished most of the planting yesterday, I'll have Andy and Marvin's help today." He motioned toward the house. "Why don't you come inside and have some breakfast with the family? After we eat, me and the boys will get right to work on your buggy wheel. You can sit on the front porch and visit with Pop, if he don't have too many other things to do, that is."

Bishop Swartley smiled, revealing a gold crown on one tooth that sparkled in the sunlight. "That sounds right gut to me."

Caleb grinned and followed the bishop inside. On days like today and despite the pain in his shoulder, he felt really good about the occupation he'd chosen. Truth was, he didn't think he'd be happy doing anything else.

"Hand me that packet of peas, would you?" Naomi said to Mary Ann.

"I'll get it." Nancy grabbed for the package, which had been left on the grass, while Naomi made furrows in the dirt to plant the peas. It should have been done weeks ago, but there hadn't been time.

"Hey, Naomi asked me to get those!" Mary Ann

grappled for the peas, and in so doing, spilled the whole packet.

"Now look what you've gone and done," Nancy said, shaking her finger at her younger sister.

Naomi stood and arched her aching back. She was in no mood to referee a quarrel between the girls. "Please, pick up those peas, and be quick about it— both of you."

"But it was Mary Ann who spilled them," Nancy protested.

"It wouldn't have happened if you hadn't grabbed for 'em first," Mary Ann countered.

"Enough!" Naomi shouted. "I've had about as much as I can stand."

The girls became silent, but Naomi could see by the frowns on their faces that neither was happy with the other. They were probably miffed at her, too.

Papa had closed the store today so he could help the brothers get some of the plowing and planting done in the fields. Naomi thought at first he would expect her to take the kinner to the store and manage things on her own, but he'd suggested she stay home and get caught up on things needing to be done. She'd been hard at work since breakfast, and nothing had gone right. She'd dropped a shoofly pie on her clean kitchen floor, Zach had been difficult to get down for a nap, and ever since she and her sisters came to the garden, all they'd done was bicker.

I wish I'd been an only child, Naomi fumed. She was tempted to haul both girls into the kitchen and give them a bletsching but figured that wouldn't help things any. Maybe it would be best to separate them awhile.

"I'll tell you what," Naomi said as she knelt next to Mary Ann and helped rescue the peas. "Why don't you and I finish this job, and Nancy can go inside and start lunch?"

Nancy thrust out her lower lip. "By myself?"

Naomi nodded. "You're ten years old now and gettin' quite capable in the kitchen. I think you'll do a gut job making lunch for everyone."

Her sister's eyes brightened. "You really think so?"

"Sure do."

"I'll ring the dinner bell when the meal's ready." Nancy hopped up, brushed the dirt from her apron, and sprinted for the house.

Naomi released a weary sigh. At least that problem had been solved.

"I don't see why we can't use Midnight in the fields," Norman complained to his father as they walked toward the house for their noon meal.

Abraham gave an exasperated moan. "If I've told you once, I've told ya a hundred times. That horse is not yet broke. Have you forgotten the way he acted up the other day when you tried to hitch him to the buggy?"

"How's he ever gonna learn if we don't put him to work?"

"He'll be put to work when he's broke."

"Papa's right," Matthew put in. "I've been workin' with Midnight whenever I have free time, but it'll be awhile before he's ready to pull a buggy."

"All good things take time," Jake put in.

"I'll be glad when I'm on my own," Norman grumbled. "Then I can do whatever I want."

Abraham grabbed Norman by the shirttail. "What was that?"

The boy shook his head. "Nothin', Papa."

"Seems here of late, all you do is gripe and complain. If you're not careful, I'll be sendin' you to the store with Naomi every day, and I'll stay here to help Matthew and Jake." The thought of farming appealed to Abraham more than he cared to admit, but he'd made a commitment to run the store, and for Sarah's sake, he'd see it through. She'd loved the place, and he was committed to keeping the business going in memory of his precious wife.

If only life weren't so full of disappointments. Norman might think he'll be able to do whatever he wants when he's a grown man, but he's in for a big surprise.

Naomi and Mary Ann had just finished planting the last of the peas when Papa and the brothers walked into the yard. Papa, Norman, and Jake headed straight for the house, but Matthew stopped at the garden patch. "How's it goin'?" he asked. "Any trouble with Hildy today?"

Naomi shook her head. "If I had my way, she'd be

gone." She wiped the perspiration from her forehead and grimaced.

"I begged Papa not to kill the goose, so he made me promise to stay out of her way and try not to act scared whenever she comes around," Mary Ann put in.

Matthew nodded at Mary Ann, then turned back to Naomi, offering her a sympathetic smile. "Wish I could help you in the garden, but there's a lot to be done in the fields yet."

"I know." Naomi turned to her little sister. "Run up to the house and get washed. If Nancy doesn't have everything ready, see what you can do to help."

The child skittered away, and Naomi faced Matthew again. "Sure wish I didn't have so much to do. Between workin' at the store most every day and all the chores to do here, I'm plumb tuckered out."

Matthew shuffled his feet, and a wisp of dust curled around his boots. "I'm sorry you're so miserable, Sister. Things have been kind of hard since Mama died. Sorry to say, but you've had to shoulder more than your share of the work." He patted her arm with his solid, calloused hand.

Naomi smiled through her tears. "It means a lot to know someone cares."

"Of course I care. Papa cares, too—he just has a funny way of showin' it."

She sniffed. "You really think he cares?"

"Jah."

"Then how come he never says so? If Papa cares, why does he yell so much and expect me to do every-

87

thing like Mama used to?"

Matthew shrugged. "Don't know. Why don't you ask him?"

"I did, and he said he wasn't tryin' to compare me to Mama."

"Maybe he's not then."

"He is so. All the time he's saying, 'Your mamm didn't do it this way or that.'" Naomi looked away. There was no point saying anything more. If she broke down in front of Matthew, he'd probably think she was a big boppli.

"Things between you and Papa will work out, Naomi. You'll see."

She stared at the toes of her sneakers. "I hope so. I surely do."

CHAPTER 7

By the first week of May, Naomi wondered how she would make it through the summer. The store had been bombarded with customers, many of them curious tourists, and the garden was growing weeds faster than she could keep up. Every evening after they returned home from the store, Naomi and her sisters tackled the weeds. It was backbreaking, especially when Naomi was already tired from doing her regular chores and helping out at the store.

Tonight, as she prepared for bed, tension pulled the muscles in her neck and upper back. *Will things ever get easier? It's been a year since Mama died, yet I still struggle to get everything done. How did you do it all, Mama?*

Naomi took a seat on the edge of her bed, pulled the pins from her hair, and brushed the golden brown waves cascading across her shoulders. Tomorrow was an off-Sunday, and there would be no church. Maybe she could get caught up on her rest, since they had no company coming and no plans to go calling.

Zach stirred from his crib across the room, and Naomi went to check on him. He'd kicked off the covers, exposing his bare feet.

"Sleep well, little one, and may your days ahead be trouble free," Naomi murmured as she pulled the boy's quilt over his body. *The quilt Mama made before Zach was born. It's all my little brother has of our mamm now.* Naomi's nose burned with unshed tears. *I won't cry. There's been enough tears already.* She leaned over and kissed the baby's forehead, then tiptoed across the room.

Letting the weight of exhaustion settle over her body like a heavy blanket, she flopped onto her bed. As soon as her eyes closed, a vision of Caleb came to mind. What would it be like if they could marry and start a family? Would she be happier raising her own children than taking care of her siblings?

"Guess I'll never know," she murmured before drifting off to sleep.

Holding a single red rose in one hand and his lunch pail in the other, Jim stepped into the kitchen. "Honey, I'm home!"

When there was no response, he decided Linda might be upstairs taking a nap. She'd been doing that a lot lately, and he suspected it had something to do with her depression over not having a baby.

"That's about to change." He dropped his lunch pail on the counter, opened the door under the sink, retrieved a small glass vase, and inserted the rose. Eager to share his good news, he headed upstairs.

As Jim expected, he found his wife on the bed. She wasn't sleeping, though—just lying there staring at the ceiling.

He bent over and kissed Linda's forehead, then held up the rose.

"What's that for?"

"We're celebrating."

"Celebrating what?"

"Our lawyer, Max, called this afternoon, saying a young woman in Bel Air, Maryland, has agreed to give us her son. If you're agreeable, we can head east by the end of next week. That'll give me time to get some jobs lined out and be sure my foreman knows what to do in my absence."

Linda sat up, her eyes wide and her mouth open. "A baby? We're finally going to get a baby?"

"Not exactly a baby. He's a year old, but—"

"A year isn't that old, Jim. He's almost a baby,"

she said excitedly.

Jim smiled. "I was hoping you'd see it that way."

She clambered off the bed. "The end of next week, you said?"

"I think we can be ready by then, don't you?"

She nodded and wrapped her arms around him, almost crushing the rose. "Will we fly or drive?"

"I thought it would be best if we drove. It's been several years since we've had a real vacation, and we can see a few things on our way to and from."

Linda rushed over to their closet and pulled out a suitcase. "There's so much to do between now and then. I'll need to pack, make motel reservations in Maryland, buy some baby things, get the nursery ready—"

"Whoa! Slow down, sweetie. I'll take care of the motel reservations, we can go shopping together, and you can pack. How's that sound?"

She grinned, reminding him of the carefree young woman he'd married eight years ago. "This is going to be the best vacation ever!"

"Yeah, I think so, too."

Naomi stood at the stove, stirring a pan full of scrambled eggs. Papa, Matthew, Norman, and Jake were still outside doing chores. Samuel and Mary Ann had gone to the henhouse to gather eggs. Zach sat in his high chair across the room, while Nancy spoon-fed him cereal.

"Is breakfast ready yet?" Nancy asked. "I'm so

hungry I might start eating the boppli's mush."

Naomi chuckled. "The eggs will be done soon. I think you can wait."

"Since there's no preaching today, can we do somethin' fun?"

Naomi considered her sister's question. She'd planned to rest most of the day, but doing something fun might be a better way to relax.

"What would you like to do?" she asked.

"How about if we go over to the Beechys' place? I hear they have a batch of new piglets and a couple of baby goats."

The idea of spending time in the company of Anna Beechy did have some appeal. The woman was old enough to be Naomi's grandmother, and since Naomi had no grandparents living nearby, Anna was the next best thing. Always cheerful and bursting with good advice, Anna was a joy to be around.

Naomi sprinkled salt over the eggs. "If Papa says it's okay, then I'll take you, Mary Ann, Samuel, and Zach over to the Beechys' after our noon meal."

"Then I hope he says yes, 'cause I'm ready for some fun." There was a pause before Nancy added, "I'm sick of workin' so hard, aren't you?"

"We've all been working hard, and with summer upon us, it's not likely to get much better," Naomi replied. "The garden will soon be producing, and then there will be canning to do."

Nancy groaned. "I don't like to can. It gets too hot in the kitchen."

"I know, but it has to be done. We can always cool our insides with some of Papa's homemade root beer, you know."

"That's true. Do ya suppose he'll be askin' us to sell some to neighbors and English folks who see our sign at the end of the driveway?"

Naomi added a bit of pepper to the scrambled eggs. "No doubt he will be wantin' us to do just that."

"Hey! Cut that out, you little rascal!"

Naomi turned in time to see a blob of cereal fly out of Zach's grubby little hands and hit Nancy in the middle of her nose. She chuckled. "At least it's not me feeding the stinker this time."

Naomi had no sooner pulled their buggy into the Beechys' yard, when Samuel, Nancy, and Mary Ann scrambled down and hurried to the barn.

She smiled as she hoisted Zach into her arms and stepped out of the buggy. Even though it had been a long time since she'd felt the exuberance her younger siblings obviously felt, she could still remember how wonderful it was to see newly born critters on a farm.

As she strolled across the Beechys' lawn, Naomi couldn't help but notice the weed-free garden bordering the house. Colorful flowers danced in the breeze, making Naomi mindful of her own flowerbeds choked with weeds. It wasn't the way of the Amish to allow their gardens to be neglected. But then, most families had many helpers, not just three younger siblings who pulled more pranks on each other than they did weeds.

"It's gut to see you," Anna called from her rocking chair on the front porch. She waved and beckoned Naomi to join her. "Did you come for a little visit, or were you needing something?"

"I brought the younger ones to see your baby animals." Naomi stepped onto the porch, holding Zach against her hip. "They've already headed to the barn, so I hope that's okay."

"Oh, sure. Abner's out there, and he'll be glad to show off his new piglets and the twin goats born last week." Anna's wire-rimmed glasses had slipped to the end of her nose, and the strings of her white head covering draped over her shoulder. "Have a seat, won't ya?"

Naomi sat in the wicker chair beside Anna's rocker and placed Zach on her lap. He squirmed restlessly, but she held on tight. "You're not gettin' down, ya hear?"

"Is the boy walkin' yet?" Anna asked.

"No, but he crawls plenty fast, and I'm afraid if I put him down, he might try to follow the others out to the barn."

"You can take him there now if you'd like. We can always talk later." Anna leaned over and chucked Zach under his chubby chin. "You're sure growin', ya know that?"

"I think we can stay here awhile," Naomi said. "It won't hurt him to learn how to sit still."

"Would ya mind if I hold him?" Anna asked with an eager expression.

Naomi handed Zach over and smiled as he nestled against the older woman's chest. "You're sure good with kinner. I can tell he likes you."

Anna chuckled. "I'd better be good with 'em, for I've had plenty of practice over the years, what with raisin' my own young'uns and now havin' *kinskinner*."

Naomi couldn't imagine having grandchildren. Since it wasn't likely she'd ever marry, she would probably never have any children, much less grandchildren.

"Your flowers are sure beautiful. Not a weed in sight," she said, changing the subject.

"My daughter Lydia helps some, but mostly the flowerbeds are my job." When Anna smiled, her wrinkles seemed to disappear. "I love the feel of dirt beneath my fingers, not to mention the wonderful gut aroma of the flowers as they come into bloom."

"Who takes care of the vegetable garden?"

"It's a joint effort, with me, Lydia, and my older granddaughters, Peggy and Rebecca, taking turns at weed pullin' and the like." Anna chuckled. "Leona doesn't help yet 'cause she's too little and would just be in the way."

Naomi thought about three-year-old Leona and how she often came with her father, Jacob Weaver, to the store. Jacob had been Papa's friend for as long as she remembered. His oldest boy helped in his painting business, his two older daughters assisted their mother at home, and Leona, the youngest, was a real cutie.

"Our vegetable patch doesn't look nearly so good," Naomi admitted, bringing her musings to a standstill.

Anna pushed the rocker back and forth, and Zach giggled. "Have you got much celery planted this year?" she asked.

"Not much a'tall. Why do you ask?"

"Thought maybe somebody at your house might be gettin' married come November."

Naomi shook her head. "Not unless one of my brothers decides to find himself a wife, and then it would be her family who'd need to supply the celery for the wedding supper."

Anna clucked her tongue. "I figured a young woman your age would have a serious beau by now and be thinkin' of marriage."

Naomi's voice lowered to a whisper. "That's about as likely as a cat makin' friends with a dog."

"I've known that to happen a time or two."

Naomi smiled. Anna Beechy always looked on the bright side of things.

"There's no special man in your life then?"

"Not really." An image of Caleb Hoffmeir popped into Naomi's head. "Even if there were, I'd never have enough time to court."

Anna shook her head. "Such a shame your daed hasn't found himself another wife by now. If Abraham were to get married, you wouldn't have so many responsibilities and would be free to court."

Naomi opened her mouth to reply, but Zach's high-pitched scream cut her off.

"I think the little guy's hungry," Anna said. "Why don't I take him inside and see if I can find something he might like while you walk out to the barn and check on the others?"

"You wouldn't mind?"

"Not a'tall." Anna stood. "Now run along and have a little fun. Me and the boppli will be just fine."

"All right then. I'll be back soon." Naomi jumped up, took the stairs two at a time, and sprinted toward the barn, determined to make the most of her unexpected free time.

A few minutes later, she found her sisters and brother kneeling in the hay beside the twin goats.

"Look, Naomi," Samuel announced. "They like us already."

"Well, sure they do," Abner Beechy agreed. He sat on a bale of hay nearby, his straw hat tipped at an odd angle, a wide smile on his weathered face.

Mary Ann looked up at Naomi and grinned from ear to ear. "We seen the new piglets, too."

"Come, pet Floppy. She won't bite." Nancy motioned for Naomi to join them.

She knelt between her sisters. "You've already named the twins?"

"Yep. This here's Floppy 'cause his tail flops around," Samuel said, pointing to the smaller of the two goats. "And this one we've decided to call Taffy, since her skin's the color of taffy candy."

Naomi stroked each of the goats behind the ears and touched the tips of their wet noses. They were soft and silky and awfully cute. She laughed when one of the kids made a *baa*-ing sound and licked her finger. Maybe there was some joy in life, after all. Maybe she just needed to look for it more often.

"I still don't understand why we couldn't have flown to the East Coast. It would have been much quicker than driving."

Jim glanced at his wife, sitting in the passenger seat of their minivan. "I told you before—this will give us a chance to see some beautiful country between here and there."

She frowned. "I just want to bring our little boy home. Didn't you say you'd set up an appointment for us to meet with the woman and her lawyer on Saturday morning?"

He nodded. "This is only Monday, Linda. That gives us five whole days to get there."

"And we can stop in Lancaster to see the Amish?"

"Bel Air's only a few hours from Lancaster," he said, feeling his patience begin to wane. Wasn't Linda listening the first time he'd explained all the details, or was she becoming forgetful like her mother? "I told you we can stop in Lancaster before we head to our hotel in Bel Air."

"Okay."

"I called my folks the other day and told them we'd be coming to Ohio soon after we picked up the boy.

They're eager to meet their new grandson." Jim flicked on the blinker and headed up the ramp taking them to the freeway. "Think how much fun it will be to see the Amish. And you can finally buy that hand-made quilt you've been wanting, Linda."

"Amish quilts are expensive, you know."

He shrugged. "You're worth it."

They rode in silence for a while, then Linda spoke again. "What if he doesn't like us, Jim?"

"Who?"

"The baby."

"You worry too much. What's not to like? You've got enough love in your heart for ten babies, and I'm . . ." Jim chuckled. "Well, what can I say? I'm gonna be the world's best dad."

She reached over and touched his arm. "I know you will."

"You're not disappointed because he isn't a new-born?"

She shook her head. "I can't wait to hold our son and tell him how much I love him."

CHAPTER 8

Naomi pushed an errant strand of hair away from her face as she washed a new picking of peas. Today had been busier than usual at the store, and she was so tired this evening she could barely stand at the sink, much less prepare supper.

"The family's counting on me, and it won't get done unless I do it," she mumbled with renewed determination.

"You talkin' to yourself, Sister?"

Naomi turned her head. She'd thought she was alone in the kitchen.

Nancy stood near the back door with another basket of peas in her hand. This was the third one she'd brought in for Naomi to wash.

"Guess I was talking to myself," Naomi admitted. She nodded toward the counter. "Just put 'em over there, and then you need to get washed and start setting the table. Papa and the brothers will be in soon, and they'll expect the meal to be ready and waiting."

"Why can't Mary Ann set the table?"

"She's in the living room with Zach at the moment—hopefully keepin' him out of trouble."

"I'll be glad when Saturday comes and we can stay home. I'd rather be sellin' root beer at home than workin' at the store all day."

"There'll be plenty of work to do here, as well," Naomi reminded. She poured the clean peas into a kettle and placed it on the stove. "Remember, we won't just be sellin' root beer on Saturday."

Nancy set the basket on the counter. "Jah, I know."

"If things go well, maybe we can take time out to have a little picnic."

"Can we have it down at the creek?"

"I don't think so. We've gotta stay close to the house

100

in case we get any root beer customers."

Nancy scowled. "Then how are we gonna have a picnic?"

"We can eat it at the picnic table on the lawn. That way we can watch for customers, and if there's time, maybe we can play a game of croquet."

"Sounds gut to me." Nancy started for the stairs. "I'm goin' upstairs to wash, but I'll be back to set the table."

Naomi blew out her breath. She didn't have the heart to tell Nancy they might not have time for a picnic lunch if they had a lot of customers or didn't get all their chores done on time. She figured the child needed something to look forward to. All work and no play was bad for any soul, especially the kinner.

Jim stood at the window, looking down at the hotel parking lot. They had arrived in Lancaster, Pennsylvania, that morning; but after only a few hours of shopping and sightseeing, Linda developed one of her sick headaches and begged Jim to stop. He'd been fortunate enough to find a hotel with a vacancy and had canceled their reservation in Bel Air. They would leave the hotel in Lancaster at eight in the morning and be in Bel Air by ten. By this time tomorrow evening, they'd be a family of three.

Jim's cell phone rang, and he pulled it from the clip on his belt. His conversation lasted only a few minutes, and during that time he kept glancing at the bathroom door, where Linda had gone to take something for her headache and to try to relax in a warm bath.

A few seconds after he hung up the phone, she returned to the room with a questioning look on her face. "I thought I heard your cell phone ring."

He nodded.

"Who was it?"

"Carl Stevens. The lawyer representing the baby's mother."

Linda's face paled. "Please tell me there's nothing wrong. She didn't back out or anything, did she, Jim?"

"Mr. Stevens called to let me know our meeting tomorrow is still on schedule."

Linda frowned. "I wish it had been today."

"The way you're feeling, you wouldn't have been up to it today, Linda. You'll feel better by tomorrow." Jim took Linda's hand and led her over to the bed. "Please, lie down and try to relax. You look all done in."

She flopped down on the bed, pulling her legs underneath her and leaning against the pillows. "I am kind of tired, and this headache doesn't seem to be going away. It's been a long five days on the road."

"I know, honey, but it'll be worth it when we get the baby. You'll be so excited you'll forget you were ever tired or had a migraine."

"I hope so." Linda rubbed her forehead.

Jim massaged her shoulders and neck. "Lie down now and rest awhile. You hardly slept last night, and I'm afraid you're going to feel worse if you don't get some sleep."

She yawned. "You're right. I haven't slept well since we left home. A nap might really help."

"That's my girl. You'll feel better after this is all behind us and we're heading to Ohio with our boy."

She nodded and scooted farther down on the bed. "We've waited so long for a baby. I just want to hold him."

He pulled the cotton bedspread over her. "Soon, Linda. Just one more day and we'll have our son."

As Caleb headed for home, he felt a renewed sense of determination. He'd been in town on errands today and had gone by the Fishers' store in hopes of seeing Naomi. Just like the other times he'd dropped by lately, she was busy. Too busy to talk, she'd informed him. Even if she hadn't been busy, Caleb knew Naomi's father was there, watching Naomi's every move and listening to whatever she and Caleb said.

Caleb clucked to the horse to get him moving faster. "Probably shouldn't have left Andy alone at the buggy shop while I went to town, but I wanted the chance to see Naomi again."

The only good thing that had happened during his visit to the store was the minute he'd spent talking to Nancy Fisher, when she'd given him the news that Naomi and the younger ones would be staying home on Saturday to sell root beer from their front yard. Abraham would probably be working at the store all day, which meant Caleb could drop by the Fishers' place for some root beer and the chance to speak to

Naomi without fear of her dad eavesdropping. He hadn't given up on their relationship yet and was determined to find a way for them to be together.

"Maybe I'll see if Mom has a nice plant I could take Naomi," he mumbled. "That oughta make her take notice of the way I feel."

Caleb talked to his horse the rest of the way home, and by the time he pulled up to the mailbox beside the driveway, he was feeling pretty confident. He opened the box and withdrew the day's mail. Smiling, he noticed a letter from his cousin, Henry, who owned a buggy shop in Holmes County, Ohio. He tore it open and read the letter out loud.

Dear Caleb:

I've been to an auction and have acquired some antique buggy parts—wheels, axles, springs, moldings, a couple of old seats, and a surrey top. If you're interested in buying some, hop a bus and come take a look. Don't be too long, though, 'cause a couple of other people are interested. Wanted to give you first pick.

Your cousin,
Henry Stutzman

Caleb grinned. He would leave Andy and Marvin in charge of his shop for a few days, and come Saturday, he'd be on a bus bound for Berlin, Ohio. He would have to see Naomi some other time.

Whistling a happy tune, Caleb entered the buggy

shop a short time later, but he stopped inside the door, shocked by the sight that greeted him. Andy was sitting on the floor, moaning and grasping the palm of his left hand.

"What's wrong?" Caleb dashed over to his brother and dropped to his knees.

Andy's face contorted. "It's my thumb! Shot a nail straight into it."

"How'd ya do somethin' like that, and where was Marvin when it happened?" Caleb reached for Andy's hand, and his stomach churned at the sight. A three-inch nail was partially embedded in his brother's thumb.

"I was usin' that new air gun you bought awhile back—and guess my aim was off." Andy's lower lip jutted out, making him look much younger than his eighteen years. "Marvin's still out in the fields helpin' Pop, John, and David." He grimaced. "This sure does hurt like crazy."

"I can only imagine." Caleb put his arm around Andy's waist. "Here, let me help you up. Then we'd better get one of our neighbors to drive us to the emergency room."

Andy's dark eyes widened as he shook his head. "The hospital?"

Caleb nodded. "You need to get this taken care of right away. Can't go around with a nail stickin' out of your thumb for the rest of your life."

"But I hate hospitals. They use big needles and do things to folks that hurt somethin' awful."

"Nothing they do to you at the hospital could be much worse than what you've done to yourself. Now let's go."

Andy allowed Caleb to lead him out of the shop and into Caleb's open buggy. As soon as he had his brother settled in the passenger seat, Caleb ran into the house to tell Mom what had happened and let her know they'd be driving to the Petersons' to see about getting a ride to the hospital. So much for doing any more today. At the rate things were going, Caleb wondered if he'd be able to go to Ohio on Saturday.

Abraham took a seat on a bale of straw and leaned his head against the wooden planks of the barn. The sweet smell of hay tantalized his senses, and he drew in a deep breath. *Too bad I can't enjoy my farm all the time. If only I weren't so tired after workin' at the store all day.*

"I have learned, in whatsoever state I am, therewith to be content." Abraham thought about the verse of scripture Bishop Swartley had recently quoted from Philippians 4:11. Just this afternoon, his friend Jacob Weaver had reminded him that Hebrews 13:5 said, "Let your conversation be without covetousness; and be content with such things as ye have: for he hath said, I will never leave thee, nor forsake thee."

Of course, Jacob was talking about the need for Abraham to be content with his family and learn to enjoy them more. He said it was time for Abraham to quit grieving over Sarah's death and realize God hadn't left him and would never forsake him.

Abraham closed his eyes, and a vision of his sweet wife burst into his mind. He blinked and tried to dispel the image, but it only became stronger.

It was the day of their wedding, and he could hear Sarah's voice and feel her soft touch. Sarah's dark eyes revealed the depth of her love for him, and they had promised to cherish one another until death parted them.

"Papa, are you sleepin'? The supper bell's chimin', and it's time to eat."

Abraham forced his eyes open, reluctantly letting go of Sarah's image. Little had he known on their wedding day that she would be the first to pass on.

When he looked up at his oldest son, he noticed a worried frown on Matthew's face.

"You okay, Papa?"

"Fine. Just restin' my eyes." He stood and arched his back.

Matthew started for the barn door. "You comin' then?"

"Right behind you." Abraham took one more look around the barn. He'd been grieving for Sarah long enough. It was time to move on. Jacob was right. He needed to be content with what he had. Maybe tomorrow, after he got home from the store, he'd set up the tent in their backyard, and they'd have themselves a little campout. He figured the younger ones would like it, and truth be told, he was looking forward to it, as well.

CHAPTER 9

"Linda, are you awake? It's time to get up. Our appointment is in three hours."

Linda's only response was a deep moan.

Jim touched his wife's forehead. She wasn't running a fever; that was good. "What's wrong, honey? Are you still feeling sick this morning?"

She nodded but kept her eyes closed.

"Maybe you'll feel better once you've had some breakfast."

Linda rolled onto her side. "My head is pounding, and my stomach's so upset, I don't think I could keep anything down."

Jim climbed out of bed. "I'll go take my shower and check on you when I get out."

"Okay."

Ten minutes later, when Jim returned to the bedroom, he discovered that Linda was no better.

"Honey, I think you're gonna have to stay here while I go to Maryland to pick up the baby."

"I have to go with you." She lifted her head but let it fall back on the pillow.

"You don't have to go, Linda. It will be better if you sleep off that migraine."

"What about the papers? Won't I be expected to sign something?"

"We both signed the necessary papers in Max's office several weeks ago. He faxed them to the woman's lawyer, remember?"

"Oh, that's right." She opened her eyes, and when she looked up, Jim noticed there were tears ready to spill over.

Linda's face looked pale and drawn, and he knew she would never make the two-hour trip to Bel Air without throwing up. He bent over and kissed her forehead. "Close your eyes and get some sleep. By the time you wake up, you'll be feeling better, and I'll be here with our boy."

She nodded, and a tear trickled down her cheek. "Don't stop anywhere on the way back. Bring him straight to the hotel, okay?"

"I will, honey."

Before Papa and Samuel left for the store in the morning, he'd nailed a sign to the fence at the end of their driveway, and Naomi placed several jugs of root beer on the picnic table. By nine o'clock, they'd had a few English customers who said they'd driven by the farm and seen the sign. A couple of their Amish neighbors also dropped by. Naomi wondered how she would get any chores done when she had to race back and forth from the house to the yard to wait on customers. Nancy wasn't good at making change, so Naomi put her and Mary Ann to work inside while she handled the root beer sales. During the slack times, she rushed into the house, tended to Zach, did some cleaning, and instructed her sisters on what they should be doing. At the moment, they were supposed to be cleaning their bedroom while she mopped the kitchen floor. Instead, they were arguing, and Naomi was afraid they would wake Zach, who was taking his morning nap.

She set the mop and bucket aside and trudged up the stairs.

"What's the problem?" Naomi asked when she entered the girls' room.

Mary Ann sat on the hardwood floor with a stack of papers in her lap, and Nancy stood off to one side, her hands on her hips and a scowl on her face.

"Mary Ann won't help me clean," Nancy tattled. "She's been sittin' there goin' through old school papers for the last ten minutes."

"Mary Ann, please get up and help your sister clean this room," Naomi instructed.

The child pointed to the garbage can a few inches away. "I am cleanin'. I'm throwin' out all the papers I don't want."

"You can do that later, after the room is clean." Naomi grabbed the broom, which had been leaning against the wall, and handed it to Nancy. "You sweep, and Mary Ann can hold the dustpan. After that, the windows need to be washed, and your throw rugs should be shaken."

A horn honked in the yard, signaling another root beer customer.

Naomi turned and started for the door. "I'll be back

soon to check on your progress." She left the room, praying she'd have enough patience to get through the day without losing her temper or having to spank someone.

Jim was glad traffic was light that morning, and he had no trouble finding his way to Carl Stevens's office in Bel Air. He parked the minivan in the parking lot, and a few minutes later he entered the building and introduced himself to the receptionist. The middle-aged woman invited him to take a seat, asked if he'd like a cup of coffee, and said Mr. Stevens would be with him in a few minutes.

As Jim sat in a straight-backed chair, holding a mug of coffee in his hands, he wished Linda were with him. Would the lawyer be reluctant to hand the boy over to Jim without meeting his wife first? Would the child willingly go with Jim, or would he make a fuss?

I sure am glad I bought that car seat for the baby before we left Washington. I'm so nervous, I'd probably have forgotten to get one if we'd waited to buy it until we got here.

Jim was more than a little anxious about becoming a father. After eight years of marriage, he and Linda had developed a pleasant routine. Their whole life was about to change, and he hoped it would be for the better and that he wouldn't regret his decision to adopt this little one-year-old boy.

"Mr. Scott?"

Jim's thoughts came to a halt, and he looked up. A

tall man with thinning gray hair and rimless glasses offered him a halfhearted smile.

Jim stood and extended his hand. "You must be Carl Stevens."

"That's right." The man glanced around. "Where's your wife? Linda, isn't that her name?"

"She's at the hotel with a bad headache."

The lawyer raised his eyebrows, but before he could ask any questions, Jim quickly added, "It's just a tension headache. She'll be fine in a couple hours."

"I see. Well, please come into my office." The older man led the way, and Jim followed.

When they entered his office, Mr. Stevens nodded toward a chair. "Please, have a seat."

As he sat down, Jim scanned the room. He and Carl Stevens seemed to be alone. He cleared his throat. "Excuse me, sir, but where's our baby? Will I be meeting the child's mother?"

The lawyer took a seat in the leather chair behind his desk and leaned forward, his hands tightly clasped. "There's been a change in plans."

"Change in plans? What do you mean?" Jim's heartbeat picked up momentum, and a trickle of sweat rolled down his forehead. He didn't like the fact that there was no mother or baby waiting to greet him, and Mr. Stevens's grim look gave no comfort, either.

"Shelby, the boy's mother, phoned me this morning."

"And?"

"I'm sorry to say she's changed her mind."

"About the adoption?" Jim's face heated, and it was all he could do to remain seated.

The lawyer nodded solemnly. "I'm afraid so, and as you already know, she has the right to do that."

Jim jumped up. "But she can't back out now! Linda and I were counting on this adoption. We've come a long way to get the boy."

"I'm aware of that, but you knew there was a chance this could happen. I'm sure your lawyer advised you of the birth mother's rights."

"Yes, he did, but we hadn't heard anything to the contrary since we signed the papers on our end, so we assumed—"

"I'm sorry, Mr. Scott. I'm sure once you explain the details to your lawyer, he will try to find you another child."

Jim trembled as he fought for control. "What details? Why did the birth mother change her mind at the last minute? I need to have something to tell my wife when I show up without the baby."

Mr. Stevens nodded toward the vacant chair. "Please be seated, and I'll explain."

Jim remained firmly planted in front of the desk with his arms folded.

The lawyer shrugged and took a sip of his coffee. "Shelby said after thinking it over, she's not able to part with her son. She's had him a whole year and has grown quite attached."

"Then why in thunder was she planning to give him up for adoption?"

"If you wish to hear the rest of the story, then I insist you calm down."

Jim drew in a deep breath and sank to the chair. "I'm listening."

"The birth mother and the baby have already bonded, and she feels her son will be better off with her."

"That's ridiculous! What can an unwed mother give a child that my wife and I can't?"

"In a material way, probably nothing, but she does have a mother's love to offer her son."

"We would have loved him." Jim clenched his fingers until they were digging into the palms of his hands. "I own a successful painting business. We could give the boy a good upbringing, and he would lack nothing in the way of material things."

"I'm sure that's true, which is exactly why your lawyer should have no trouble finding you another child."

"So that's it then? There's nothing more to be said?"

"No. I'm sorry."

As Jim stood, a sense of defeat crept into his soul and wrapped itself tightly around his heart. How could he face Linda and tell her they had no son? There would be no grandbaby to show off to his folks in Ohio. The truth was, there might never be.

Without another word, Jim stormed out of the lawyer's office, slamming the door behind him. When he climbed into his van and drove away, it felt like a fifty-five-gallon drum of paint rested on his shoulders.

He headed out of Bel Air, up Interstate 1, and onto Highway 222 toward Pennsylvania, wondering what he could tell Linda that might soften the blow.

He gripped the steering wheel and clenched his teeth. "If there's a God in heaven, why would He have allowed this to happen?"

Two hours later, when Jim drove into Lancaster County, he was still fuming. "I need to get myself calmed down before I go back to the hotel." He rolled down his window, but a blast of hot, humid air hit him full in the face.

Snapping on the air conditioner, he turned off the main road and drove aimlessly along the backcountry roads. Over a covered bridge, past several Amish farms, he went farther and farther. A sign nailed to a fence at the end of a driveway caught his attention: HOMEMADE ROOT BEER—$3.00 A GALLON.

He turned in. "Root beer won't solve my problems, but it might take care of my thirst."

Since Zach was happily crawling around on the clean floor, Naomi decided to tackle the kitchen cupboards. The girls had finished cleaning their bedroom and were downstairs in the cellar gathering canning jars, which would be put to use next week.

Naomi pulled out a step stool and was carrying it to the cupboard when she heard a horn honk.

"Ach! Why now?" She turned toward the door and was about to open it, when Zach let out a howl. Her first thought was to ignore him, but then she remembered her sisters weren't able to watch the little guy while she waited on the customer.

Scooping Zach and his small quilt into her arms, Naomi grabbed a tissue from her apron pocket and swiped it across his nose. The horn blared again, and she hurried outside.

An English man stood near the picnic table.

"Can I help ya?" she asked, balancing Zach on her hip.

"I was wondering if you have any cold root beer."

Naomi nodded. "There's some in the house."

"Do you sell it by the glass or only in gallon jugs?"

"Just in jugs, but I'd be happy to give you a paper cup if you're wantin' to drink some now."

The man looked awfully tense, but he did return her smile. "Cute baby you've got there. Is it a boy or girl?"

"He's my youngest brother. Just turned one in April." She plopped Zach in the center of the picnic table, wrapping the quilt around his bare legs. "He weighs a ton, and I'll sure be glad when he starts walkin'."

"Do your folks have many children?" the man asked.

"My mother was hit by a car and died when this little guy was only two months old. That left eight kinner—I mean, kids—for my dad to raise."

He raised his eyebrows. "That's too bad about your mother."

Naomi was about to comment, but a loud shriek

116

caught her attention. "That must be one of my sisters. I'm guessing our crazy goose is chasing one of them again. As soon as I see what's up, I'll be right back with your cold root beer." She dashed off, leaving Zach on the picnic table.

Jim waited patiently for the young woman to return with the root beer, the whole time keeping an eye on the diaper-clad boy sitting in the center of the picnic table. At first the child never moved, but after a few minutes, he began to squirm.

"Sit still, little guy, or you might fall," Jim said.

When the baby grabbed hold of his blanket, scooted to the edge of the table, and tried to climb down, Jim's heart slammed into his chest. "No, no, little boy. You'd better stay put until your sister gets back."

The child's legs dangled precariously over the edge of the table, and Jim knew if he didn't do something, the kid would fall. He grabbed the boy around the waist and lifted him into his arms.

The baby giggled and kicked his chubby feet as a blob of drool rolled down his chin.

Jim grabbed the edge of the colorful quilt and blotted the boy's face with it. "There, that's better, isn't it?" He looked back at the house. *Where is that girl, and what could be taking her so long? Does she think I came here to buy root beer or baby-sit her brother?*

When the child burrowed his downy head into Jim's chest, his heart welled with an emotion he'd never felt before. *So this is what it feels like for a father to hold his son.*

Jim cast another quick glance at the house. All was quiet, and not a soul was in sight. With no thought of the consequences, Jim made an impulsive decision. He whirled around and dashed for the car.

Jerking open the back door, Jim slipped the child into the car seat and buckled him in. He glanced at the house again, and seeing that the coast was clear, he hopped into the driver's side. He slammed the door, turned on the ignition, then sped out of the yard.

CHAPTER 10

Inside the kitchen, Naomi found her sisters standing in the middle of a big mess. Broken glass and some of last year's peaches were splattered on the floor. Nancy swept at it with a broom, while Mary Ann sat at the table, sobbing.

"What happened here? I cleaned this floor once already." Naomi pointed to the sticky linoleum. "I thought you two were supposed to be bringing up jars from the cellar for canning."

"We were, but Mary Ann wanted some peaches, and even though I said no, she took a jar anyway," Nancy said.

Naomi turned to face her youngest sister. "How come?"

"I—I—was hungry, and seein' all those jars of fruit made my stomach want food." Mary Ann hiccupped. "I cut my hand on the glass when I tried to pick up the pieces."

It was then that Naomi noticed Mary Ann's hand was wrapped in a napkin and there was blood seeping through. Naomi hurried to her younger sister and gently took her hand. "You'd better let me take a look at that."

"Don't make it hurt more." Mary Ann's lower lip quivered.

"I'll be careful." When Naomi pulled the napkin aside, the child winced. "This needs some antiseptic and a bandage." She clicked her tongue. "Don't think it's gonna need any stitches, though."

Mary Ann sniffed. "I'm glad. I don't wanna go to the hospital; that's for sure."

Naomi nodded at Nancy. "As soon as you get the glass picked up, would you mind gettin' a jug of cold root beer from the refrigerator? I've got a customer outside waiting."

"Jah, okay."

As Nancy finished her job, Naomi led Mary Ann upstairs to the bathroom, where the first-aid supplies were kept.

When they returned to the kitchen a short time later, the floor was still a mess and Nancy was gone.

Probably took the root beer out like I told her. Naomi grabbed a mop from the utility closet and tackled the sticky floor. "Is there no end to my work today?" she muttered.

The back door opened, and Nancy sauntered in, holding a jug of root beer and looking kind of miffed. "You sent me outside for nothing. There was no customer waitin'."

"Sure there was. He asked for cold root beer, and I told him there was some in the house. Maybe he's in his car." Naomi grabbed the jug of root beer from Nancy and handed her the mop. "Finish this up while I go check."

When Naomi turned, she stubbed her bare toe on the rung of a chair. "Ach!" She limped out the back door and around the side of the house.

When she reached the front yard, Naomi came to a halt. The man was gone, and there was no car in the driveway. "Guess he got tired of waitin'." Her gaze swung back to the picnic table, and she felt the blood drain from her face. Zach was gone, and so was his quilt.

Naomi's stomach clenched as a wisp of fear curled around her heart. She set the jug on the picnic table, willing herself to breathe. *It's okay. Zach's here someplace. He just climbed down from the picnic table and crawled off.*

"Zach! Where are you, baby?" She scanned the yard and strained to hear anything that might give some indication that her little brother was nearby. "He has to be here—just has to be." The only living thing in sight was a chicken wandering up the driveway.

Naomi's knees, decidedly unsteady, threatened to

buckle beneath her. She clutched her midsection and held herself in order to keep from collapsing. *Why was I so stupid? I should never have left Zach sitting on the picnic table with a stranger. What am I gonna tell Papa if I can't find him?*

Ignoring the pain in her foot from her stubbed toe, Naomi rushed back to the house, calling her sisters to come quickly.

Nancy ran out the front door. "Was is letz, Naomi? You look upset."

"Zach's missing, that's what's wrong," Naomi panted.

Mary Ann followed Nancy onto the porch, her dark eyes huge as saucers. "What do you mean, he's missin'?"

Naomi swallowed hard as a raw ache settled in her stomach. "I left him on the picnic table when I came inside to get cold root beer for the man and to see which of you was screaming." She pointed to the table. "But he's gone now. I don't see him anywhere."

Nancy glanced around the yard. "Who was the customer, Naomi? Was it someone we know?"

Naomi shook her head. "It was an English man."

"How come you didn't bring Zach along when you came to the house? What made you leave him all alone?"

Nancy's question was nearly Naomi's undoing. Guilt clung to her like a fly trapped in a spider's web, and tears she'd been fighting to keep under control rimmed her eyes. "I wasn't thinkin' straight. When I heard the scream, all I could think of was getting to the house to see what happened." She shook her head. "I never dreamed Zach would try and climb down or crawl off somewhere while I was gone. Besides, he wasn't alone. I figured the English man would see that Zach stayed put."

Nancy tipped her head and gave Naomi a look that sent shivers up her spine. "How do ya know the boppli crawled away?"

"He sure enough didn't walk, unless he's learned something new without us knowing." Naomi was in no mood for these silly questions. They needed to find Zach, and she knew it had better be before Papa got home.

Naomi's shoulders were tense, and a jolt of pain shot up her neck. "I need you two to help me look for him. He couldn't have gone far."

For the next half hour, the girls searched in the garden, the woodshed, the chicken coop, and all through the house, even though Naomi didn't see how Zach could have crawled there without her or one of the sisters seeing him.

With a sigh of resignation, she finally sent Nancy out to the fields to get the brothers. They needed more help looking.

After Naomi explained to Matthew how she'd left Zach on the picnic table, everyone spread out, searching a second time in every nook and cranny and calling Zach's name.

"I'm hitching up the buggy," Matthew announced.

"I'll look for Zach along the road."

"Come now," Naomi said with irritation. "There's no way he would have crawled up the driveway. Not with the sharp rocks and all."

"Did you ever think maybe that English man took him?" Norman said, squinting and looking at Naomi like she didn't have half a brain.

Reality settled over Naomi like a dreary fog. She didn't want to acknowledge the possibility that her little brother had been kidnapped. "The man seemed so nice, and—"

"Did you get a good look at the car he was driving?" Jake asked.

The thought that Zach could have been taken by the English man pierced Naomi to the core of her soul, and her head began to spin. She grabbed hold of the porch railing. "I—uh—think it was a van, but I can't be sure. It could have been a station wagon or even a truck."

"Didn't you see it parked in the driveway? Think, Naomi. Surely you must have noticed."

Matthew's words weighed on Naomi like a sack of grain. "I—I did see it but barely took notice. I'm not sure if it was a van or not, and I don't even know the color of the vehicle."

"Then I suppose you didn't pay attention to the license plate, either?" This question came from Norman.

Naomi's only response was a slow shake of her head.

"Well, did ya see what direction the car was headed when it left?" Matthew asked.

She blew out her breath. "Now how could I have noticed when I was inside the house when it left? I already told you, Matthew."

"I'm goin' out to search the roads just the same." Matthew turned to Norman. "You'd better come along, and Jake can stay here and keep looking."

As she headed for the barn to look one more time, a sense of dread weighed heavily on Naomi's shoulders. How she wished she could erase what had happened and start her day over again. She would have done everything differently if she'd only known the way things would turn out.

"Oh, Lord," she prayed, "please keep my little brother safe, and help us find him real soon."

Jim glanced in the rearview mirror. No police cars. No Amish buggies in pursuit.

If I get caught, I'll be arrested for kidnapping. If I go back to the hotel empty-handed, Linda will be devastated. He gripped the steering wheel with determination. *Just keep on driving, and don't think about what you've done.*

The child in the backseat gurgled, and Jim turned his head for a brief look. "You okay, little guy?" Could it have been fate that took him to the Amish farm for root beer? After all, he needed a baby, and that family had plenty of kids to go around. The little boy was just one more mouth to feed, and he didn't even have a mother. *Maybe I did them a favor by taking the baby off their hands.*

When he caught another glimpse of the boy, his thoughts turned to more expedient matters. "Clothes. The kid's gonna need to be wearing more than a diaper before I take him to see Linda. Otherwise, she'll ask a bunch of questions."

A short time later, Jim pulled into the parking lot of a Wal-Mart store. As soon as he turned off the engine, he hopped out of the car and went around to open the back door. The baby giggled when Jim lifted him out of the car seat. "Sure are a trusting little fellow, aren't you?" Not once since Jim grabbed the boy off the picnic table had the baby cried or even fussed. In fact, the baby seemed perfectly at ease with Jim, which only confirmed in his mind that he'd done the right thing by taking the child.

"Out you go," Jim said as he hoisted the baby into his arms. "We're off to do some shopping, then you're going to meet your new mom."

It had been a long day, and Abraham was eager to get home. A few minutes ago, he'd sent Samuel out back where they kept the horse, telling him to give the animal a couple of apples. Abraham would close the store at five, then go out to hitch the horse to the buggy. They'd be home in half an hour or so, then he would tell the family about the campout he'd planned for tonight.

At two minutes to five, Abraham turned down the

kerosene lamps he used to light his place of business. He'd just gotten to the last one when someone entered the store. It was Virginia Meyers, his least favorite customer.

"Hello, Mr. Fisher," she called with a wave of her hand. "Is Naomi here?"

He shook his head. "She and the girls stayed home today to sell root beer and do some cleanin' and such."

She pursed her pink lips and gave her ponytail a flip. "That's too bad. I was hoping to speak with her."

Abraham moved toward the young English woman. "Mind if ask what about?"

"Just girl stuff. You know—stamps and things."

Abraham wasn't sure why, but he didn't believe her. He had a feeling Virginia wanted to talk to Naomi about more than just rubber stamps. He'd heard the two of them a time or two and gotten the gist of the conversation on more than one occasion. Virginia wanted to show Naomi the world—her modern, English world. As far as he knew, Naomi had declined the invitations to do something fun, and he prayed she always would.

"Is there something I can help ya with?" he asked, feeling more impatient by the minute. "I'm about to close, so if you're needin' something, then you'd best hurry and get it."

She glanced around the store. "No new stamps yet, I take it."

"Nope."

"Okay then. Tell Naomi I dropped by."

"Right, Virginia."

"It's Ginny. Remember?"

He shrugged his shoulders. "Ginny then."

"Guess I'd better get back to the restaurant. The supper crowd will probably be filing in by now. See you later, Mr. Fisher." Ginny bounded out the door, and Abraham heaved a sigh of relief.

He grabbed his hat from the wall peg, locked the front door, and headed for the back of the store.

Thirty minutes later, Abraham pulled the buggy into his yard, and Samuel jumped down. "Run inside and tell Naomi she can put supper on," he told the boy. "I'll get the horse unhitched and be right in."

"Sure, Papa." Samuel scampered toward the house, and Abraham went around to the front of the horse. He'd only begun to take the harness off when Naomi came running toward him with the older boys, Mary Ann, and Nancy right behind her.

"Hey, there!" he said with a smile. "Guess what I've got planned for tonight?"

"Papa, I think you'd better hear what I have to say before you share any plans," Naomi said with a catch in her voice. She looked downright flustered, and Abraham wondered if she'd had a rough day with the kinner.

"Is everything okay here? Did the girls do their work as you asked?"

Tears splashed onto Naomi's cheeks, and she grasped his arm.

"Daughter, what is it? Tell me what's wrong."

"It's Zach, Papa." There was a note of panic in her voice, and Abraham steeled himself for the worst.

"What about the boy? Is he sick?"

"Please, take a seat at the picnic table, and I'll tell you everything."

He shook his head. "Tell me now."

"Papa, I think it might be best if you sit down," Matthew interjected.

Abraham looked at Naomi, then back at Matthew. They both had awfully grave looks on their faces. He was sure something terrible had happened in his absence, and he dreaded hearing the news.

Stumbling over to the picnic table, he dropped to the bench. "Tell me now, and be quick about it."

Naomi rattled off a story about how she'd been asked by an English man to get some cold root beer and said she'd heard one of the girls scream and how, fearing Hildy the goose might have been chasing them, she had left Zach sitting on the picnic table while she rushed off to see about things.

"When I discovered Mary Ann's hand was cut, I sent Nancy outside with the cold root beer while I tended the wound. When Nancy came back in, she said the man was gone." Naomi took a deep breath and rushed on. "Then I went out to have a look-see, and sure enough the man wasn't there." She gulped. "The worst part of all was when I realized Zach was missing, too."

Abraham's eyes darted back and forth. "Is this true?"

Matthew nodded. "I'm afraid so. Naomi thought Zach might have climbed down from the picnic table and crawled off, so she sent Nancy to the fields to get me, Norman, and Jake." He swallowed hard, and his Adam's apple bobbed up and down. "We searched and searched but couldn't find Zach anywhere."

"Yeah, we even drove out on the road a piece," Norman added.

Abraham sat there several seconds, feeling as though he were in a daze. This couldn't be happening. It had to be a dream—a horrible nightmare. Soon he'd wake up and find everything as it had been that morning.

He shook his head as though it might help him think straight. "That man took our boppli, didn't he?"

No one said anything, but everyone nodded.

Abraham stood on trembling legs. "Matthew, you'd better go to our English neighbors and ask them to phone the police."

CHAPTER 11

As Jim pulled into the hotel parking lot, his head swirled with confusion. He'd been told a few hours ago that the son they planned to adopt was no longer available—the mother had changed her mind. Then, in a moment of desperation, he'd stolen an Amish baby right off the picnic table where his older sister had left him sitting. Since she hadn't returned right away, it had been so easy. It almost seemed as if she had no intention of returning. This only confirmed in Jim's mind that his going there had been predestined. He and Linda were meant to have the boy, and he would be better off living with them than he would be growing up Amish. The young woman had told Jim her mother died and there were eight children in the family. As far as Jim was concerned, that was too many for one man to raise alone.

He climbed out of the van and went around back to retrieve his new son. "Your mommy and I can give you so much," he said as he unbuckled the boy's seat belt and started to take him out of the car seat. The Amish baby quilt was tucked around the child's legs, and Jim removed it. "Can't leave this bit of evidence for Linda to see. She'd ask a ton of questions for sure."

For some reason, when Jim had dumped the boy's cloth diaper into the garbage at Wal-Mart, he couldn't throw the quilt out. He'd been tempted to, but it didn't seem right to pitch the child's only link with his past life.

I'll hide the quilt for now and decide what to do with it later. Jim set the baby back in the car seat, grabbed the blanket, and stuffed it inside his toolbox behind the backseat.

The child started to wail.

"Okay, okay, I'm coming." Jim lifted the baby into his arms and grabbed the bag of diapers he'd purchased. A few minutes later, he inserted his key card into their hotel room door and let himself in. *I wonder if Linda's awake and feeling better.*

He was pleased to see that she was up, sitting on the small couch in front of the television. She jumped up when she saw Jim and ran to greet him.

"You're back—with our baby!" Linda reached for the child, and Jim felt relief when the boy went willingly to her.

Her eyes filled with tears. "He's even more beautiful than I'd imagined." She returned to the couch, muted the TV, and hugged the boy. "I take it everything went well?"

Jim sat beside her. "Without a hitch."

"Did you get all the paperwork? His birth certificate and the adoption papers?"

Jim froze. In his haste to pull off this little charade, he hadn't given any thought to the legal papers they might need. If the baby didn't have a birth certificate, how could they enroll him in school?

Linda can homeschool. Yes, she should do that anyway. She's home all day, and it will be better for the boy to learn from her. Still, when the child grows up and wants to get a driver's license, passport, or marriage license, he'll need some proof of his identity.

Jim clenched his teeth. Why hadn't he thought about all this before?

"Jim, you didn't answer my question about the papers."

He gently squeezed Linda's arm. "Not to worry. It's all taken care of. The adoption papers and new birth certificate for our boy will be mailed to my paint shop address."

"Why there and not our home?"

"Because that's where our safe is kept, Linda."

"Oh, right."

I'll have to see my friend Hank when we get home. He has connections, and I'm sure he'll be able to get exactly what I need. We can apply for the baby's Social Security number as soon as I get a phony birth certificate.

"Let's call him Jimmy," Linda said, breaking into Jim's thoughts.

"Sure, honey. Whatever you want."

"Are you ready to go shopping now?"

He blinked. "Huh?"

"Shopping. You said we came to Lancaster County so I could look for a quilt and tour Amish country. My headache is gone, and I'm ready to do some sight-seeing." Linda kissed the top of the baby's head. "Besides, he's sucking on my hand, which probably means he's hungry. We'll need to get him some food, Jim."

Jim groped for the right words. Shopping and sight-seeing was not a good idea—at least not here, where the baby might be recognized. What if the boy's sister had gotten a good look at his van? The police could be out looking for him.

"We can stop somewhere for some food for Jimmy,

but I think we should head for Ohio today. Right away, in fact."

Linda looked at him like he'd lost his mind. "You're kidding."

He shook his head and stood. "I'm anxious to show Mom and Dad our new son."

"What about the Amish quilt you promised me?"

"You can get one in Holmes County. I'm sure Mom will know the best places to look."

"You think so?"

"Yep. Now let's pack our things and get going."

As Linda stood, she held Jimmy against her chest. "You make it sound critical that we leave. Is there something wrong, Jim? Something you're not telling me?"

Each lie Jim told seemed to roll right off his tongue, yet each seemed to complicate things that much more. He leaned over and kissed her cheek. "Of course not, honey. I'm just excited to see my folks and have them meet Jimmy."

She gazed lovingly at the baby. "He's so cute, but I wonder why his hair is cut so funny. It almost looks like a bowl was set on his head and someone cut around it."

Jim gulped. "Uh—it's—probably the boy's birth mother couldn't afford a real haircut."

"That makes sense." Linda touched the back of Jimmy's ear. "Look at the cute little heart-shaped birthmark."

Jim only glanced at the red blotch. "Uh-huh. Interesting." He hurried to the closet and retrieved their suitcase.

"My parents will want to see him soon, too. Can we go to Idaho after we get home?" Linda asked.

"Sure, but not right away. I've got a business to run, you know. After taking this much time off work, there'll be lots for me to do."

Linda nodded. "Okay, but let's try to make a trip there as soon as we can."

"Right. I promise we'll do that." Jim plunked the suitcase on the end of the bed. "I'll pack our clothes, and you can get the cosmetic bag ready."

"What about the baby? Who's going to hold him if we're both packing?"

"Why don't you put him on the bed?"

"But he might fall off."

Jim's mind flashed to the moment the baby had been left sitting in the middle of the picnic table. He'd tried to climb down and would have probably fallen if Jim hadn't been there to catch him. "Put him on the floor then. He can do a little exploring while we get ready to go."

"I wonder if he can walk. He's a year old, and many children walk by their first birthday. Did the mother say whether he's walking yet or not?"

"Uh—no, she didn't say." *The boy's sister mentioned that he's not walking yet, but I sure can't tell Linda that.* "If you put him on the floor, we'll find out if he can walk."

She did as he suggested, and the boy crawled off to

investigate Jim's slippers, sitting on the floor near the bed. "I guess he either can't walk or doesn't want to right now."

He shrugged. "Guess so."

Linda gave Jim a lingering kiss. "Thank you for coming all this way so we could adopt our precious child."

He swallowed around the lump in his throat. What he'd done was illegal in the eyes of the law, but as far as he was concerned, it had been the right thing. Jim had never seen Linda so happy. She was fairly glowing.

Naomi took a seat in the rocker next to Zach's playpen and tried to pray. The police had come awhile ago, followed by reporters from the local newspaper. With no information about the vehicle the man had been driving, the police said it would be difficult to track him down. Not only that, but the Fishers had no pictures of Zach, since it went against their beliefs to own a camera or have their picture taken. Naomi knew a few Amish teenagers who owned cameras and kept them in secret, but Papa would have punished anyone in his family who tried something like that.

"Zach ain't never comin' back, is he?"

Naomi jerked her head. Nancy stood by the back door with tears coursing down her cheeks. Mary Ann stood beside her, looking like she'd lost her best friend.

"Things aren't lookin' so good, but we have to pray

believing." Even as she said the words, Naomi knew she didn't believe them. She'd been praying all afternoon and into the evening, and it hadn't brought Zach home.

The tension Naomi felt in her neck earlier mounted with each passing moment. She was scared. Even more so than when her mother was hit by a car and she worried Mama might not live. If God had done nothing to prevent her mamm from stepping into the road to retrieve some mail, what made Naomi think He would bring her little brother home?

"Papa's still outside talking with the police and those newspaper reporters," Nancy said, moving across the room. She dropped into a chair and leaned her elbows on the table. Mary Ann followed and did the same. "They want to take pictures of the family, but he won't let 'em."

"That's right. Papa said, 'Absolutely no,'" Mary Ann put in.

Naomi shook her head. "I wouldn't think he'd agree to anyone takin' pictures." Tears clouded her vision. She was the cause of all this. *How can I go on living, knowing it was because of my carelessness Zach was taken? What if I never see my little brother again? What if something awful has happened to him?*

Naomi remembered reading an article awhile back in the Amish newspaper, *The Budget*. It told about two little Mennonite girls who'd become trapped inside a cedar chest. Three days later, they were found smothered to death.

She feared the worst for her baby brother, and visions of Zach being mistreated threatened to suffocate her. What if the English man planned to hurt the boy? She knew that many children who'd been kidnapped were either killed or physically abused. She'd read accounts of such things in the newspaper. There were many evil people in the world, and for all she knew, that English man who'd asked for root beer could be one of the worst.

Naomi spotted Zach's bib draped over his high chair. It looked the same as always, as though Zach would be sitting in the chair at supper, wearing the bib tied behind his chubby little neck. She could almost taste the sweetness of her little brother, but he wouldn't be here tonight. Truth was, he might never sit in that high chair again.

A renewed sense of loss rocked Naomi, and she doubled over, letting her head fall onto her knees. Her world was spinning out of control, and she was powerless to stop it. *Oh, Zach, my sweet little brother, what I have done to you? What have I done to this family?*

Someone touched her head, and she looked up.

"Don't cry, Naomi. Please, don't." The sorrowful look on Mary Ann's face only made Naomi feel worse.

"*Ball wollt's besser geh*—soon it will go better," Nancy said as she left the table.

Naomi wanted to be brave in front of her younger sisters. She wanted to believe things would go better.

She wished she could offer words of comfort and be strong for the others. It was her job to look after the family. She'd promised Mama she would, and now it seemed she was incapable of caring for anyone. She had proven that by leaving Zach on the picnic table.

Oh, Mama, I've let you down. I'm so sorry.

The back door squeaked open, and Papa marched into the room. She could see the pain behind his dark eyes and knew she was the cause.

"Are the reporters and policemen gone?" Naomi asked.

He nodded curtly and stalked across the room, stopping a few feet from where she sat in the rocker. "Matthew and Norman are out on the road looking again, but I'm sure it's no use. Zach's gone. They won't find him."

The look of defeat on Papa's face was nearly Naomi's undoing.

"Where are Jake and Samuel?" Nancy asked. "I thought they'd be asking for something to eat by now."

"Yeah, I'm gettin' hungry, too." Mary Ann glanced at Naomi. "When are ya plannin' to start supper?"

Papa shot the girl a look that sent shivers up Naomi's spine. "How can you think about food at a time like this? Don't ya care that your baby brother's been kidnapped?"

Naomi stood. "Mary Ann's only a child, Papa. She doesn't fully understand what's happened today, and I'm sure she didn't mean she doesn't care."

She cringed when her father shook his fist and hollered, "This is all your fault, Naomi! You were supposed to be in charge of the kinner, and leavin' Zach outside with a stranger was downright *schlappich*."

"I know I was careless, Papa, but I—"

He shook his head. "You weren't just careless. What you did was *narrisch*."

"Naomi ain't crazy, Papa," Mary Ann defended.

He whirled around, and for a moment, Naomi was afraid he would strike the child. "When I want your opinion, I'll ask for it! I didn't say Naomi was narrisch. I said what she *did* was crazy."

Nancy grabbed hold of his shirtsleeve. "What are we gonna do now, Papa? How can we make things right?"

He released a deep moan. "The newspaper is plannin' to run a story about our missing boy, so all we can do is pray and hope the English man brings Zach home or that somebody saw him drive away from our place and can identify the vehicle." He shook his head. "I fear the worst. If I ever see my baby again, it'll be a miracle."

The room began to spin, and Naomi grabbed for the chair to steady herself. "*Der Herr, bilf mir*—the Lord help me. Please, help us all."

CHAPTER 12

Naomi sat in the rocking chair long after Papa went upstairs. He'd said some hurtful things earlier, yet she felt she deserved every cutting word. It was her fault Zach was missing, and if they didn't get the baby back, she would never forgive herself. As much as it hurt, she couldn't blame her daed or anyone else in the family if they chose not to forgive her.

"Naomi, I'm gettin' awful hungry," Mary Ann complained. "Can't we please have some supper?"

Naomi stood as though in a daze and moved slowly to the kitchen cupboard. "Jah, okay. Maybe some sandwiches then." She would feed the younger ones, but she doubted Papa would want anything to eat. Truth was, she had no appetite for food, either, and wondered if she would ever feel like eating again. Her body felt paralyzed with grief. She didn't want to eat, talk, or even move, yet she knew she must do all three.

If Zach comes home, everything will be all right, she told herself. *I need another chance to prove I'm responsible. That's all I want. Just one more chance; is it too much to ask?*

Naomi's heart pounded when she heard a horse and buggy trot into the yard. Were her brothers back so soon? Had they found Zach? Oh, she hoped it was so.

She lifted the shade and strained to see who was outside. It was getting dark, and the yard, lit only by the moon, was full of shadows.

A knock sounded at the back door, and Naomi realized it wasn't Matthew or Norman. They would never have knocked.

"Want me to get it?" asked Nancy, who had begun setting the table.

"If you wish."

A few seconds later, the door opened, and Marvin Hoffmeir stepped into the room.

Naomi squeezed her eyes shut as she leaned heavily against the cupboard. *What's he doing here, especially at a time like this when our world's been turned upside down? We don't need company now; that's for certain sure.*

"Naomi, are you okay?" Marvin asked.

She forced her eyes open and turned to face him. "Something terrible happened here today."

He nodded, and she noticed his blond hair was sweat-soaked around the edges where it met his straw hat. Marvin was two years younger than Caleb and had the same color hair, but his eyes were dark brown, not clear blue like his brother's.

"I know about Zach," Marvin said. "I ran into Matthew and Norman on the road when I was returning from the bus station."

"What were you doin' at the bus station?" Nancy asked.

Marvin removed his hat. "Took Caleb there so's he could go to Berlin, Ohio. Our cousin Henry has a buggy shop there, and he wrote a letter saying he got in some old parts he thought Caleb might like to have." He took a step toward Naomi. "Sure sorry to hear about Zach, and I wanted to drop by and say so."

"Danki. It's appreciated," Naomi murmured.

"Wish there was something I could say to make your family's pain a bit less."

"You can pray," Mary Ann piped up. "It's what we're all doin'; ain't that right, Naomi?"

Naomi opened her mouth to respond, but her dad's booming voice cut her off before she could speak. "What are you doin' here, Marvin?" Papa asked as he marched into the room. "This isn't a good time to come calling."

Marvin explained about running into Matthew and Norman on the road. "Matthew mentioned how upset everyone was, and I thought maybe I could offer some words of comfort or maybe help in some way."

"Who went and made you the new bishop?" Papa asked mockingly.

Naomi flinched. She could hardly believe her father had said such a thing. "There's no call to be rude, Papa."

"It's okay. I understand," Marvin said. "You've had a terrible shock today."

"You know nothin' about what we've been through!" Papa shouted. "My boppli's been snatched by a stranger. Can you understand the pain of losin' your son? Well, can ya, boy?"

Marvin shook his head. "No, but my brother Andy

ran a nail through his thumb the other day, and—"

"A hurt hand is nothin' compared to our loss. I think you'd better head home. We don't need your sympathy." Papa drew in a deep breath and clenched his fists at his sides. He was visibly shaking, and Naomi knew he was taking out his frustrations on Caleb's brother.

She took a few steps toward her father. "Papa, Marvin only wanted to offer his support. He knows we're upset and feels our pain, just as the others will when they hear what's happened."

Papa pulled out a chair at the table and lowered himself into it with a groan. "Jah, well, it ain't you I'm mad at, Marvin. Sorry for speakin' thataway."

Naomi swallowed around the lump in her throat. She knew *she* was the one her papa was angry with. He'd already made that clear enough. *Well, he can't be any angrier with me than I am with myself.* The pain of losing Zach was like having a sliver in her thumb. She'd felt its presence ever since she discovered her little brother was missing.

Marvin shuffled his feet a few times. "I—uh—guess I should get goin'."

"Wanna stay and have supper with us?" This came from Mary Ann, who had taken a chunk of ham out of the refrigerator. "Naomi's gonna make sandwiches."

Naomi frowned at her youngest sister. "I never said that."

"Did, too."

"I did not. I only agreed to fix you something to eat.

I never said what it would be." Naomi couldn't believe she was arguing with Mary Ann—and over something so petty. *What's wrong with me? I'm not thinking straight right now. I'm not myself at all. Maybe I did agree to make sandwiches and just don't remember.*

Naomi took the ham from her sister. "All right. I'll fix a plate of sandwiches." She glanced at the back door. "Matthew and Norman will probably be hungry when they get home, too."

Papa's fist pounded the table, clattering the silverware and almost toppling over the glasses. "This talk about food is ridiculous! Our Zach has been stolen, and all anyone can think about is eatin'? What's wrong with the lot of you?"

Mary Ann's lower lip quivered, and Nancy cringed. The children weren't accustomed to seeing their father so agitated. They weren't used to losing their brother, either, yet it had happened, and they would have to deal with it. Starving the children sure wasn't the way. Naomi knew that much.

Marvin cleared his throat, and Naomi swung her gaze back to him. She'd almost forgotten he was still here, what with all the fuss about sandwiches and Papa's angry outburst. "I—uh—appreciate the offer to stay for supper, but I need to get home. Mom will be expectin' me," Marvin mumbled.

"I'll see you to the door," Naomi said, moving in that direction.

He shook his head. "That's okay. I know my way

144

out." Marvin took two steps, then looked back. It was as though he wanted to say something more but was afraid to say it. Maybe it was for the best. Everyone had said enough already.

"Good night, Marvin. It was kind of you to stop by," Nancy said, surprising Naomi and causing Papa to glare at her.

"Night," he mumbled. "I'll be prayin' for you. Please keep me and the family posted." With that said, Caleb's brother walked out the door, closing it quietly behind him.

Naomi turned to her father. "Papa, is it all right if I fix something for the girls to eat?"

He stood and headed for the back door. "Do whatever you like."

"Where ya goin'?" Mary Ann called.

He never replied, only slammed the door behind him.

Naomi's hands trembled as she reached inside the cupboard and retrieved a loaf of bread. This didn't make sense, her fixing supper as though it were any other night of the week, the brothers out combing the roads in hopes of finding Zach, and Papa outside probably ruing the day Naomi was born.

"I—I—don't know if I can do this," she whimpered.

"Here, let me help." Nancy took the bread from Naomi and buttered several slices. "Why don't you fix yourself a cup of herb tea? Might help to calm you down. Mama always said tea was like a soothing balm whenever she was tired or had a bad day."

Naomi didn't feel like drinking a cup of tea any more than she did eating a ham sandwich. All she wanted to do was reach into Zach's playpen, lift him into her arms, and drink in the sweetness of her little brother until she felt dizzy from the joy of holding him. She glanced at the playpen, filled only with a couple of Zach's homemade toys. The reality that they might never see him again hit her one more time. She stifled a sob and stumbled out of the room.

Caleb would be glad to get off the bus and stretch his legs. He had called Henry from the bus station in Lancaster to let him know what time he'd arrive in Dover and ask if he could arrange for him to get a ride to Berlin. It was nice Henry had a phone in his buggy shop. It was much easier to make contact that way.

"Too bad Pop's against the idea of me having one," he muttered.

"Were you talking to me?" the elderly woman who sat beside Caleb asked.

He'd thought she was asleep. Her eyes had been closed, so he figured . . . "I—um—sorry to disturb you. I've got a habit of talkin' to myself."

"That's all right," she said, pushing a wayward strand of silver gray hair back into place. "My husband, rest his soul, used to talk to himself all the time."

Caleb leaned his head against the seat back and closed his eyes. He didn't mean to be rude, but he wasn't in the mood to talk to anyone right now.

"You're one of those Plain people, aren't you?"

He opened his eyes. "Yes, ma'am. I'm Amish."

"Are you from Holmes County?"

"No, Lancaster County, Pennsylvania."

"But you're heading to Ohio?"

"Jah. My cousin has a buggy shop there."

"Isn't that interesting? Arnold, my late husband, used to own an old Student Buggy, made by G. & D. Cook & Co. Carriage Makers."

Caleb's ears perked up. "Is that so? I'm a buggy maker, too, and I also repair antique carriages."

"Really?"

Caleb nodded. "I bought a book on antique buggies the other day, and there was a picture of an antique Student Buggy in it. Looked a little like the open carriages we Amish sometimes drive."

"Do you make a good living selling buggies?" she asked.

"Fair to middlin'. Make enough so's I could support a wife and family." Caleb thought about Naomi. He sure wished she were free to court. He wished she didn't have to work so hard, either. Maybe when he got back to Pennsylvania, he'd finally get over to see her, like he'd planned on doing today. *Of course, I'd better wait 'til her daed isn't at home.*

Jim knew he was pushing hard, stopping less often than he usually did, but he was in a hurry to leave Pennsylvania and get to Ohio. They had stopped to get something for Jimmy to eat as soon as they left Lan-

147

caster County. Linda stocked up on formula and bought two baby bottles, not knowing if the boy had been weaned. She'd also purchased several jars of baby food, as well as some teething biscuits, juice, and a few outfits. She made a comment about how odd it seemed that the baby's real mother hadn't sent more than a package of diapers and one outfit with him.

I can hardly tell her the truth about that, Jim thought as he glanced in the rearview mirror. He hadn't seen any cops, or at least none had paid him any mind. That was good. Must mean no one had identified him or the van. Hopefully, he was in the clear.

As he took another look in the mirror, Jim caught a glimpse of Linda. She hummed while she stroked the baby's golden brown hair. She had insisted on riding in the back with the boy. "I can care for his needs better this way," she'd said when they left the hotel in Lancaster.

That was fine with Jim. It gave him a chance to think; and since Linda was preoccupied with the baby, she wouldn't be likely to pester him with a bunch of questions he didn't feel like answering.

Jim glanced at his watch. It was almost four o'clock. Pittsburgh was four hours from Lancaster, and they'd been traveling two hours, so they were halfway there. *Maybe we should stop for the night and get a hotel in Pittsburgh. We can have some dinner, get a good night's rest, and arrive at Mom and Dad's in Millersburg a few hours after breakfast.*

He smiled and turned on the radio. Everything was

going to be fine. By this time tomorrow, they'd be sitting in his folks' living room, watching TV, and playing with their son.

CHAPTER 13

Naomi spent a fretful night. It didn't seem right trying to sleep when her baby brother wasn't in his crib across the room.

She awoke with a headache and wished she could stay in bed—wished, in fact, she could stay there forever and never have to deal with anything again. But she couldn't. Nancy was pounding on the door, telling her it was time to start breakfast. She rolled over and punched the pillow around her head.

"Naomi, are you awake?" Nancy knocked again. "Naomi?"

"I'm comin'. Just give me a few minutes to get dressed."

"Jah, okay. I'll go downstairs and get things started."

"Danki."

Naomi sat up and glanced at the baby's crib. It was empty. Same as it had been last night when she'd crawled into bed. "What have I done?" she moaned. "Life will never be the same without Zach."

Ten minutes later, Naomi entered the kitchen. Nancy was mixing pancake batter, and Mary Ann was setting the table. Zach was gone. His empty playpen was a constant reminder.

"I take it Papa and the brothers are still outside chorin'?" Naomi asked, grabbing a jug of milk from the refrigerator and forcing her mind off her missing brother.

"As far as I know," Nancy answered. "Haven't seen any of 'em this morning."

Naomi glanced at Mary Ann. She'd finished setting the table and stood beside Zach's empty high chair, staring at it as though he were sitting right there.

"You won't bring the boppli home by starin' at his chair." Naomi's voice sounded harsh, even to her own ears, but she seemed powerless to stop the cutting words.

Mary Ann hung her head. "It's my fault Zach's gone, and I'm afraid God's gonna punish me for it."

"It ain't your fault," Nancy hollered from across the room.

"That's right; it's not," Naomi agreed. "What would make you say such a thing, Mary Ann?"

The little girl kept her eyes downcast as she slid her bare toes back and forth across the linoleum. "If I hadn't dropped the jar of peaches and screamed 'cause I cut my hand, you might not have rushed into the house without Zach." She looked at Naomi with tears in her eyes. "And if you'd gone outside sooner, Zach might not have been kidnapped."

Before Naomi could voice her thoughts on the matter, Mary Ann spoke again. "I'm afraid, Naomi.

Are you gonna let some Englisher take me, too?"

Naomi's mouth fell open. "What are you talking about?"

Mary Ann closed her eyes and drew in a shaky breath. "If you think I did a bad thing, you might want me to go away, same as Zach."

Her little sister's comment was nearly Naomi's undoing. She took hold of Mary Ann's arm, flopped into a chair, and lifted the child onto her lap. Rocking back and forth, Naomi let her tears flow. "It wasn't your fault, Mary Ann. I'm the one to blame, and I'll never let anyone take you away."

After a sleepless night, Abraham had gone to the barn before daylight, thinking he might get the animals fed and do a few other chores. How could he go to bed and rest when his youngest son was in the hands of a stranger? What did the Englisher want with Zach? Did he plan to hurt him? It happened to other children who were kidnapped; he'd read terrible things in the newspaper about little ones who'd been taken from their families and were abused by the abductor. Many had been found dead, with their little bodies mutilated beyond recognition.

Abraham trembled as he sank to his knees in front of a bale of hay. He bent into the pain that threatened to squeeze the life out of him. "Father in heaven, please keep my boy safe. Even if Zach never comes home, I pray You'll protect him from harm."

Tears coursed down Abraham's cheeks, and he

swiped at them with the back of his hand. Yesterday afternoon he had hoped to start over with his family by having a surprise campout in the backyard. A few days ago, while praying and reflecting on God's Word, he'd come to the point of accepting Sarah's death and thought he could do better by his children. That had all changed now. He couldn't deal with the second tragedy that had befallen them. God could have prevented it from happening, same as He could have saved Sarah.

"This is your fault, Naomi," he wailed. "You were supposed to be watching the boy. I trusted you to care for my kinner, and look what happened." He sniffed deeply and nearly choked on his saliva. Naomi was in the house and couldn't hear his tirade, but he didn't care. His heart was full of bitterness, and she was the cause. "I'll bet you were thinking about Caleb Hoffmeir or that English girl, Virginia Meyers, instead of watchin' out for Zach. You probably don't care a mite for this family—thinkin' about yourself, that's all."

As the angry words spewed out of his mouth, Abraham grew even more tense. He clenched his teeth and fought for control. Deep in his soul, he knew Naomi did care for the family, yet he couldn't find it in his heart to forgive her carelessness. If Zach wasn't returned, Abraham didn't know if he could ever look at his oldest daughter again without feeling she was to blame for his misery.

"Sorry to disturb you, Papa, but I was wonderin' if

you're about ready for breakfast? The bell rang a few minutes ago."

Abraham jerked upright at the sound of Jake's voice. "You go ahead, Son. I ain't hungry."

Jake moved closer to the spot where Abraham knelt. "You okay? Ya haven't hurt your back again, have you?"

Abraham remembered the last time his back had gone into spasm, and he'd been forced to crawl from the barn to the house. That had been painful, but nothing compared to the way he felt right now.

He made a fist and touched his chest. "Hurtin' here but no place else."

Jake's brown eyes revealed obvious concern. "I'll leave you to your prayin' then. That's all we can do, isn't it, Papa? Pray and ask God to bring Zach home."

Abraham nodded. "And to keep our little boy safe."

"Oh, look, Jim. There's a quilt shop across the street. Let's stop." Linda, still in the backseat with Jimmy, leaned forward and tapped Jim on the shoulder.

"I thought we'd go straight to Mom and Dad's. Besides, it's Sunday, and most of the shops are closed," Jim said as he kept driving. "You and Mom can go shopping tomorrow."

"I really want to stop now. It would feel good to stretch my legs, and I'd like your opinion on which quilt to get."

"Wouldn't you rather have Mom's opinion? She knows more about that kind of thing than I do."

"She wouldn't know how much money you're willing to let me spend."

Linda had a point. Mom would probably tell his wife to get whatever she wanted—that money was no object. It would be easy for her to say; it wasn't her money she'd be spending. Still, he thought it would be better if the women went shopping while he and Dad stayed home and visited over a cup of coffee or watched TV. They could keep an eye on the baby, too. Surely Linda didn't want to shop for a quilt while holding a fidgety child.

"Please, Jim," she pleaded. "Won't you turn around and head back to Fannie's Quilt Shop so I can see what they have in the window?"

"What about Jimmy?"

"What about him?"

"Wouldn't you rather shop tomorrow, without him?"

"No. I don't want to leave him alone."

"He wouldn't be alone. He'll be with me and Dad while you and Mom come to town."

They had entered the town of Berlin, and Jim had to stop for an Amish buggy that had pulled away from the curb. Seeing the buggy made Jim think of the Amish farm where he'd gone for root beer. Root beer he'd never gotten. He'd left with a child, instead.

"Jim, are you going to go back to that quilt shop or not?"

Linda's pleading voice pulled his thoughts aside, and he was grateful. No point dwelling on the past. Especially one he wasn't free to talk about.

"Okay, okay. Just let me look for a good place to turn around."

"It looks like there are a lot of tourists, doesn't it? Even for a Sunday," she remarked.

"Yeah, plenty of people like us who want to find something made by the Amish to take home." Linda would not only be taking an Amish quilt home after this trip, but an Amish baby, as well. She just didn't know it.

"I'll meet you at the Subway place on West Main Street," Caleb called to his cousin.

"Okay, but don't be late. Cleon, my driver, will be pickin' us up later this afternoon, and then we'll drive over to Dover so you can catch the bus."

Caleb waved at Henry and strolled up the sidewalk. He'd decided to take a walk before they ate and check out some of the shops in the area. He would have to sit for a long time on the bus, so stretching his legs beforehand would be good.

Caleb had arrived at Henry's last night, and they'd spent the evening getting caught up on one another's lives. Since today was an off-Sunday and there'd be no church, first thing this morning, they'd gone to the buggy shop to look at the antique parts Henry had recently acquired. Caleb chose to buy a set of wheels, some spokes and hubs, a couple of shaft bars, and one old seat that was sturdy but would need to be reupholstered. He'd have them shipped to his place; and if he decided to stay in Holmes County a couple more days, the parts would probably be waiting for him when he got home.

However, Henry said he had a lot of work to do this week, and Caleb was eager to get home, so he decided to catch the evening bus back to Pennsylvania. He should arrive in Lancaster early Monday morning.

As Caleb neared a store called "Fannie's Quilt Shop," he saw a young couple with a baby looking in the window.

He squinted against the glaring sun. *That little guy looks kind of like Zach Fisher. He's dressed in English clothes, but his hair is cut like an Amish baby's would be. Don't rightly see how it could be, though. Zach's at home with his family, whereas this baby has English parents.*

"Yes, honey, I promise to bring you back sometime tomorrow so you can buy a quilt," he overheard the man say to the woman.

Caleb stared at the baby a few more minutes, then finally moved on. *I'd better find myself somethin' cold to drink, 'cause this hot, humid weather must be gettin' to me. Naomi's baby brother dressed in English clothes, bein' held by English folks outside a shop in Ohio? No, it couldn't be. I'm just missing Naomi, that's all.*

CHAPTER 14

Naomi stood at the kitchen sink, washing dishes. It was hard to think about working at the store today, but she knew it would be expected of her. They had to make a living, and that wouldn't happen if they all stayed home worrying about Zach and blaming themselves for his disappearance. Of course, Naomi knew she was the only one to blame. She'd let everyone down—Mama most of all, since she hadn't kept her promise to care for the family. Naomi had failed miserably, and now she feared nothing would ever be the same.

As she placed the clean dishes into the drainer, Naomi's thoughts continued to spiral. Where was Zach now? Was he safe and being cared for, or had he been abandoned somewhere? Worse yet, could her baby brother have been murdered?

She shuddered. *Oh, Lord, give me a sense of peace about this. Some word—anything—that will let me know Zach is okay.*

The roar of a car's engine drove Naomi's thoughts to the back of her mind. She dried her hands on a towel and went to see who had driven into their yard.

Outside, Naomi spotted a police car, and Papa came running from the barn. Did the police have information about Zach? If so, she hoped it was good news.

Naomi stepped off the porch and hurried toward the car. "I'm sorry, Mr. Fisher," she heard one of the men say. "I'd like to say we're hot on the suspect's trail, but the truth is, there is no trail. We don't have a single lead on your son."

"Nothing a'tall?" Papa asked with a catch in his voice.

The policeman shook his head. "We spoke with all your neighbors, and no one saw anything out of the ordinary on Saturday. Some said they'd seen cars going in and out of your place, but nobody noticed an English man with a baby."

Papa's forehead wrinkled, and he stared down at his boots. "Guess it's hopeless then."

"It's not hopeless, Mr. Fisher. The local newspaper and TV station have run a story on the kidnapping, so we're hoping someone will come forward with helpful information."

"Without any pictures of your son or a good description of the man and his vehicle, it's going to be difficult to solve this case," the other police officer said.

Naomi felt as if her heart had plunged clear to her toes. She breathed in and out slowly, trying to calm her fears. So it *was* hopeless. Zach was gone for good. The days ahead looked bleak and frightening. Without Zach, nothing would ever be the same.

Papa nudged Naomi's arm. "Now that you've had more time to think on it, can you remember anything else?"

She shook her head and blinked against the tears

that sprang to her eyes. "Sorry."

"Was the man old or young?" the first officer asked.

"I told you Saturday night, he wasn't old. I'm sure of that much."

"But you have no idea if he was in his twenties, thirties, or forties?"

"And what color was the man's hair?" the other policeman asked.

Naomi wanted to scream. She'd been through these questions the other night and told them all she knew. Why did they keep on asking?

"Answer the man, Naomi," Papa instructed.

She swallowed hard. "I–I'm not sure. I think it was brown, but it could have been black. The man was younger than Papa, but to tell ya the truth, I didn't pay close attention to much of anything. I'd had a busy morning, and—"

"That's just an excuse. You should've been payin' more attention," Papa barked. "You wouldn't have left Zach on the picnic table if you had been."

Will I ever hear the end of this? Does he have to keep reminding me of what I've done?

"I'm sorry. Sorry for everything." Naomi whirled around and dashed for the house.

Caleb entered his house, ever so glad to be home. Leaving Marvin and Andy in charge of the buggy shop was okay for a day or two, but much longer and things might not go well. He knew Andy's hand was still bandaged after getting that nail stuck in his

159

thumb, so he couldn't do much to help if they got busy. Marvin sure wasn't able to do all the work by himself.

When Caleb first arrived in Lancaster, he'd called Ken Peterson for a ride home; and from the smell that greeted him as he entered the kitchen, Caleb figured he'd arrived in time for breakfast.

"I'm home," he called.

Mom, who stood in front of the stove with her back to him, whirled around. "Caleb! We didn't expect you for another couple of days."

He grinned and hung his straw hat on a wall peg. "Couldn't stay away from my mom's great cookin'."

She smiled. "You would say something like that."

"Caleb always did like to eat," Levi, his eleven-year-old brother, put in from his place at the table.

Caleb crossed the room and ruffled the boy's blond hair. "What would you know about it, huh?"

Levi chuckled and reached for his glass of milk.

Caleb glanced around. "Where's everyone else?"

"Your daed's in the fields with John and David," Mom replied. "Andy and Marvin went out to the buggy shop a few minutes ago."

"They've had breakfast already?"

"Jah."

"And the sisters? Where are they?"

"Irma and Lettie are down in the cellar gettin' canning jars. We've got a bunch of peas to put up later today."

"Thought the peas were done," Caleb said, taking a

seat across from Levi.

"This is the last picking."

"So am I too late for breakfast?"

"Not a'tall. Haven't eaten myself yet, and as you can see, Levi's waitin' for seconds."

Levi patted his stomach. "I'm a growin' boy."

Caleb laughed. "How's things around here? Everything okay in the buggy shop?"

Mom set a plate of scrambled eggs in front of Caleb and frowned. "Things are okay at our place, but it's really bad over at the Fishers' right now."

"How so?"

"Baby Zach's missing."

"What do you mean, Mom? How can the little guy be missin'?"

"Seems he was kidnapped right out of their yard early Saturday afternoon. Some English man came askin' for root beer, and they're sure he's the one who took him."

Caleb's thoughts flashed to the quilt shop outside of Berlin, Ohio. He'd seen an English couple there with a baby who looked like Zach. Was it possible? Could it be? If there was even a chance . . .

Caleb pushed his chair away from the table and stood. "I've gotta go, Mom."

"What about breakfast?"

"I can eat something later."

"But where are ya off to?"

"I'll be back as soon as I can, and I'll explain everything then." He grabbed his hat and raced out the door

161

before his mother could say another word.

Abraham didn't know how he was going to go about business as usual today, but somehow he must. Staying home and moping around or railing at God for His unfairness wouldn't bring in any money. It wouldn't bring Zach home, either.

He lit the gas lanterns near the front of the store, placed the OPEN sign in the window, and went to the back room to fetch the box of children's books that needed to be set out. Naomi could tend to any customers coming in, and he would enlist the help of his two youngest daughters with the books. He'd left Samuel home today to work in the fields with the older boys.

As soon as he and the girls entered the storage room, Abraham spotted Zach's empty playpen. A sting of pain sliced through his body, and he winced, feeling like he'd been stabbed with a pitchfork. *Zach. Zach. Oh, my sweet little boy, how my soul pines for you.*

Nancy and Mary Ann must have noticed the place where Zach had taken so many naps, for they both stood like statues, staring at it.

"I miss my little brother." Mary Ann touched the railing of the playpen and whimpered.

"You think we'll ever see Zach again, Papa?" Nancy questioned.

Abraham wished he could offer his daughters some comfort or hope that Zach would be returned. He couldn't. Not when he knew, short of a miracle, they

162

would never see their precious boppli again.

"Papa, will Zach come home?"

Abraham clenched his teeth to keep from snapping at Nancy. Since Saturday night, he'd said too many unkind words and knew his attitude was wrong.

"I'll carry this box of books into the next room for you," he mumbled, "and while you two are settin' them on the shelf, I'll come back here and do some rearranging."

Nancy and Mary Ann looked at each other, then back at him. *Are they expecting me to say more? Maybe offer some reassurance that Zach will be coming home?*

He bent down and lifted the cardboard box into his arms. "Go on now."

The girls followed him to the other room, and as soon as they started on the books, he returned to the storage area and shut the door.

Abraham grabbed the playpen and folded it up. *No use leavin' this out as a reminder of what can't be undone.* With the toe of his boot, he kicked one of the wooden blocks that had fallen out of the playpen along with several other toys. "Besides, it's only in the way."

He shoved the playpen behind some containers against the wall, then grabbed an empty box and tossed all of Zach's toys inside. As he was finishing that chore, someone knocked.

"Come in."

The door squeaked open, and his friend Jacob

Weaver entered the storage room. "The girls said I'd find you in here. What are ya up to?"

"Cleanin'. Organizin'. Tryin' to forget." Abraham flopped onto the cot where he sometimes took a nap, as a feeling of despair washed over him like a drenching rain.

Jacob's hazel-colored eyes showed compassion. He took a seat beside Abraham, and in quiet solitude they sat there.

After several minutes, Jacob cleared his throat. "'O Lord of hosts, blessed is the man that trusteth in thee.' Psalm eighty-four, verse twelve."

Abraham grunted. "Jah, well, the Bible also says, 'The Lord giveth and the Lord taketh away.'" He clasped his hands tightly together. "He's taken my youngest son, Jacob, and I don't think Zach's ever comin' back."

"It wasn't God who took your boy. It was an English man who was probably desperate and didn't know right from wrong."

"*Humph!* Everyone knows right from wrong."

"Maybe here," Jacob said as he touched his head, "but not necessarily here." He laid his hand against his chest.

Abraham swallowed around the lump in his throat. "I'm thinkin' you oughta be our next bishop. You always seem to know what to say."

Jacob gave a small laugh. "We have a bishop, remember?"

"Andrew Swartley won't be around forever. He's in

his eighties now and gettin' pretty forgetful at times."

"Don't matter how forgetful the man is; as long as he's alive, he'll be our bishop."

Abraham knew a bishop was chosen by lot and remained the head leader until his death. Still, no one lived forever, and when Andrew Swartley passed on, there would be a need for a new bishop.

"Never know what the future holds," Abraham said, elbowing his friend in the ribs.

"That's true enough."

"If I had known my boy was gonna be kidnapped, I sure would have done things differently."

"No one can foresee the future, only God," Jacob said. "And He can take something bad like Zach's disappearance and turn it into something good."

Abraham groaned. "The only good that'll ever come outta this would be if Zach is returned to us."

Naomi sat on the wooden stool behind the counter near the front of the store, trying to insert figures from receipts into the ledger. It was hard to concentrate. Hard to think about anything other than Zach. Over the last couple of days, a sense of sadness had pervaded every step she took, every thought that popped into her head. Her heart felt as dark as the night sky.

She was glad when Jacob Weaver showed up, asking to see her dad. He and Papa had been close friends for a good many years, and if anyone could help Papa through his grief, it would be Jacob. *Sure wish someone could help me with mine.*

She glanced at the clock on the wall across the room. Jacob had been in the storage room with Papa for half an hour already. *Wonder what they could be talking about? Jacob must be takin' a break from his painting business. I'm sure he knows Papa is hurting real bad right now.*

Mary Ann and Nancy had finished unloading the books from the box Papa had brought out, and they'd wanted to ask him what they should do next. Naomi caught them before they knocked on the door, telling the girls they could go outside for a while, as long as they stayed on the front porch. From her spot behind the counter, she could see the entire porch through the window, so if anyone bothered her sisters, she would know about it.

The front door suddenly swung open, and Caleb rushed in.

"Naomi, I came as soon as I heard the news."

She fought against the urge to dash around the counter and throw herself into Caleb's arms. His gentle expression gave evidence of his concern, and she felt sure he wouldn't judge her the way Papa had done.

Naomi held herself in check and managed a brave smile. "It's been rough since Zach was kidnapped."

"I'm awful sorry it happened, but I think I might have some information that could be helpful." Caleb stepped closer. "I don't want to give anyone false hope, but I may have seen Zach."

"What? Where?" Naomi's mouth fell open, and her

heart thumped so hard she feared it might burst.

"Just outside of Berlin, Ohio," he said. "I went there to look at some buggy parts my cousin was selling."

"And?"

"On Sunday I went for a walk in town before my driver took me to the bus station in Dover."

Naomi jumped off the wooden stool and skirted around the counter. "And you saw Zach there? Is that what you're sayin', Caleb?"

He gave his earlobe a couple of tugs. "I can't rightly say it was Zach, but it sure enough looked like him."

"Was there an English man with him?"

Caleb nodded. "A woman, too. She was holding the baby, but the little guy was wearin' English clothes, so I told myself it couldn't be Zach." He shrugged. "Besides, I thought he was home with you. I had no idea he'd been snatched right off your farm. When I got home this morning, Mom told me what happened."

"Stay here while I get Papa. He's in the back room with Jacob Weaver."

Naomi bolted for the rear of the store and pounded on the storage room door. "Papa, it's me! Caleb Hoffmeir's here with some news about Zach."

The door swung open, and Papa and Jacob emerged.

"Where's he at? What'd he say?" Papa's eyes were wide, and he looked downright befuddled. It was the first time he'd spoken to Naomi since that morning, when the police stopped by their house.

"He's up front by the counter. He thinks he may

167

have seen Zach in Berlin, Ohio."

Papa rushed past her, with Jacob Weaver following. Naomi was right on his heels.

"What's all this about you seein' Zach in Ohio?" Papa asked Caleb, who stood with his back against the counter.

"Not sure it was him," Caleb answered, "but he had the same dark brown eyes and light brown hair cut in a Dutch bob. If I hadn't thought he was home with his family, I probably could have convinced myself it was him."

"Who was he with? Where exactly did you see him? Was he okay?"

Caleb held up one hand. "Slow down, Abraham, and I'll try to answer your questions one at a time."

Papa gripped the edge of the counter with both hands. "Okay, I'm listening."

"I went to Berlin to see about some buggy parts, and—"

"Forget the buggy parts! Just tell me about my son!"

Jacob stepped forward and laid his hand on Papa's shoulder. "Calm down once, and let the boy talk."

Papa sucked in a deep breath, and Naomi could tell he was fighting hard for control. "Go on," he mumbled.

"On Sunday, before I headed home, I decided to take a walk." Caleb paused a moment. "I was goin' past this quilt shop, when I noticed an English couple looking in the window. The woman was holding a little boy who looked sort of like Zach."

"Did you say anything to 'em?"

"No. Didn't see a need."

"Did you get a look at the vehicle they were driving?" This question came from Jacob, but Caleb shook his head.

"I kept on walking, so I didn't even see if they had a car."

"But you're sure it was a quilt shop they were in front of?" Papa asked.

Caleb nodded. "The sign out front said FANNIE'S QUILT SHOP. I'm sure of that much. Also heard the man say they'd be goin' back on Monday to buy a quilt."

Papa paced back and forth, making sounds like "*Hmm* . . . Well now . . . I wonder . . ." Finally he halted, turned to face Naomi, and announced, "You're gonna have to mind the store a few days 'cause I'm goin' on a trip."

"Where are you going, Papa?"

"To Ohio. To Fannie's Quilt Shop."

CHAPTER 15

Naomi couldn't believe her dad planned to leave her in charge of the store, much less the children while he went to Ohio. She wanted to believe he trusted her again but figured more than likely he was just desperate for any news of his missing son. It could be a trip made in vain, however, and what if something bad happened while Papa was gone?

"Do you have to leave right away?" Naomi asked, touching her father's arm.

He pulled away. "Don't be tryin' to tell me what to do."

She blinked. "I—I wasn't. I just thought—"

"I need to go to Berlin," Papa said. "Don't have a moment to lose."

"Would you like me to give you a ride home so you can pack and find a way to the bus station?" Caleb asked.

Naomi had almost forgotten he was still there, standing on the other side of the wooden counter. He offered her a brief smile, but she looked away, afraid she would break down in front of him.

Papa hesitated and gave his beard a couple of tugs. "Well, I suppose I would need to leave my horse and buggy here so Naomi and the girls have a way home."

"I can call my cousin Henry who runs a buggy shop near Berlin and see if he'd be willing to put you up for a couple of nights."

"I'd be much obliged," Papa said with a nod.

"Want me to see about gettin' you a bus ticket and a ride to the station?" Jacob Weaver asked.

Papa nodded. "Jah, sure. That would be a big help."

"Richard, one of the English fellows who works for me, was gonna drive me into Lancaster today, so we can drop you off at the bus station first, if you like."

"I appreciate the offer, Jacob. Danki."

"I'd better get a move on then," Papa said. He glanced over at Naomi. "Don't know how long I'll be gone but probably won't be more than a few days at the most."

She opened her mouth to respond, but he turned his back on her. "Ready, Caleb?"

Caleb nodded.

"Can you and your driver pick me up in an hour at my place?" Papa asked Jacob.

"Sure, no problem."

Papa opened the screen door, and the three men stepped onto the porch. Naomi heard her father say something to Mary Ann and Nancy, and when she glanced out the window, she saw him hug them.

She sniffed and fought for control. *Papa never gave me a good-bye hug. He's still angry with me, and I fear unless Zach is found, he always will be.*

On a sudden impulse, Naomi darted for the front door. Papa was already in the parking lot, heading for Caleb's open buggy. She hurried after him, a surge of guilt giving power to her legs. She had asked God for a sign that Zach was all right. Maybe Caleb's news was that sign. "Papa, wait!"

He stopped and whirled around. "What's wrong?"

"Take me with you. I want to be there when you find out if the quilt shop owner has any information about Zach."

Papa's forehead wrinkled, and his eyebrows disappeared into the creases. "Who would watch the kinner if you came along?"

She gulped back the sob threatening to explode from her lips. "I don't know. I'm sure the older boys could manage on their own, and maybe we can ask Anna Beechy to care for the younger ones."

"What about the store, Naomi?"

"Couldn't we close it for a few days?"

"No. This is something I need to do alone." Papa turned away as though the matter was settled.

With a heavy heart, Naomi watched him climb into Caleb's buggy. She knew he couldn't be persuaded to change his mind. When Papa said no, that was it, plain and simple.

Caleb waved as he pulled out of the parking lot, but she didn't respond. He was being so nice, yet she couldn't even find the words to thank him.

"What's wrong with me?" she moaned. "I'm not acting right anymore." Hunching her shoulders, Naomi trudged back to the store. Maybe, just maybe, Papa would return from Ohio with good news.

"Papa said he's goin' to Ohio to see someone about Zach," Nancy said when Naomi stepped onto the porch.

Naomi nodded. "That's right. Caleb was there on Sunday, and he saw a little boy who looked like Zach."

"Will Papa be bringin' the boppli home with him?" Mary Ann questioned, her expression hopeful.

"I don't know what Papa will discover in Ohio," Naomi answered as honestly as she knew how. Truth was, she didn't hold out much hope that the person

172

who ran the quilt shop would know anything helpful.

"Can me and Mary Ann stay out here awhile?" Nancy asked, changing the subject. "It's hot inside, and we like watchin' the people go by."

Naomi nodded. "If we get lots of customers, you'll have to come back in the store. I can't watch you and wait on people at the same time."

"You don't hafta watch us," Mary Ann said with a huff. "We're big girls, and we can look out for ourselves." She thumped her older sister on the arm. "Ain't that right, Nancy?"

"Yep. We'll be just fine."

"I'll keep the door open so you can call if you need anything."

Naomi pushed on the screen door and entered the store. She figured she might as well get to work unloading the shipment of rubber stamps that the UPS man had delivered first thing this morning. Maybe Ginny Meyers would drop by later today, and she could show her what came in. She needed something to take her mind off Zach—and Papa heading to Ohio for what could very well be a complete waste of time.

Half an hour later, Naomi gathered up the garbage and headed outside with the idea of giving the plastic sack to Nancy to deposit in the trash bin. She was surprised to see her sisters leaning against the porch railing holding red lollipops in their hands.

"Where'd you get those?"

Flash!

Naomi jumped.

Flash! Flash!

She pivoted to the right. A middle-aged English man stood on the far end of the porch with a camera in his hands. He nodded and grinned at Naomi. "They said I could take their pictures, and I offered them candy as payment."

A jolt of heat shot up Naomi's neck, and her stomach rolled. She dropped the sack of garbage and yanked the candy from her sisters' hands. "You two know better than to accept anything from a stranger." She shook her finger in Nancy's face. "You also know how we stand on picture takin'. What were you thinking?"

"Didn't figure there'd be any harm. Sarah Graber said she let someone take her picture a few days ago."

"If Sarah jumps off the barn roof, are you gonna follow?" Naomi's voice was shrill, and her hands shook as she clenched the candy she held at her sides. Didn't her sisters have any idea how dangerous talking to a stranger could be? And allowing the man to take their pictures . . . She was sorely disappointed in them.

"Get inside, both of you," she hollered. "The shelves need dusting, and the windows could use a good washing, too. Now get to it!"

The girls stomped off, slamming the screen door as they went inside.

Naomi dropped the lollipops into the garbage sack she'd left on the porch and turned to face the photographer, ready to give him a piece of her mind. Before she could get a word out, he lifted his camera and snapped a picture of her. She gasped. "How dare you!"

He slipped the camera into a canvas satchel and slung it over his shoulder. "Looks like somebody got up on the wrong side of the bed this morning."

Naomi whirled around and stomped into the store, leaving the garbage sack where it lay. She found Nancy washing windows, but Mary Ann was crouched behind the counter, crying.

Naomi dropped to her knees in front of her youngest sister. "I didn't mean to make you cry, Mary Ann, but you should know better than to do what you did out there."

The child wiped her eyes with the back of her hand. "I only wanted a piece of candy."

"Then you should have come inside and asked for one."

Mary Ann looked up, her brown eyes reminding Naomi of a wounded animal. "I figured you'd say no."

Naomi pulled the little girl into her arms. "When you're done with the dusting, you can help yourself to a lollipop from the candy counter."

Mary Ann sniffed. "Nancy, too?"

"Jah." Naomi grabbed the broom and started sweeping the floor. *What was Papa thinking, leaving me alone to care for his children? I can barely function, much less take charge of things 'til he gets back home.*

"Mom, if you don't need me for a while, I think I'll

take my lunch and go out back to the picnic table," Abby said.

Fannie nodded. "Sure, Daughter, go right ahead. Since it's almost noon, there probably won't be too many customers."

Abby smiled, her dark eyes gleaming. She was such a sweet girl, always helpful and ever so pleasant. And Abby was mighty good with a needle and thread. She'd done her first piece of quilting when she was ten years old and had been making beautiful quilts ever since. Fannie didn't know what she would have done without Abby's help after her husband, Ezra, had a massive heart attack two years ago, leaving her a widow. Fannie's son, Harold, had married Lena Graber two years ago, and they lived next door to her, so Fannie knew she could rely on them, as well. Fannie hoped she'd have her only daughter around awhile. Abby was only eighteen and didn't even have a serious boyfriend yet.

"I'll trade off with you when I'm done eating," Abby said, breaking into Fannie's musings. "You've worked hard all morning and could use some time in the fresh air."

Fannie grunted. "Hot and sticky air, that's more like it."

"It's much cooler under the shade of the old maple tree."

"That's true, and I'll probably take your suggestion." Fannie pointed to the back door. "Now go eat your lunch. Time's a-wastin'."

176

When Abby hurried away, Fannie returned to her job at the cutting table. She had a Log Cabin quilt she was planning to work on, and it sure wouldn't get done by thinking about it.

She'd only taken a few snips when the bell on the front door jangled. She looked up and saw an English couple enter the store. The woman held a little boy in her arms. *Probably not much more than a year old,* Fannie figured. The baby had light brown hair and eyes so dark it made her think of chocolate syrup.

Fannie fought the urge to ask if she could hold the baby. It had been too long since her kinner were little. She'd always wished for more children, but the Lord must have thought two were enough. After Abby was born, Fannie never conceived again. Since she had no husband now, it wasn't likely she'd ever have any more children, either.

"May I help ya with somethin'?" she asked, moving toward the English couple, who glanced around the store with confused expressions.

The man fidgeted and glanced out the front window. "We—uh—need a quilt," he mumbled.

"What size are you needin'?"

He looked at the woman. "Queen?"

She nodded. "That's the size of our bed, so that's what we want."

"All the quilts are hung on racks, according to their dimensions," Fannie said, pointing across the room. "Do you have any particular style or color in mind?"

The woman shook her head. "No, not really. I guess

177

maybe something with blues would be nice. Our bedroom is blue and white."

"There are several quilts with blue in them. Would ya like to browse, or do you want me to show them to you?"

"You'd better show us, or we'll be here all day," the man said. Fannie figured his edginess was probably because he'd rather be doing something other than looking at quilts. Most men didn't like shopping. Leastways, Ezra never had.

"Right this way." Fannie led, and they followed.

The woman handed the baby over to the man while she looked at quilts.

"Sure is a cute baby," Fannie said. "How old is he?"

"He's—uh—one."

"What's the name of this pattern?" the woman asked, pulling Fannie's attention back to the job at hand.

"That one's called Lone Star. My daughter, Abby, made it."

"Do you make every quilt here in the shop?"

"Oh no. We'd never have time to make 'em all." Fannie waved her hand. "There are several Amish and Mennonite women in the area who sew for us."

"They're all lovely," the woman said, "but I think I'll take this one." She glanced at her husband and pointed to the price sticker. "It's six hundred dollars, Jim. Can we afford that much?"

He grimaced but nodded. "I think we can swing it."

"Will you take a credit card?" the woman asked.

"We'll be paying cash," her husband said, reaching into his pants' pocket and retrieving a brown wallet.

"But, Jim, that's a lot of money and—"

"It's fine. I've got enough cash left to get us home."

"Where you folks from?" Fannie asked as she lifted the quilt off the rack.

"We're here visiting family," the man answered before the woman could open her mouth.

Fannie figured that was all the information he cared to give, so she dropped the subject. Some English folks were sure odd. So close-mouthed about things.

She took the quilt to her work counter and carefully wrapped it in tissue paper, then placed it inside a light-weight cardboard box.

Obviously pleased with her purchase, the woman fairly beamed. She took the baby from her husband, and he picked up the box.

Fannie followed them to the front door. "I hope you'll get many years of enjoyment from the quilt you bought. Have a good day now."

"Yes, thank you," the man muttered. "You, too."

For the next few hours, Naomi and her sisters cleaned and stocked more shelves. When that was done, she sent Nancy and Mary Ann to the back room so they could play while she inserted more figures into the ledger.

She had just seated herself behind the counter when Ginny Meyers entered the store. Naomi looked up and feigned a smile. "We got a new shipment of rubber stamps in this morning. You'd probably like to have a look-see."

Ginny raced over to Naomi. "I can't even think about stamps right now. I read about Zach's kidnapping in the newspaper this morning and came by to offer my support."

Naomi nodded. "It happened on Saturday."

"That's what the paper said." Ginny reached across the counter and took hold of Naomi's hand. "I'm sorry, Naomi. It must be awful for you."

Naomi blinked back the tears threatening to spill over. Having someone's sympathy was awful nice, but for some reason, seeing Ginny and hearing her kind words made Naomi feel worse.

Ginny released Naomi's hand and clicked her tongue. "You've got dark circles under your eyes. I'll bet you haven't slept hardly at all since Zach was taken, have you?"

"No," Naomi admitted. "Truth is, I haven't been able to do much of anything since then."

"What I want to know is, what kind of maniac would drive onto an Amish farm and snatch a baby right out from under his family's nose?"

Naomi drew in a deep breath and almost choked on her words. "I don't know, but it's my fault Zach was taken, and Papa is furious with me."

"Why's it your fault?"

"The man who stopped by for root beer asked if I had any that was cold." She gulped. "I was going to get him some from the refrigerator when I heard one of the girls scream. So I raced to the house, leaving Zach on the picnic table. When I returned, the man was gone, and so was Zach."

Ginny's mouth dropped open. "You're kidding?"

Naomi shook her head. "If Zach isn't found, I don't think I'll ever forgive myself, and Papa sure won't."

"He's upset right now, but I'm sure in time he'll realize something like that could have happened to anyone."

"I didn't leave the boppli there on purpose; surely Papa must know that."

Ginny's clear blue eyes seemed full of understanding. "Of course you didn't."

"I'd had such a busy morning, and I just wasn't thinking."

Ginny nodded. "I understand. You're overloaded with too many responsibilities and can't do them all. If your dad would hire a maid and give you some time to yourself, you could probably function a whole lot better."

Naomi sniffed and blew her nose on a tissue she'd pulled from under the counter.

"You know what I think you need?"

"Uh-uh."

"You need to get away for a while and do something fun." Ginny smiled. "Why don't you make up some excuse to leave the store for a couple hours and sneak away with me to see a movie? It might help take your mind off your troubles."

"I can't. Papa's headed to Ohio today, and that

leaves me fully in charge."

Ginny's pale eyebrows lifted. "Ohio? Why'd he go there?"

Naomi explained about Caleb's recent trip and what he'd seen outside the quilt shop near Berlin. "Papa thinks if he talks to the shop owner, he might learn something about the couple with the baby who looked like Zach."

Ginny tapped her pink, perfectly manicured fingernails along the edge of the counter. "Maybe the man who stole your little brother lives in Ohio. If your dad gets a lead on him and calls the cops, you could have Zach home real soon."

Naomi managed a weak smile. "I hope so, Ginny. Jah, I truly do."

CHAPTER 16

Fannie opened the front door of her shop and held it for Abby, whose arms were full of quilting material.

Abby stepped inside. "Thank you, Mom. I'll put these on the shelves in the back."

Fannie was about to reply when she heard footsteps on the stairs behind her. She turned around quickly and nearly bumped into a tall, middle-aged Amish man with the bluest eyes she had ever seen. She didn't recognize him and figured he was probably from another district.

"Can I help you?" she asked.

"I'm lookin' for the owner of this quilt shop."

She smiled. "That would be me. I'm Fannie Miller."

He cleared his throat. "I've got some questions."

"About quilting? Are ya lookin' to buy a quilt?"

He glanced around, kind of nervouslike. "Don't need no quilts. Would it be all right if I came inside?"

"Yes, yes, of course." Fannie stepped into the shop, and she knew he was right behind her, for she could hear the *clomp clomp* of his boots against the wooden floor.

"I was here yesterday evening, but you were closed for the day," the man said.

"Must have been after six."

"Jah. My bus didn't get in 'til seven, then it took me some time to get a driver and make my way over here." He removed his straw hat, and Fannie was amazed at how thick and shiny his brown hair appeared to be. Not a sign of gray, either, although his full beard had a sprinkling in it.

She moved toward the counter where they waited on customers, and he followed. "If you're not here about a quilt, what can I help you with?"

He gave his beard a couple of pulls. "I heard there was an English couple outside your store on Sunday. Since your shop was closed that day, they said they'd be back Monday morning to buy a quilt."

"Who'd they say it to?"

"The man told the woman, and Caleb Hoffmeir, the

young buggy maker from my district in Lancaster County, was walking by and heard their conversation."

"I see."

"So, I'm wonderin' if they did come to your store on Monday."

Fannie smiled. "Lots of English come here, Mr.—"

"Abraham. Abraham Fisher." He shifted his weight from one foot to the other. "The English couple had a little boy. Would have been about a year old."

"Hmm . . . let me think." Fannie tried to picture some of the customers she'd had yesterday. It had been a busy day, full of tourists, as well as several of her regular customers.

"Please, try to remember. This is awful important."

Fannie took a seat on the wooden stool and tried to concentrate. "Do you know this English couple?"

He shook his head. "No, but when Caleb told me he'd seen them, I bought a bus ticket and came right here."

"Could you explain things better, Abraham? Why would you be so interested in an English couple with a baby, who you don't even know?"

Abraham clasped his hands tightly together. "I live near Paradise, Pennsylvania, and my baby was kidnapped out of my yard on Saturday afternoon."

Fannie's heart clenched. She could hardly fathom such a horrible thing. "I'm so sorry. You and your wife must be frantic with worry."

"My Sarah died a little over a year ago when she

184

was hit by a car. Our baby, Zach, was only two months old at the time."

Fannie could almost feel the man's grief. "I lost my husband when he had a heart attack two years ago, so I sympathize with your loss."

He paced back and forth in front of the counter. "Losin' Sarah was hard enough, but now that I've lost my boppli, too, the pain's nearly unbearable."

"I can imagine."

"Caleb Hoffmeir said the boy with the English couple looked like my Zach." He grimaced. "I'm thinkin' maybe they could be the ones who kidnapped him."

Fannie clasped her hands. "You must be beside yourself with worry."

He nodded. "If you could help me on this, I'd be much obliged."

She drew in a deep breath and tried to focus her thoughts. "Let's see now . . . Mary Zook and her sister Catherine came in first thing Monday morning. They bought some material for a new quilt they wanted to start. And then a young English mother and her daughter stopped by." Fannie smiled. "They live in the area and are regular customers."

Abraham's eyebrows furrowed deep into the folds of his forehead. She could tell he was growing impatient and wanted some answers.

Fannie licked her lips. "After Carol and her daughter left, about ten women arrived. I think they were with a tour bus."

When Abraham made no comment, she continued. "Then later, around lunchtime, an English couple came in, asking to buy a queen-sized quilt." She snapped her fingers. "Say, they did have a little boy. Fact is, I couldn't get over how sweet he was. Cute as could be and seemed to be quite even tempered. Never fussed a bit the whole time they were here."

Abraham leaned across the counter until she could actually feel his warm breath on her face. "What'd the boy look like? How old would you say he was? Did he have a Dutch bob?"

Fannie sat up straight and moved away from Abraham. It made her nervous to have him breathing on her that way. "I'd guess he was around a year or so, and he had such pretty hair—golden brown, I'd say it was. Don't know if it was Dutch bobbed or not, though. It was slicked back away from his face."

"And his eyes? What color were the boppli's eyes?"

"Brown. Dark brown, like chocolate."

Abraham's breathing intensified. "Did ya get a look behind his right ear?"

She shook her head. "Can't say that I did. Why do you ask?"

"Zach has a small heart-shaped birthmark there."

Fannie rubbed her forehead and tried to get a better picture of the little boy in her mind. "I'm sorry to say, but I didn't notice behind his ear. Fact of the matter is, I was more concerned with showin' the woman the right color quilts than anything else."

"Did they buy a quilt?" he asked.

"Jah. Got a nice Lone Star pattern with shades of blue."

"Did you happen to get their names?"

"No, but I heard the woman call the man 'Jim' a couple of times."

"No last name?"

She shook her head.

"If they bought a quilt, you must have made out a receipt."

"I did, but they paid cash, so I had no reason to get their name and address." Fannie frowned. "Funny thing, though, I did ask 'em once where they were from, and the man only said they were here visiting family."

"Did you get a look at the car they were drivin'? Maybe the color or license plate?"

"Sorry, but another customer came in as they were leaving, so my attention was turned to her. Truth is, I never saw the Englishers' car."

Abraham groaned. "And that's all you know?"

"Afraid so." Fannie skirted around the counter. "Sure wish there was more I could do to help. I know this must be awful frustrating for you."

Abraham rubbed the bridge of his nose. "Don't know how I'm gonna return home and tell the family I came all this way for nothin'."

"I'll be praying for you, Abraham." She paused. "You said you live near Paradise, right?"

He nodded.

"I've got a cousin who lives near that area, and she's

been after me to spend some time with her this summer."

"You should do it. Lancaster County is a right nice place to visit."

"Jah, I've been there before, but not in many years."

"If you do get over our way, feel free to stop by my store and say hello. It's called Fisher's General Store and is located just outside the town of Paradise."

"I might do that. I'd like to see how things are, and I pray by then you'll have found your boy."

He smiled, but she could tell it was forced. The creases in Abraham's forehead gave indication that he was deeply troubled. "I'm prayin' for the same thing," he said, turning toward the front door. "Thanks for being willing to speak with me, and I'm sorry for takin' up so much of your time."

She followed him to the door. "It was no trouble. I only wish I had more information to give."

"You told me what you knew, and I appreciate it." Abraham pulled the door open and stepped onto the porch. "Good day to you, Fannie Miller."

"*Da Herr sei mit du*—the Lord be with you," she said in return.

"Who was that man?" Abby asked when Fannie shut the door. "I stayed at the back of the store because I could see you two were in deep conversation."

Fannie nodded. "He was askin' about an English couple who bought a quilt yesterday."

Abby tipped her head. "Mind if I ask why?"

"The man and woman had a little boy, and someone

188

who knows Abraham Fisher saw them outside our store on Sunday." She pursed her lips. "Seems Abraham's boppli was kidnapped off his farm Saturday afternoon, and the young fellow who noticed the English couple window-shoppin' thought their child looked like Abraham's boy."

Abby's dark eyes revealed her usual compassion. "That's awful. I can't imagine such a thing."

"Me neither." Fannie sighed. "Sure wish there was something I could have said to make Abraham feel better. He seemed so distraught over the disappearance of his son."

"You can pray for him, Mom. Pray the people who took his baby will come to their senses and return the boy home."

Fannie gently squeezed her daughter's arm. "You're sure a smart one; ya know that?"

Abby smiled. "Well, what can I say? I'm only followin' in my dear mamm's footsteps."

Abraham figured there was probably no use in him hanging around Berlin. If he had a lick of sense, he'd catch the next bus home and be done with it. Still, he had a strong feeling the English couple who visited Fannie's Quilt Shop yesterday were the ones who took Zach. At least the man. Naomi never mentioned anything about a woman being involved. Of course, she'd been so befuddled that day she didn't seem to remember much of anything.

He meandered down the sidewalk, heading for the

other side of town. *Might as well take a look around, just in case those people are still in town.*

For the next couple of hours, Abraham wandered up and down the streets of Berlin, looking inside stores, checking out every English person he saw. He scrutinized each car parked along the street, as well as those passing by. He saw lots of English people, many with children. None looked like Zach, however.

"It's hopeless," he mumbled. "Might as well head back to Henry's Buggy Shop and ask him to call someone to take me to the bus station in Dover."

Abraham turned and started down the street in the direction of Henry's place, which was about a mile out of town. Henry had dropped him off this morning, saying he'd be happy to come back for Abraham if he knew what time and where he wanted to be picked up. Abraham declined the offer, telling Caleb's cousin the walk would do him good.

As he plodded along, Abraham noticed he was coming to Fannie's Quilt Shop again. He fought the urge to go inside and ask a few more questions. *That would be dumb,* he decided. *Fannie said she didn't know anything more.*

Feeling a muscle in his back begin to cramp, Abraham took a seat on the wooden bench outside the quilt shop. He'd rest awhile before continuing his journey to the buggy shop. While he sat, he would watch every car going past and check each person who walked by.

Maybe if he begged God hard enough, his prayer

would be answered. He leaned forward and rested his chin in his hands. *Please, Lord, let it be so.*

Time passed, and Abraham continued to watch and pray. He didn't know how long he'd been sitting there, but the touch of someone's hand on his shoulder jolted him upright.

"Abraham, are you all right?"

He turned his head. Fannie Miller stood behind him, her hazel-colored eyes looking so sincere. Two little wisps of dark brown hair had escaped her white covering. He ignored the sudden urge to push them back in place.

"I–I'm okay," he sputtered. "Just sat down for a spell to rest my back. Guess I lost track of time, 'cause from the way that sun feels, I'd have to say it's past noon."

Fannie nodded. "My daughter just finished her lunch break, and I was lookin' to take mine. Took a quick glance out front before I did and saw you sitting here." She moved around to stand beside the bench. "I was worried about you."

"It's nice of you to be concerned," he replied. "I've been walkin' up and down the streets of Berlin all morning with the hope of spotting the English couple I told you about."

She stared down at him, compassion evident on her round face. "I take it you saw no one with a child who looked like your son?"

He shook his head.

"Have you had lunch?" she asked suddenly.

"Naw, I wasn't in the mood to eat."

"How would you like to share my lunch? There's a picnic table under a maple tree behind the store, and I'd be glad to have you join me."

"I couldn't ask you to do that."

"It's no bother." She chuckled and patted her stomach. "I packed way too much food this mornin', and you might save me a few added inches if you share it with me."

He smiled in spite of his dismal mood. "Jah, okay. I'd be happy to then."

"Let's go into the store first," Fannie said. "My lunch basket's there, and we can go out the back door." She led, and he followed.

There was a young woman with dark brown hair cutting a piece of material at one of the tables near the back of the store. She was younger than Fannie and several pounds lighter, but he could tell they were related.

"This is my daughter, Abby," Fannie said as they approached the young woman. "Abby, this is Abraham Fisher from Lancaster County, Pennsylvania."

Abby looked up from her work and smiled. She had a dimple in her right cheek, just like her mother's. "It's nice to meet you, Abraham. Mom told me you were here earlier, asking about an English couple with a little boy who looked like your son."

A renewed sense of hope welled up in his chest. "Do you remember them? Did you get any information

192

about who they were or where they were goin'?"

She shook her head. "Sorry, no. I was outside havin' lunch when the couple came in. Mom told me about it later."

He released a heavy sigh. "Sure wish someone knew something."

"God knows, Abraham," Fannie said sincerely. "I'm sure He feels your pain."

She held up a wicker basket. "I've got our food right here. You ready?"

He nodded. "Ready and feelin' hungrier by the minute."

For the next half hour, Abraham and Fannie got better acquainted as he told her about his family and the way it had been since Sarah's death. He was amazed at how understanding and sweet she was, offering words of encouragement and saying she would keep him and his family in her prayers.

Fannie shared a bit about her life, too: how she'd only been able to have two children—a boy, now married, and Abby, who helped at the quilt shop.

Abraham studied Fannie as she sat on the other side of the picnic table smiling at him. *Too bad there aren't any widows like you in my area,* he mused. *If so, I might change my mind about gettin' married again.*

CHAPTER 17

Naomi glanced out the kitchen window. Half an hour ago, she'd sent Nancy and Mary Ann to the garden to pick strawberries, and they still hadn't returned. Didn't they realize she was in a hurry?

She placed two pie pans on the counter and slipped the flattened dough inside each one. After another long day at the store, she didn't feel like baking, but the girls had been begging for strawberry pie, and the garden was overflowing with ripe berries. "Sure hope Papa gets here soon," Naomi muttered. He'd been gone two full days, and she had no idea when to expect him. Had he found the English couple with the baby who looked like Zach? If so, had the police been called? How she hoped Papa would return with her little brother. "Everything will be all right if Zach comes home."

"You talkin' to yourself again?"

Naomi whirled around. Norman stood inside the kitchen door, his face and arms covered with dust.

"You shouldn't be sneaking up on me like that."

He sauntered across the room and opened the refrigerator door. "Wasn't sneakin'. Just came in to get a glass of lemonade."

"You're dirty as a pig," she scolded. "Should have washed up outside before you came into the house."

He grunted. "Don't tell me what to do, Naomi. Just because Papa's gone don't mean you can boss everyone around."

She balled her hands into fists and planted them on her hips. "I'm not."

Norman set the pitcher of lemonade on the table and went to get a glass from the cupboard. "Jah, you are. Ever since Mama died, you've been kinda bossy, and now that Papa's gone to Ohio, you think you can tell everyone what to do."

Heat crept up the back of Naomi's neck, and she struggled to keep her tears at bay. She didn't understand why her brother was being so mean, but she had to keep control of her emotions, especially in front of her siblings.

"Norman, do this," he taunted. "Nancy, do that. All you ever do is order folks around."

"I'm only doing what I was asked to do," she countered. "Papa said I should look after things, and that means—"

"Ha! Look after things? Were ya lookin' after Zach when he was snatched off the picnic table last Saturday?"

She winced. The pain of her brother's words sliced through Naomi like a knife. She opened her mouth to defend herself, but she couldn't. Norman was right. She hadn't done a good job of looking out for Zach that day, but she didn't need to be reminded of her error. Naomi had berated herself aplenty these last few days, but to be told she was negligent by one of her family members was like a slap in the face.

She turned back to the pie shells. What was keeping those girls? Tears slipped from her eyes and landed on the counter with a splash.

"Don't see how you can expect anyone to do what you say anymore," Norman went on. "You'd better quit bossin' and start being more responsible."

Naomi choked on a sob, pushed the pie pans aside, and rushed out the back door. She stopped long enough to blow her nose and gulp in a deep breath, and then hurried to the garden.

The sound of children's laughter drifted on the wind, and she halted at the edge of the grass. Nancy and Mary Ann ran back and forth between the rows of strawberries, laughing, hollering, and throwing berries at one another.

Naomi cupped her trembling hands around her mouth and hollered, "Stop that!"

When the girls ignored her and kept on running, she marched into the garden, picked up one of the half-empty plastic containers, and shoved it at Nancy. "*Des is mer gen greitz*—this is annoying to me."

Mary Ann screeched to a halt and hung her head. "Aw, Naomi, we was only havin' a little fun."

"I sent you out here to pick strawberries, not have fun! I've got pies to bake, and there aren't nearly enough berries in this container for even one pie."

Nancy scrunched her nose. "How come you're always yellin' at us?"

"I wouldn't have to yell if you did as you were told."

"Norman said we don't hafta mind you anymore," Mary Ann said.

Naomi clenched her teeth. "Oh, he did, did he?"

Her little sister nodded soberly.

"You should know better than to listen to Norman. He's only trying to make trouble."

Nancy's lower lip quivered. "Why can't we ever please you, Sister? Ever since Zach was taken, you've been cranky and shootin' orders all the time."

Overcome with remorse, Naomi bent down and grabbed both girls in a hug. "I love you so much, and I'm sorry for takin' my frustrations out on you," she said tearfully. "It's just that I'm feeling awful about Zach being kidnapped, and I want to take good care of you girls—see that you do things right and are kept safe."

Mary Ann buried her face in Naomi's neck. "It ain't your fault Zach was taken."

"That's right," Nancy agreed, "and Papa's gonna bring him back home; you'll see."

"I hope so. I truly do." Naomi sniffed. "Forgive me, girls—for being such a grump?"

"Jah," they said in unison.

"All right then. Please get busy and fill these containers with berries. I want to get the pies started before we have supper."

Nancy and Mary Ann grabbed their plastic tubs and started picking right away. Naomi turned and headed back to the house. She hoped Norman had returned to the fields. She was not in the mood to listen to more

197

of his unkind remarks.

She had only taken a few steps when she heard a horse and buggy pull into the yard. It was Caleb.

He waved and stepped down from his buggy. She noticed right away that he held a book in his hands. "This is for you," he said as he approached her.

She tipped her head. "What for? It's not my birthday or anything."

"It's my way of letting you know I've been thinkin' about you. I wanted to come by yesterday and see how you were doing, but I had so much work in the shop I couldn't get away." He handed the book to Naomi. "This is about all the sights out west. I remember once when we were kinner, you said you'd like to see Mount Rainier and what's left of Mount St. Helens."

Naomi blinked against threatening tears. "That was kind of you."

"How are things going? Heard anything from your daed yet?"

She shook her head and moved toward the house. "Would you like a glass of lemonade or something?"

"That'd be nice."

"Have a seat on the front porch. I'll take the book inside and be right out with the lemonade."

Caleb plunked himself down on the top step, and Naomi went into the house. When she entered the kitchen, she was relieved to see that Norman was no longer there. She placed the travelogue on one end of the counter and went to the refrigerator. A few minutes later, she returned to the porch with two glasses of lemonade and handed one to Caleb. "Here you go."

"Danki." He smiled when she took a seat beside him. "So ya don't have any idea when Abraham might be home?"

"Nope. I'm hoping his bein' gone these three days means he might have discovered something about Zach."

"I could go to one of the English neighbors and call my cousin in Berlin."

Naomi sucked in her bottom lip. "I suppose you could, but Papa might not like it if he thought we were checkin' up on him. Besides, he's not too keen on makin' phone calls that aren't absolutely necessary."

Caleb shrugged. "Guess he'd call one of your neighbors and ask them to get you a message if there was anything important to tell."

She sighed and set her glass down on the step. "Jah, which probably means he hasn't found Zach."

"If he does find your little brother, maybe he'll come home and surprise everyone."

"That would be wonderful—the answer to my prayers."

Caleb took hold of Naomi's hand, and the contact of his skin made her flesh tingle. "I know there are some in our district who feel you were negligent by leavin' Zach on that picnic table." He gazed into Naomi's eyes, and she could see the depth of his understanding. "Some, like me, know it was just an accident. Could

199

have happened to any one of us if we'd been distracted."

Her eyes filled with tears, and she nodded. "That's what happened all right. I'd been awful busy that morning, which probably didn't help things any, but when I heard Mary Ann's scream, I lost track of what I should be doin'." She pulled her hand from his and reached up to wipe the tears on her cheeks. "Even so, I can't quit blamin' myself for what happened, and the worst of it is, Papa blames me, too."

Caleb frowned. "Wish there was some way I could get him to let you start goin' to singings and the like. Maybe then we could begin courtin'."

Naomi opened her mouth to respond, but a car pulled into the yard, and she and Caleb both stood.

"Looks like Mr. Peterson, the man we often call for rides when we can't take the horse and buggy," Naomi said.

The door of the passenger side opened, and Naomi's father stepped out, holding his suitcase. A chorus of cheers went up from the garden patch as Naomi's sisters rushed out to greet him. Naomi and Caleb followed.

Naomi's heart sank when she realized Papa was alone. No precious little brother to hold and welcome home.

"How was your trip?" she asked Papa after he told Mr. Peterson good-bye and shut the car door.

He looked tired, and his face was drawn. "Long. It's gut to be home."

"Any news about Zach?" She had to ask, even

though it was obvious he'd returned empty-handed.

He shook his head. "Fannie didn't have much information to give me."

"Who's Fannie, Papa?" Nancy asked.

"She's the woman who owns the quilt shop on the outskirts of Berlin, Ohio."

"Did she say whether an English couple had come to her store with a baby who looked like Zach?" Caleb questioned.

Papa frowned. "Caleb, what are you doin' here?"

"I dropped by to see if the family had received any news from you yet."

Naomi was glad Caleb made no mention of the book he'd brought. That probably wouldn't set well with her daed.

"I see," Papa said. "That's nice of you, but there is no news. None that's good anyways."

"So the woman at the quilt shop didn't know a thing?" Caleb asked.

"The description of the baby she saw seemed to fit Zach. Same as what you said, Caleb."

"Did she know who the English people were or where they were going?" Naomi asked.

"I just said she didn't have any real information," Papa snapped.

She stared down at her bare feet. "Sorry. I thought maybe—"

Papa started moving toward the house. "Where's the rest of the family?"

"The boys are still out in the fields," Nancy replied.

"Want me to ring the dinner bell so they'll come up to the house?"

He shook his head. "Naw, let 'em keep workin' awhile longer. Since I have no good news to share, there's not much point to callin' them in 'til suppertime."

Naomi was surprised at Papa's attitude. Despite his abruptness with her a few minutes ago, he didn't seem near as edgy as before he left for Ohio. After making the long trip and not finding Zach, she thought he'd be cranky as all get out.

"Let's go inside. I'm bushed," Papa said.

The girls started to follow, but Naomi stopped them before they got to the porch. "What about the berries? Have you got both containers filled?"

"Just about," Nancy answered.

"Please get it done. I've still got those pies to bake."

"Ah, do we have to?" Mary Ann whined. "I wanna go inside with Papa."

"Do as your sister says," he scolded. "We can talk when you're done pickin' berries."

The girls walked away with their shoulders hunched, and Papa stepped onto the porch. He stopped before he got to the door and turned around. "Caleb, would ya like to join us for supper?"

Naomi was even more surprised by her father's question than she was by his easygoing attitude. What in the world would make Papa invite Caleb to supper? As far as she knew, he didn't want the buggy maker hanging around.

Caleb shuffled his feet. "That's a real nice offer, and I'd sure like to, but Mom's expectin' me back right away. Maybe some other time."

Papa lifted his hand. "Just want to say thanks for tellin' me about those English people you saw in Ohio and also for settin' things up so I could stay with Henry while I was there."

"You're welcome." Caleb turned to Naomi and gave her a quick wink. She was glad Papa's back was to them. He wouldn't have liked Caleb flirting with her, even if he were in a better mood than she'd seen him in some time.

"Thanks for the book," she whispered to Caleb.

He smiled, waved, and headed for his buggy.

Naomi followed her father into the house. Things might be looking up. Leastways, she felt as if they were somewhat better now that Papa was back home. She didn't know why he seemed less agitated than before, but she might as well enjoy the change for as long as it lasted. Come tomorrow, like as not, they might all sink into depression again.

CHAPTER 18

Naomi climbed the stairs to her bedroom, feeling the burden of weariness with each step she took. It was nearly midnight, and as usual, she was the last one to bed.

The past two weeks had gone by quickly as the garden brought forth an abundance of produce that needed to be either canned or frozen. Each evening after they returned from the store and every Saturday, Naomi and her sisters tended the garden. Samuel had been put to work helping with the picking, but he flatly refused to do anything in the kitchen. "Canning is women's work," he'd boldly announced.

Naomi sighed deeply as she entered her room. She was still having trouble getting the children to mind, even the youngest like Samuel and Mary Ann. Ever since Zach's disappearance, they had been hard to deal with.

Maybe it's me who's hard to deal with, she considered. *Maybe I expect too much. I'm not their mother, after all. If I were, Zach would have been better cared for.*

Naomi glanced at her little brother's empty crib. It was a constant reminder of her loss and the remorse she felt for being so incompetent. At Papa's insistence, the high chair and playpen had been dismantled. Yet Naomi couldn't seem to part with the crib in her room. If she kept it there, it would remind her to pray for Zach. And if God took pity on them and returned her baby brother, his bed would be ready and waiting.

Naomi removed her kapp and placed it on the dresser. She pulled the pins out of her bun, and soft brown waves cascaded down her back and around her shoulders. She picked up the hairbrush and sank to the bed as a vision of her mother came to mind.

"Always brush your hair one hundred strokes every night, and it will stay healthy and shiny for years to come," Mama often said. Even when Naomi was so weary she could barely find the strength to lift her arms, she had followed her mother's suggestion. It made her feel closer to Mama, thinking about how she used to watch the dear woman brush her own silky tresses until they shone like a new penny.

Tears welled up in Naomi's eyes and clouded her vision. "Oh, Mama, I miss you so much."

Plink.

Naomi tipped her head and listened. What was that strange noise? It appeared as if something had hit her bedroom window.

Plink. Plink. There it was again. It sounded like pebbles being thrown against the glass.

She hurried to the window and lifted the dark shade. A man stood in the yard below her room. When he stepped out of the shadows, she realized it was Caleb.

He waved at her, and Naomi's breath caught in her throat. *What's he doing here? Doesn't Caleb know Papa could hear the noise and go outside to investigate?* Of course, her father had been the first to go to bed that night, saying he was tired and his back hurt. More than likely, he was sound asleep, and since Naomi had been the last person to head for bed, she was probably the only one still awake.

She tiptoed out of her room and down the stairs, listening for any sounds coming from the other bedrooms. There was nothing but quiet and the subtle creaking of the stairs as she slowly descended them.

With her heart pounding, Naomi slipped out the back door and into the night. Caleb stood beside a shrub, still gazing upward.

"What are you doing here?"

He whirled around. "Don't scare me like that."

"Were you throwin' pebbles at my window?"

He nodded. "Came to see you, and when I saw the light, I figured that was the best way to get your attention."

She stifled a yawn. "Jah, and it could have caught Papa's attention, too. Caleb Hoffmeir, what were you thinking?"

He took hold of her hand and led her across the yard. "I was thinkin' about you and how I wished I'd accepted your daed's invitation to supper a couple weeks ago."

They stood under the old maple tree now, and Caleb nodded at the swing hanging from its branches. "Have a seat, and I'll give you a few pushes."

She glanced around, half expecting to see Papa or one of the brothers come charging out of the house, but all was quiet.

Naomi sat on the wooden seat and grasped the rope handles. This was crazy, her sitting here in the middle of the night, allowing Caleb to push her on the swing as though they were a courting couple.

"I've waited so long for this chance to be alone with you," Caleb murmured against her ear.

Naomi filled her lungs with fresh air and tried not to shiver.

"You're tremblin'," Caleb whispered. "Are ya cold? Want me to get a buggy robe out of my rig?"

She shook her head. "I'm okay. Just a little nervous is all."

"Afraid your daed might catch us?"

"Jah."

"He's been much friendlier to me lately, so maybe he wouldn't mind if he did find us together."

"Something must have happened in Ohio. When Papa returned, he seemed softer," Naomi said. "I'm sure he hasn't forgiven me for leavin' Zach on that picnic table, but he's not been quite so harsh when he speaks to me, either."

"Have you tried talking to him about things? Explain the way you feel and all?"

"No. I doubt it would do much good. Papa's always been pretty closemouthed about his feelings, and this thing with Zach has put a barrier between us that might never come down." She released a heavy sigh. "Truth is, it's affected the whole family. None of the kinner acts the same toward me anymore."

"Sorry to hear that, Naomi. Wish there was somethin' I could do to make your life more pleasant."

"I'm afraid there isn't much anyone can do. What we need is a miracle—to have Zach come home."

Caleb continued to push the swing back and forth. The musical rhythm of singing crickets filled the night air, and for a few moments, Naomi felt a sense of peace, as though it had permeated the air she breathed.

"Naomi, will you continue to see me like this—after it's dark and everyone's asleep?" Caleb asked.

She moistened her lips with the tip of her tongue. How she wanted to say yes, but what would be the point in leading Caleb on? If they began to secretly court, soon he'd be talking of marriage, and she knew that was impossible. Papa would never give his consent. She had a responsibility to the family, a promise to Mama that must be fulfilled. Naomi had already messed up by allowing her busyness to cloud her thinking. She sure couldn't allow thoughts of love and romance to lead her astray.

"Naomi?"

She jerked her head. "Jah?"

"What have you got to say about me comin' by like this again?"

Naomi opened her mouth to respond, but her words were cut off.

"*Net*—never!"

Naomi swiveled around. There stood Papa, his arms crossed and his face a mask of anger. He'd looked at her the same way the day Zach was kidnapped.

Papa turned to face Caleb. "I give you a foot, and you take three yards! What's the meaning of all this huggin' and kissin' going on behind my back?"

"Papa, we weren't. Caleb just came by so we could talk."

"*Humph!* I know all about the thoughts on a young man's mind, and the buggy maker didn't come here in the middle of the night to talk!"

"That's not true, Abraham. I only wanted to speak with Naomi about her and me courtin'."

Papa smacked his hands together, and Naomi jumped right off the swing. "I thought I made myself clear on that subject awhile back. Naomi's not courtin' you or anyone else. She's needed here. Plain and simple." He pointed at the house while he glared at Naomi. "Get on to your room. We'll discuss this more in the morning."

He turned to face Caleb. "And you'd better get back in your buggy and head for home!"

A sob caught in Naomi's throat, but she did as her father commanded. Was there never to be any peace in this family? Would she ever be free from her guilt or experience the joys others her age felt when they were courted by some special fellow?

"Have you got the baby's car seat? I don't want to leave it in the car, where someone might steal it," Linda called as Jim was about to close the garage door.

He clenched his teeth. The whole time they'd been in Ohio visiting his folks, Linda had been overprotective of Jimmy, barely allowing Mom and Dad to hold the baby. On their trip home, she'd insisted on sitting in the backseat with him. Now she was acting paranoid over the boy's car seat. *What next?*

"Linda, it's not likely someone's going to break into our garage, get into the locked car, and steal a kid's car seat, for pity's sake."

She stood at the door leading to the house and frowned. It was that "I want my way, and I'll cry if I don't get it" kind of scowl she had learned so well.

They had been driving all day, it was almost nine o'clock, and Jim was too tired to argue. "Fine. Whatever."

Jim opened the back door of the van and unhooked the car seat. He lifted it out, set it on the concrete floor, and went around to open the hatch in order to get their luggage. In the process, he spotted a piece of the baby quilt sticking out of his toolbox. He glanced at the house. Linda had already gone inside with Jimmy.

"Whew! I've gotta ditch this thing." He opened the toolbox, withdrew the quilt, and headed into the room adjoining the garage, where he kept some of his painting supplies.

"Don't know why I didn't throw this silly quilt out when we were in Pennsylvania." Yet even now, Jim had no inclination to permanently dispose of the small blanket. It was weird, the way he felt when he looked at the little quilt. Jim knew if he threw it away, he'd be getting rid of the last shred of evidence to link him with the kidnapping of an Amish baby. Yet, he couldn't bring himself to throw the colorful blanket away.

Maybe later, he decided. *After Jimmy's older and I feel more like he actually belongs to Linda and me.*

Jim grabbed the canvas bag where he kept his paint rags and stuffed the quilt deep inside. Linda never went into his shop, so there was no danger of her discovering the quilt there.

A short time later, he was inside the house. He'd brought in their luggage, as well as the car seat. "Where do you want this thing?" he called to Linda, who had gone into the living room with the baby.

"How about the hall closet?"

"Sure, okay."

When Jim stepped into the room, he saw Linda sitting on the floor in front of the couch, and Jimmy stood by the coffee table, holding onto the edge. The child pivoted toward Linda, let go, and took two steps forward.

"He's walking!" Linda shouted. "Jim, our little boy took his first steps!"

Jim smiled at his wife's exuberance. She was going to make a great mother, and he'd done a good thing by providing her with the chance.

I sure wish there were some way I could notify the baby's family that he's safe and in good hands. If my child disappeared, I'd be worried and wondering if he was okay. That was another part of this whole thing that bothered Jim. How was the boy's family taking his disappearance? Jim had made an impulsive decision when he'd grabbed Jimmy off that picnic table. At the time, he hadn't felt much remorse. Truth was, when the adoption fell through, taking the baby seemed like an answer to his problem. He also convinced himself that he'd done the Amish family a favor. There were eight kids, the young woman had said. *That's too many for anyone to raise, let alone a man with no wife.*

"He's doing it again!" Linda's excited voice drove Jim's thoughts to the back of his mind.

He smiled as the baby took two more steps, flopped onto the floor, and giggled.

Jim leaned over and helped Jimmy to his feet. "There you go, little guy. Let's see if you can take a couple more steps before we call it a night." He held the boy's chubby hands and walked him a few feet from where Linda sat. "Trot on over to your mommy. Come on, I know you can do it."

He let go, and the baby toddled toward Linda's extended arms. She grabbed him in a hug. "Good job, Jimmy! That's my big boy.

"He's certainly adjusted well, don't you think?" she said, looking up at Jim. "It's as though he's always been ours."

He nodded and took a seat on the couch.

"When did you say the papers should arrive?"

"What papers?"

"His birth certificate and the final adoption papers."

"I told you before, they're being sent to my paint shop, where I plan to put them in our safe."

"I trust you to take care of everything, just like you always have," she said sweetly.

"I do my best." Jim pinched the bridge of his nose, feeling a headache coming on. *Thanks for the reminder, Linda. I'd better see about getting some phony papers drawn up—and soon.*

"I think I'm going to take this little fellow to his new room. It's been another long day of travel, and he's probably ready for bed." Linda yawned. "For that matter, I'm ready to call it a night, too."

"I'll put the suitcases in our rooms, and then I'm gonna give my foreman a call and see what he's got lined up for tomorrow."

"Oh, Jim, I hope you're not planning to go back to work right away."

"I've got to, Linda. My business won't run itself."

"But I thought you'd want to rest a few days and spend some quality time with me and Jimmy."

"We'll do something fun over the weekend. I don't have the luxury of taking any more time off to rest."

She sighed. "All you ever do is work. Sometimes I think you care more about your painting business than you do me."

His face heated. "What do you mean? I just spent three weeks with you, didn't I?"

"Yes, but—"

"And I made sure you got the Amish quilt you've always wanted. Doesn't that count for anything?"

"Of course it does, but *things* don't make up for time spent with those you love." Linda kissed the top of Jimmy's head. "I can't believe how much love I feel for this little guy already."

Jim stood and went to her side. "I love you more than you'll ever know, Linda." He bent to kiss her cheek. *Enough to steal an Amish baby so you could be a mother.*

"I know, and I love you, too. Guess I'm just tired and not quite ready to let go of our vacation."

"I understand." He took hold of the baby's chubby hand. "Let's get Jimmy settled in, then we can take a dip in the hot tub and head for our room."

Her eyes widened. "You want me to leave him alone on his first night?"

"Well, I thought—"

"Jim, he might be frightened sleeping in his new crib. And what if he wakes up during the night and needs me?"

Jim massaged his forehead. "You're not planning to sleep in the kid's room, I hope."

She nodded. "I thought maybe I'd sleep on an air mattress. Just for tonight, of course."

"Yeah, okay. Whatever you want to do." He grabbed the suitcases and trudged up the hall behind her.

CHAPTER 19

By the middle of August, Naomi felt defeated. The days were longer, the work was harder, the children became more difficult, and Papa seemed crankier than ever. Naomi was irritable, too; and no matter how many times she said, "I love you" or "I'm sorry for snapping," her siblings still acted as though she shouldn't be the person in charge.

Except for Sunday services, Naomi hadn't seen or

spoken to Caleb since the night her daed caught them under the maple tree. Papa had made it clear when he spoke to her the next morning that she could not be courted by Caleb or anyone else.

Naomi leaned against the wooden counter and groaned. A little boy and his mother had just left the store. Every time Naomi saw a child about Zach's age, she thought of him. It had been two months since her little brother had been kidnapped, and in all that time, the police hadn't had any leads. Since there was nothing to go on, Naomi was sure they had quit looking.

She clutched the notebook lying in front of her. *After this much time, we may as well give up on the idea of Zach ever coming home. If that English man was gonna bring our boppli back, he would have done so by now. All we can do is hope and pray Zach's okay.*

The bell above the front door jingled, and in walked Ginny Meyers. Naomi's gaze darted to the back of the store, where Papa and the girls were stocking shelves. The last thing she needed was for him to see her talking with Ginny. He'd made it clear he didn't care much for the young English woman, and he didn't like Naomi talking to her.

"Hey, how are you?" Ginny asked, leaning across the counter. "Haven't been able to get away from the restaurant much lately, and I've missed our little visits."

Naomi sighed. "Things are pretty much the same around here."

"No news on Zach?"

"Not a word."

"Sorry to hear that." Ginny leaned closer. "Can you meet me for lunch today? We can talk better if we're away from here."

Naomi turned her head toward the back of the store. She could only see Mary Ann and Nancy. Papa must have gone to the storage room for more boxes. "I—I don't see how I could get away."

"Tell your dad you want to go for a walk or something. Say you're bringing your lunch and will eat it somewhere along the way." Ginny smiled, her blue eyes twinkling with mischief. "I'll meet you in the park at noon."

Naomi's hands grew sweaty. She hadn't done anything so bold since she crept out of the house to see what Caleb wanted. What if someone saw her with Ginny and told her father? And what about the girls? Would Papa mind her leaving them at the store with him while she went off by herself for a while?

"I can't make any promises, but I'll see if I can get away," she whispered. "If I'm not there by twelve fifteen, you'll know I'm not coming."

Ginny winked. "Fair enough. See you soon." Her long, blond hair hung down her back this morning, and it swished back and forth as she swaggered toward the front door. Naomi couldn't help but wonder how she would feel if she could let her hair down in public. She'd been thinking about the English world a lot lately. The worse things got at home, the more appeal the modern world had for her. If she were English and not Amish, she'd be allowed to do more—probably wouldn't have so many brothers and sisters to look after, either.

The door closed behind Ginny, and Naomi took up her work again. She had to make a list of things they needed to order. Papa would be expecting it to be ready by the time he was done at the back of the store.

Half an hour later, Naomi was finished, and just in time.

"Have ya got that list done yet?" Papa asked as he stepped behind the counter and peered over her shoulder.

She lifted the tablet and without turning around handed it to him. "Say, Papa, I was wonderin' if it would be all right if I take my lunch pail and go for a walk. I sure could use some fresh air."

"*Humph!* The thermometer in the window shows it's almost ninety outside. Most likely the humidity's at ninety percent, too. Nothin' refreshing 'bout that."

She nodded. "I know, but it seems even hotter inside the store."

"Jah, well, I don't mind if ya eat your lunch outside, but you'll have to take the girls along."

Naomi swiveled on the stool. "Why can't they stay here with you? Won't you be needing their help if a bunch of customers shows up?"

Papa gave his beard a quick tug and stared over the top of her head, refusing to make eye contact. "Guess you've got a point."

"I can go then?"

He nodded curtly. "Don't be gone long. I've got some errands to run later, and I can't leave Nancy and Mary Ann in charge of the store while I'm gone."

"I won't be late. I promise."

Jim entered the house through the garage door. He and his crew had started painting an apartment complex nearby, and Jim thought he'd swing by the house and get a couple jugs of iced tea. They were having unusually warm weather here in the Northwest, even for the middle of August. The last thing he needed was for any of the guys to keel over with heat exhaustion.

"Linda, I'm home for a few minutes!" he called.

When there was no response, he headed down the hall to their room. He discovered Linda asleep on the bed with Jimmy curled up next to her. At the foot of the bed was a stack of things they'd picked up on their trip to the East Coast in June.

He tiptoed out of the room. No point in waking Linda or the baby. Besides, he needed to get some aspirin from the medicine cabinet. He had another headache and wondered if it was from the heat. The guy on the radio said the temperature had reached almost eighty degrees. It was only eight o'clock in the morning, so Jim figured it might be in the high nineties later in the day.

When he emerged from the bathroom a short time later, Linda and Jimmy were still asleep. Jim scooped up the brochures and headed for the kitchen. He was surprised after all this time that Linda hadn't thrown the stuff away.

Jim grabbed two jugs of iced tea from the refrigerator and decided to take the time to pour himself a glass. His painting crew was already hard at work, and he figured he could take a few minutes before heading back to the job site.

Dropping into a chair at the table, he flipped through the stack of magazines and other papers. A newspaper called *The Budget* was at the bottom of the pile. It was published in Sugarcreek, Ohio, for the Amish and Mennonites. Jim discovered there were numerous articles written by Plain people all over the nation. There was even a want-ad section. *Hmm . . . this might be a way I could let Jimmy's family know he's okay.*

Jim jotted down the address and information needed to place an ad and stuck it inside his shirt pocket. He'd get something drafted soon and send it off. *Better not mail it from here, though. Don't want to take the chance of anyone tracing its origin.*

Jim decided he would write up the announcement tomorrow, and when they went to Boise next weekend to see Linda's folks, he'd take the ad and mail it from there, along with cash. *I'm not dumb enough to send a check, that's for sure.*

"What are you doing home, Jim? I thought you were at work."

Jim jumped up, dropping *The Budget* to the floor. "Don't scare me like that, Linda."

"Sorry. I thought you heard us come into the room."

She held the baby, and Jimmy smiled and said, "Da-Da-Da."

"Yep, that's me. I'm your daddy, little guy." Jim extended his arms, and the child went willingly to him.

"What are you doing with all our vacation stuff?" Linda asked.

"I—uh—found the brochures at the foot of our bed and thought I'd take a look." He sat down at the table, balancing Jimmy on one knee. "I was surprised to see all this stuff. Figured by now you'd have thrown out the junk you brought home from our trip."

She wrinkled her nose and took the seat across from him. "It's not junk, Jim. There's a lot of interesting things about the Amish in those brochures." She bent over and picked up *The Budget*. "Look, there's even an Amish newspaper."

"Yeah, I noticed."

"Earlier today, I was reading some of the articles written by Amish and Mennonite people," she said. "They sure live a different lifestyle from the rest of America."

He nodded and kissed the top of Jimmy's head.

"I'd like to visit Pennsylvania Dutch country again sometime. Maybe try to learn a little more about the Amish people's unusual culture. When do you think we might make another trip to Pennsylvania?"

Jim nearly choked. The last thing he needed was to bring his wife and boy back to Lancaster County so he could be snagged for kidnapping. "I—uh—think

Mom and Dad are planning to make a trip out here next summer, so there's not much point in us making plans to go to the East Coast for a few more years."

Linda's lower lip protruded, but it wasn't going to work this time. Her whining, pouting, or cajoling would not get her a trip to Pennsylvania or even Ohio—not if Jim had anything to say about it.

"Naomi, I'm glad you could make it."

Naomi looked over at Ginny, who had flopped onto the picnic bench. "I was surprised Papa had no objections to me leavin' the store."

Ginny smiled. "That is one for the books."

"Maybe he's sick of seeing me." Naomi stared down at her clasped hands. "Ever since Zach was taken, he's had trouble lookin' me in the eye."

Ginny clicked her tongue. "Well, shame on him. Doesn't your dad realize you didn't leave Zach sitting on that picnic table on purpose? It's not like you were hoping he'd be kidnapped or anything."

Naomi swallowed the bile rising in her throat. "I've never admitted this to anyone, but the truth is, I've often wished I could be free of caring for my family—even daydreamed about how it would be if I were an only child."

Ginny elbowed Naomi in the ribs. "Get real, girl! Anyone with brothers and sisters has wished that more than once. I can't tell you how many times I've wondered how much better my life would be if my brother, Tim, had never been born."

Tears welled up in Naomi's eyes, and she sniffed in an effort to hold them back. It seemed like all she did anymore was cry. Cry and feel sorry for herself.

"I'm here to tell you that just because you wished you had no siblings to care for doesn't mean you were the cause of your brother being abducted."

"But I'm the one who left him in the yard with a complete stranger." She gulped on a sob. "If Zach never comes home, I don't think I'll be able to forgive myself."

"If your family was more supportive, you could probably deal with this a lot better." Ginny squeezed Naomi's hand. "Want to know what I think?"

Naomi shrugged, knowing Ginny would probably give her opinion no matter how she replied.

"I think you need to get away from this place."

"What place? The park?"

Ginny snickered. "No, silly. Lancaster County and your accusing family."

Naomi's mouth fell open. "What are you saying?"

"I'm saying you and I should hit the road—jump in my sports car and head for parts unknown." Ginny frowned. "I'm getting sick of helping out at my folks' restaurant. If I don't strike out on my own pretty soon, they'll have me tied to that place."

Naomi trembled. Just the thought of leaving home sent shivers up her back. She had never been any farther north than East Earl and no farther south than Strasburg. Truth was, the Fishers were a stay-at-home kind of family. They didn't hire English drivers to take them on vacation trips like some in their community were fond of doing.

"Promise me you'll think about what I said. Your family doesn't appreciate you, and my advice is to get away. Put as many miles between you and them as you can."

"What about the promise I made to Mama before she died? I told her I'd look after the family, and if I leave, I'll be breakin' that vow."

"Get real, Naomi. Nobody in your family listens to what you say anymore. You've told me that several times. You wouldn't be reneging on your promise; you'd be setting your family free."

Naomi swiped her hand across her damp cheeks. "You think they'd see it that way?"

Ginny nodded.

Naomi filled her lungs with the humid air clinging to her clothes like flypaper. Would she be dishonoring her mother's wishes if she left? Could she do it? She grabbed hold of her lunch pail and squeezed the handles. "I'll think about it. That's all I can promise."

CHAPTER 20

Naomi awoke in a cold sweat. She'd been dreaming about Zach again. She'd done that several times since his disappearance, but this dream was the worst. In the nightmare, Zach sat on the picnic table, his arms outstretched, tears coursing down his rosy cheeks. She stood in the doorway, wanting to go to him but unable to move her legs. She'd tried calling Zach's name but couldn't find her voice. A thick fog settled over the baby, and when it lifted, he was gone.

Naomi closed her eyes and drew in a deep breath. She was glad it had only been a dream. The vision of Zach with his arms extended still disturbed her. "Be with him, Lord," she prayed. "Be with my baby brother wherever he is."

Naomi sat up and swung her legs over the side of the bed. Maybe it was time to take down the crib. Seeing it sitting there empty was a painful reminder that her baby brother was gone. Maybe this was the reason he haunted her dreams so often. She'd left the crib up at first, hoping Zach would be returned. Then she justified it by telling herself that leaving it there was a reminder to pray for him.

"I'll remember to pray for Zach even without seeing his crib," she murmured.

Naomi tasted salty tears as she dismantled her little brother's bed. "I'm such a failure," she moaned. "Maybe Ginny's right. My family would be better off without me."

She hauled the crib across the hall and positioned it behind several boxes in the storage closet. *Guess Ginny didn't actually say they'd be better off if I was gone. She just said I'd be setting them free. But that adds up to the same thing in my estimation.*

Naomi tiptoed back to her room. It was only five in

the morning, and she didn't want to wake the younger ones, who were still asleep in their beds. *I need to have a heart-to-heart talk with Papa before I make any decisions that could affect the rest of my life. I have to find out how he really feels about me. If there's even a chance he thinks we can iron things out, I'll keep trying to make it work.*

Naomi slipped a dark green dress over her head, quickly did up her hair, and put her white head covering in place. She padded across the room in her bare feet and grabbed the doorknob. Papa would probably be doing his morning chores in the barn by now. If her brothers weren't working near him, she'd go there and talk to Papa before starting breakfast.

Several minutes later, Naomi stepped into the barn. It was dark and quiet, with only the occasional nicker of the horses to break the peaceful silence. She made her way toward the goat pen, knowing Papa usually started milking the goats first thing.

Soon she heard his muffled voice, and the steady *ping, ping, ping* of milk spurting into the bucket confirmed that Papa was there. She halted at the door when she perceived his first words.

"Oh, Lord God, You know how hard I've been tryin'," he wailed. "I want to forgive the man who stole Zach from us. I want to forgive Naomi for her part in Zach's disappearance, too, but it's ever so hard." He sniffed, and Naomi could tell from her dad's quavering voice that he was close to tears.

"I thought if I kept praying and trusting, You'd bring

Zach home to us, but that hasn't happened. Where is Your goodness, Lord?" There was a pause, followed by a deep moan. "Naomi hasn't been happy since Sarah died and she was left to care for the kinner. Truth is, I think all my oldest daughter wants is to be free of us . . . to marry the buggy maker and forget about her responsibilities here. I have to wonder if she didn't leave Zach outside with that English fellow on purpose, hopin' he might take him. Then she would be shed of one little brother." He grunted. "Maybe she'd like to get rid of the rest of her brothers and sisters, too."

Naomi covered her mouth with the palm of her hand and steadied herself against the wall in order to keep from toppling over. Papa was baring his soul to God, and she was witness to it. For the first time since Zach's kidnapping, she'd heard her daed say what had been buried deep in his soul. Papa not only blamed her for the kidnapping, but he thought she'd done it on purpose.

"Truth is, Lord, I can barely look at Naomi anymore," Papa continued. "Sometimes I wish—"

Naomi couldn't stand to hear another word. She choked on a sob, spun around, and rushed out of the barn.

Abraham felt washed out as he trudged toward the house. He'd been up since before dawn, done all his chores, and had spent more than an hour in the barn, praying and telling God everything on his heart. It

226

hadn't helped. He felt as miserable now as when he'd begun praying. If only there was a way to relieve his pain. If he could just make things right again.

When Abraham entered the kitchen, he thought it was strange that none of the gas lanterns were lit. Naomi was usually up by now, scurrying around the kitchen and yelling at Nancy and Mary Ann to get the table set for breakfast. There was no sign of her, and none of the children were around.

Maybe she overslept. If Naomi isn't up yet, there's a good chance the others are still in bed, too. His three youngest children relied on their older sister to rouse them each morning. They'd probably sleep 'til noon if she didn't make them get up.

Abraham ambled across the room and set the pail of goat's milk on the kitchen table. When he lit the lantern overhead, a piece of paper came into view. It was lying on the table, right where he sat for every meal. *Looks like some kind of a letter.*

He sank into a chair and began to read.

Dear Papa:

I came to the barn earlier, hoping we might talk. We never got that chance because I overheard you speaking to God. I've known for many weeks, ever since Zach was taken, that you blame me for everything. I understand. I blame myself, too.

After hearing the rest of your conversation with the Lord, I was hit with the cold, hard fact that you believe I wanted Zach to be taken. It's not so,

Papa. I would never want harm to come to any of the kinner, and I sure didn't wish for that English fellow to take my baby brother.

I've come to the conclusion that it would be best for the family if I left home. I'm no good to anyone, and none of the children want to mind me anymore. I'm heading out with Ginny Meyers into the English world. Don't know where we're going, but it'll be far from here.

Please know that I love you and the rest of the family, and I pray someday you'll find it in your heart to forgive me. I'll never stop praying for Zach and his safe return, but if God doesn't answer that prayer, then I'm askin' Him to give Zach a good life with the one who took him.

Your oldest daughter,
Naomi

Abraham let the paper slip from his fingers and fall to the floor. He sat there for several minutes as though in a daze. This couldn't be happening. It had to be a horrible dream. Naomi always looked out for the kinner. Surely she wouldn't set out with that spoiled English girl and leave her brothers and sisters to fend for themselves. And what about the store? Who would help him run the place now?

Abraham fell forward, his head resting on the table. *First, I lost my dear wife in death, then my baby boy was snatched away, and now my oldest daughter has run off.* He lifted his head as hot tears streamed down his face and dripped onto his beard. *Dear Lord in heaven, I've lost them all. Oh, God, help me! What have I done?*

Naomi stood trembling at the back door of Meyers' Family Restaurant. It was still early, but she knew someone was inside because there were lights on. *Probably getting ready for the Saturday morning breakfast crowd.*

She drew in a deep breath, trying to steady her nerves. She should be at home, getting breakfast on and lining out the chores she and the children needed to do for the day. Instead, she was about to embark on a journey that would likely change the rest of her life. Her family's life would be different now, too. *Will Samuel, Nancy, and Mary Ann be better off without their big sister telling them what to do? And what of Matthew, Jake, and Norman? Will they be relieved to hear I've run off?*

She gulped in another breath and sank to the concrete porch. Her legs were still wobbly from running most of the way to town. *What will Papa think when he reads my note? Will he be glad I'm gone? Will he hire a maid to help out now, or will he try to do everything alone?*

After hearing the hurtful words her daed said to God in the barn, Naomi had made a beeline for the house, where she scrawled a note to Papa and hurriedly packed a few clothes and personal things. Then she'd headed out on foot, not wanting to take the time to hitch up the horse and buggy and knowing Papa might have heard if she had. Besides, taking the buggy would have complicated things. She would have had to leave it somewhere in town for Papa or one of the brothers to pick up later on. No, it was better that she'd come on her own.

Naomi stared across the empty parking lot. No customers yet, so it must be too early. Would Ginny be working today? What if she wasn't? How would Naomi let her friend know she was ready to leave Lancaster County behind? She knew Ginny lived somewhere in the nearby town of Soudersburg, but she didn't know the address.

Maybe I could ask her folks or someone else who works at the restaurant. Naomi got to her feet, and the back door suddenly opened. Relief flooded her soul when Ginny stepped onto the porch carrying a sack of garbage. She wore a pair of blue jeans and a yellow T-shirt with a white apron tied around her waist.

"Naomi! What are you doing here at this time of the day?"

Naomi's knees threatened to buckle. She sat back down with a moan.

Ginny tossed the plastic sack into the dumpster beside the porch and took a seat on the step. "What's wrong? I can tell by your swollen eyes and red cheeks that you've been crying."

"I—I—came to see you."

Ginny pointed at the suitcase sitting on the other side of Naomi. "You've run away from home?"

Naomi nodded as tears streamed down her cheeks. "I can't go back, Ginny."

"Why? What happened?"

Naomi quickly related the story of how she'd overheard her father praying in the barn. "He believes I left Zach on the picnic table on purpose. He thinks our family would be better off without me."

Ginny draped her arm over Naomi's shoulder. "You did the right thing by leaving. I've told you many times that your family doesn't appreciate you." She sighed. "Truthfully, I don't think my parents appreciate me, either. They've got me doing kitchen duty this morning, and Mom knows how much I hate it."

Naomi swiped her hand across her face and sniffed. "If you're still wantin' the two of us to run away together, I'm more than ready to go."

"Now?" Ginny looked over her shoulder as though someone might come out of the restaurant and catch the two of them making plans.

"Jah, if you can get away."

Ginny chewed on her bottom lip. "Let's see. . . . I drove my own car to work this morning, so transportation's not a problem. However, I would need to go home and get some clothes and my bankbook. Can't very well leave town without any money."

"But today's Saturday, and the bank's not open," Naomi reminded. "I have a little money with me— took it from my dresser drawer where I'd been savin' up to buy a present for Jake. His birthday is two weeks from today."

Ginny scrambled to her feet. "That's going to be one birthday you'll have to miss."

Naomi didn't need the reminder. The pain of not being there to help celebrate any of her family's birthdays smarted like a bee sting.

"I doubt you have enough money to take us very far, but I've managed to save up a pretty good sum." Ginny smiled. "And for your information, the bank we use in Lancaster is open 'til one today, and even if it weren't, there's always an ATM machine."

"After you get some money, then what?"

"First off, I'm going into the restaurant to get my purse. It's got my car keys and driver's license, which are both vital items. Then I'll leave a note for my folks. When I'm sure nobody's looking, I'll come back outside; we'll jump in my sports car, head for the house, grab a few things, and be off to the bank." She grinned as though she was finding great joy in all of this. "From there, it's hit the road and never look back!"

Abraham sat up. He didn't know how long he'd been leaning over the table with his head resting on his arms. Rays of light streamed through the kitchen windows, bouncing off the walls and sending swirls of tiny dust particles through the air.

The older boys must be outside doing their chores yet, but he was sure the younger ones were still in bed. If there was ever a day when Abraham felt like closing the store and staying home, this was that day. Not since Zach's kidnapping had he felt such anguish. How could he go about business as usual when Naomi had run off? How could he have let such a terrible thing happen? All Abraham wanted to do was climb the stairs to his room, crawl into bed, and pull the covers over his head.

But I have a family to support, he reminded himself. *Besides, closing the store won't bring Naomi home. Only God can do that, same as with Zach.* He grimaced. Would God answer his prayers where his two children were concerned? He'd obviously failed them—probably failed God, too. If only he'd hired someone to help out after Sarah died. If he hadn't been so stubborn and tightfisted, Naomi wouldn't have had to work so hard. If she'd had more free time—time to do some fun things with others her age—maybe she wouldn't have been preoccupied and left Zach alone in the yard.

"I've been too hard on her," he moaned. "Now it's too late."

"Who ya talkin' to, Papa, and what's it too late for?"

Abraham turned in his chair. Samuel stood inside the kitchen door, a lock of blond hair in his eyes, his cheeks still rosy from sleep.

"Where are your sisters?" Abraham asked. "Are they up yet?"

Samuel shrugged. "Don't rightly know. I woke up and didn't smell anything cookin', so I thought I'd come down here and have a look-see."

Abraham pushed his chair away from the table.

"You'd better wake 'em. Nancy and Mary Ann are gonna have to fix breakfast."

Samuel's blue eyes reflected his obvious confusion. "What about Naomi? Why ain't she in here cookin'?"

Abraham grabbed the pail of goat's milk he'd set on the table earlier and lumbered across the room. He jerked open the refrigerator door, placed it inside, and withdrew a bottle of cold milk. "Naomi's gone."

"Gone? What do you mean, Papa? Where'd she go?"

Abraham opened his mouth to respond, but Nancy's shrill voice cut him off. "Papa, when I woke up, I looked in Naomi's room 'cause she didn't wake us like she usually does. The door was open, and most of her clothes were lyin' on the bed." She wrinkled her forehead. "Zach's crib wasn't there no more, and I'm thinkin' it's all kind of strange."

Mary Ann, who stood beside her older sister, nodded. "Where is Naomi, Papa? How come she don't have breakfast started yet?"

Abraham set the bottle of milk on the table and pulled out a chair. He motioned his children to do the same. "I'm afraid I've got some bad news concerning your older sister."

"What's wrong? Is Naomi sick?" The question came from Mary Ann, and she looked mighty worried.

Abraham drew in a deep breath as he prayed for the right words. He bent down and retrieved Naomi's note, which had fallen to the floor after he'd read it. "Naomi left me this," he said, waving it in the air.

"Says here she's leavin' home because she feels guilty about Zach being taken." Truth was, there was a lot more to it than that, but Abraham didn't have the courage to admit to his children that he was the primary cause of Naomi going.

"She's run away? Is that what you're sayin', Papa?" Nancy's eyes were wide, and her mouth hung slightly open.

He nodded as a lump formed in his throat.

"Why would she do such a thing? Don't Naomi love us no more?" Samuel's chin quivered as he spoke.

"I'm sure she loves us," Abraham said, "but she blames herself for Zach's kidnapping, and she thinks we'd be better off without her."

"That ain't true!" Nancy hollered. "I love my sister, and since Zach left, we've needed her more'n ever."

It was a fact. They did need Naomi, but no one in the family had shown her that—least of all Abraham. He placed the note facedown on the table. "We're gonna have to find a way to deal with this, ya know."

"Let's go after her!" Samuel yelled. He jumped up from the table and grabbed his straw hat from the wall peg where he'd hung it last night.

Abraham shook his head. "Slow down once, Son. We can't go runnin' all over the place hunting for Naomi when we don't have a clue where she's gone."

"But she must've said somethin' in that note," Samuel argued. "Sure as anything, she'd want us to know where she was goin'."

"All she said was that she was taking off with Virginia Meyers, the flighty English gal who hangs around the store always askin' for rubber stamps."

"Ginny?" Nancy's eyebrows lifted.

He nodded. "Jah. Said the two of 'em were headin' into the English world and didn't know where they were goin'."

Mary Ann dropped her head to the table and sobbed. Nancy whimpered and patted her sister's shoulder. Samuel stood at the door with his arms folded.

"All we can do is pray for Naomi, same as we've been doin' for Zach," Abraham said with a catch in his voice. He hated to see how miserable the children were. More than that, he couldn't understand how he had let such a shocking thing happen.

CHAPTER 21

"I'm glad we're about the same size and you could wear some of my clothes," Ginny said, reaching over to tap Naomi's jeans-clad knees. "It would have looked like you'd hired me as your driver and were going on vacation if you'd kept wearing your plain, long dresses and head covering." She glanced over at Naomi and smiled.

Naomi sat in the passenger's seat of Ginny's fancy red sports car, uncomfortable with the speed they were going and unaccustomed to the cold air blasting her in the face from the air-conditioning. She stared down at the faded blue jeans and pink T-shirt Ginny had loaned her. The items of clothes were one more thing that felt foreign. "I'm not so sure about this. It feels odd wearin' men's trousers and havin' my hair hanging down my back with no kapp."

"You'll soon get used to it."

Naomi wasn't sure she would ever become accustomed to the English world. She and Ginny had only been on the road a few hours, and already she felt out of place and missed home.

"Anytime you're ready to stop for lunch, just say the word." Ginny tapped the steering wheel with her long fingernails. "Since we left in such a hurry this morning, I didn't get breakfast."

"Me neither." Truth be told, Naomi had no appetite for food. Things were so mixed up, and her brain felt muddled. She doubted she could eat a bite of food, much less keep it down.

"Do you know where we're heading?" Naomi asked.

Ginny nodded. "West."

"How far west?"

"All the way."

"You mean clear to the Pacific Ocean?"

"Yep. I've always wanted to stick my feet in the frigid waters along the Washington or Oregon coast. I've got a friend living in Portland, and we can probably stay with her awhile."

Naomi shivered. Just thinking about being that far from home and staying with strangers gave her the chills. Had she done the right thing by leaving? Would she be able to adjust to life in the modern world? Going English seemed like the best thing to do, since she had no other place to go. Ginny was her only friend right now, and Naomi knew she couldn't make it on her own.

"You'll be fine once we get out of Pennsylvania. This will be such an adventure that soon you'll forget about your unappreciative family and the nasty way they've treated you."

Naomi stared at the passing scenery, forcing her tears back. She'd left home feeling it was the thing to do, but she would never forget her family. How had Papa and the rest of them taken the news of her leaving? Did they feel sad, or were they glad she wouldn't be around to tell them what to do?

"You think you'll miss your folks?" she asked her friend.

Ginny wrinkled her nose. "I think they'll miss me more than I do them. After all, they won't have my help at the restaurant anymore. To tell you the truth, I believe that's all they think I'm good for."

Naomi could relate to that feeling. Ever since Mama died, she'd felt unappreciated.

"I've got enough money to take us to Oregon, but we'll have to get jobs after we get there," Ginny said. "My friend Carla used to live in Pennsylvania, but she works at a fitness center in Portland now. I'm hoping she can get me a position there."

"But what can I do? I only know how to work at the

store and around home."

"Guess you could get a job at a restaurant, waiting tables or doing dishes in the kitchen."

Naomi grimaced. The last thing she wanted to do was wash dishes.

"Mom, the mail's here, and there's a letter addressed to you from your cousin Edna in Pennsylvania." Abby waved the stack of letters and placed them on the kitchen table. Fannie rinsed the last dish in the sink full of clean water, grabbed a towel, and quickly dried her hands. "Guess I'd better take a peek. I haven't heard from Edna in several weeks."

Abby pulled out a chair for her mother. "Have a seat, and I'll pour you a cup of mint tea."

Fannie smiled appreciatively. "That'd be nice." She ripped open her cousin's letter and withdrew a note card with a hand-drawn picture of a chocolate cake on the front. Inside was written: "Count your age by friends, not years. Count your blessings, not your tears. Hope you'll help me celebrate my fiftieth birthday on Saturday, September sixth, with a picnic by the pond."

Fannie smiled. "Leave it to Cousin Edna to plan her own party. She always was one to do things a bit differently than others."

Abby chuckled and handed her mother a cup of hot tea. "You thinkin' about going?"

Fannie took a sip, enjoying the unique flavor of her homegrown lemon mint tea. "Sure would be nice, but who would mind the store while we were gone?"

"Not *we,* Mom," Abby corrected. "Edna invited you, and I can look after the store for the few days you'd be gone."

"Hmm . . ." Fannie pursed her lips. "What if things got really busy? Sometimes it's hard for both of us to wait on customers when the tourists come by."

Abby shrugged. "I could always call on Lena to help. I'm sure she wouldn't mind bringing her quilting to the store to work on. That way, she'd be available to help whenever I might need her."

Fannie stared into her cup, watching the steam curl, lift, and disappear into the air. It would be nice to see Edna again, and since she'd be in the area, she might even be so bold as to drop by Abraham Fisher's store and see how he was doing. Ever since his visit to the quilt shop, she'd been praying for him and his kidnapped boy. She'd never admit it to anyone, but truth was, she'd thought of Abraham quite often. She could tell he was hurting bad. Even though he'd seemed kind of terse when they first started talking, underneath it all, she sensed he was a man with a tender heart.

"Mom, what do you think?" Abby's sweet voice broke into Fannie's thoughts.

"Think about what?"

"Me mindin' the quilt shop while you go to Pennsylvania?"

Fannie drank the rest of her tea and set the cup aside. "I'll pray about it. How's that sound?"

Abby smiled. "I'll be prayin', too. Prayin' you'll realize how badly you need to get away." She patted her mother's hand. "You work too hard, ya know that?"

Fannie pushed her chair away from the table. "I like to work. Keeps my hands busy and my mind off things I'd rather not be thinkin' about."

"Like Dad? Are ya still missin' him, Mom?"

Fannie stood. "I'll always miss your daed, but as time goes by, the pain gets less, and only the pleasant memories of the past remain. Besides, as my mamm used to say, 'There's no sense advertising your troubles, 'cause there's no market for 'em anywhere.'"

"Guess that's true enough." Abby sobered. "I miss Dad, too. I can't imagine what it must be like for you, Mom. Losin' the man you'd loved so much must have felt like someone put a hole in your heart."

Fannie nodded. "That's the way it was at first. I couldn't understand why God would allow your daed to die of a heart attack. After searching the scriptures, I came to realize God could use my grief for good if I let Him."

Abby placed the cups and saucers in the sink and quickly washed them. "Guess we'd better hurry if we're gonna get to the store on time."

Fannie glanced at the clock on the far wall. "Yep. We've spent more time blabberin' than we usually do in the morning, but it's been good, don't ya think?"

Abby dried her hands and grabbed her head covering from the back of the chair. "I always enjoy our time together." She leaned over and kissed her mother's cheek. "And I thank the Lord every day that He gave me a special mamm like you."

Tears welled up in Fannie's eyes, but she blinked them away. "Go on with you now. Let's get the buggy hitched."

Caleb climbed out of the open carriage and headed for the Fishers' store. Mary Ann and Nancy sat on the front porch, eating their lunches. "Got anything good in those pails?" he called.

"Just a sandwich and a few cookies," Nancy answered. "Everything was so confusing at our place this mornin', we didn't have a chance to put much together."

"Jah, Papa seemed pretty upset, and so was we."

Caleb leaned against the porch railing. "What's the problem? No one's sick, I hope."

"Naomi left."

He squinted at Nancy. "Left?"

"She's run off with that English girl, Ginny."

Caleb could hardly believe his ears. "Would you repeat that?"

"She's run off with Ginny Meyers. Left a note on the kitchen table this mornin'." Nancy shook her head. "I still can't believe she'd do something like that. I think it's a sin and a shame the way she ran out on us."

Caleb was sure there was more to the story. Naomi wouldn't just run off and leave her responsibilities for no good reason. Her obligation to care for the family was why she couldn't go to young people's functions or court. She'd told him so several times. "What exactly did her note say?"

"Said she feels guilty about Zach bein' kidnapped and that she was takin' off with Ginny Meyers out into the English world."

Caleb thought this was the worst possible news. Naomi didn't know how to function in the fancy, English world. She was in for a rude awakening, and leaving her family didn't make a lick of sense. If Naomi didn't come home, all his plans and dreams for them getting married would vanish like vapor from a boiling pot.

Caleb had come to the Fishers' store in hopes of trying to talk Naomi into seeing him in secret again. That wasn't going to happen. Not today and maybe not ever.

I'd go after her if I knew where she was goin', but I don't. He turned and clomped down the steps, his boots echoing against the wooden planks.

"Where ya headed, Caleb?" Mary Ann called. "I thought you was goin' into the store."

He shook his head but kept on walking toward his buggy. "No need to now."

Abraham sank onto the wooden stool behind the counter in his store. He didn't know how he had made it through the morning. As soon as he'd come to town, he had gone to Meyers' Family Restaurant, hoping Virginia's parents knew where the girls had run off to.

Their daughter had left them a note, same as Naomi had, but it said nothing about where they planned to go, how long they would be gone, or how they would survive. Abraham knew the words Naomi had heard him speaking to God had been the cause of her outlandish decision.

He glanced at the clock on the opposite wall and tried to concentrate on the invoices in front of him. It was a little past noon, and the girls had taken their lunches outside to eat on the front porch. Normally, he'd be ravenous by now, but not today. Abraham had no interest in food. All he wanted to do was find his missing children. If he could have Zach and Naomi back home, he'd be happy and would change. No more pushing Naomi to get things done. No comparing her to his wife. No expecting his oldest daughter to take charge of the kinner without any outside help.

Abraham leaned over and massaged his aching head. *I'd love on my boy lots, too. Should have spent more time with him when he was here.* He closed his eyes and tried to focus on the work he needed to do today. It was no use. All he could think about was how badly he'd messed up.

"You don't look like you're gettin' much work done. What's the matter; have you got a headache?"

Abraham looked up. Jacob Weaver stood on the other side of the counter, holding his straw hat in one hand and a fishing pole in the other. "Jacob, I didn't hear ya come in."

"No, I guess not. Been standing here for several seconds. I'm taking the day off, and I was hoping the two of us could go fishin'."

"Sorry, but I can't."

"Isn't it time to put aside your memories of the day Sarah was killed and quit blaming yourself because you went fishing? I thought you were giving things over to God."

Abraham shook his head. "This isn't about that. Things are really bad for me and the family right now."

Jacob leaned the pole against the counter and hung his hat on the nearest wall peg. "What's the trouble, my friend? Have you heard something about Zach that's not good news?"

Abraham shook his head. "Haven't heard a word about the boppli, but now Naomi's gone, too."

Jacob's dark eyebrows lifted. "What do you mean? Where is she?"

"I don't know. She left a note on the kitchen table sayin' she was leaving—running off with that English friend of hers, Virginia Meyers."

"Did she say why?" Jacob's question pierced Abraham clean to his soul.

He hung his head, unable to look his friend in the eye. "It's because of me. She overheard me talkin' to God this morning out in the barn."

"Mind if I ask what you were saying?"

"I told the Lord I haven't been able to forgive the man who took my boppli or Naomi, either, for leavin' Zach out in the yard with that English man. Said I thought she might have done it on purpose and that she wanted to be free of us in order to marry the buggy maker."

Jacob's sharp intake of breath was enough to let Abraham know what his good friend thought about that kind of prayer. More than likely, the man thought he was not only a bad father but also a wayward Christian, talking to God that way.

"I didn't mean all those things," Abraham was quick to say. "Just got confused about the way I was feelin' and all." He drew in a shaky breath. "I thought maybe if I had a little heart-to-heart talk with my Maker, I'd feel better."

"Naomi heard your prayers, left a note on the table, and has run away?"

"That's about the size of it, and I feel like I've been kicked in the stomach."

"I imagine you do."

"Isn't it bad enough that God took my little boy? Does He have to punish me further by taking my oldest daughter?" Abraham felt a burning at the back of his eyes, and he squeezed them shut as he fought for control.

Jacob stepped around the counter and placed his hand on Abraham's trembling shoulder. "Give it to God, Abraham. He's not the cause of all this, ya know."

Abraham shook his head. "No, I don't know. He could have stopped it from happening. He could have—"

"God don't work that way, and we must remember His ways are not our ways." Jacob squeezed Abraham's shoulder. "God loves you. Focus on His person and His goodness. Wait for Him to act. Allow Him to heal your heart and help you forgive those who have trespassed against you."

"I—I don't know if I can do that."

"You can, and you must. Release the anger. Pray for the man who took your boy. Give Zach and Naomi over to the Lord and rest in Him." Jacob paused. "First Corinthians ten, verse thirteen reminds us that He will never suffer us to be tested above what we are able to bear. God told Paul, 'My grace is sufficient for thee.'"

"I feel more like Job than Paul," Abraham said. "Everything I dearly loved has been snatched away from me. Sarah—Zach—and now Naomi."

"That's not true, Abraham. You still have six other kinner who love you and need your support."

Abraham cleared his throat, trying to dislodge the lump. "Wish I knew for sure that Zach and Naomi are all right. I could rest a lot easier if I had the assurance they're both safe."

Jacob's eyes were watery as though he, too, were fighting tears. "Maybe God has plans for your boy— and Naomi, too. Might could be one or both of 'em has a job to do out there in the English world."

"A job? What kind of job?"

"Maybe the man who took Zach will find his way to God because of something Zach says or does."

"But how could that be? Zach's only a year old.

What does he know about God?"

Jacob shrugged. "Probably nothin' yet, but in the days ahead, a lot could happen."

"And Naomi? How do you think God will use her running away to bring about something good?"

"Can't rightly say, but I do know if you turn them both over to the heavenly Father, trust Him in all things, and picture the two of them livin' healthy, happy lives, you'll have a lot more peace." Jacob smiled. "Isaiah forty, verse thirty-one: 'But they that wait upon the Lord shall renew their strength.'"

"'They shall mount up with wings as eagles; they shall run, and not be weary; and they shall walk, and not faint.'" Abraham finished the verse of scripture with tears rolling down his cheeks. "I'll wait, Jacob. Wait on the Lord and ask Him to protect my kinner and use them in a mighty way. It won't be easy, though."

CHAPTER 22

Before boarding the bus, Fannie hugged her daughter one last time as a knot rose in her throat. She and Abby hadn't been apart more than a few hours since Abby was a young girl and used to spend the night with her friend Rachel. Ever since Abby's dad passed away, she had preferred to be with her mother. Fannie hoped Abby would be okay during the few days she would be gone.

"It's all right, Mom," Abby said, as though sensing her mother's concerns. "I'll be fine, and so will the quilt shop."

"I'm sure you're right, and I've asked your brother to check in on you, so if you need anything, be sure to let either Harold or Lena know."

"I will, Mom." Abby handed her mother a newspaper. "Here's the newest issue of *The Budget*. I thought you'd like to take it along so you'll have something to read on the bus."

"Danki." Fannie forced her tears to stay put. "See you in a few days. Be well, and don't work too hard."

Abby smiled. "I won't. Have a good time, and tell Cousin Edna I said hello and to have a right nice birthday."

"I'll tell her." Fannie turned and stepped onto the bus. She was sure she would feel better once she was on the road. She found a seat near the back and was glad when no one sat beside her. Though normally quite talkative, this morning she wasn't in the mood to engage in conversation. All she wanted to do was read *The Budget* and relax.

As the bus pulled away from the station in Dover, she settled herself in the seat and opened the newspaper. Usually she read it from front to back, but today Fannie felt inclined to check out the classified ad section first. One never knew when they might find a good deal on quilting material or notions, and sometimes there were auctions advertised, asking for quilts.

She scanned the want ads first, and sure enough, there was an ad telling about a quilt auction to be held in Indiana next month. When she got back home, she'd have to see if she had anything she might want to send.

From there, Fannie's gaze went to the notice section. One notice in particular caught her attention. It was titled, "To the Amish Boy's Family." Her interest piqued, Fannie read on. "This is to notify the family of the Amish baby taken from a farm in Lancaster County in June of this year—the boy is fine. He's healthy, happy, and well cared for."

Fannie let the paper fall to her lap. *This could be Abraham Fisher's boy. Sure sounds like it's so. After all, how many Amish babies could have been kidnapped in Lancaster County during the month of June?* Goosebumps erupted all over her arms, and she shivered. *Has Abraham read this? Does he subscribe to* The Budget? She knew immediately where her first stop in Lancaster County had to be. She should arrive at the bus station in Lancaster sometime this afternoon. A friend had given her the number of a woman who lived in the area and drove for the Amish, so the first thing she planned to do was phone the English woman. She would ask to be driven to Fisher's General Store outside the town of Paradise. If Abraham hadn't read this ad, he certainly needed to. If this was his boy, he had to know the child was safe.

"Don't get me wrong. Our trip has been a blast, and I

loved seeing all the sights with you in Chicago and along the way as we came out west, but I'm ready to get off the road now and settle in. I bet you are, too. I think we should be in Portland in about three hours." Ginny turned up the volume on the radio, and a country-western song blared through the speakers. "I sure do like this type of music, don't you?"

Naomi frowned. "It's kind of loud, don't ya think?"

"I prefer it that way. Helps me stay awake."

"Maybe we should stop awhile and stretch our legs."

Ginny glanced at Naomi. "Are you needing a rest stop?"

Naomi didn't really have the need, but it would feel good to walk around and get away from the annoying music for a while. It might also help Ginny to wake up, which was important since she was their only driver. "Jah, I'm thinkin' it would be nice to stop."

"I'll pull into a rest stop then. The sign I saw back a ways said the next one was ten miles. Should be seeing it soon, I imagine."

Naomi pushed the button to make her window roll down and tried to relax. Did her family miss her as much as she missed them? What were they doing in her absence? It was September already, and toward the end of August, the younger children had no doubt gone back to school. Were they managing all right? Night and day, so many unanswered questions plagued her, but she kept reminding herself that leaving home had been for the best. She'd mailed Papa a postcard last week to let him know she was okay. She had made no mention of where she and Ginny were or where they were heading. He probably wouldn't care anyway.

Naomi leaned over and pulled a notebook and a pen from the small canvas bag at her feet. The day after they'd left Lancaster County, she began keeping a journal. At first she'd only written about places they'd seen along the way, but then she started writing down her private thoughts. It helped some, yet there was still a deep ache in her soul that no amount of note taking could dispel. If only she could change the past—go back and make things right. But that was impossible. All Naomi could do was make a new life for herself. She was convinced her family didn't want her anymore.

"We're almost to Oregon," she wrote. *"Clear across the country we've come. Everything looks different on this end of the United States. Lots of tall mountains, like beautiful Mount Rainier. Even though it's warm right now, there's no humidity. Ginny says we'll be in Portland in a few hours. Guess she's lined things up with her friend, Carla, for us to stay at her place until we both get jobs."*

Naomi sighed. Would she even be able to find a job in the big city? It seemed like Ginny might be working at the fitness center Carla had told her about, but Naomi had no prospects at all.

"I used to envy Ginny and think I might want to be part of the English world," she wrote in her journal. *"Now I'm not so sure. Truth is, I feel like a chicken*

tryin' to build a nest on top of a hot stove. It's like I don't belong anywhere now. I'm not Amish 'cause I left that behind, yet I'm not really English, either." She glanced down at her faded blue jeans, which used to be Ginny's. *"I'm dressed in English clothes, wearin' my hair down, and have started to use some makeup, but inside I still feel Plain."*

"We're here. You ready to use the rest room?"

Ginny's question drove Naomi's thoughts to the back of her mind, and she quickly returned her notebook to the canvas bag.

Naomi got out of the car and followed Ginny up the path toward the women's rest room. She glanced over her shoulder and caught a glimpse of a man heading to the men's side of the building. She halted and stood there, her heart pounding like a hammer. Was that him—the Englisher who took Zach? But how could she be thinking such a thing when she'd told the police she barely took notice of the man who'd come to ask for root beer? Had she seen and remembered more than she realized, not recalling it until now, or was her mind merely playing tricks on her?

"Naomi, are you coming or not?"

Naomi jerked her head. Ginny glared at her as though she'd done something wrong.

"What are you standing there for? I thought you had to use the rest room."

"I—I—do, but—" Naomi turned to take another look at the man, but he was gone.

Ginny furrowed her brows. "What's the matter with

you, girl? You look like you've eaten a bunch of sour grapes."

"Nothin's wrong. I'm fine." Naomi started walking again. The stress of leaving home and trying to make her way in a foreign world must be getting to her. Jah, that's all it was.

Abraham was glad the kinner were back in school. He didn't have to worry about watching out for them at the store during the day. Only trouble was, he had no one's assistance now. Even though his younger girls weren't nearly as much help as Naomi had been, Nancy and Mary Ann could stock shelves and do some cleanup around the place. Now he was faced with doing everything himself, and there was certainly no time for naps.

Today was one of those days when he really needed a rest. He'd been stocking shelves all morning when there were no customers, and he barely had enough time to choke down a sandwich at noon. It would be nice if he could head for the back room and lie down on the cot. Just a few minutes to close his eyes and let the weariness drain from his body.

"Maybe I should close the store for a day or two. Then I could stay home and get caught up on my sleep." He grabbed a dust rag from under the counter and attacked the accumulated grime on the shelves behind him. "That wouldn't make much sense. If I closed the store, then I'd be losin' money. Besides, there's as much work at home, and unless I decide to hire a maid, it'll just keep piling up."

"I see you're talkin' to yourself again."

Abraham whirled around. Jacob Weaver stood inside the door with a smile on his face. "I admit it. I was talkin' to myself." Before Jacob could comment, he added, "How's the painting business, and what brings you to my store in the middle of the day?"

"We're paintin' the outside of the bank in Paradise," Jacob replied. "I've got the crew all set up, so I thought I'd stop by and see how you're doing." He glanced around the store. "Guess there's no customers at the moment, huh?"

"Nope, but it was sure busy this morning. Can't hardly handle things by myself—here or at home."

Jacob leaned on the counter. "I'm sure some of the women in our community would help out if you weren't too stubborn to ask."

Abraham put the dust rag away and sank to the wooden stool on his side of the counter. "What's the point in askin' when it would only be temporary? Sooner or later they'd have to stop helping and take care of their own families."

"I've told you before that you should hire a maad."

"I know, and I've been thinkin' on it." Abraham sighed. "Trouble is, I don't know who's available or who would work out good with the kinner. They can be a handful. Been worse since Naomi up and ran off."

"Have you heard anything from her?" Jacob asked.

"Just a postcard, and that didn't tell much."

"She never said where she and Virginia Meyers were heading or how she was doing?"

Abraham shook his head. "Just that she was fine and didn't want me to worry. I checked with Virginia's folks again, and they haven't heard a word from their daughter."

"At least Naomi had the decency to let you know she's all right."

"Jah, but that don't tell me if she's ever comin' back."

"Do you want her to?"

Abraham's defenses rose, and he clenched his teeth. "Of course I do. Been prayin' every day that she'll come back and we can make amends."

"You're not casting blame on her now?"

Abraham shrugged.

"Jesus commanded us to forgive others the same way He forgave us. Until you forgive Naomi and the man who took Zach, it will be like someone tied a stone around your neck and is pulling you down."

"Are you tryin' to goad me into an argument this afternoon, Jacob Weaver?"

"Why would you think that?"

"You keep sayin' things that make me believe you're against me now."

Jacob shook his head. "You know better than that, Abraham. You're my gut friend, and I want you to find peace within your soul."

"I doubt that'll ever happen. Not unless Naomi and Zach come home again."

Jacob groaned. "We've had this discussion before, and I thought you were gonna turn things over to God. You need to work on your faith, my friend. Allow yourself to forgive, trust the Lord to do His will in your children's lives, and wait on Him."

Abraham slapped his hand down on the counter, causing several pieces of paper to fall to the floor. "That's easy for you to say! All your kinner are safely at home. If young Leona or one of the others was snatched away, I'll bet you'd be singin' another tune."

Jacob shrugged his shoulders. "Maybe so, maybe not. I'd like to think I'd be praying every day, studyin' God's Word, and having the faith to believe He would bring something good out of the mess I was in."

Abraham massaged his forehead. He was sure the escalating pain would burst his head wide open. He knew all the things Jacob said were true, but he was tired and discouraged and couldn't muster enough strength or faith to believe in miracles anymore.

"I can see I've upset you," Jacob said, leaning over the counter and touching Abraham's arm.

Abraham was about to comment when the front door opened and an Amish woman walked in. He blinked. She looked familiar, but he couldn't quite place her.

"Can I help ya with somethin'?" he asked.

She smiled and nodded. "Remember me . . . from the quilt shop on the outskirts of Berlin?"

"Well, sure enough, I do remember you." He skirted around the counter and nearly bumped into Jacob.

"Never thought I'd see you again, though."

"My cousin, Edna Yoder, who lives near Strasburg, invited me to come for her fiftieth birthday. I just arrived in the area, but I wanted to drop by your store and see you before I headed out to Edna's place."

Abraham grinned. She wanted to see him, even before her cousin. Now that was a fine howdy-do. He turned to Jacob then. "This is Fannie Miller. I met her when I went to Ohio awhile back."

Jacob shook Fannie's hand, then he cleared his throat and gave Abraham a silly-looking grin. "Well, I'd best be goin'. It was nice meeting you, Fannie."

"You, too."

He waved and hurried out the door.

Abraham smiled at Fannie. "Would ya like a cup of cider? I have some in the back room, in the small cooler I usually bring to work."

She shook her head. "Thanks anyway, but I don't have much time. My driver is waitin' outside, but I have something I need to show you before I go."

"What is it?"

Fannie pulled a newspaper out of the canvas bag she held in one hand. "Have you seen the most recent issue of *The Budget*?"

"Can't say that I have. Don't have much time for readin' anymore." He frowned. "Things have really gotten bad around here since Naomi took off."

"Who's Naomi?"

"She's my oldest daughter—the one who left Zach sittin' on the picnic table back in June."

"Oh, yes, I believe you mentioned her. Just couldn't remember the name."

"She overheard me prayin' out in the barn one morning, tellin' God I blamed her for Zach's disappearance." Abraham swallowed hard. Just talking about it brought back all the pain. "The worst part is, I told God I thought she may have done it on purpose."

"Why, Abraham? Why would Naomi have left her little brother alone on purpose?" Fannie questioned.

"I thought she wanted to marry the buggy maker so bad she'd do most anything to get out of her responsibilities at home." He stared at the toes of his boots, feeling too ashamed to look at Fannie. "I was only speakin' out of anger and frustration. Didn't mean all that, not really."

She patted his arm tenderly, the way his wife used to do. It felt warm and comforting, and he looked into her eyes. "Sorry for dumpin' all my troubles on you. I know you didn't come here for that."

"No, I didn't, but I'm glad you felt free to share with me." Fannie smiled. "I think my visit might give you a ray of hope about your missing boy, too."

"Oh, how's that?"

Fannie snapped the newspaper open and laid it on the counter. "See here, in the classified ad section?"

Abraham stared at the part where she'd placed her finger, and he read each word out loud. "To the Amish Boy's Family . . . This is to notify the family of the Amish baby taken from a farm in Lancaster County in

259

June of this year—the boy is fine. He's healthy, happy, and well cared for." Abraham's knees almost buckled, and he had to grab hold of the counter to keep from toppling over. "Zach. This has to be about my missing son."

CHAPTER 23

Abraham couldn't believe he hadn't been able to track down the origin of the ad in *The Budget*. Thanks to Fannie showing him the paper, he felt closer to finding Zach than ever before. Yet the lead took him nowhere. He and Fannie had walked down the street to use a payphone, but when he called *The Budget* and asked about the ad, he'd been told the person placing the notice had mailed it and paid cash. There was no return address, and the postmark had been smudged beyond recognition.

"It's hopeless," Abraham said to Fannie as they headed back to his store.

She shook her head. "Nothing is hopeless. All things are possible with God."

"My friend Jacob says I should accept this tragedy and move on with my life. He thinks God will use Zach's and Naomi's disappearances for His good."

"Jacob could well be right." Fannie stopped in front of Abraham's store. "I should go now. My driver's quite patient, but I've kept her waitin' long enough."

"Sure wish you didn't have to run off. How long will you be in the area?" He felt a sudden need to be with this woman in whose presence he felt remarkably relaxed.

"Edna's birthday is tomorrow evening, and I had planned on catching the bus home the next day since it's an off-Sunday and there won't be any preaching."

Disappointment flooded Abraham's soul. "So soon? I'd kinda hoped we could see each other again. Maybe visit over a nice meal, the way we did at the picnic table out behind your shop."

Fannie's face lit up. "Say, I have an idea. Why don't you bring your family and come over to Edna's party tomorrow night? We're gonna eat outside on picnic tables, and I'm sure there will be plenty of food, so you needn't worry about bringing anything."

"But I don't even know your cousin. Wouldn't she think it a bit odd if a bunch of strangers showed up at her party?"

Fannie shook her head. "Edna's turning fifty this year and has planned her own party. She's always done things differently than others and loves surprises." Fannie chuckled. "I'm sure she'd be happy if my surprise was a few unexpected guests."

Abraham wasn't sure about all this, although he had to admit it did sound like fun. "That's awful nice, but—"

Fannie held up her hand. "Now I won't take no for an answer. I'd like to meet your family, so please say you'll come."

"Well, I—"

Fannie reached into her black handbag and pulled out a small notebook and pen. "I'm gonna jot down the directions to her place, and I'll expect to see you there. It begins at six o'clock."

Abraham took the piece of paper and said he and his family would try to make it. He didn't know why, but for the first time in many weeks, he was actually looking forward to something. It probably wasn't the party nearly as much as it was thinking about seeing Fannie again.

Fannie waved and headed for the English woman's car, still parked in the graveled lot next to the Fishers' store. "See you tomorrow night, Abraham," she called over her shoulder.

Abraham strolled up the steps to his store, surprised at how much energy he felt. He'd been tired earlier in the day, but now he could probably clean the whole store and not feel the least bit winded. "Sure hope the rest of the family will be eager to go to Edna Yoder's party, for I don't want to miss another chance to spend time with Fannie."

Jim had just finished lining out a job his crew would be doing tomorrow. It involved painting the trim on a three-story office building, which meant they'd have to use scaffolding. It wasn't something he used that often, but lately he'd been getting more jobs like this one in Tacoma, so he was glad he'd recently bought the necessary equipment.

"Guess we've got everything pretty well ready," he told Hank, his foreman. "Make sure the guys know to be on the job by seven tomorrow morning. I want to get an early start because Saturday's supposed to be another warm day."

"I'll see to it." Hank sauntered off as Jim's cell phone rang.

"Scott's Painting and Decorating," he said into the mouthpiece.

"Jim, where are you? I thought you'd be here by now. You said you were coming home for lunch today, remember?" Linda's tone was high-pitched and whiny.

"We worked a little later than usual this morning, and I'm just now ready to take a break," he said patiently. "I had to get a job lined out for tomorrow."

"You're working on Saturday again?" He could hear the disappointment in her voice.

"It's the only way I could fit the paint job in Tacoma into my busy schedule, and we have to take advantage of this good weather when we're doing an outside job. Never know when it will turn rainy again."

"I guess Jimmy and I will have to go to the park by ourselves."

"I'll be home soon, honey," Jim said, making no further comment on either of their Saturday plans.

"I was wondering if you could stop by the store and pick up a couple of things on your way here," Linda said.

"Sure, what do you need?"

"Jimmy's cutting another tooth and could use some of that numbing gel to rub on his gums."

"No problem."

"Also, we're almost out of disposable diapers."

"Got it."

"And could you buy a new thermometer? I believe Jimmy's got a fever, but our old one reads normal, so I think it must be broken."

Jim groaned. "If it says the baby's temperature is normal, then it probably is, Linda." She was too protective and had been since they got Jimmy. Jim thought things would settle down after a few weeks, but they'd had the boy for three months now, and still she acted paranoid about anything concerning the child. Jim had even installed one of those baby intercoms so Linda could keep tabs on Jimmy when he was sleeping. If he hadn't, she probably would have insisted on sleeping in the baby's room, the way she had the first night after they returned from Pennsylvania.

"Get a new thermometer anyway, just in case," she pleaded.

"Okay. Tell my boy his daddy will be home soon, and we'll eat our lunch together." Jim turned off the phone.

"She'll probably be holding our son's hand until he's old enough to leave home," he mumbled as he headed for his van. Jimmy was a special kid, and Jim loved him as if he were his own, but he didn't think it was good for Linda to smother the boy. *He'll either grow up to be a mama's boy, or he might end up rebelling. Neither would be good. I guess I'm going to have to do something to prevent that from happening.*

Jim opened the door and climbed into the driver's seat. He had been feeling much better about taking Jimmy since he'd gotten some phony papers drawn up and tucked safely in his deposit box. Also, placing an ad in the Amish newspaper when they'd gone to Boise to see Linda's folks had given him a sense of peace.

"Sure hope the little guy's Amish family sees that notice. If they know he's okay, maybe they won't miss him so much."

Jim rubbed his temples, feeling as though a headache might be forthcoming. "Who am I kidding? A notice in the paper wouldn't make me feel much better if someone took my baby."

He slipped the key into the ignition and started the van. "I can't admit to Linda what I've done or take Jimmy back to his rightful home. Linda's become too attached to him, and so have I. Just need to put it out of my mind, that's all. The longer he lives with us, the more it will seem like he's always been ours." Jim pulled out into traffic. "Besides, I took him to make my wife happy, and she is. That's all that counts, and I'm sure Jimmy's better off with us than he would be living among the Amish."

Naomi sat on the couch in Carla Griffin's apartment, looking through the want ads and feeling completely out of place. Truth be told, she wasn't sure she would ever feel comfortable again. Since they'd arrived in Portland, she'd felt like a fifth wheel. Until they came here, Ginny had acted like she was her friend. Now Ginny seemed more interested in Carla than she did Naomi. The two young women had gone off to the fitness center this morning, leaving Naomi alone.

"Naomi, you need to find a job," Ginny had said before they walked out the door. "There's a newspaper in the living room. Why don't you browse the want ads and see what you can find?"

Before Naomi could reply, Ginny added, "We should be back by noon, and it would be nice if you had some lunch waiting for us."

Naomi sniffed and reached for a tissue from the little square box on the table by the couch. Despite having access to fancy clothes, TV, and modern appliances, she felt alone and misunderstood. Not only was she lonely and discontent, but as she scanned the paper, she soon discovered there didn't seem to be any jobs she was qualified to do. Nothing except waitress work, and she wasn't sure she would even be good at that. Waiting on customers in a crowded restaurant was not the same as serving her family back home.

She circled a couple of restaurant jobs and tore them out of the paper. Would Ginny or Carla have time to drive her there later today? Would anyone want to hire a Plain girl from Pennsylvania who knew so little about the modern way of doing things? She wondered if she could find her way around the large town of Portland. No doubt she'd have to take a bus to and from work, as she didn't have a car or know how to drive.

Doubts mingled with her misery as she shed one tear after another. What if she couldn't make it in the English world? What if she felt forced to return home, knowing she was the object of her father's anger?

Naomi stood, forcing her tears to stop. "I won't know if I can make it here until I try to get a job, so in the meantime, I'll head for the kitchen and see what there is to eat. Might as well find something to do while they're gone, even if I don't appreciate Ginny's attitude and her bein' so bold as to ask me to have lunch ready when they get back."

When she entered the small kitchen, Naomi went straight to the refrigerator. One side was full of canned soft drinks and a few bottles of beer. She wrinkled her nose. "Hope Ginny's not gonna drink that awful stuff, and I won't be tryin' any, that's for certain sure."

By the time Ginny and Carla returned, Naomi had lunch ready to serve. She'd made ham and cheese sandwiches and fixed a tossed green salad. She would have liked some pickled beets, but of course, there were none. Once more, she found herself wishing for the things she'd had at home.

"How'd the job interview go?" she asked Ginny as the girls took a seat at the table.

"Great. They said I could start on Monday."

"That's gut. I mean, good," Naomi replied. If she was going to live among the English and try to become one of them, she knew she'd have to quit saying Pennsylvania Dutch words. Nobody would want to hire someone who used to be Amish; she felt sure of it. She would try hard to keep that part of her life a secret and do all the things expected of her in the fancy, English world.

"Did you find anything in the paper you can apply for?" Carla asked. She combed her fingers through the ends of her shoulder-length auburn hair.

"Yeah, did you?" Ginny chimed in.

Naomi felt their scrutiny piercing her bones. She grabbed the newspaper off the table and pointed to one ad. "I believe this one's not far from here. Maybe I'll see about it first."

Carla nodded. "Good idea. Everyone pulls her weight here, so you are going to need a job."

When Abraham arrived home from the store that evening, he was aggravated by the sight that greeted him. Not only was supper not ready, but the girls hadn't even started cooking. He found them both sitting at the kitchen table, drawing pictures of colored leaves.

Mary Ann looked up when he cleared his throat. "Oh, hi, Papa. Did ya have a good day?"

"It was all right 'til now," he grumbled.

"How come? What's wrong?" Nancy asked, never looking up from her work.

"I come home after a long day at the store and find you two sittin' at the table drawing, and there's no supper ready. That's what's wrong."

Nancy pushed her chair away and stood. "Sorry, but we got busy and lost track of time. Is it okay if we just have cold sandwiches?"

"I guess if I don't want to wait all night for something to eat, then sandwiches will have to do." Abraham trudged across the room and set his lunch pail on the cupboard. "Naomi would have had supper goin' by now, ya know. She always fixed something hot to eat for the evening meal."

"But Naomi ain't here," Mary Ann said.

"Don't get smart with me, girl! I know perfectly well where Naomi is."

Nancy rushed to his side. "Really, Papa? Have you had word from her?"

Abraham frowned. "No, haven't had nothin' but that one postcard. I only meant—oh, never mind. Just get busy fixin' us something to eat, and be quick about it!" He grabbed a glass from the closest cabinet and turned on the cold water at the sink. "Where are the brothers? Shouldn't they be inside by now?"

"I think the older ones are still out in the fields," Nancy said as she pulled a loaf of bread from the breadbox. "Samuel said he was gonna play in the barn awhile."

"I see. Well, let me know when supper's ready, and I'll ring the dinner bell." He gulped down the glass of water and was about to head for the living room when the back door swung open, and all four of his sons sauntered into the room.

"Is supper ready yet? I'm hungry as a bull,"

Matthew announced.

"Don't smell nothin' cookin'," Jake added. "That's not a good sign."

"Supper ain't ready?" Norman asked with a scowl.

"I'm workin' on it," Nancy said sharply. "For your information, I'm making cheese sandwiches."

"Is that all we're havin'?" This question came from Samuel, who had a chunk of straw stuck to his hair.

Abraham reached down and plucked it out, then handed it to the boy. "Be glad for what you're gonna get and take this back where it belongs."

Samuel opened the door and flung the straw outside. When he stepped into the kitchen again, he wore a smug expression on his face. "We've got us a batch of new kittens in the barn, did ya know that, Papa?"

Mary Ann jumped up from the table. "Were they just borned?"

Samuel shook his finger. "Born, ya *glotzkeppich* girl. Ain't ya learned nothin' in school?"

Mary Ann stuck out her tongue. "I'm not block-headed, and I've learned aplenty." She pointed to the pictures still on the table. "See there, I know how to draw really good."

Abraham's patience was waning, and he'd had about as much as he could take. He clapped his hands together, and everyone in the room jumped, including Matthew, the oldest. "It riles me when my kinner can't learn to get along. Samuel and Mary Ann, you ought to be ashamed of yourselves."

Mary Ann hung her head, and Samuel dragged the

toe of his boot across the floor. "Sorry," they said in unison.

"That's better. Now I have some gut news."

All eyes focused on Abraham.

"Is it about Zach or Naomi? Has either one been found?" Matthew questioned.

"I'm afraid not, although Fannie Miller came to the store today and showed me a notice in *The Budget* that gave me some hope Zach might be okay."

"Fannie Miller? Who's she, Papa?" Jake asked.

"She's the woman I met in Berlin, Ohio. The one who runs the quilt shop."

"Right," Nancy put in. "Papa told us about her after he came home."

Abraham nodded and pulled out a chair. "Why don't you all have a seat?"

Everyone did as he suggested, and Norman leaned forward, his elbows on the table. "What'd the notice say about Zach?"

Abraham gave his beard a couple of tugs before he answered. He wanted to be sure he worded it just the way it had been written in the paper. In his eagerness to get home, he'd left it at the store. "Let's see now. . . . It said something like: 'This is to notify the family of the Amish baby who was taken from a farm in Lancaster County in June that the boy is fine. He's happy, healthy, and bein' well cared for.' "

Nancy's eyes were huge as the sugar cookies Naomi used to bake. "You think they were talkin' about our Zach?"

He nodded soberly. "I'm nearly sure. How many other Amish babies did you hear about bein' kidnapped from our area back in June?"

"None. Only Zach." Matthew rubbed his chin as though deep in thought. "Is there any way we can find out who placed that notice?"

"Fannie and I called *The Budget*, but nobody there knows. The ad was sent in the mail and paid for with cash. There was no return address on the envelope, and the postmark was smudged."

Jake let out a low whistle. "So near, yet so far away."

Abraham didn't need that reminder. He tapped his fingers along the edge of the tablecloth. "At least we know Zach's all right and not bein' mistreated or—" His voice trailed off. He couldn't bring himself to say the words.

"Did Fannie Miller come all the way from Ohio just to tell you about that ad?" Matthew asked.

Abraham shook his head. "She's in the area to attend her cousin's birthday party. She just happened to get ahold of *The Budget* before she left home. Said after she read it, she thought of me and my missin' boy. That's why she dropped by the store."

"Fannie must be a right nice woman," Nancy said.

"Jah, she is. Which brings me to another topic. She—uh—invited us to attend her cousin's party tomorrow night at six."

The room got so quiet that Abraham was sure he could have heard a feather land on the floor.

"Do we know Fannie's cousin?" The question came from Mary Ann, whose blue eyes were fairly gleaming. "We haven't been to a party in a long time, and I think it would be fun."

"I'm not sure whether we've met Edna Yoder or not. She lives up near Strasburg, so she could've come into the store if she was near Paradise, but we don't actually know her."

"Why would ya wanna go to some woman's party you don't even know?" Norman asked.

"Because we were invited by Fannie, that's why."

"Well, the younger ones can go, but I'm stayin' home," Jake said with his arms folded across his chest.

"Me, too," Samuel agreed.

Abraham pushed his chair away from the table. "We're all goin', and that's the end of it. Plain and simple."

CHAPTER 24

Naomi was glad one of the restaurants she had circled in the newspaper yesterday was only a few blocks from Carla's apartment. She could walk and wouldn't have to bother Ginny or Carla for a ride. Besides, Ginny had just announced that they'd already made other plans for their Saturday.

"Carla and I are going shopping at the mall, then we

plan to take in a show. If you've got any money, you're welcome to come along, Naomi," Ginny said as she grabbed a donut from the plate in the center of the table.

Naomi shook her head. "I had planned to see about a job today."

"That's a good idea." Ginny gulped down a glass of milk and wiped her mouth on a napkin. "I don't want to impose on Carla much longer, and in order for us to afford an apartment of our own, we'll both need jobs."

"Jah—I mean, yes, I know. A couple of restaurants are looking for waitresses, and one's not far from here, so I thought I'd check on it sometime today."

"That's great. I hope it works out." Ginny stood. "I'd better go see if Carla's out of the shower yet. She said she wanted to get an early start, and it's almost ten."

"Do you think I look all right?" Naomi asked. "I wasn't sure what to wear when I went lookin' for a job." She stared down at the blue jeans and white cotton blouse, on loan from Ginny. "If I had enough of my own money left, I'd buy a dress or skirt and blouse."

"I think what you're wearing is fine. After all, it's not like you'll be applying for a job at some fancy office where you'd be expected to dress up every day." Ginny balled up her napkin and tossed it across the room. To Naomi's surprise, it landed right in the garbage can. "Some restaurants provide their employees with a uniform anyway, so I wouldn't worry about what you have on today."

"Okay, I'll try not to worry."

Ginny started for the door to the living room but turned back around. "That's your biggest fault; do you know that?"

Naomi pushed her chair away from the table and grabbed her dishes. "What is?"

"You worry too much." Ginny left the room, and Naomi headed for the sink to wash her plate and glass.

Ginny's words stung like fire ants, but even so, she wondered if they might be true. Did she worry too much? Was it a fault? A passage of scripture from the book of Matthew came to mind. "Which of you by taking thought can add one cubit unto his stature? And why take ye thought for raiment?"

Naomi turned on the faucet and allowed a stream of warm water to pour over the dishes as memories of home flitted through her mind. She had left the Amish faith when she ran away from home, but the things she had learned about God were still embedded in her mind. She might be able to turn her back on the responsibility to her family, but Naomi didn't think she could ever reject God. Only trouble was, she felt like He had rejected her.

"Say, Caleb, are you going to the singin' on Sunday night? I hear it's gonna be out at Jacob Weaver's place."

Caleb handed Andy a piece of sandpaper for one of the new buggy wheels they had been working on.

"Nope. Hadn't planned on goin'."

"Why not? Seems like all you ever do is work. You need to get out and have a little fun." Andy winked. "Maybe find a pretty girlfriend and start courtin'."

Caleb clenched his teeth. "Now you sound like Mom. She's always sayin' I should be married and raising a family by now."

"Maybe she's right. Ever think about that?"

Sure, he'd thought about it aplenty. Trouble was, there was no one he wanted to marry except Naomi Fisher, and that was about as unlikely as the moon falling from the sky.

Andy glided the sandpaper back and forth, and Caleb did the same with the other buggy wheel. "No comment?"

Caleb shook his head. "Nope."

"You're still pinin' for Naomi, aren't ya?"

He shrugged.

"Have you heard anything from her since she left home?"

"Not a word. 'Course I didn't really expect to."

Andy clucked his tongue. "Still can't believe she took off and left her family like that. Always thought Naomi was more dependable."

Caleb dropped the piece of sandpaper and frowned at his younger brother. "She is dependable. Naomi's a wonderful woman, who stood by her family long after her mamm died."

"That may be true, but what about now? Where's Naomi when her family still needs her?"

Andy's point was well-taken. Where was Naomi, and what had happened to drive her away? Caleb was sure it had happened that way. Somebody must have said or done something to make her run off with Ginny Meyers. It wasn't like Naomi to do something so rash.

Caleb noticed an unpleasant odor, and he wrinkled his nose. "Smell that? There must be a stinky old skunk nearby."

"Sure hope it's not someplace in the buggy shop," Andy said with a scowl. "If it sprays our equipment, we'll be in a fine fix."

"It's most likely outside, but it sure does stink." *Just like this whole mess with the storekeeper and his daughter.* If only Abraham Fisher had given Naomi the freedom to court, she might still be here. In fact, Caleb and Naomi could very well be published by now. If Caleb had been allowed to have his way, come November they would have become man and wife.

He grabbed a fresh piece of sandpaper and gave the wheel a couple of good swipes. He might not be able to do anything about his future with Naomi, but he sure enough had the power to make this wheel look as smooth as glass.

As Fannie checked her appearance in the mirror, she grinned at her reflection and patted her hair to be sure it was still in place. She felt like a teenager getting ready for her first suitor to come a-calling. It was silly, really. She was a grown woman, forty-two years old to be exact. Even though tonight wasn't a date, she hoped Abraham Fisher and his family would show up for Edna's party. There was something about the man that fascinated her.

Fannie had been thinking about Abraham ever since she'd gone to his store yesterday afternoon. She was worried about him and felt bad he couldn't get any answers from *The Budget* regarding the origin of that ad. Then there was the situation with his daughter leaving home. It really put Abraham in a bind. Who was helping care for his children, and what about the store? Was he able to run it by himself? If he did come to the birthday party, she planned to ask him those questions.

Abraham seems nothing like my husband was, she mused. Ezra had been short, a few inches taller than Fannie's five foot two. Abraham was tall, maybe six feet or better. Ezra was thin and wiry. Abraham had muscular arms, even though he was a bit portly around the middle. That didn't bother Fannie in the least, since she was on the plump side herself.

"You've got to quit comparin' the two men," she fumed. "Abraham lives here, and I make my home in Ohio, so there's no chance of us gettin' together, even if I might wish it were so."

Abraham's bearded face popped back into her mind. His eyes were so blue she felt she could drown in them.

Abraham's personality seems the opposite of my Ezra's, too. He appears to be strong-willed and a bit

278

harsh, whereas Ezra was the quiet, placid type. She shook her head. *I loved my husband. Loved him a lot. So why am I fascinated with Abraham when he's nothing like Ezra? Besides, I barely know the man.*

A forceful knock brought Fannie's musings to a halt. "You about ready, Cousin?" Edna called through the door. "My guests will be arrivin' 'most any minute."

Fannie turned away from the mirror. "I'll be out shortly."

"Jah, well, don't take too long."

"I won't." Fannie smiled. Edna always had been the impatient one. Impatient but sure could be a lot of fun. It was a wonder she never married after Joseph died. Ten years Edna had been without a husband, but she seemed to be getting along okay. Shortly after Joseph passed away, their son Aaron got married, and Edna gave him the house. She and her two other children, Gretchen and Gerald, lived with Aaron and his wife, Irma, until the twins were both married. Once they were settled into homes of their own, Edna moved into the small house behind her place. Edna's grandparents had built the home many years before, but for a long time it sat empty. Edna was determined not to rely on family to care for her, so she supported herself by taking in sewing. She made a lot of head coverings for women in the area who didn't have time to sew for themselves.

Fannie sighed and picked up the quilted pillow she'd made to give her cousin as a birthday present. It was time to head outside for Edna's party.

By six o'clock, the serving tables on the lawn were covered with an array of delicious food. Friends and relatives had brought everything from baked beans and potato salad to pickled beets and dilled green beans. Fannie scanned the crowd of people. The only thing missing at this party was Abraham and his family. Had he changed his mind about coming? Maybe he'd been delayed or couldn't find the place. Edna's home was rather out of the way.

"You look as nervous as a bird tryin' to escape the claws of a cat on the prowl. What are ya pacin' for?" Edna asked, as she gave Fannie a nudge to the ribs.

"I told you I had invited a guest, remember?"

Edna nodded. "The storekeeper up near Paradise— isn't that what ya said?"

"Right. I told him to bring his whole family, so if they do come, we might need another picnic table."

"Not a problem. Aaron has more sawhorses in the barn, and he can always lay plywood over the top. In fact, I'll go ask him now if you're sure the man's comin'."

Fannie smoothed the folds in her dark green dress. "He never actually said he'd come, just that he'd try to."

Edna gave her a knowing look. "I'd say you're a mite smitten with the storekeeper."

"What makes you think that?"

"You've got the look a young woman gets when she's expectin' her beau to arrive." Edna wiggled her eyebrows. "If the love bug has bit you, then I guess there's still hope for me at my old age."

Fannie shook her head. "I haven't been bitten by love, and fifty's not old, Cousin."

"I guess not, if you consider I might live another fifty years yet." Edna chuckled. "You know what middle age is?"

"Turnin' fifty?"

"Uh-uh. It's when ya know all the answers, but nobody asks you the questions."

Fannie laughed. "You always come up with the silliest things." She fidgeted with the cape on her dress. "Think I look okay?"

"Of course you do."

"I don't look too fat?"

Edna's pale eyebrows drew together. "You ain't fat, just pleasingly plump, as my dear mamm used to say."

"I've put on a few pounds since Ezra died, and I've been trying to watch what I eat, 'cause I don't want to gain any more weight."

"Maybe you should try the garlic diet. I've got a friend who's been on it a year already." Edna giggled like a schoolgirl and slapped her knee. "She hasn't lost a pound, but she has a few less friends now, that's for sure."

Fannie shook her head. It was easy for Edna to make jokes about people being fat. She was skinny as a twig. Had been since they were young girls.

"Tell me now, how much do you weigh?" Edna whispered in Fannie's ear.

Fannie pondered that question a few seconds, then

turned to her cousin and said, "Oh, one hundred and plenty."

Edna roared, and Fannie did, too. It felt wonderful to be having such a good time. Too bad Abraham wasn't here to share in the lively banter. With all his problems, he probably needed a good laugh.

Fannie glanced at the driveway and sighed. She so hoped he would show. "Well, guess I'll get some food and find myself a seat."

"Good idea. I'm headed that way, too."

Fannie followed her cousin to the serving table and had filled her plate half full when a vehicle pulled into the yard. It was a van driven by an English man, and when she saw Abraham Fisher get out of the passenger's side, Fannie almost dropped her plate. "He's here," she whispered to Edna.

"Then go greet him," her cousin said, giving Fannie a little nudge.

"Why don't you come with me? After all, this is your party, and I'd like to introduce him to the guest of honor."

"All right." Edna followed Fannie up the driveway, and by the time they reached the van, three young children, two girls and a boy, stood by Abraham's side. Then the back door opened, and three older boys, almost men really, climbed out of the vehicle.

"Abraham," Fannie said breathlessly. "I'm glad you could make it." She turned to Edna. "This is my cousin, Edna Yoder. She's the one havin' the birthday."

Edna smiled and held out her hand. Abraham shook it, but Fannie couldn't help noticing how he kept his focus on her. "It's nice to meet you, Edna. Happy birthday."

"Danki."

"How old are you?" the youngest girl asked.

Abraham raised his eyebrows. "Mary Ann, it ain't polite to pose such a question."

Edna laughed. "It don't bother me none. I'm fifty years old, but I'm not over-the-hill yet. Just runnin' a little harder, that's all."

Everyone but the younger ones laughed. Fannie figured they probably didn't know much about being over-the-hill. She smiled at the children . . . Abraham's kinner. It sure was nice to finally meet them.

"This is Matthew, my oldest," Abraham said. "Then there's Norman, Jake, Nancy, Samuel, and Mary Ann."

"It's good meetin' all of you," Fannie said. "Won't ya come fill your plates now? The rest of Edna's guests are already eatin'."

"I'll be right there. Just need to tell our driver what time he should come back for us." Abraham looked over at Edna, as though he was waiting for her to give the word as to when the party might wind down.

"Tell him to drop back around nine or so," she said with a nod.

"All right then." Abraham headed for the driver's side of the van.

"Why don't you wait for him?" Edna said to Fannie. "I'll take the rest of his brood over to the food." She started toward the tables, and the children willingly followed.

Fannie held back, feeling more nervous than ever. What did Abraham's children think of their father bringing them to a party for a woman they didn't even know? Had he told them how he and Fannie met? Did they think she might be after their daed?

Am I?

The question in Fannie's mind frightened her. She'd never been the kind of woman to throw herself at a man. Had she been too forward, asking him here tonight?

When Abraham stepped up beside her, she shivered.

"You cold?" he asked.

"No, no, I'm fine. You ready to eat?"

He nodded. "Jah, sure. Always ready for some gut food."

"Who's doin' the cookin' at your place now that your oldest daughter's gone?" Fannie asked as they strolled down the driveway, side by side.

"Nancy, but she's only ten and can't cook nearly as good as Naomi." He stopped walking and kicked a small stone with the toe of his boot. "Sure has been hard to keep things goin'."

"I'm sorry to hear that," Fannie said, feeling an ache in her heart for Abraham. "Do you have help at the store?"

He shook his head. "Not since Naomi left."

"That's a lot of responsibility for one man. I know, because I run my quilt shop with the help of my daughter. Don't know what I'd do if Abby ever quit helpin' out."

"I've thought about hiring someone, but I don't know who. It would have to be a person I could trust to do a good day's work and not fool around like some of the young ones are apt to."

"I understand," Fannie said. "Have you put the word out that you're lookin' to hire someone?"

"Nope. Thought I could manage on my own awhile yet. Been hopin' and prayin' Naomi might come to her senses and return home."

When Fannie looked into Abraham's blue eyes, she could see the depth of his pain. She wished there was something she could do to help. But what would it be?

As they continued walking toward the group of people gathered at the tables, an idea popped into Fannie's head. "Say, I was thinkin' maybe I could help at the store. Just 'til you're able to hire someone more permanent," she blurted out.

His eyes grew large, and he looked at her as though she'd offered him a special gift. "You mean it, Fannie?"

She nodded. "I'll phone the English gift shop next to our store tomorrow morning and ask them to get word to Abby. If she's agreeable for me to stay here a few weeks, I'll be free to help you."

He tipped his head to one side. "But if you're

helpin' me, won't that leave your daughter alone at the quilt shop?"

Fannie pursed her lips. "My daughter-in-law, Lena, would probably be willing to help Abby during my absence."

A huge smile spread across Abraham's face. "Fannie Miller, I believe you're an answer to my prayers!"

CHAPTER 25

Fannie had never seen the time pass so quickly. It was hard to believe she'd left Ohio two months ago and had been helping Abraham ever since.

"I sure like your little house," Fannie said to Edna as the two women cleared their breakfast dishes one morning.

"Danki. I think it's kinda cozy and comfortable."

"It's nice you can live close to your family yet be off by yourself. It's not like it is with most *grossdaadi-haus*—grandparents' houses—where you are right next door."

Edna grinned. "I'm afraid my family couldn't put up with me livin' that close. My joke tellin' and silliness might bother 'em to no end."

Fannie shook her head. "I doubt that, Cousin. I think your happy attitude is a real pleasure, and I've enjoyed our time together more than I can say."

Edna poured liquid detergent into the sink and

turned on the faucet. "When you came for my birthday, I never expected you to stay so long."

"Have I been a bother?"

Edna clucked her tongue. "Goodness, no. I'm right glad you're still here." She leveled Fannie with a serious look. Too serious for Edna. "That storekeeper must have some hold on you, that's all I've gotta say."

Fannie grabbed a dish towel, in readiness for the clean dishes. "Abraham doesn't have any kind of hold on me. He needs my help, and since Abby's been more than willin' to let me stay on—"

"He couldn't have hired someone in the area to work at the store?" Edna interrupted.

Fannie shrugged. "Guess he likes the way I do things."

"*Humph!* I'd say it's you he likes."

Fannie's face heated up, but she didn't argue. Truth was, she had a hunch Abraham was beginning to see her as more than someone to help at the store. They'd become good friends, and she'd even gone to his house for supper a time or two. Of course, she usually ended up doing the cooking, since Nancy's meals were pretty bland.

If she were truly honest, Fannie had to admit she'd agreed to stay on longer for more than Abraham's need of help. She enjoyed the man's company and hoped . . . *What exactly am I hoping for?*

"Looks like it might snow," Edna said, breaking into Fannie's thoughts. "Sure is cold enough for it." She chuckled. "When my twins were little, they used to think the clouds were giant pillows leakin' feathers all over the earth."

Fannie smiled and nodded absently.

"Do you think it's safe to take my horse and buggy to the store today? I could always run next door and ask my Mennonite neighbor to drive you."

Fannie shook her head. "That's all right, Edna. I rather enjoy driving my own buggy, and I know how to get around in the snow, should the clouds decide to let loose of their feathers."

"You be real careful crossing Route 30, ya hear? There was a bad accident out there last week."

"I never go against the light, and I'll take every precaution."

The women finished the dishes as they engaged in light conversation, and a short time later, Fannie had Edna's horse and buggy hitched and ready to go.

"Take care, ya hear?" Edna called as Fannie got the horse moving down the lane.

"I will!"

A short time later, Fannie headed down Fairview Road toward Paradise. By the time she got to Paradise Lane, the buggy started shaking.

"Was is letz do—what's wrong here?" she mumbled, trying to hold the reins steady.

The buggy wobbled, lurched, then unexpectedly tipped to the right.

"Ach!" Fannie halted the horse and climbed down to evaluate the problem. It took only a moment to realize the right back wheel had fallen off and was lying in the ditch.

The frosty November wind whipped against Fannie's dress, and she shivered, wrapping her woolen shawl tightly around her shoulders. "This isn't good. Not good a'tall. I sure can't put the wheel in place, and even if I did know how, I have no tools to fix it."

Fannie climbed back into the buggy. At least she was out of the cold. She'd have to wait until someone came along who might be willing to help—wait and pray it would be soon. She'd left Edna's place later than planned and had no idea how long it might be before help arrived. She was going to be late showing up at the store, and Abraham would probably be worried.

Fannie closed her eyes and prayed. *Father in heaven, send someone who can fix my buggy. Help Abraham not to worry, and please be with his daughter and baby boy today.*

At the sound of a horse's hooves, Fannie opened her eyes. A young Amish man driving an open buggy pulled in front of her rig. He hopped down and came around to the right side where Fannie sat holding the reins. She opened her door and greeted him.

"Looks like you've got a problem with your buggy. Maybe I can help," he said with a smile.

"Oh, I surely hope so. I was travelin' along fine one minute, and the next, I'd lost a back wheel."

He extended his hand. "I'm Caleb Hoffmeir, the buggy maker in this area. I've got some tools in the back of my rig, so if the wheel's not badly broken, it shouldn't take me long to fix."

"I'd be much obliged," she said, stepping out of the carriage.

Fannie stood off to the side as Caleb picked up the wheel and set it in place. When he headed to his buggy to get some tools, she remembered something Abraham had told her one day at the store. "Caleb Hoffmeir, the buggy maker, wanted to court Naomi, but I wouldn't give my permission for her to even go to singings. If I'd allowed them to court, Naomi might still be with us," he'd said with a look of regret.

As she watched Caleb work on the wheel, Fannie decided they needed to have a little talk. "My name's Fannie Miller, and I own a quilt shop outside of Berlin, Ohio."

"I know the place. Was there awhile back and saw some English folks in front of your shop." He grunted. "Thought maybe the baby they had with 'em was Abraham Fisher's boy."

"Abraham told me. I've been helping in his store the last couple of months, but I don't believe I've met you before."

Caleb grunted. "I haven't been in Fisher's store for quite a while."

"Abraham's mentioned you several times."

"I bet whatever he said wasn't good. The store-keeper and me don't see eye to eye, especially concerning his oldest daughter."

Fannie shifted from one foot to the other, praying for

the right words. "Actually, I think Abraham regrets not allowin' Naomi to be courted by you."

Caleb looked up from his job and frowned. "It's a little late for that, wouldn't ya say? Naomi's gone, and there's no chance of us ever courtin' now."

Fannie offered up another quick prayer. "Abraham believes if he'd given Naomi more freedom, she might not have run off like she did."

Caleb stood and pushed his hand against the buggy wheel. "Seems like it's in good shape now."

Fannie was amazed at how quickly he'd fixed it. She was also stunned by his lack of interest in what Abraham had to say. *Maybe it's not a lack of interest,* she decided. *I fear the young buggy maker has a bitter heart toward Naomi's father.*

"Danki, for fixin' the wheel. How much do I owe you?" she asked.

He shook his head. "No charge. I was passin' by anyhow, and I'd never leave anyone stranded."

She smiled. "I can see why Naomi was so taken with you."

He shrugged. "I ain't so sure about that. If she'd been taken with me, then she wouldn't have run off with her English friend. She left the Amish faith and her friends and family behind. Truth be told, I think she's probably much happier now."

Fannie wished there was something she could say to make Caleb feel better or at least offer him a ray of hope. She moistened her lips with the tip of her tongue and decided to make one last attempt. "I want you to know that I've been praying real hard—prayin' God will take this situation with Abraham's two missing kinner and turn it into something good."

Caleb's Adam's apple bobbed up and down as he swallowed, and Fannie could see he was struggling to keep his emotions in check. "That'd be right nice if God could make something good come from the whole mess, but to tell ya the truth, I ain't holdin' my breath for no miracle." He grabbed his tools and turned toward his buggy. "It was nice meetin' you, Fannie Miller."

"Same here," she called. "And I'll continue to pray for everyone concerned."

Naomi arched her back and wiggled from side to side, trying to dislodge the kinks that never seemed to go away. It was cold and raining outside, which Carla said was typical for November in Portland, Oregon. Between the chilly rain and her aching back, Naomi had been tempted not to come to work today. However, she needed the money.

Naomi donned her monogrammed apron and massaged the muscles in her lower back. She was grateful for her job as a waitress here at Jasper's Café, but she hated the work. She had been waiting tables for the last two months and still hadn't gotten used to the expectations placed upon her. Naomi had plenty of chores to do at home, but she could do them as she found the time and was pretty much in charge of things. Here at the restaurant she had a boss telling her what to do and criticizing every time she messed up.

Of course, she reasoned, *I did have Papa tellin' me what to do—especially at the store.*

Thoughts of her family sent a wave of homesickness through Naomi so sharp she felt as if her knees could give way. She missed Mary Ann's silly questions, Samuel's curious nature, and even Nancy's sometimes defiant attitude. She longed to listen to Matthew's mellow voice, telling her things would work out all right, and she would give most anything to have a little chat with Jake, or even Norman, who often got on her nerves.

She sighed. *I miss Papa, too, even though he does blame me for Zach's disappearance. Maybe my daed was right when he said some of the English like Ginny are spoiled. Seems to me most of 'em I've met have way too many things to take up their time. I'd much rather be sittin' out on the front porch, eating home-made ice cream and visiting with the kinner and Papa than I would rushin' off to movies, dances, and what-ever else Ginny and Carla do on the weekends.*

Naomi had thought she and Ginny would be able to pool their money and get an apartment of their own. But as it turned out, Ginny decided the kind of place she wanted was too expensive, so they were still staying at Carla's.

At least Naomi had her own bedroom, which was something to be grateful for. Ginny and Carla shared a room with twin beds, and that was fine with Naomi. She felt out of place around Carla, who drank beer and smoked cigarettes. Back in Pennsylvania, Ginny seemed to care about Naomi and acted like she wanted to be her friend. Here, she only seemed worried about her own needs and practically ignored Naomi unless she wanted something. Being able to escape to her room at the end of the day was one small comfort. For the most part, she felt removed from everything—like she didn't really belong.

Not only had Ginny and Carla become best friends, often leaving Naomi out of things they'd planned, they expected her to prepare most of the meals and keep the apartment cleaned and picked up. Already they were talking about Thanksgiving and Christmas and how they looked forward to the meals she would cook. Naomi wondered if she could make it through the holidays away from her family, while she catered to the whims of Carla and Ginny.

As she neared the restaurant's kitchen, Naomi smelled spaghetti sauce cooking. She closed her eyes and inhaled deeply. The aroma reminded her of the scalded, peeled tomatoes she and Mama used to make for homemade, savory tomato sauce. It was nothing like the plain old canned stuff that came from the grocery store.

"Sure wish I could go home," she mumbled.

"Are you gonna stand there all day rubbing your back and talking to yourself, or did you plan to start working sometime in this century?" Dennis Jasper's dark, bushy eyebrows drew together as he planted his beefy hands against his wide hips.

"I—I was only trying to get the muscles in my back to relax," Naomi replied, making no mention of the private conversation she'd been having with herself.

His thin lips turned into a scowl. "Make an appointment with a massage therapist, or see one of them bone crackers, but do it on your own time!"

Naomi nodded, grabbed her order pad, and headed for the dining room. This was not a good way to begin the day.

Jim had thought if he gave Linda more time, she would relax and not be so overprotective with their son. Two months had passed since he'd decided to take charge of things, yet so far he hadn't done a thing to let Linda know her actions were unacceptable and would only lead to trouble for Jimmy later on.

"Today's the day I lay down the law," Jim told himself as he headed across town to bid another job. "As soon as I get home tonight, I plan to tell Linda the way it's going to be from now on."

Jim's cell phone rang. "Probably the owner of the house I'm supposed to bid," he grumbled. "I'm only a few minutes late, but some customers can be so demanding."

"Scott's Painting and Decorating," he said into the phone.

"Jim, it's me."

He shook his head. Didn't she know by now that he recognized her voice? "What's up, Linda?"

"Jimmy fell and split open his lip. I think you should come home so we can take him to the emergency room for stitches."

"How deep is the cut?" Jim asked, feeling immediate concern.

"Not very deep, but it's bleeding."

"A lot or a little?"

"Well—"

"Linda, is the cut really bad or not?"

"I—I—think it could be."

"You think or you know?"

There was a pause.

"Linda?"

"I'm here. Just taking another look at Jimmy's lip."

"Is it still bleeding?"

"It does seem to be slowing up. I put a cold wash-cloth on it."

"That was a good idea."

"Are you coming home or not?"

"I really don't see the need." This was one of those times Jim wished his wife was willing to drive. It was ridiculous that she had to take the bus everywhere or call a taxi if Jim wasn't available to take her. Once in a while, she'd rely on a friend, but since they'd gotten Jimmy, she didn't socialize much anymore.

When Jim and Linda first got married, she had driven. But then she'd had an accident not far from their home. Even though it was only a fender bender and she hadn't been seriously hurt, Linda refused to drive the car from that day on.

"Please . . . Jimmy needs his daddy right now," she pleaded.

"Look, honey, if he was seriously hurt, I'd rush right home, but from what you've told me, it's just a little cut. Keep the washrag on it awhile longer, and if the bleeding stops, you'll know it doesn't need any stitches."

"Does that mean you're not coming home?"

He groaned. "That's exactly what it means. I'm on my way to bid a job, and I'm already late, so—"

"Fine then. If Jimmy bleeds to death, it will be your fault."

"He's not going to bleed to death from a split lip." Jim's patience was waning, and if he didn't hang up now, he knew he would say something he might regret later on. "I've got to go, Linda. I'll call you later and see how Jimmy's doing."

"But—"

He hung up before she could finish her sentence and clicked the button to silent mode. He may not have won the match, but he felt sure he'd won this round.

"You about ready to take a break for lunch?" Abraham asked Fannie as she reached under the counter and put the dust rag in place.

She smiled, and his heart missed a beat. Fannie had come to mean a lot to him. Truth of the matter, he'd been taken with her from the day they'd met at her quilt shop in Ohio. Since she'd been helping out at the general store, they'd had a chance to get to know each other. It still made him wonder why she'd been so willing to stay and help these past two months. In the beginning it was only supposed to be a couple of weeks—until he could find someone else. But the longer Fannie stayed, the more he wanted her to. She was a big help at the store, had a wonderful way with his kinner, and he'd fallen in love with her sweet, gentle spirit.

"You're lookin' at me awful funnylike," she said, pursing her lips.

He cleared his throat, feeling self-conscious all of a sudden. "I—uh—was admirin' your smile."

"Is that so?"

"Jah."

"I think your smile is nice, too."

"Danki. I'm also glad your bein' late today wasn't anything worse than a buggy wheel fallin' off."

"I agree."

"I was worried when you didn't show up at the usual time."

"I've got the buggy maker to thank for gettin' me back on the road again. If Caleb Hoffmeir hadn't come along, who knows how long I might have been stranded?"

Abraham's heart clenched at the thought of Fannie sitting on the road by herself on such a blustery November day. "I'd have come a-lookin' for you if you'd been much later," he said.

She offered him another smile. "I believe you would."

He grinned back at her.

"Now about lunch," she said. "Would you like to take your break first today? You look kind of tired, Abraham."

He shook his head. "Actually, I was thinkin' of closing down the store for an hour or so and takin' you to lunch at the Good 'n Plenty."

"Eat out? You and me together?"

He winked, feeling like he used to when he was a teenaged boy flirting with one of the girls in his community. "That's how I'd like it. Kinda like a date, don't ya know?"

She smoothed her navy blue dress as though there might be wrinkles. "Aren't we a bit old to be courtin'?"

He laughed. "Ask your cousin Edna what she thinks about gettin' old."

Fannie waved her hand. "I'm not askin' Edna anything, 'cause I already know how she stands on the subject of middle age."

"She's got a good attitude about things. Always positive and cracking jokes."

"That's true. It wonders me that she's never remarried."

"How about you, Fannie? How come you've not married again?"

She shrugged. "I could ask you the same question, Abraham Fisher."

He chuckled. "You got me there."

She touched her fingertips to the sides of her hips.

Hips that were a little wide, but he didn't mind one bit. "Are you gonna say why or let me guess?"

He gave his beard a few pulls, the way he always did when he was thinking. "The truth is, I never found anyone I thought I could love as much as my Sarah."

She nodded. "Same with me and Ezra."

He took a deep breath and decided to throw caution aside. "Here of late, I've been feelin' differently, though."

Her dark eyebrows raised a notch. "Oh? How so?"

"You're bound and determined to make me say it, aren't you, Fannie Miller?"

"Say what?" she asked in a teasing tone.

He reached for her hand and was glad when she didn't pull it away. "I've come to care for you, Fannie. You've brought joy into my life and helped me learn to deal with the pain of losin' two of my dear kinner."

Fannie glanced at the floor, but then she lifted her gaze to rest on him. "I feel the same way, Abraham. I enjoy your company a lot."

"You think it might be possible you'd consider stayin' on here permanently so's we could do some courtin'?"

She held up two fingers. "I've already been here two months longer than I'd planned to be. I can't expect Abby to keep runnin' the quilt shop by herself."

"Why not? She's done well in your absence, ain't it so?"

Fannie nodded. "Jah, but she's had to rely on my

daughter-in-law, Lena, when things have gotten real busy."

"Would Lena be willing to keep helping Abby—if you stayed here in Lancaster County, that is?"

"She might. I really couldn't say without speakin' to her first."

"Will you do that, Fannie? I surely want you to stay on." He wiggled his eyebrows. "I think my kinner are rather fond of you, too, and they'd probably turn cartwheels if I was to tell 'em you were gonna stay and maybe become their new mamm."

Fannie's mouth fell open, and she stood there gaping at him. "Are you sayin' what I think you're sayin'?"

A trickle of sweat rolled down Abraham's forehead and onto his cheek. Was he ready to answer that question? Should he have said anything about her becoming a mother to his children? "I—that is—if we were to court for a while, I think maybe we'd soon know if we're ready to make that kind of commitment to one another."

"I agree. We mustn't rush into anything."

"Right." He leaned forward, and with no thought for what he was doing, Abraham grabbed Fannie in a hug and kissed her right on the mouth.

She responded favorably, but when they pulled away, he noticed her face was as red as a ripe tomato.

"Sorry for takin' liberties that weren't mine," he mumbled.

She slapped his arm lightly. "No apology needed. I rather liked it."

Relief flooded his soul. Maybe there was hope for the two of them to start courting. Might could be Fannie Miller would one day soon become Mrs. Abraham Fisher.

CHAPTER 26

Abraham took a seat in the rocking chair near the woodstove. It was quiet here in the living room, and he hoped to spend a few minutes alone in prayer. Fannie had offered to cook their Christmas dinner, and she'd arrived early this morning. Ever since then, she and the girls had been in the kitchen.

He breathed in the aroma drifting through the house. A nice fat turkey as well as a shank of ham roasted in the oven. There would also be mashed potatoes, stuffing, creamed corn, pickled beets, chow-chow, and whatever else Fannie decided to place on the table. He had an inkling she'd brought a couple of apple-crumb pies, which he'd told her were his favorite. Yesterday, Nancy had made two pumpkin pies and one cherry cream, but unless her baking skills had improved here of late, he knew the crusts would either be burned or too tough.

Abraham patted his stomach, anticipating the meal that would be served in another hour or so. He'd been pleased when Fannie told him her daughter wouldn't be spending the holiday alone. Fannie had talked about returning to Ohio for Christmas, but Abby wrote and told her it would be fine if her mother wanted to be with Abraham and his family. Abby said she'd be having Christmas dinner with her brother and his wife, and she'd also mentioned she was being courted by a young man named Lester Mast, who Abraham figured might have more to do with her being okay with things as they were.

"Seeing as how Fannie's daughter is so happy and Fannie's here with me and the family, it's gonna be a much better Christmas than I'd thought it would be," he murmured. "Only thing that could make this day better would be if Zach and Naomi were home."

He leaned his head back, closed his eyes, and let memories of days gone by wash over him. Two years ago, his Christmas had been the best one ever. Sarah was pregnant with Zach and excited about the prospect of being a mother to the little one who'd be born in the spring. In Abraham's mind, he could see Sarah's sweet face as she sat in the same chair he now occupied. . . .

"You want another boy to help out on the farm, or would you be just as happy with a girl this time?" she'd asked when Abraham stepped into the room.

"I'll be content with whatever the good Lord gives us," he replied, bending over and kissing Sarah on the cheek.

She patted her bulging stomach. "Sure does kick a lot, this little one. Could be a feisty child, you suppose?"

He chuckled and took a seat on the couch across from her. "If he is, we'll have to give him twice as many chores so he doesn't have time on his hands to think up too many troublesome things to do."

"You said *he*." Sarah smiled. "I suspect that you're hopin' for another boy."

He shook his head. "It really don't matter. Just want the boppli to be healthy, that's all."

"Jah, me, too."

"Papa, you sleepin'?"

Abraham's reflections came to a halt as he opened his eyes. Samuel stood facing the woodstove, his hands held out so he could warm them.

"I—uh—was restin' my eyes." Abraham wasn't about to share his deepest thoughts with young Samuel.

"Well, I didn't hear no snorin', so I guess that means you weren't really asleep," the boy said with a snicker.

Samuel's my youngest boy livin' here now, Abraham mused. *His temperament isn't nearly as easygoin' as Zach's, but I sure do love him.*

"How old are ya now, boy?" he asked.

Samuel brought himself up to his full height. "Will turn nine soon, after Naomi's birthday next month."

A lump lodged in Abraham's throat. Naomi had been their New Year's baby, born one hour after the New Year. She'd be turning twenty-one in a week, but sorry to say, she wouldn't be celebrating the special day with her family.

Oh, Naomi, if only I could see you again and tell you the things on my heart. I've sought God's forgiveness for my mixed-up thinkin', but I need your forgiveness, too.

Thanks to Jacob Weaver's godly counsel, as well as Fannie's sweet spirit and love, Abraham had come to realize he could no longer hold Naomi responsible for Zach's disappearance. He'd forgiven the man who took Zach, too, and that hadn't been easy. The hardest person to forgive had been himself. He'd made so many mistakes since Sarah's death, but if God could pardon his sins, then Abraham knew he needed to forgive himself.

Matthew 7:1 said, "Judge not, that ye be not judged." Abraham had judged his daughter when he told God he thought Naomi might have left Zach outside with a stranger on purpose. That was wrong, and he was glad he'd finally seen the light. Only trouble was, Naomi didn't know he'd forgiven her. In Matthew 18:21, he was reminded of the way Peter had asked Jesus how many times he should forgive someone who had sinned against him. Jesus' reply in verse 22 was "seventy times seven." That was a lot of forgiving, and before Naomi left home, Abraham had refused to forgive her even once.

"Something sure smells good comin' from in there, ain't it so?" Samuel said with a nod in the direction of the kitchen.

Abraham pulled his thoughts away from the past. There was no point going over things that couldn't be changed. He had a sense of peace now, and if God allowed him to share the things on his heart with Naomi someday, he would be grateful. If not, then he prayed God would give Naomi the same feeling of peace and the knowledge she was both loved and forgiven.

"The smells are *wunderbaar schee,*" he said, smiling at his freckle-faced son.

Samuel grinned. "Jah, wonderful nice. I'm gonna eat two helpings of everything today. Fannie says I'm a growin' boy, and she's a mighty good cook, don't ya think, Papa?"

"Jah, ever so gut."

Samuel turned around so his back was facing the stove. "Sure is gettin' cold outside. Me and Jake were out in the barn playing with the kittens awhile ago, and we nearly froze to death."

"Guess we could have ourselves a white Christmas," Abraham said.

"Sure hope so. I'm more'n ready to build a big snowman. Maybe a snow fort, too, so's I can hide behind it when Jake and Norman decide it's time for a snowball fight."

Abraham chuckled. Samuel could hold his own against his older brothers. He was a determined one; that was for sure.

Samuel moved over to the living room window. "Thought I heard a car door slam. Did ya hear it, Papa?"

"Nope, can't say I did. 'Course the wood from the

stove is poppin' pretty good, so that might be what you heard."

Samuel wiped the moisture off the window and peered out. "It's a car all right. Looks like Mavis Peterson's station wagon. Wonder why she'd be comin' over here on Christmas Day."

Abraham shrugged. "Don't rightly know. Maybe she has somethin' she wants to give you younger ones."

"You think so?" Samuel raced to open the front door before Abraham could respond. A few seconds later, the boy turned around, and his eyes were huge as pancakes. "You'll never guess who got out of Mavis's car."

Abraham craned his neck to see, but the view out the front door was out of his sight.

"It's Naomi, Papa! Naomi's come home for Christmas!"

Naomi trembled as she stepped out of Mavis's station wagon. What if her family wasn't happy to see her? How would she respond if Papa was still angry and blamed her for Zach's kidnapping? That was an issue she'd been dealing with for the last few weeks—ever since a customer left her a biblical tract along with his tip. The first verse of scripture that caught her attention was from Psalm 51:3: "For I acknowledge my transgressions; and my sin is ever before me." On the back of the tract was a verse from that same chapter of Psalms, verse 10: "Create in me a clean heart, O God;

and renew a right spirit within me." That little piece of paper had been enough to make Naomi realize she needed to seek God's forgiveness and ask for a renewed heart. Returning home to ask Papa's forgiveness seemed like the next step to take. Besides, she was tired of the modern world and missed her family and friends here in Lancaster County.

"It's good to have you home," Mavis said, breaking into Naomi's thoughts. "Tell your family I said hello."

Naomi said she would and thanked Mavis for the ride from the bus station. She'd been grateful their English neighbor had agreed to come, this being Christmas and all.

Oh, Lord, Naomi prayed silently as she made her way to the house, *please give me the right words to say when I see the family . . . especially Papa.*

She'd only made it to the front porch when Samuel stuck his head out the door. She thought he'd seen her and might even come out, but instead, he ducked back inside.

Maybe I made a mistake coming home. Should I have bothered to save up my money for the long bus ride from Oregon to Pennsylvania?

Naomi had no more time to ponder the question. A chorus of voices was hollering for her to come inside out of the cold.

Matthew grabbed her suitcase, while Mary Ann squeezed her around the waist, and Nancy and Samuel clung to her hands. Norman and Jake stood off to one side, smiling like they were ever so glad she'd come

308

home. She couldn't tell what Papa was thinking, as he just stood there with his mouth hanging slightly open.

Naomi took a tentative step in her father's direction. "Papa, I'm sorry about everything. I don't want to be English anymore, and I came here to beg you to let me come home." Her vision clouded with unshed tears. "Can you ever forgive my trespasses?"

He rushed forward, embracing Naomi and wetting the top of her head with his tears. "Oh, Naomi, my beautiful daughter, you're more than welcome here. As far as forgiving you . . . I've already done that, and now I'm the one who needs your forgiveness. That day in the barn, when you heard me talkin' to God, I was just spouting off. I spoke out of pain and frustration and wasn't thinkin' clear. I know you'd never leave Zach alone on purpose, and I'm sorry for what I said. Will you forgive me, Naomi?"

Overcome with emotion, Naomi could only nod. Tears coursed down her cheeks and ran onto her jacket, but she didn't care. Papa was glad to see her. That's all that mattered.

Papa held Naomi at arm's length. "Let me look at you. Oh, you've grown so thin."

She opened her mouth to reply, but everyone started talking at the same time.

"Where have ya been?"

"Why didn't you write?"

"How come you're dressed thataway?"

Naomi looked down at her blue jeans and heavy jean jacket. She'd wanted to wear her own clothes when she arrived home, but she no longer had any of her Plain dresses. When Naomi was at work one day, Ginny gave them to some charity organization. "If you're going to be English, you should set aside all your Amish ways. That means getting rid of those drab dresses and ridiculous white caps you were forced to wear back in Pennsylvania," Ginny asserted. "Why don't you all come into the kitchen? Dinner's ready, and you can visit with your sister while we eat."

It wasn't until then that Naomi realized there was someone else in the room besides her and the family. A middle-aged, slightly plump Amish woman with dark brown hair and hazel-colored eyes stood off to one side. Had Papa finally hired a maad?

Papa withdrew a hanky from his pants pocket, blew his nose, and announced, "Naomi, this is Fannie Miller."

Fannie stepped forward and held out her hand. "I've heard so much about you, Naomi. I can see how happy your family is that you came home for Christmas."

"Fannie is Papa's girlfriend. We're all hopin' she's gonna be our new mamm," Mary Ann blurted out.

Papa's girlfriend? New mamm? So the woman wasn't a maid at all. But where had she come from, and why hadn't Naomi ever seen her before?

"I met Fannie at her quilt shop in Berlin, Ohio," Papa said. "Remember, I told you about her when I got back after goin' to see if I could find Zach."

Naomi did remember. It was their first ray of hope concerning her little brother, but nothing had come of it. Fannie had told Papa she didn't know the English couple with the little boy. Did her being here have anything to do with that? Could it be Fannie now remembered something and had come to Pennsylvania to tell Papa about it?

"Fannie's been helping at the store for the last couple months," Papa said before Naomi could voice any questions. "She came here in early September to attend her cousin's birthday party, and when she saw I needed help at the store, she stayed on." He smiled at Fannie and reached for her hand. "I—uh—well— since that time, we've come to care deeply for each other."

Fearful she might topple over, Naomi grabbed the arm of the nearest chair. How could so much have happened since she left home? Papa in love? How was this possible when he'd loved Mama so dearly?

"I'm afraid we're bombarding her with too much too soon," Fannie said softly. "Come, let's go into the kitchen and eat ourselves full."

For the next hour, the Fishers and Fannie sat around the huge wooden table in the kitchen, eating a wonderful array of foods and visiting. For now, Naomi decided to set her feelings regarding Fannie aside and enjoy the time spent with her family. She was glad she hadn't been baptized and joined the church yet, for if she had they would have surely shunned her.

"Tell us where you've been these nearly four months," Matthew said as he reached for another piece of apple-crumb pie.

"Out west—in Portland, Oregon."

"How'd ya get clean out there?" Jake asked.

"In Ginny Meyers's car. She has a friend who lives in Portland, so we were able to stay with her."

Papa leaned forward with his elbows on the table. "Where's Virginia now? Did she come back to Pennsylvania, too?"

Naomi shook her head. "Afraid not. Ginny's got a job workin' at a fitness center in Portland, and she seems to like it there."

"What about her folks? They're worried about her, ya know," Nancy put in.

"Ginny said she had contacted them, saying she'd decided to stay in Oregon for good."

Papa shook his head. "That's not what Bob Meyers told me. He said they'd not heard a single word from Virginia since she left a note saying she was going. They didn't even know you'd gone with her until I told 'em."

Naomi felt awful about that bit of news. At least she'd told her daed she was heading out with Ginny. Then she'd mailed him a postcard, but of course, that didn't make up for not writing again.

"How come you didn't send but one postcard?" Norman asked. "Don't ya know how worried we all were?"

Her face heated up, and she stared down at the table. "I'm sorry about that, but I convinced myself none of the family would want to hear from me again."

"That ain't true, Naomi," Samuel spoke up. "We've

missed ya somethin' awful."

She lifted her head. "I've missed you, as well."

"Tell us what it's like out west," Matthew said. "Is Oregon much different than here?"

Naomi nodded. "It rains a lot there, and Portland's awfully crowded. I worked as a waitress in a café near Carla's apartment, and the traffic on that street was horrible."

Fannie pushed her chair away from the table and grabbed several pie plates. "Naomi's probably tired from her long bus trip, so why don't we let her rest awhile?"

Papa stood, too. "Fannie's right. Naomi, why don't you go upstairs and take a hot bath, then climb into bed? Tomorrow we can hear more about your adventures in the English world."

Naomi could hardly believe this was the same father she'd left a few months ago. He wasn't harsh or yelling at anyone. He didn't seem distant or irritable. He had said earlier that he'd forgiven her and asked for forgiveness in return. Something had happened to Papa since she'd been gone, and she had a feeling it had a lot to do with Fannie Miller.

Naomi picked up her plate and a few others, then hauled them over to the kitchen sink.

Fannie smiled and shooed her away. "Nancy and Mary Ann can help do the dishes. Why don't you go upstairs like your daed suggested?"

"Jah, maybe I will. I am kind of tired." Naomi started for the door leading to the stairs, but she turned back around. "Has there been any word on Zach?"

"Nothing a'tall," Nancy said. "I don't think he's ever comin' home."

Papa moved across the room and opened one of the cupboard doors, then reached up and withdrew a newspaper. "That's not entirely true. We have had some word."

Anticipation welled within Naomi's chest. "What do you mean?"

"When Fannie came for her cousin's party, she stopped by the store to give me this." He walked over to Naomi and handed it to her.

"*The Budget*? Fannie gave you a copy of the newspaper?"

He nodded. "Read what I've highlighted, right here."

Naomi studied the part where Papa's finger lay, the section he'd colored with a yellow highlighter pen. By the time she'd finished reading the notice, her heart was pumping extra hard. "This has to be Zach." She looked up at her father. "You think it's him, don't you, Papa?"

He nodded. "I do."

"Then the man who took him must have placed this notice." A ray of hope seeped into Naomi's soul, and she squeezed her eyes shut in prayer. *"Let it be Zach, Lord. May this be the tool that leads us to him."*

"I called *The Budget* as soon as I saw the ad," Papa said, "but they had no information to give me."

Naomi's hopes were dashed as quickly as they had

soared. She blinked back tears. "All this tells us is that Zach's with someone, but we don't know who. Not very good news if you ask me."

"But it says Zach is okay and being well cared for," Papa said in a calm voice. "Somewhere out there among the English your little brother is living, and even though I still miss him terribly, this ad in *The Budget* is something to hold on to, don't you think?"

"I—I guess so."

"Even if we never see Zach again, at least we have the assurance he's not hurt or anything."

She nodded.

"I think this notice is an answer to prayer." Papa smiled, despite the tears in his eyes. "Our little boy is spending Christmas Day with someone who cared enough to place the ad so we wouldn't worry. Even though we don't know where Zach is, I feel peace in my heart about it." He nodded at Fannie. "I've come to believe, thanks to Fannie and Jacob's good counsel, that God will use this whole thing to bring something good for our family." He took Naomi's hand and gave it a gentle squeeze. "He brought you home, and that's one good thing. If He can give us a Christmas miracle like that, I'm gonna trust Him where Zach's concerned, too."

Naomi marveled at the peace she saw on her father's face. If he could rely on God like this, maybe she could, as well. He'd brought her home again, and Papa was right, it was like a Christmas miracle.

She handed the newspaper back to him. "I'll see you

in the morning, for we've surely got a lot more catchin' up to do."

CHAPTER 27

"Naomi! Are you up?" A child's high-pitched voice, followed by the sound of determined knocking, roused Naomi from her sleep. Groggy and disoriented, she rolled over in bed, noticing a ray of light streaming through a hole in the dark window shade.

"Naomi?"

"Jah, I'm awake." Naomi recognized Nancy's voice and realized this wasn't a dream. She was home in her own comfortable bed. A renewed sense of joy flooded her soul as she burrowed deeper into the feather pillow she had missed for too many nights. It was much softer than the flat, lumpy pillow she'd slept on for the last several months. The heavy quilt that covered her was warm and invited Naomi to linger awhile. Even the pungent aroma of kerosene from the lantern she kept near her bed was comforting. How she'd missed this familiar room, their big drafty house, and especially the family whom she had never stopped loving.

"You comin' downstairs soon?" Nancy asked. "Or do ya want me to get started on breakfast without you?"

With great effort, Naomi sat up. She glanced at the

clock on her dresser and grimaced. This was her first morning home, and she'd slept later than she had planned. "I'll be there as soon as I'm dressed," she called.

"See you in the kitchen." Naomi heard her sister's footsteps pad down the hall, and she smiled. Outside, the old rooster crowed raucously. These sounds were a lot more pleasing than the loud music Carla used to play every morning or the noisy cars that whizzed by in front of their apartment.

Naomi climbed out of bed and headed for the window. Lifting the shade, she peeked out. The ground below was covered with a blanket of radiant white. If more snow came, there would soon be bonfires, sledding, and sleigh rides. Courting couples in their community would be having all kinds of fun.

Naomi's thoughts went immediately to Caleb. Had he found someone to court during her absence? She couldn't blame him if he had. After all, Naomi had told Caleb on several occasions not to wait for her and to look for someone else. She'd often reminded him that as long as she was responsible for her family, there was no chance for them to court.

Naomi shook her head. *Leaving the way I did probably told Caleb I had no interest in him.* Naomi had never allowed herself to give in to the feelings she'd had for Caleb ever since they were kinner. There was no point in leading him on when they had no future together.

She blinked away sudden tears. Naomi hadn't

written to Caleb even once while she was away, even though she'd been tempted to. "There was a good reason for that," she mumbled. Besides not wanting to give Caleb hope that she might care for him, Naomi had convinced herself she would never return to Pennsylvania. Until she'd found the tract left by a customer at Jasper's Café, she had given up hope of ever reconciling with God, herself, and especially Papa.

Has Caleb thought about me or missed the times he used to come into the store and talk to me when we were alone? She shivered against the cold and hugged herself. *Caleb deserves to be happy, so if he did find someone while I was gone, I'll make an effort to set my feelings for him aside and share in his joy.*

Tap. Tap. There was another knock on the door. "Naomi, are you in there?" This time it was Mary Ann calling to her.

"I'm about to get dressed. I'll be down in a few minutes."

Naomi knew there was no more time for reflections. Her family was waiting for breakfast, and she needed to hurry and see that it was on the table. "At least some things haven't changed 'round here," she said with a shake of her head. "But that's all right. I'm just mighty glad to be home."

Jim jerked the pillow over his ears in an attempt to drown out the shrill cry of their fussy child vibrating through the intercom. Yesterday, since it was Christmas, they had allowed Jimmy to stay up later than usual, playing with his new toys. Now Jim was paying the price for that decision. Linda's folks had come for the holidays, and all day, Jimmy had been passed from Grandma to Grandpa and back again. Between them and Linda, the kid was spoiled rotten. He'd received way too many gifts, eaten far too much junk, and had been up running around when he should have been sleeping.

When Jim heard Linda slip out of bed, he groaned. "What time is it?"

"Three in the morning," she whispered. "Jimmy's crying again."

"I'm well aware of that. The kid's been screaming every hour on the hour since he went to bed at eleven. Probably has a stomachache from all the candy he ate."

"Go back to sleep, honey. I'll tend to him."

Jim only grunted in response. If he didn't have to get up for work in three hours, he might not care about lost sleep or a screaming child in the room down the hall.

Jim had just dozed off again when he heard a familiar sound.

"Da-Da-Da."

When he rolled over and sat up, Jim could see Linda's silhouette at the foot of the bed. She had Jimmy in her arms.

"What's he doing here?"

"I couldn't get him to settle down, so I thought he could sleep with us."

"That's not a good idea, Linda."

"Why not?"

"I've got to get a few hours' sleep before it's time to get ready for work."

"Which is exactly why I brought the baby into our room." She moved to her side of the bed, placed Jimmy between their two pillows, and crawled in beside him.

Jim turned on his side toward the wall. If this didn't work out, he might have to sleep on the couch.

"Da-Da."

"Yeah, right. Go to sleep, Jimmy. Da-Da needs his rest."

Jim had no more than closed his eyes when he felt a small foot connect to his ribs. "Ouch!"

"What's wrong, honey?"

"The kid's kicking me."

"Jimmy, no-no," Linda said sweetly.

Another jolt with the boy's toes.

Jim moaned. "Can't you move him to the other side of the bed?"

"He might fall out if he's not between us. Close your eyes and try to sleep."

"Ma-Ma-Ma! Da-Da!" A small, wet hand touched Jim on the back, and he jerked away.

"Take the boy back to his own room, Linda."

"He's lonesome, Jim. After the excitement of yesterday and being the center of attention, he needs us."

"And I need my sleep!"

"There's no reason for you to yell. You might wake Mother and Daddy."

"If they're not already awake, it's a miracle," he grumbled.

"You don't have to be sarcastic."

"I'm just stating facts."

"Our first Christmas with Jimmy was wonderful, wasn't it?" she asked, changing the subject.

"It was great."

"Wasn't it cute when the baby tried to give his bottle to the teddy bear my folks got him?"

"Yeah, real cute. Jimmy shouldn't be taking a bottle anymore."

"I think he still needs it. It offers him comfort."

"Then why isn't he taking one now?"

"I tried that, but he wasn't interested. He's probably full."

"Uh-huh." Jim's breathing slowed as the need for sleep overtook him.

Whap! Jimmy's clammy little hand slapped the side of Jim's head.

He bolted upright. "That's it. I'm putting the hammer down."

"The hammer? Jim, what on earth are you talking about? Are you having a bad dream?"

"No, it's more like a nightmare." Jim jumped out of bed, swooped Jimmy into his arms, and stumbled for the door.

"Where are you taking my baby, and what's all this about a hammer?" Linda shouted.

He halted and turned toward the bed. "My dad used to say he was putting the hammer down whenever he made up his mind to take control of a situation. So I've decided it's time for me to do the same, because this whole thing is totally out of control."

"I don't understand why you're so upset." Linda's voice shook with emotion, but he wasn't going to give in. Not this time. He'd done it too much in the past, and where had it gotten him? Jim usually took the easy way out, opting not to answer his cell phone when he knew it was Linda calling or sleeping on the couch when she was determined to bring Jimmy to bed with them. He was putting the hammer down once and for all, and it was going to stay down this time!

"Naomi, there was really no need for you to come in this mornin'," Abraham said as she moved around the store, lighting the gas lanterns. "I figured you'd want to stay home and get caught up on your rest."

She shook her head. "I want to be here, Papa. I've missed helpin' you, and it's a lot nicer workin' at our store than waiting tables at a crowded, noisy restaurant."

"I doubt we'll have many customers today, what with it bein' the first Monday after Christmas and all." He nodded toward the closest window. "Besides, it's snowing like crazy, and folks aren't likely to brave the storm just to come into our store."

She smiled at him. "Then why'd we open at all today?"

"Out of habit, I guess." He chuckled, then shrugged.

"Never know when someone might have a real need for somethin'."

"That's true. I remember last winter when it got so cold that folks were comin' in here to buy kerosene for their lanterns, woolen scarves, hats, and gloves. We sold plenty of snow shovels, too."

"Good point. Which is exactly why I felt I couldn't close the store today."

"When did you start selling quilts, Papa?" Naomi asked, as she fingered a stack of colorful coverings on the shelf a few feet away.

"Those are Fannie's. She made them, and I suggested she try selling 'em here." Abraham put the OPEN sign in the door window and grabbed the broom. "It wonders me so the way this place can get so dirty. Sure wish folks would learn to wipe their feet before comin' inside."

Naomi left the quilts and came to stand at his side. "Mind if I ask you a personal question?"

"Ask away."

"Just how serious are you and Fannie?"

He stopped sweeping and turned to face her. "I'm hopin' to ask her to marry me soon."

Naomi's mouth fell open. "I never thought you'd marry again. You and Mama—well, I know how much you loved her."

"I did, and there will always be a spot in my heart for her. You can't live with someone over twenty years and not keep that love in here." He placed his hand against his chest.

"Do you love Fannie more than Mama?"

Abraham's throat constricted. The way he felt was hard to describe. He scuffed the toe of his boot against the floor. "What Fannie and I have is special. I won't deny it. As far as lovin' her more than your mamm— I don't think I could ever love anyone more than Sarah." He shook his head. "Maybe the same, but in a different way. Does that make sense to you?"

Naomi nodded, and her dark eyes filled with tears. "I—think so, Papa."

He set the broom aside and gave her a hug. "It's so gut to have ya home, Daughter. I surely did miss you."

"I missed you, too."

Abraham was going to say more, but the front door opened, and Fannie stepped into the room.

"Gude mariye," she said with an easygoing smile. "Sure is nasty out there." The top of Fannie's black bonnet was covered with white flakes, and Abraham was sorely tempted to brush them away.

Instead, he returned her smile and said, "Didn't expect you'd be in this mornin', what with the snow and all."

She waved a hand. "Wouldn't let a little bad weather keep me from comin' to the store when I figured you'd be here all alone."

He nodded toward Naomi. "Couldn't persuade her to stay home and rest up today."

Fannie removed her heavy shawl and bonnet and hung them on a wall peg. "Knowing Matthew, he'd probably have been grateful to give you the job of babysitting after school," she told Naomi.

Naomi's forehead wrinkled. "Matthew's been watchin' the kinner while I was away?"

"Only after school and on Saturdays," Abraham explained. "Nancy does most of the cooking and cleaning these days, but Matthew's good at keepin' the peace when the younger ones start scrappin'."

Naomi smiled. "Jah, I know how that can go."

Fannie cleared her throat. "Abraham, I was wonderin' if I could talk with you a minute—in private."

He glanced over at Naomi. "Would ya mind waitin' on any customers who might come into the store?"

"I'd be happy to, Papa."

Abraham took hold of Fannie's arm and led her to the back of the building. They stopped in front of a rack full of seeds and gardening supplies. "What's up?" he asked.

She shifted her weight from one foot to the other, kind of nervous-like. "I've been thinking that since Naomi is home now, maybe I should head on back to Ohio."

He stood there for several seconds, feeling numb and not knowing how to respond. "You want to go?" he finally mumbled.

She stared at the floor. "I've been gone for several months now, leaving Abby on her own at the quilt shop."

"I thought she was managing pretty well with Lena's help."

Fannie nodded. "She is, but—"

"And I thought you enjoyed workin' here with me." Abraham fingered his beard, wishing this conversation had never taken place.

"I do, but I miss my quilts, and—"

He pointed to the front of the store. "I cleared off a shelf so you could sell some of your quilts."

"I know, and I appreciate that." She smiled, but it never quite reached her eyes. "Your daughter's back, Abraham. You don't need me anymore."

With no thought of anyone seeing them, Abraham pulled Fannie into his arms. "I'll always need you, Fannie Mae. I love you and want to make you my wife."

Her beautiful eyes, which reminded him of acorns in the fall, filled with tears. "You really want to marry me?"

He kissed the top of her white head covering. "I thought you knew how I felt. I've told ya often enough lately that I love you."

"I know, but with Naomi comin' home and all, I thought you might feel you could get along without me now."

"I could never get along without you, Fannie. I want you to be my *fraa*."

She sighed against his chest. "*Ich lieb du*—I love you, Abraham Fisher."

"Does that mean you'll marry me?"

She nodded. "If Abby's willin' to take over the shop completely."

Abraham stiffened. "And if she's not?"

Fannie smiled and reached up to gently pinch his cheek. "I'll suggest she move here. Maybe we can find a building nearby and set up a quilt shop."

Suddenly, an idea popped into Abraham's head, and he snapped his fingers. "Say, I'll tell ya what."

"What's that?"

"I could add on to my store, then you'd have your own quilt shop. How's that sound?"

She tipped her head back and looked up at him. "It sounds wunderbaar gut to me."

Caleb couldn't believe his mother had sent him out in weather like this just to get some kerosene, which she'd said she was only low on. And why did it have to be him and not Andy or Marvin? Was it the fact that he was older, and she felt he knew better how to handle the horse and buggy in the snow?

Pop had hired a driver this morning to take him to a dental appointment in Lancaster, and both John and David had gone off to see their girlfriends. Since Mom had insisted Caleb head to the Fishers' store right away, he'd left Andy and Marvin at the buggy shop. They'd begun work on a new carriage for an English man in the area who ran a bed-and-breakfast and offered free buggy rides to the tourists. Caleb could only hope his brothers wouldn't mess up the job while he was away. Marvin was careless at times, and Andy tended to be accident-prone. No telling what might happen in Caleb's absence.

By the time he arrived at Fisher's General Store,

Caleb was pretty worked up. He hadn't been to the store in many months. Not since Naomi left home.

Caleb stomped the snow off his feet and entered the store. A blast of warm air hit him in the face, and he rubbed his hands briskly together. It felt good to be out of the cold, even though he'd driven a closed-in buggy, which had a portable heater inside.

"Gude mariye," he said, nodding at Abraham, who sat behind the counter, looking at a large blue ledger.

"Jah, it surely is a gut morning."

Caleb shoved his hands into his pockets. *The store-keeper seems to be in an agreeable mood today. Don't recall that he's ever been so friendly to me before.*

"Did ya have a gut Christmas?"

"It was fine. How about yours?"

Abraham nodded and smiled. "Better than I ever expected."

Hmm . . . maybe the man's cheerful attitude has something to do with Fannie Miller. Caleb's mother had recently told him that she'd heard from her friend Doris, who knew someone acquainted with Fannie's cousin Edna Yoder, that Fannie and the storekeeper saw a lot of each other these days. Edna told her friend she thought there soon might be a wedding between Abraham and Fannie, and the word had been passed along.

"Me and the family had the best Christmas present," Abraham continued.

Caleb leaned against the counter. "What was it?"

The storekeeper pointed toward the back of the

room, and Caleb's gaze followed the man's finger. Two Amish women stood side by side with their backs to him. One he figured was Fannie, but he didn't know whom she was waiting on.

Suddenly, the smaller of the two women turned around, and Caleb nearly passed out from the shock of seeing her. "Naomi!"

She made her way to the front of the store, and her radiant smile lit up the whole room. "It's nice to see you, Caleb."

"I—I had no idea you were back," he stammered. "How long have ya been here?"

"I came home on Christmas Day."

He studied Naomi intently. She was dressed in Plain clothes, although they hung loosely on her. She was obviously not English anymore or she wouldn't be here, dressed as an Amish woman. There were dark circles beneath her luminous brown eyes, but he thought she looked beautiful.

"Have you come home for good?" he asked hopefully.

"Jah, I've seen the error of my ways."

He smiled. "I'm so glad—about you comin' home, that is."

Abraham cleared his throat a couple of times. "Ahhem."

Caleb whirled around. In his joy over seeing Naomi again, he'd almost forgotten her daed was right there. No doubt the man was scrutinizing everything he'd said, just waiting to ask Caleb to leave his store.

"I—uh—came by for some kerosene," Caleb mumbled. "Mom's almost out, and with the bad weather settin' in, she thought she'd better have plenty on hand."

"Makes sense to me." Abraham had a funny kind of grin on his face, and Caleb didn't know what to make of it.

Fannie joined the group then. "It's nice to see you, Caleb."

"Likewise." There was an awkward silence, then he asked, "How's that buggy wheel holdin' out? It didn't fall off again, I hope."

Fannie shook her head. "Been stayin' right in place."

"That's gut. Real gut."

Fannie glanced at Abraham and winked. "Don't ya have somethin' you want to tell the buggy maker?"

Abraham's forehead wrinkled. "I do?"

She went around the back of the counter and whispered in his ear, which quickly turned pink, while a slow smile spread across his face.

"Fannie reminded me of somethin' I told her awhile back . . . when Naomi left home and I wasn't sure if we'd ever see her again."

"What was that?" Caleb asked.

"I'd like to hear whatever it is, too," Naomi put in.

The storekeeper gave his beard a couple of yanks, leaned slightly forward, and announced, "Caleb Hoffmeir, I give you permission to court my daughter."

CHAPTER 28

Naomi pulled on a clean dress and secured her head covering in place. She'd been home a week already, and here it was New Year's Day—her twenty-first birthday. Would her family remember? Would they do anything special to celebrate?

She smiled at her reflection in the mirror. "It doesn't matter. Just being home with those I love is birthday present enough for me." She thought about Ginny and wondered if she ever missed home. Her first day back at the store, Naomi had gone to Meyers' Restaurant to see Ginny's folks. She felt they deserved to know where their daughter was living and that she was okay. They had appreciated the information but said their hearts were saddened by their daughter running off that way.

A knock on her bedroom door drove Naomi's thoughts aside, and she called, "Come in."

Nancy and Mary Ann stepped into the room, each with their arms held behind their backs.

"Hallich Neiyaahr un Hallich Gebottsdaag!" Mary Ann announced.

"Jah, Happy New Year and Happy Birthday!" Nancy echoed.

Before Naomi could respond, they both handed her a gift. Mary Ann's was in a white envelope, and

Nancy's was inside a small brown paper sack.

Naomi struggled not to cry. Her sisters had remembered today was her birthday, and even if no one else in the family acknowledged it, this display of love was enough for her.

She took the gifts, went over to her bed, and seated herself. Her sisters followed and sat on either side of Naomi.

"Open mine first," Mary Ann said excitedly. "I made it myself."

Naomi tore the envelope open and withdrew a piece of heavy paper folded like a card. There was a picture of a tulip on the front, colored with red crayon. The words HAPPY BIRTHDAY were above it. Inside Mary Ann had written a note. "To my big sister: I'm glad you didn't stay gone like Zach. We all missed you! Love, Mary Ann." Tucked inside the card was a blue felt bookmark that had been cut out with pinking shears.

Tears sprang to Naomi's eyes as she hugged her little sister. "The card's so nice, and I'll put the pretty bookmark inside my Bible."

Mary Ann smiled. "I knew you'd like it."

"I do. Danki."

"Now mine," Nancy said, nodding at the paper sack Naomi had placed in her lap. "Fannie helped me make it."

Naomi reached inside the bag and pulled out a pot holder, quilted in various colors using a simple nine-patch pattern.

"It's for your hope chest," Nancy explained. "For when you and Caleb get married."

Naomi wrapped her arms around Nancy. "It's ever so nice. You did a gut job, and it would definitely go in my hope chest, if I had one." She sighed. "As far as me ever marryin' Caleb . . . Well, that remains to be seen. We only got permission to court a week ago."

Nancy nodded, looking suddenly grown up. "It'll happen, just you wait and see."

Naomi stood. "Right now the three of us need to head downstairs and get breakfast started. The menfolk will be in from chorin' soon, and if I know Papa and those brothers of ours, they'll be hungry as a bunch of mules."

Mary Ann and Nancy both giggled, and Naomi followed them out of the room.

"After breakfast is over, I'm gonna bake you a hurry-up cake," Nancy announced. "I've learned to cook since you were gone."

Naomi opened the refrigerator door and withdrew a carton of eggs. "I'm sure you've become right capable in the kitchen."

"Nancy can't make blueberry pancakes as good as yours," Mary Ann put in. "She always burns them around the edges."

Nancy stomped her foot. "Do not!"

"Do so!"

Naomi held up one hand to silence the girls before their disagreement got out of hand. "Let's not spoil the New Year by arguing, okay?"

"Yeah, Papa don't like it when he hears us yellin'," Mary Ann said as she began setting the table.

"Then don't yell," Nancy shot back at her.

Naomi was about to say something when the back door swung open and in walked Samuel, carrying a wicker basket with a strip of cloth draped over the top. Believing it was freshly collected eggs, she pointed to the refrigerator. "Set 'em in there 'til we've had a chance to be sure they're clean enough."

Samuel's eyebrows shot up. "I ain't puttin' your birthday present in the refrigerator. It'd kill him."

"Him?" Naomi moved to where Samuel stood by the table. "What have you got in there?"

Samuel grinned and handed her the basket. "This is my present to you."

Mary Ann and Nancy crowded around as Naomi pulled back the piece of cloth, and a ball of white fur poked its tiny head up. *Meow!*

"It's one of Snowball's kittens, ain't it so?" asked Mary Ann.

Samuel nodded, looking right pleased with himself. "I named this one Speckles 'cause he's white with gray spots on his legs and head." He touched the kitten's pink nose with the tip of his finger. "Ya like him, Naomi?"

She gently squeezed his shoulder. "He's real nice, Samuel. Danki."

"You better put that cat outside," Nancy said in her most bossy voice. "Papa don't like animals in the house; you know that."

334

Samuel started to protest, but Naomi came to his rescue. "I think it might be best if Speckles stays in the barn with his mother for a while, don't you, Samuel?"

He shrugged. "I guess so."

"He'll still be my pet, though," Naomi assured the boy. "I'll play with him whenever I'm in the barn, and when he's old enough to leave his mamm, he can run all over the yard."

Samuel grinned from ear to ear. "I like that idea." He took the basket from Naomi. "Speckles is gonna be one good mouser, you'll see."

"I'm sure he will be."

As Samuel headed out the door, Matthew, Jake, and Norman entered the kitchen. They were carrying something under a large piece of canvas.

"What have you got there?" Naomi asked, her curiosity piqued.

"It's your birthday present," Matthew said. "We've been fixin' it ever since you came back home a week ago."

Naomi crossed the room and lifted one corner of the canvas. Her breath caught in her throat when she saw what was underneath. "This is our mamm's old cedar chest, isn't it?"

Norman nodded. "You like what we did with it?"

"Oh, yes." Naomi knelt on the floor beside her mother's beloved hope chest. Her brothers had sanded away all the old scratches and gouges and given it a new coat of stain with clear varnish brushed over the top.

"We thought with you bein' courted by the buggy maker and all, you'd be needin' a hope chest now," Jake announced.

Tears slipped out of Naomi's eyes and rolled down her cheeks. "Caleb and me haven't had even one date yet, but I surely do appreciate all the work you three did on Mama's cedar chest." She stroked the lid, which felt as smooth as glass. "Even if I never marry, I'll treasure this all of my days."

"Why not start by fillin' it with this?"

Naomi looked up. Papa stood inside the door, holding a quilt in his hands. "This was your mamm's, and I want you to have it for your twenty-first birthday," he said with a catch in his voice.

Naomi stood. "Oh, Papa. Mama's Double Wedding Ring quilt has been on your bed ever since I can remember. Her mamm gave it to you as a wedding present. How can you part with it?"

He stepped forward, holding it out to her. "She'd want you to have it, Naomi, and I sure wouldn't think of sellin' it."

"Why would ya be sellin' anything of Mama's?" The question came from Nancy, who stood beside Naomi, fingering the edges of the blue and white quilt as though it were made of spun gold.

"Fannie and I have decided to get married in the spring, and it's customary for a widower to sell his wife's things before he remarries." Papa smiled at Naomi. "Of course, I'll be giving you and the sisters a chance to pick whatever you're wantin' first."

The joy of Naomi's birthday and all the wonderful presents faded as the stark reality set in that her daed really was planning to marry Fannie Miller. Soon Fannie would be in charge of the house, and since he'd said he wanted to add a quilt shop on to the store, it would probably mean Fannie would continue to work there, as well.

Wonder where that leaves me? Naomi asked herself. *From what I can tell, Fannie seems like a nice enough woman, but I don't really know her yet. The thought of her takin' Mama's place hurts real bad, and it would appear she'll soon be fillin' my shoes, as well. Even so, my burdens will be lighter once Papa and Fannie are married. Now there'll be a chance for me to finally think about marriage—should Caleb ask.*

"I have somethin' else for you," Papa said, forcing Naomi to set her thoughts aside.

"Oh, what's that?"

"It's right here." Papa handed Naomi a black Bible, which she recognized as also having belonged to her mother. "I thought, as the oldest daughter, this ought to go to you."

Naomi gulped back a sob. Everything was happening too fast, and she felt so confused about her father's plans to be married. She would treasure Mama's hope chest, quilt, and especially the Bible, but could she really accept Fannie as her stepmother?

As Caleb guided his horse and sleigh down the road, he kept glancing at the box on the floor by his feet.

Inside was a delicate purple and white African violet, one his mamm had grown. She had a way with plants and things—had them growing in pots all over the sunporch and into her sewing room. Caleb had offered to buy the violet, telling his mother he wanted something special to give Naomi for her birthday. Mom flatly refused, saying he did so many favors for her—always running to town to fetch things and whatnot. Besides, there was no way she would take money from one of her sons for a plant she'd so easily grown. She only sold them to the customers who visited her booth when the farmers' market was open.

"Sure hope the cold doesn't get to the violet before I arrive at the Fishers' place. Wouldn't do to present Naomi with a dead plant for her twenty-first birthday," Caleb mumbled.

The horse whinnied as if in response, while the sleigh glided across the snow-packed road as easy as a duck sets down on water.

"This is gonna be the best New Year's," Caleb shouted into the wind. He'd been given permission to court the storekeeper's daughter, and nothing could be any better than that. Nothing but marrying Naomi, and he hoped that would come about next fall.

A short time later, Caleb pulled into the Fishers' yard, hopped down from the sleigh, and tied his horse to the hitching rail near the barn. He grabbed the box housing the African violet and chanced a peek inside. It looked fine, and he breathed a sigh of relief.

Caleb took the porch steps two at a time and knocked on the back door. It was still early, and he figured Naomi might be in the kitchen doing up the breakfast dishes.

The door swung open on the second knock, but instead of Naomi, it was Abraham who greeted Caleb. "Hallich Neiyaahr," he said with a nod.

"Happy New Year to you, too," Caleb replied. "Is— uh—Naomi at home? I came to wish her a happy birthday and give her this." He held out the box, feeling kind of nervous all of a sudden.

Abraham nodded and stepped aside, pushing the door all the way open. "Naomi, there's someone to see you."

Caleb still couldn't believe the change that had come over the storekeeper in the last few months. Mom had mentioned a few times that ever since Fannie Miller started helping at the store, Abraham had been much more agreeable. Now that Naomi was back home again, her daed seemed downright friendly. Caleb couldn't believe the man had actually given him permission to court his oldest daughter. It seemed almost too good to be true.

He shifted from one foot to the other, hugging the box close to his chest.

"Well, you comin' inside or not, boy?"

"I—uh—sure." *Guess some things haven't changed. Abraham still sees me as a boy, not a man.* Caleb stepped into the warm kitchen, and the sight of Naomi standing at the sink washing dishes made his heart pound. Her cheeks were flushed, and a wisp of golden brown hair had worked its way free from the bun at the back of her head. He stared at Naomi several seconds, imagining what it would be like to be married to her and come into their own house, knowing she was his and his alone.

"Happy birthday," he said, extending the box toward her.

She smiled and wiped her hands on a dish towel.

Nancy, who had been drying the dishes, spoke up. "You're sure gettin' a lot of presents today, Sister."

"Why don't you set it there?" Naomi said, motioning to the table. She finished drying her hands and joined him a few seconds later.

"Sure wasn't expectin' you to give me a gift," she said breathlessly. "What is it?"

He chuckled. "Open the box and take a look for yourself."

She lifted the flaps, and her sharp intake of breath made him wonder if she believed the plant was as pretty as he thought she was. "It's beautiful, Caleb. Danki."

"Sure can't put that gift in your hope chest," Nancy announced.

Naomi's face flamed, and she gave her sister a warning look.

"If you don't have other plans, I was hopin' you'd go for a ride in my sleigh," Caleb said, coming to Naomi's rescue. No doubt some of her other birthday presents had been meant for her hope chest.

Naomi glanced at her father. "Would that be all right with you?"

He nodded. "Jah, sure, as long as you're back in time for our afternoon meal. Fannie's comin' by soon, and she plans to fix us a big pot of sauerkraut and pork to eat around one o'clock."

"I'll have her back in plenty of time," Caleb assured him.

"But shouldn't I be here to help with the cooking?" Naomi asked. She looked kind of flustered, and Caleb wondered if maybe she didn't want to go with him.

Abraham shook his head. "Fannie can call on Nancy if she needs any help."

Naomi shrugged, but Caleb could see by the wrinkles in her forehead that she wasn't too happy. Did she prefer to be here cooking rather than go for a ride in his sleigh? Maybe she wasn't all that anxious to be courted by him.

"If you'd rather not go sleigh ridin', I'll head for home." Caleb held his breath and waited for her answer.

She shook her head and offered him a smile. "A sleigh ride sounds like fun. I'll get my heavy shawl and gloves." She left the room, and Caleb shuffled to the back door to wait for her.

Naomi returned to the kitchen a few minutes later, wrapped in a long black shawl and wearing her dark bonnet and a pair of heavy gloves. "I'm ready to go."

Caleb opened the door and followed her outside. Maybe her problem had more to do with Fannie Miller than it did him. He looked over his shoulder, calling, "We'll be back soon."

When Fannie drove into the Fishers' yard, she spotted Caleb Hoffmeir in an open sleigh. Naomi sat beside him, and as their rigs passed in the driveway, Fannie waved and called, "Hallich Neiyaahr!"

"Happy New Year to you, as well!" Caleb hollered in response.

Fannie grinned. Things were working out real nice for her and Abraham these days. Spring would be here soon, and after their wedding, she'd be living in his house permanently. *Sure hope everything works out equally well for Naomi and the buggy maker. After all this family's been through, there needs to be a time of peace and happiness.*

Fannie pulled her buggy beside the barn and climbed down. Before she had a chance to unhitch the horse, Matthew stepped out of the barn and took charge of things. "I'll put your horse away. That way you can hurry inside out of this cold."

"Danki. That's right nice of you," she said with a smile. "Some woman's gonna be lucky to call you 'husband' someday."

Matthew's face turned pink. Fannie figured it was a result of embarrassment rather than the cold weather. From what she'd been able to tell, he seemed kind of shy around women. Abraham had told her that so far Matthew showed no signs of wanting to pursue a serious relationship with anyone, either.

"I saw Naomi and Caleb heading out in his sleigh," Fannie said, changing the subject. "Looks like the beginning of their courting days."

"It would seem so."

"After all Naomi's gone through, I'm glad to see her finding some happiness."

"She's been through a lot; there's no denying that." Matthew stroked the horse behind his ear. "Uh— Fannie, I want you to know I'm real glad you and Papa are plannin' to get married come spring."

"Thank you for saying so," she said, a feeling of joy bubbling in her soul. "I hope to make your daed feel happy and content. He's been through more in the last couple years than many men face in a whole lifetime."

Matthew nodded. "You're right about that, too." He touched Fannie's arm, and she knew at that moment she'd made a friend. "Papa's changed a lot since he met you, and we're all grateful."

Tears sprang to Fannie's eyes, but she blinked them away. "It's God who gets the thanks, Matthew. He's done a mighty work in Abraham's life, but it's only because the man allowed God's Word to take root in his soul."

"I understand Jacob Weaver has shared a good many scriptures with Papa, too," Matthew said. "The verses and his friendship with Jacob have also been gut, but being in love with you has brought joy back into my daed's life."

"I love Abraham very much, and he's brought a good deal of happiness into my life, as well."

"Glad to hear that."

Fannie turned toward the house. "See you later, Matthew. And don't forget . . . pork and sauerkraut at one o'clock sharp!"

CHAPTER 29

The remainder of winter flew by like flurries of snowflakes, and spring was ushered in with blustery winds and a sprinkling of rain. Naomi had recently been baptized and joined the church. With a sense of peace, she enjoyed each moment, whether she was working at the store, doing chores at home, or having fun with Caleb in his courting buggy. They'd gone ice-skating, taken several leisurely drives, spent time at her house playing games and visiting, and attended a few singings. Tomorrow night, another one would be held, only this singing would be at the Fishers' place. Caleb wouldn't be driving Naomi to or from the young people's event, and Matthew, who was usually shy around women his age, would be there, since Papa had insisted on it.

Naomi couldn't believe her father had agreed to host the singing in their barn. It was the first time he'd ever allowed anything like that. There seemed to be a lot of "firsts" for Naomi's daed these days, and she was pretty sure Fannie Miller was the reason he'd become so agreeable.

As she moved away from her bedroom window, Naomi spotted the letter she'd received from Ginny Meyers that morning. This was the first Naomi had heard from Ginny since she'd returned to Lancaster County three months ago without her English friend.

She plucked the letter off the dresser and read it aloud.

Dear Naomi:

You've probably been wondering why I haven't written before now. To be honest, I was mad at you for leaving the way you did and then compounding it by giving out Carla's phone number to my folks. I'm okay with that now, though. I talked to Mom and Dad last week, and they've finally come to accept my wanting to live out here and be on my own.

Naomi smiled as she reread that part. She was glad things were better between Ginny and her folks. At least they were keeping in touch now.

She drew her attention back to the letter and continued to read.

Since you left Portland, I've been dating Chad Nelson, the guy who manages the fitness center where I work. He's already talking about marriage and says he's hoping we can buy our own fitness center someday. That would be so great. As you know, I've wanted to have my own fitness center for some time.

I want you to know that I harbor no ill feelings toward you. I'd hoped you would make it in the English world, but apparently you're not cut out for it.

All the best,
Ginny

Naomi sighed and flopped onto her bed. It was late, and she should be asleep by now, but she wasn't tired. There were too many thoughts rolling around in her head. Things with Ginny seemed to be settled, but there was still one more item she needed to deal with.

"If only Mama were here," she whispered. "She was so full of wisdom and would surely have some answers for my confusion."

As Naomi rolled over, her gaze came to rest on the black Bible she kept on the nightstand by her bed. "Mama's *Biewel*. Maybe I can find a solution in there."

She reached for the worn, leather book but had no idea where to look for the specific answers she wanted. "Something to make me feel better about Papa marrying again," Naomi murmured. "Jah, that's what I'm needin' the most right now."

Naomi's mother had placed several bookmarks inside the Bible, so she opened to the place where the first one was marked. "Genesis chapter two, verse twenty," she read aloud. " 'And Adam gave names to all cattle, and to the fowl of the air, and to every beast of the field; but for Adam there was not found an help meet for him.' "

Tears slipped out of Naomi's eyes and rolled down her cheeks. She sniffed and wiped them away with the back of her hand. *Oh, Papa, you've been like Adam ever since Mama died. You had plenty to do but have been lonely and needed a help meet.*

Naomi knew Fannie would make a good wife for Papa. She'd proven that already by the way she'd helped out, both here at the house and working at their store. She had taught Nancy how to quilt, given Mary Ann and Samuel the love and attention they needed, become a friend to the older boys, and most of all— she loved Papa and made him happy. Naomi had also taken notice of Fannie's gentle, positive spirit, which she felt sure came from her deep devotion to God. Fannie was much more outgoing than Mama had been, but she had the same qualities in many other ways.

Naomi set the Bible aside and closed her eyes. *Heavenly Father, help me love Fannie the way the rest of my family does. I don't know what my future holds regarding workin' at the store, but help me learn to be content in whatsoever state I shall find myself.* She paused, about to close her prayer, when a vision of Zach popped into her mind. He would be two years old in a few weeks, probably celebrating his birthday with his new family—whoever they were. It was looking more and more like Naomi would never see her little brother again, but as long as she lived, she would not forget him.

And Lord, she continued, *please, protect Zach and let him know how much he's loved, even if it has to be through someone other than his real family. Give him a happy birthday and see that he gets plenty of hugs. Amen.*

As Naomi crawled under the covers, a sense of peace settled over her like a soft blanket. Things would work out in the days ahead. She felt certain of it.

"It's so good to have you home. I've missed you, Mom."

Fannie smiled at Abby and gave her another hug. "It's good to be here, but remember, it's only for a few weeks. I'll be returning to Pennsylvania soon to get ready for my wedding to Abraham."

Abby nodded. "I know, but I'll enjoy the time we do have together."

Fannie glanced around the quilt shop. She'd missed this place and all the activity of customers coming in to look at quilts, pillows, potholders, and wall hangings. Not only that, but one day a week, a group of Amish ladies from their community came here to spend several hours making quilts, which would then be sold. She and Abby had enjoyed many days with the women as they stitched and chatted about the weather and one another's lives.

"I wish you would consider moving to Lancaster County with me," Fannie said. "I think you'd like

Abraham's family, and you could help me in the quilt shop Abraham plans on adding to his store."

Abby shook her head, and her cheeks turned slightly pink. "I have a boyfriend, Mom. If I left, what chance would there be for me and Lester to court?"

"There are many eligible young men in Lancaster, you know."

Abby sank to a chair in front of the quilting rack. "Oh no, Mom. I couldn't think of letting anyone else court me. Lester is special, and I—"

"He's not been comin' over to the house when you're alone, I hope," Fannie said, a feeling of concern welling up in her chest.

"'Course not. With Harold and Lena livin' right next door, I always make sure Lester comes a-callin' at their place, which is where I've been taking my meals since you've been gone."

"That's gut. I wouldn't want anyone thinkin' ill of my daughter."

"You should know I'd never do anything to embarrass you." Abby's dark eyes shimmered with tears.

"I know you wouldn't, sweet girl." Fannie patted her daughter's hand. "However, I've been thinkin' it might be better for all concerned if you moved in with Harold and Lena. They can either rent out my place or close it up 'til you're married."

Abby's forehead wrinkled. "I'd miss the old house if I had to move out."

"It would only be temporary."

"Jah, okay. If Harold and Lena have no objections,

I'll move in with 'em." Abby jumped up. "Now let's talk about your wedding plans, shall we?"

Fannie grinned. "The date's set for May nineteenth. I'm hoping you, Harold, and Lena can all be there."

Abby leaned over and kissed her mother's cheek. "I wouldn't miss it for the world, and I'm sure my big brother and his wife will feel the same."

"You'll like Abraham," Fannie said, pushing her chair back.

Abby smiled. "I've only met him once, when he came here to see about the English couple who had a little boy he thought might be his. He seemed like a nice enough man."

"Abraham and his family have been through a lot the past couple of years." Fannie's throat clogged, and she had to pause in order to gain control of her emotions. Just thinking about the pain Abraham had endured made her feel all choked up.

"From what you've said in your letters, he's come to grips with the loss of his son. Isn't that right?"

Fannie's fingers traveled over the top of a Lone Star quilt. "Don't rightly think he'll ever completely get over losin' Zach, but he is dealin' with it pretty well these days."

Abby touched her mother's arm. "I believe you might have somethin' to do with that, Mom."

"It's the Lord who gets the credit for Abraham's change of heart," Fannie asserted.

Abby grabbed a large cardboard box from under the counter. "Guess we've had ourselves enough of a chitchat. If you want to pick out some quilts to sell in your new shop, we'd better get to work, don't ya think?"

Fannie smiled. "I can sure tell who's in charge of this shop these days."

Abby's cheeks flushed a bright pink. "Sorry, Mom. Didn't mean to sound so bossy."

"It's all right. You're used to bein' on your own now, and that's perfectly understandable." Fannie pulled a Log Cabin quilt out of the stack and placed it inside the box. "Think I'll give this one to Naomi when she and Caleb get married next fall."

Abby's eyebrows shot up. "There's to be another wedding in the Fisher family?"

"It would appear so." Fannie shrugged. "But only time will tell what the future holds."

Caleb felt mighty good about going to the singing. Since the event would be held in the Fishers' barn, he wouldn't be driving Naomi home tonight, but he had every intention of spending time alone with her. In fact, he hoped to get the chance to discuss their future.

He clucked to his horse to get him trotting faster. Wouldn't pay to be late—not when he was planning to spend every minute with the woman he loved.

"Sure hope she feels the same way about me," Caleb said to the gelding. "I've waited so long to court Naomi Fisher, and I don't want us to waste one single moment."

When Caleb pulled into the Fishers' yard, he noticed there were already several buggies lined up beside the barn. He climbed down from his open rig and secured the horse.

"Hey, Caleb, how are you?" Norman called as he stepped around the corner.

"I'm gut. And you?"

"Doin' fine, and I'll be even better once all the girls get here."

Caleb chuckled. "Anyone in particular you're waitin' for?"

Norman shook his head. "Not really. Still lookin' for the right one."

"Jah, well, I wouldn't wait too long if I were you. You ain't gettin' any younger, ya know."

Norman snickered. "Look who's talkin'. If I'm not mistaken, we're not that far apart in age, and you ain't married yet, neither."

Caleb thrust out his chest. "I hope to remedy that soon enough."

"Ha! I'll bet I know who you're on the verge of askin', too."

"Never you mind," Caleb said, shaking his finger at Naomi's brother. He glanced around. "Where is she?"

"Who?"

"Don't play dumb. I'm talkin' about Naomi. Is she in the barn or still up at the house?"

Norman shrugged. "How should I know? I ain't my sister's keeper."

Caleb slapped Norman on the shoulder. "Very

funny." He started to walk away, but Norman stepped in front of him.

"She's in the barn, if you must know. I believe she brought out a jug of lemonade."

"I worked up quite a thirst on the drive over here," Caleb said with a wink. "I think I'll head in there and see about gettin' myself a glass."

"You do that, Caleb." Norman leaned against the side of the barn. "I'm gonna stay out here and watch the rest of the buggies come rollin' in. That way I can check out the competition."

Caleb sauntered off, chuckling to himself.

Just inside the barn door, Caleb bumped into Matthew, who carried a bale of straw. "Need any help?" Caleb asked.

"No, I'm fine. Just haulin' this across the barn so there'll be more room." Matthew's face was kind of red, and Caleb noticed he seemed nervous and out of place. In all the time Caleb had been attending singings, he'd never seen Matthew at one. From what he knew of Naomi's oldest brother, Caleb doubted he was here to choose a girlfriend. Truth be told, Matthew's daed probably asked his son to hang around, since Matthew was a few years older than most of the young people who would be here tonight and could act as chaperone without being too obvious or intrusive.

Caleb spotted Naomi on the other side of the room. She held a glass in one hand as she visited with a couple of women her age. He felt funny about interrupting, but if he didn't say what was on his mind right away, he might lose his nerve.

"Caleb, I'm glad you could make it," Naomi said as he approached her. "Did some of your brothers come to the singing, too?"

He nodded and reached up to wipe the trickle of sweat dripping down his face. "Marvin and Andy said they were comin', but I didn't see any sign of their rigs when I pulled in. Guess that means I beat 'em here."

"You look flushed," Naomi said. "Would you like a glass of cold lemonade?"

"That'd be nice," he said, reaching out to take the glass she offered. "Danki."

Clara and Mabel, who stood next to Naomi, giggled, and she wrinkled her nose at them.

"Want to take a walk before things get started?" he asked, feeling his courage begin to mount. "I'd like to talk awhile, if it's okay with you."

"I'd like that." Naomi set her glass down on the wooden table, said good-bye to the two young women, and headed for the door.

Caleb gulped down a swig of lemonade, placed it on the table, and followed quickly. Once they were out-side, he suggested they go to the creek behind the Fishers' place.

They walked in silence until they reached the water's edge. Taking Naomi's hand, Caleb turned to face her. He moistened his lips. This was going to be more difficult than he'd thought. Things always seemed simpler when rehearsed in one's mind, but when it came down to the actual saying, Caleb felt like his mouth had been glued shut.

"Sure is a nice night," Naomi said. "Looks like we'll have us a hot summer, what with spring bein' so warm and all."

"Yep."

"Hope we have a good turnout tonight."

"Uh-huh."

"I'm glad Matthew agreed to help out. It's good for him to be with young people other than those in his own family."

"Right."

Naomi sighed. "Caleb, you said you wanted to take a walk so we could talk. Only trouble is, I'm doin' all the talkin'."

He let go of her hand and bent over to scoop up a flat rock, which he promptly pitched into the water. "Guess I'm a bit nervous."

"How come? It's not like this is our first date or anything."

"I know, but it's the first time I've ever proposed to a woman."

Naomi's mouth dropped open, and her eyes were wide. "You mean propose marriage?"

He nodded. "If you'll have me, I'd be pleased to make you my wife come November."

"Really?"

"You don't believe me?"

She laughed lightly. "Of course. It's just so sudden.

We've only been courting a few months."

Caleb took both of her hands this time. "You've known for some time how I feel about you, right?"

"Jah."

"I've loved you ever since we were kinner, but until the Monday after Christmas, when your daed said we could court, I never thought I'd have the chance to ask you to marry me."

Naomi's eyes filled with tears. "To tell you the truth, I never thought I'd be asked to marry anyone."

He could hardly believe his ears. Naomi was everything a man could possibly want in a wife. She was beautiful, smart, a hard worker, and ever so sweet. "Well, I'm askin' now, and if you think you could love me even a little bit, it would make me the happiest man in all of Lancaster County."

Naomi smiled, and he thought he could drown in the joy he saw on her face. "Caleb Hoffmeir, I love you, and not just a little bit. I'd be honored to be your wife."

CHAPTER 30

"I don't see why you're making such a fuss over Jimmy's birthday. You bought enough balloons and crepe paper to decorate the whole house." Jim motioned to the pile of decorations Linda had placed on the kitchen table. "He's only turning two and won't even remember this day when he's grown up."

She frowned. "We'll take lots of pictures. He'll have those to look at and know his mommy and daddy cared enough to give him a party."

"Who are you inviting to this shindig?" he asked.

"Just my folks—and maybe my sister and her husband."

"No other kids besides Jimmy will be here?"

She shook her head. "He doesn't really know any children."

Jim groaned. "That's because you shelter him too much, Linda. The boy should be around kids his age."

Linda pulled out a chair and took a seat at the table. "He's too young for preschool, and he has no cousins living nearby, so how can you expect him to have other children to play with?"

He shrugged. "Why don't you enroll in an exercise class at that new fitness center across town? I hear they have a great nursery for kids." Linda opened her mouth, but before she could reply, Jim added, "It would be good for both you and Jimmy."

She scowled. "Are you saying I'm fat and need to exercise in order to lose weight?"

Now where did that come from? Jim rubbed his forehead, glad Jimmy was taking a nap and couldn't hear the shouting that was probably forthcoming.

"Is that what you were insinuating, Jim?" she asked, her voice rising a notch.

Jim took the chair opposite Linda and grabbed a package of blue balloons. "You're not fat, and I wasn't hinting you needed to lose weight."

"What then?"

"I just think you stay cooped up in this house too much. You and Jimmy need to get out more."

"I take him for walks to the park, and we go shopping when I feel up to catching the bus."

"I'm not talking about going for a trek to the park or shopping. You need to socialize more."

"I would if we still lived in Boise. All my friends and family live there."

Jim didn't need reminding. She'd told him often enough that she didn't like western Washington and wished they were still living in the town where they'd both grown up.

"We moved here because of my job," he reminded. "You said back then you were in agreement with me starting my painting business here."

She sighed. "I know, but I thought we'd have two or three children by now and would be so busy raising them that I wouldn't have time to miss my family back home."

"This is your home now, Linda, and you do have Jimmy to raise."

"But he's only one child. I'd like more. Wouldn't you?"

"We aren't able to conceive, remember?"

"I know, but we adopted Jimmy, so why can't we adopt more children?" She pushed her chair back and stood. "I can give our lawyer a call right now and ask him to get the proceedings started."

Jim jumped up, knocking his chair over but catching it before it hit the floor. "That's not a good idea!"

She whirled around. "Why not?"

"We've had Jimmy a couple months shy of a year. He needs more time as an only child."

"Why? Because you were?"

He squinted, feeling his defenses rise. Was she trying to goad him into an argument? "That's not what I meant, Linda, and you know it."

"Isn't it?"

"No. I think we need to allow ourselves and Jimmy the luxury of enjoying one another awhile." He motioned toward the boy's high chair. "When we first learned we couldn't have children, you said you'd be happy with just one child . . . that it would be enough if I agreed to adopt. Well, I got you a baby, so why don't you appreciate it and ease up on me?"

Linda's forehead wrinkled, and she tipped her head in question. "You make it sound as if you grabbed a kid off the street and presented him to me as some kind of peace offering."

Jim swallowed hard. Linda had nearly hit the nail on the head. He had taken their son, and there was no legal adoption involved whatsoever. The adoption papers in the safe were phony. He didn't even know when the boy's real birthday was. The Amish girl selling root beer had said her brother turned one in April, so he'd made sure the birth certificate listed April fifteenth as Jimmy's birth date. He had done everything involving Jimmy out of love for Linda. He wasn't simply trying to appease her.

Jim stepped around the table and took his wife into his arms. "Let's not fight, okay?"

"I didn't start it," she reminded.

"It doesn't matter how it started. We need to set this disagreement behind us and go on from here." Jim had been putting the hammer down on several things concerning Jimmy lately, but he figured he should back off on the issue of the boy's party.

Linda's chin quivered. "And where exactly is *here?*"

He kissed the top of her head. Those golden tresses that had enticed him when they were teenagers were still shiny and inviting. If he let her know how much she was loved, maybe Linda would calm down. "You can have as big a party for Jimmy as you want," he relented, "but what would you think about me inviting a couple of my employees who have little kids? That way Jimmy will have someone to play with at the party."

"Are you saying my family isn't good enough for Jimmy?"

Jim blew out an exasperated breath. "I like your family, and I know your folks are good grandparents, but I wish you'd quit reading things into what I say."

Linda leaned into him. "I'm sorry, Jim. I'm feeling uptight right now."

"Yeah, I know." As much as Jim had come to care for that little boy asleep in his crib upstairs, there were moments like now when he wished he'd never driven onto that Amish farm nearly a year ago.

Abraham leaned the pitchfork against the barn wall and breathed in the scents he had enjoyed since he was a boy. All the while he'd been growing up, Abraham figured he would end up a farmer like his daed. He'd been one for a while—until he married Sarah and she took over her folks' general store after their passing. He couldn't let his wife run the place by herself. There were too many heavy boxes to lift, figures and book-work that never seemed to end, and often more cus-tomers than one person could handle. Besides, when the kinner came along, Sarah had more duties at home than ever before, which meant she sometimes couldn't go to the store at all. Abraham had exchanged his pitchfork for a broom, and instead of riding an old hay baler pulled by a team of horses, he'd become co-owner of his wife's family business. At that time he'd changed the name from Raber's to Fisher's General Store.

"No point in thinkin' about the past or wishing for things that can never be," Abraham murmured as he settled himself on a bale of straw. At the end of a long day, it was relaxing to come out to the barn and muck out the horses' stalls or feed them some hay. It wasn't the same as being out in the fields with his boys, but at least he could enjoy hearing the horses nicker, smell the aroma of hay bales stacked along one wall, and imagine he was a farmer again.

Speckles, Naomi's cat, jumped into his lap and began to purr.

"Matthew, Norman, and Jake are the farmers now—carryin' on a Fisher tradition that began many years ago when my ancestors first settled in Lancaster County," Abraham said, stroking the furry creature's head.

Speckles responded with more purring and a few licks to Abraham's hand with his wet, sandpapery tongue.

"Wonder if Samuel will follow in his brothers' footsteps and take to the plow, as well," he continued, as though the cat were listening to his every word. "The boy already helps in the fields whenever he's not in school. Seems to like it well enough, and might could be he'll also become a farmer."

The cat's only response was a faint *meow*.

"And what about Zach? If he were still livin' here, would he have grown up with a love for the fields? Or would my youngest boy have developed other interests, as so many of the young people in our area are now doin'?" Abraham closed his eyes as he scratched Speckles behind one ear. "I'll never know 'cause Zach won't be growin' up on this farm. His birthday's tomorrow, and he'll be turnin' two. Only he won't be celebrating with his real family, if at all."

Abraham's eyes snapped open. Did the folks who took Zach even know how old he was? Would they make up a birth date for the boy and celebrate it then?

A pang of regret stabbed Abraham's heart, as sharp as any pitchfork piercing a bale of hay. In just a few weeks, he would be marrying Fannie Miller, and she made him happier than he ever dreamed possible. However, there would always be a part of him that would remain empty and void—the chunk of his heart that had been ripped away when Zach was kidnapped.

Fannie slipped into the dark blue dress she had recently made. She could hardly believe today was actually here. Her marriage to Abraham Fisher would take place in a few hours, and she was as nervous as she had been when she married Ezra twenty-three years ago.

Edna had wanted to host the wedding, but her house was too small, even though only family and a few close friends had been invited. So Abraham agreed to have it at his place, which had a lot more room.

"Mom, you're shaking," Abby noted as she helped her mother with her cape and apron. "You're not havin' second thoughts about marrying Abraham, are you?"

Fannie turned away from the mirror to face Abby. "Of course not. I love that man dearly and can't wait to become his wife."

"Then why so nervous?"

Fannie twisted her hands together. "Guess I'm feelin' prewedding jitters like most brides do." Her vision clouded as tears gathered in her eyes. "I hope I can make him happy—and his family, too."

Abby hugged her mother. "You've been a wonderful mamm to me and Harold, and I know you'll do fine with Abraham's kinner, as well. And as far as makin' him happy . . . I've seen the look on that man's face whenever the two of you are together. I'd say he loves my mamm beyond measure."

Fannie dabbed at the corners of her eyes and smiled. "I'm glad you could be here to witness my special day. Havin' you, Harold, and Lena at the wedding will make it even more wunderbaar."

Abby sniffed and swiped at the tears running down her cheeks. "I love you so much, Mom, and it makes me glad to see you this happy."

"You don't think I'm being untrue to your daed by marrying again?"

"Definitely not. I know you'll always love Dad, but I think there's more than enough room in your heart to love Abraham, too."

Fannie nodded. "How'd you get so smart, anyway?"

Abby grinned and took hold of her mother's hand. "Guess it runs in the family, 'cause you're one of the smartest people I know."

Fannie clicked her tongue. "Go on with ya now."

"No, I mean it, Mom. You're the person who taught me how to quilt and run the shop so efficiently, and you instilled the love of God in Harold and me from the time we were little. I'd call that real smart."

"Someday you'll marry and do the same with your own children," Fannie said as she set her head covering in place.

Abby's cheeks turned pink, and her eyes glistened. "I hope it's Lester I marry, for I surely do care for him, Mom."

This time it was Fannie who initiated the hug. "God will show you if Lester's the one He wants you to wed. Pray about it, okay?"

"I will. You can be sure of that." Abby pulled back and studied her mother intently. "I'd say the bride's ready to meet her groom. Shall we go see if the others are all set?"

Fannie nodded. "If I know Edna, she's probably got the horse hitched to the buggy and is sittin' in the backseat, ready and waiting." She chuckled. "That fun-lovin' cousin of mine enjoys any kind of party. Truth be told, she's probably got all sorts of tricks up her sleeve to give me and Abraham a good laugh during our reception today."

Abby slipped her hand through the crook of her mother's arm. "Then we'd best not keep Cousin Edna waiting—or your groom, either."

Naomi stood in the living room, appraising each nook and cranny to be sure there wasn't a speck of dust. She'd been up since early this morning and had worked until late last night, making certain the house was clean and everything was ready for Papa and Fannie's big day.

Fannie and her daughter, Abby; her daughter-in-law, Lena; and her cousin, Edna had come over yesterday to help cook and clean. The women dusted, washed windows, scrubbed floors, and made huge pots of chicken corn soup, Papa's favorite. At the reception dinner, they would also serve potato cakes, cucumber salad, deviled eggs, and the spiced layer cake Edna had promised to bake. The meal wouldn't be nearly as elaborate as a first-time wedding, but the food would be tasty and filling, nonetheless.

Naomi thought about how Fannie's daughter had pitched right in and worked hard all day with a smile on her face. Naomi had taken a liking to Abby when they'd first met, and even though Abby was two years younger than she was, Naomi could tell the woman was mature and responsible. Abby wasn't quite nineteen, yet she had taken on the task of running her mother's quilt shop in Ohio, and according to Fannie, she'd done well with it, too. Now that Fannie was marrying Naomi's daed and would be staying in Lancaster County, where she'd be running the quilt shop Papa added to his store, Abby planned to remain in Berlin and keep that shop open.

Naomi shook her head. "As much as I love workin' at the store, I doubt I could run the place alone."

"You talkin' to me or yourself?"

Naomi whirled around. Her father stood by the bookcase with a huge smile on his face. "Papa, you scared me half to death. I didn't hear you come into the room."

He chuckled. "No, I expect you didn't or ya wouldn't have been chattering out loud."

A warm flush of heat spread across Naomi's cheeks. "You got me there."

"What makes you think you'll have to run the store by yourself?" Papa asked.

"I was thinkin' about how Abby's taken over her mamm's quilt shop in Ohio and marveling at how she's doin' so well with it."

"Jah, she seems like a capable young woman. A lot like her mother, I expect."

Naomi took a seat on one of the wooden benches that had been set up in the room. "You think everything looks okay, Papa? Is the place clean enough for this special day?"

He nodded and sat down beside her. "Looks gut to me, and I thank you for workin' so hard to make it just right."

She reached for his hand, noting the warmth and strength of it. "I'm so glad you and Fannie found each other, and I know you're gonna be real happy in the days ahead."

He sat there for several seconds as though contemplating something. Then he squeezed her hand and said in a shaky voice, "I'm lucky to have a daughter like you. You've done your best to keep the deathbed promise you made to your mamm, but now that commitment's been fulfilled. It's time for you to find happiness with Caleb, and I know when you two are married in the fall, you'll feel every bit as blessed and happy as me and Fannie."

Naomi swallowed around the lump lodged in her throat. "Oh, Papa, that's ever so nice of you to say."

He let go of her hand and slipped his arm around her back. "As the old saying goes, 'We grow too soon old and too late smart.' I'm sorry it took me so long to come to my senses."

She sniffed back the tears threatening to spill over. "That goes double for me."

Norman stepped into the room and planted his hands on his hips. "There you are, Naomi. I thought you'd be out in the kitchen fixin' breakfast. I'm hungry as a horse."

Papa stood. "Then why don't you march right out there and fix yourself somethin' to eat? Naomi ain't the slave around here, ya know."

Norman blinked, and Naomi stifled a giggle. In all her twenty-one years, she'd never heard Papa come to her defense thataway. She stood and headed for the kitchen. "I'll have breakfast on the table in thirty minutes, but I could use some help, if you're so inclined," she said with a smile in her brother's direction.

Norman coughed and sputtered, but she heard his footsteps right behind her. This day was sure beginning on a good note.

The wedding was more special than any Naomi had ever attended. Papa looked so handsome in his dressy black suit, and Fannie was radiant, although it wasn't just her crisp new dress that made her so attractive. It was her rosy cheeks, a smile that could melt a frosty snowman, and her twinkling hazel-colored eyes that made Fannie glow like a moonbeam.

As Papa and Fannie stood in front of Bishop Swartley repeating their vows, it was all Naomi could do to keep from sobbing out loud. The emotion with which her daed said, "Jah, I do," after the bishop asked, "Can you confess, brother, that you accept this our sister as your wife, and that you will not leave her until death separates you?" was enough to make anyone cry. And when Fannie replied, "Jah," to the similar question directed at her, Naomi knew without reservation her new stepmother would love and cherish Papa for all the days God gave them together.

At the end of Bishop Swartley's blessing, which closed with "This all in and through Jesus Christ. Amen," Papa, Fannie, and the bishop bowed their knees.

The bishop's final words were "Go forth in the name of the Lord God. You are now man and wife."

Papa and Fannie returned to their seats, grinning like children and radiating a blissful glow that fairly lit up the living room.

As several of the ordained ministers from their community gave a word of testimony, Naomi's gaze traveled across the room to seek out Caleb. When he glanced her way and gave her a quick wink, she felt her face flood with a penetrating heat. In six more months, the two of them would stand before Bishop Swartley, repeat their vows, and promise their love forever. She could hardly wait.

CHAPTER 31

It was another warm summer evening, and Naomi sat in the rocking chair on the front porch with a basket of mending in her lap. She and the girls had been so busy with canning all week that there hadn't been time for much else. Fannie had helped, too, when she wasn't working in her new quilt shop at the store.

Naomi glanced at her stepmother, who sat on the porch swing with her head leaning on Papa's shoulder. They looked as happy and content as a couple of kittens sharing a bowl of fresh milk.

Matthew, Norman, and Jake had headed for bed a few minutes ago, saying they were exhausted after another long day in the fields. Nancy, Mary Ann, and Samuel were frolicking in the yard, waiting for the first set of fireflies to make their appearance. Samuel had punched holes in the lid of an empty jar, ready to capture a few shimmering bugs.

"There's one!" Nancy shouted. "Get it, Samuel, before it flies away!"

Samuel took off across the yard, running this way and that, chasing the glowing insects, and missing every time he came close to one.

Papa kissed Fannie on the cheek. "Hold my spot; I'll be back soon." He ambled down the steps and into the yard. "Hand me that jar, Samuel, and I'll show ya how it's done."

"It ain't easy, Papa. Them bugs don't wanna be caught."

"*Humph!* I'll have you know, I was an expert at catchin' lightning bugs when I was a boy." Papa grabbed the jar, squatted down on the lawn, and waited. A few seconds later, several fireflies rose from the grass. As quick as a wink, Papa's hand swooped out and snatched a couple. When he dropped them into the jar, the children all cheered.

Naomi took another stitch on the sock she was darning, as she savored the moment of peace and happiness. Since Papa married Fannie, he'd been so relaxed and easygoing. Love and marriage were obviously good for him. Even the kinner seemed happier these days. Everyone in the family had taken to Fannie, whose gentle, sweet spirit wove its way straight into their hearts—even Naomi's.

The *clip-clop* of horse's hooves on the gravel drove Naomi's thoughts aside. She looked up and smiled when she saw Caleb step down from his open buggy.

He hopped onto the porch and handed her a loaf of gingerbread wrapped in plastic. "Mom baked today and had extra. I thought you might like this."

"Danki. It was nice of you to bring it by."

"I didn't come just to give you the bread."

"No?"

He shook his head. "I was hopin' to take you for a buggy ride."

"Now?"

Caleb leaned against the porch railing. "I know it's gettin' dark, but I'll turn my flashers on, and I'll stick to the back roads where there isn't much traffic."

"I'm not concerned about that." Naomi stared into the yard, where Papa and the children were still cavorting with the fireflies. "I've got to see about gettin' the little ones to bed soon."

"That's my responsibility now," Fannie said. "You go along with Caleb and have a gut time."

Naomi felt a twinge of resentment toward her stepmother. It used to be her job to tuck the younger siblings in, but now Fannie often did it. Realizing how foolish she was, Naomi grabbed hold of her thoughts and gave them a good shake. *I should be ashamed of myself. It's been nice to have Fannie take some of the responsibilities I used to resent off my shoulders. Besides, she's only trying to be nice.*

Naomi stood, holding the mending basket in her hands. "I guess I could go, but I'll have to bring this along."

Caleb's eyebrows lifted. "On our date?"

"If I don't, I'll never get caught up."

Fannie left the swing and moved beside Naomi. "I've never heard of takin' work along on a date. Now you just leave that mending with me, and I'll have it done by the time you get home."

Naomi gave Fannie an impulsive hug. "Papa's not the only one lucky to have you."

"Sure is a nice night," Caleb commented as he guided his horse onto the main road. "Not nearly as hot as it was today." He glanced at Naomi and grinned.

"The last few days have been real scorchers," she agreed.

"How do you stay cool enough to work at the store?"

"Papa recently bought one of those battery-operated fans. It keeps the air moving pretty good."

"Might have to look into gettin' one of those," Caleb remarked. "It can get real hot inside my buggy shop."

"How's things going with your business?" she asked. "Are you keeping plenty busy these days?"

He reached for her hand. "I'm makin' a good enough living to support a wife and a family; that much I know."

She smiled and squeezed his fingers.

"Sure can't wait 'til November and our wedding."

"Me neither."

They rode in silence for a time, but Caleb was content to enjoy the camaraderie of being with the woman he loved without any conversation. It was relaxing to listen to the steady *clip-clop* of the horse's hooves against the pavement and know that Naomi sat right beside him.

When the sky grew dark, Caleb decided it was time to head back to the Fishers' place. It wouldn't be smart to upset the storekeeper by keeping his daughter out too late. Caleb figured he was in pretty good with

Naomi's daed right now, and he aimed to keep it that way.

He'd no more than turned the buggy around when he heard a snap, followed by a thud. The buggy tilted to the right, and Caleb pulled sharply on the reins.

"What happened?" He could hear the note of concern in Naomi's voice.

"I think one of the back wheels fell off. I'd better have a look-see." Caleb jumped down and went around to survey the situation. A few minutes later, he returned to the buggy.

"It's busted real bad," he said with an exasperated sigh. "I've been so busy fixin' other people's buggies, I've neglected to keep my own up to snuff."

"Can it be repaired? Do you have your tools with you?"

Caleb thought about the day he'd met Fannie on the road to Paradise and how he'd put her buggy wheel back on with no problem at all. That was different, though. The wheel had only fallen off, not broken in two places like his had. "Tools won't help. It'll have to be replaced with a new wheel."

In the moonlight, he could see Naomi's eyes were wide. "What are we gonna do? We have no phone to call for help."

Caleb reached under his straw hat and scratched the side of his head. "Never thought I'd hear myself say such a thing, but at this moment, I wish I had one of those fancy cell phones so many of the young people carry with them these days. If I did, we'd be able to call someone to come get us." He skirted around the buggy to Naomi's side. "You think you can ride bareback?"

She tipped her head. "We're gonna ride double on your horse?"

"We could walk, but it would take much longer, and that would be pretty silly seeing as how we have Ben here to carry us back to your place."

"Will he be able to hold both our weight?" she questioned.

"He pulled my buggy with both of us in it, didn't he?"

"Jah, but that's him *pulling* our weight, not carrying it all on his back."

Caleb chuckled and helped Naomi out of the buggy. He unhitched Ben, gave her a boost onto the back of the animal, and climbed up behind her. Grabbing the reins, Caleb hollered, "Get up now, boy!"

He could feel the weight of Naomi as she leaned against his chest, and he breathed in the scent of her hair. It smelled like strawberries ripening in the sun. *Sure wish I could remove Naomi's head covering. I'd give most anything to let her hair down and run my fingers through those silky tresses.*

"This is kinda fun," she murmured.

"You think so?"

"Jah. A real adventure."

Caleb smiled. At least she wasn't mad at him for ending their date with a jostling ride on the back of his horse.

It was nearly an hour later when Caleb and Naomi plodded into the Fishers' yard. Abraham sat in the rocking chair on the front porch, but no one else was in sight.

"Sure hope I'm not in trouble with your daed," Caleb mumbled as he jumped down and helped Naomi to the ground.

As soon as her feet touched the gravel, Naomi's dad bounded off the porch. "Where have you two been so long, and what happened to your buggy, Caleb?"

Caleb quickly explained about the broken wheel and apologized for keeping Naomi out so late.

Abraham's bushy eyebrows drew together, but then he smiled. "Seems to me a buggy maker oughta take better care of his own vehicle. A broken wheel—well, I never!"

"Papa, I'm sure Caleb didn't know there was anything wrong with his wheel," Naomi said.

"Don't look so worried, Daughter. I was only kidding." Abraham sauntered off toward the house, chuckling all the way.

A sense of relief flooded Caleb's soul. The cranky old storekeeper surely had changed. He turned to Naomi. "I hear tell my mamm's plannin' a quilting bee at our house tomorrow. Are you gonna be there?"

She nodded. "Both Fannie and I have been invited, and Papa plans to take Mary Ann and Nancy to the store with him, so we'll be free to go."

Caleb smiled. "Maybe you can sneak away for a bit and come out to the buggy shop to say hello."

"I'll surely try."

Naomi fidgeted in her chair and glanced around Millie Hoffmeir's dining room table. She wasn't used to sewing for hours on end, the way she and the other twelve ladies had been doing since nine o'clock this morning. Truth be told, she'd much rather be working at the store than sitting inside a stuffy room with a bunch of chattering women. The only good thing about today was the hope she might get to spend a few minutes alone with Caleb. If she could figure out some reason to go to his shop, that is.

Fannie had seemed in high spirits all morning, but then quilting was a thing she enjoyed and did very well. She scurried about with a smile on her face, handing scissors, thread, and stick pins to anyone with a need.

"Won't be long now 'til your wedding," Jacob Weaver's wife, Lydia, said. She nudged Naomi gently in the ribs and grinned.

Naomi nodded but kept her concentration on the piece of material she was stitching.

"I'm hopin' Naomi and Caleb will bless us with many kinner," Millie piped up.

Naomi's cheeks warmed. She wished someone would change the subject to something other than her wedding or how many children she might someday have.

"Naomi's had lots of experience takin' care of little ones," Fannie chimed in from across the room. "I'm sure she'll make a real gut mamm."

"While Naomi and Caleb are waitin' for their own place to be built, I'll have the pleasure of her company right here in this house." Millie glanced at Naomi and sighed. "Lettie and Irma, my two youngest girls, can be quite a handful at times, and I'm not gettin' any younger. Maybe you can help keep them in line."

"I'll do whatever I can." Naomi glanced out the window and spotted Caleb and Andy maneuvering a broken buggy in the direction of his shop. She wondered if the Hoffmeir men would be invited to join the women for lunch or if Millie planned to fix something to take out to the buggy shop, where Caleb, Andy, and Marvin worked. If so, maybe she would volunteer to carry it out. That would be the excuse Naomi needed to see Caleb. *When it's time to stop for lunch, I'll ask Millie,* she decided.

Caleb eyed the clouds creeping in from the west. It was plenty hot today, and they could use a good rain to soak the parched ground. He leaned his full weight against the back of Mose Kauffman's mangled buggy. Andy was up front, pulling and guiding the rig into the shop. Too bad Marvin had quit helping awhile ago, but Pop showed up and announced that he needed an extra pair of hands to stack hay in the barn, so Marvin volunteered.

A couple more steps and the buggy rolled between the double doors of his shop. Caleb drew in a deep breath and stood back to eye the buggy. "Sure is a mess!" he said, shaking his head.

"Yep," Andy agreed. "Old Mose can count himself lucky he escaped that accident with only a few bumps and bruises."

Caleb nodded. Many times when a buggy was hit by a car, the driver wasn't so fortunate. Just the other day an Amish man had been killed when a truck on Route 30 bumped his rig.

"This is gonna take a powerful lot of work," Caleb mumbled. "I think Mose would be better off to let us make him a new buggy."

"You know how stubborn that man can be," Andy reminded.

"Jah, kinda the way Abraham Fisher used to be."

"Speaking of the storekeeper . . . isn't Naomi supposed to be here today? Mom said she'd invited her and Fannie to the quilting bee."

Caleb grabbed a wrench off the pegboard where some of his tools were kept. "Yep, that's what I understand."

Andy snickered. "I'm surprised you haven't come up with some excuse to go inside and see your girl-friend."

Caleb shrugged. "I've been thinkin' on it."

"Figured as much."

"Maybe I'll go up to the house at noon, but in the meantime, we've got plenty to do. So let's get busy."

Andy wrinkled his nose. "Whatever you say, boss."

Naomi glanced out the window again. Caleb and

Andy had disappeared into his shop, along with the broken buggy they'd been pushing. *Sure wish I could step outside for a breath of fresh air.*

"Naomi, would you mind helping me in the kitchen?" Millie's question drove Naomi's musings to the back of her mind.

"Sure, I'd be happy to." Naomi followed Caleb's mother into the next room. "Will the menfolk be comin' inside to eat lunch today?"

Millie opened the refrigerator and withdrew a platter of sliced ham. "Don't think they'd feel comfortable in the presence of so many women. I thought maybe I'd take something out to the shop for Caleb and Andy, and one of them can haul lunch to the rest of the men workin' in the barn."

Naomi moistened her lips with the tip of her tongue. "I'd be willing to take their meal out. That is, if you want me to."

"That'd be much appreciated." Millie smiled. "I'm sure Caleb would be glad to see you."

Fifteen minutes later, Naomi stood in front of the buggy shop with two baskets of food. She set one on the stoop and rapped on the door. When no one answered, she decided the men were probably busy or didn't hear her knock, so she entered the building unannounced.

The front part of the shop, where Caleb did his paperwork, was empty, but she could hear voices coming from the back room.

"Hand me that screwdriver, would ya, Andy?" She

recognized Caleb's voice, and her heart skipped a beat. Hearing her intended talk made her all the more eager to see him. She set the baskets on the wooden desk and started across the room.

Suddenly, there was a crash, followed by a muffled cry.

"Oh, no! Caleb!" Andy shouted.

With her heart pounding so hard it echoed in her ears, Naomi rushed into the next room. She'd barely stepped through the door when she bumped into Caleb's younger brother. His face was white as a sheet of blank paper, and Naomi knew something horrible had happened.

"What's wrong, Andy?"

"We were tryin' to get the wheel off Mose's buggy, and the whole thing collapsed." Andy's chin quivered. "I've gotta get help quick. Caleb's pinned underneath."

CHAPTER 32

Naomi stood on the Hoffmeirs' front porch, holding the book she'd brought for Caleb. Ever since he came home from the hospital, he had refused to see her. Mose Kauffman's mangled buggy could have cost Caleb his life, but he'd escaped with a concussion, several broken ribs, and a hand that had been badly crushed under the weight of the buggy axle. The doctors performed surgery, but Millie Hoffmeir told Naomi that Caleb would never again be able to use his left hand for repairing buggies. He wouldn't have enough strength, and two fingers were severely damaged. It looked as though Caleb would need to give up the buggy shop and learn a new trade, unless he wanted to oversee his brothers, who might be willing to take over the business.

Naomi drew in a deep breath and knocked on the door. She hoped she could see Caleb today. It wasn't good, him shutting himself away in his room like that, refusing to see her or even talk about the horrible accident.

Life was full of disappointments; Naomi knew that firsthand. But you didn't give up or shut your loved ones out when you needed them most.

Caleb's nine-year-old sister, Irma, answered the door. "Hello, Naomi. How are you?"

"Fine. I came to see Caleb."

Irma shook her head, her blue eyes looking ever so serious. "He don't wanna see anyone. He's only allowed our mamm and daed into his room."

Tears stung the back of Naomi's eyes, and she blinked a couple of times. "Is he feeling any better?"

Irma shrugged. "Don't rightly know."

Naomi transferred the book from one hand to the other. "This is for Caleb. Would you see that he gets it? It's a fiction novel set in the Old West. I thought he might enjoy reading it."

Irma took the book, and Naomi turned to go.

"Wait up, would you?"

Naomi recognized Caleb's mother's voice, and she spun around. "How's Caleb doing? Is he feeling any better than he was the last time I dropped by?"

There were dark circles under Millie's pale blue eyes, and her ash-blond hair seemed to have developed a few more gray strands than Naomi remembered. "Caleb's concussion is better, and his ribs will heal in time, but his hand will never be the same." Millie sighed. "I fear my boy's heart is crushed as badly as those wounded fingers that will no longer hold the tools of his trade."

Naomi stared at the wooden boards beneath her feet, unable to voice her emotions. If only Caleb would see her, maybe she could say something that would help him feel better or at least offer a ray of hope. His hand might be crippled, and he probably would have to give up fixing buggies, but one thing hadn't changed. Naomi still loved Caleb and looked forward to their wedding, only a few months away.

"Won't ya come in?" Millie prompted. "I took a shoofly pie from the oven a short time ago, and I could fix us a cup of hot tea."

Naomi pondered the invitation. Shoofly pie was a favorite of hers, and it would be nice to visit with Caleb's mother awhile. Maybe she could learn more about his condition and why he refused to see her whenever she dropped by. She nodded and forced a smile. "Jah, that sounds gut."

"Have a seat, and I'll get the teapot," Millie said

when they stepped into the kitchen. "Would ya like cream or sugar?"

"I drink mine black, danki."

Millie scurried about the kitchen, and with Irma's help, soon they each had a cup of hot tea and a plate full of pie. Irma was about to take a seat in the chair beside Naomi, when her mother waved her away. "Why don't ya cut your sister a hunk of pie and take it to her?"

Irma's forehead wrinkled. "Lettie's outside playing. She probably don't want to stop for a snack."

Millie wagged her finger. "Don't be sassin' me now. Get some pie for both of you and head on out."

Irma did as she was told, but Naomi could see by the set of the young girl's jaw that she was none too happy about being forced to leave the kitchen. If Irma was anything like Nancy, she probably figured the conversation between the women at the table would be more interesting than entertaining her younger sister.

As soon as Irma left the room, Millie leaned forward and looked intently at Naomi. "I'm worried about Caleb, and I think it's important for the two of you to talk."

Naomi nodded. "I agree, but how's that ever gonna happen if he refuses to see me?"

Millie pushed her chair back and stood. "I'll go upstairs and tell him to come down to the kitchen and have a hunk of pie. He doesn't need to know there's someone waitin' to see him."

"He might not like it when he realizes I'm here."

Millie shrugged. "Maybe so, maybe not. The point is, he's put off seeing you long enough."

When Caleb's mother left the room, Naomi took a long drink from her cup. She hoped the herbal tea would help steady her nerves.

Caleb sat on the edge of his bed, staring at his bandaged hand. He clenched his teeth and struggled with the desire to holler at someone for the injustice that had been done to him. It wasn't fair. Why had the Lord allowed him to make such wonderful plans for the future, only to dash them away?

He thought about a verse of scripture the bishop had quoted from Isaiah chapter forty-nine, verse four during the last church service he'd attended. *"Then I said, I have laboured in vain, I have spent my strength for nought, and in vain: yet surely my judgment is with the Lord, and my work with my God."*

Caleb groaned. *I have labored in vain for several years while I tried to build up my buggy business so I could marry and start a family. I used all my strength, and it was for nothing. One little mistake under Mose's buggy cost me everything I loved so much.* A tear slipped out of Caleb's eye and rolled down his cheek. He wiped it away with his good hand, feeling angry with himself for giving in to his grief. All these months he'd waited for permission to court Naomi. They'd been on the brink of marriage, and now this!

A knock on his bedroom door drove Caleb's

thoughts aside. "Who's there?"

"It's your mamm."

"Come in."

Mom opened the door and peeked in at him. "I made shoofly pie. How about comin' down to the kitchen and havin' a piece?"

He shook his head. "No thanks. I ain't hungry."

"Won't you do it for me?" she pleaded. "I'm sure you won't be disappointed."

Caleb blew out his breath and stood. He winced as pain shot through his side, but he tried not to show it.

"You okay?" Mom asked with obvious concern. "You look a mite pale."

He shook his head. "I'm fine. Let's go to the kitchen."

Caleb followed his mother and took the stairs carefully, holding onto the railing with his good hand. When he entered the kitchen a short time later, he halted inside the door. *Naomi.* What was she doing here?

She smiled, and it made his heart clench. "Hello, Caleb. It's good to see you."

Caleb's gaze darted to his mother, who stood off to one side with her arms folded. "Well, I think I'll head outside and check on the girls. You two have a nice visit, ya hear?"

The back door clicked behind Mom, and Caleb fought the desire to flee to his room. He didn't, though. Instead, he marched across the kitchen and took a seat at the table. *Might as well get this over with, 'cause if I don't, Naomi will probably keep coming around.*

"I'm sorry about your accident with Mose's buggy," she said. "I wanted to tell you sooner, but everything happened so fast the day it occurred, and after that, I was always told you weren't up to company."

Caleb just sat there, staring at the shoofly pie in front of him.

"How are you feeling?" Naomi prompted. "Are ya in much pain?"

He forced himself to look directly at her. He could see the questions on her face, the look of compassion in her eyes. He didn't want Naomi's pity or to have to answer any questions. He just wanted to be left alone, to suffer his grief in silence.

She tipped her head. "Caleb? Why aren't you sayin' anything?"

He shrugged. "There ain't much to say."

"I asked if you're in pain. You could start by answering that question."

He lifted his bandaged hand. "This will never work right again, did ya know that?"

She nodded, and tears welled up in her eyes.

"I can't make or repair buggies anymore."

"Jah, I heard."

He cleared his throat. "You know what that means, don't ya?"

"I—I guess it means you'll have to learn a new trade."

"There is no trade for this cripple, Naomi." Caleb

slowly shook his head. "And since I can't do the work I've been doin', I won't be able to support a family."

"Oh, Caleb, you can't mean that. Surely one of your brothers will keep the buggy business going. Maybe you could do some light chores and keep charge of the books."

"Makin' and repairin' buggies is all I've ever wanted." He grunted. "Do you really think I could sit around doin' nothing while my two brothers took over the business I've worked so hard to build up?"

She opened her mouth to say something, but he cut her off. "I don't see how we can get married now, Naomi."

"Please, don't say such a thing. I love you, Caleb, and I'm sure we can work something out." Naomi reached out to touch his uninjured hand, but he pulled it away and stood.

"If I can't support a wife with honest work, I won't have a wife at all. It must not be God's will for us to be together, or He wouldn't have allowed the accident to happen." He turned toward the door.

"Caleb, wait! Can't we talk about this some more?"

"There's nothin' to be said. You'd better find someone else."

"I don't want anyone but you," Naomi said tearfully.

It almost broke Caleb's heart to know she was crying, but he couldn't back down now. "There will be no wedding for us." He nearly choked on his final words. No matter how much Caleb's heart ached to have Naomi as his wife, he would not take on that responsibility when he couldn't provide adequately for her. As he stumbled out of the room, the echo of the door slamming shut reminded Caleb that a chapter of his life had been closed for good.

Fannie stood at the kitchen stove, stirring a pot of bean soup. Today, things had been busier than usual at the store, and she was exhausted. Since Naomi left early to go over to the Hoffmeirs', and Mary Ann, Nancy, and Samuel were back in school, she and Abraham had been on their own all afternoon.

She added a dash of salt to the soup. *Sure hope Naomi made out okay with Caleb. I pray he agreed to see her this time.* She sighed. *That girl's been through enough, and she shouldn't have to hurt anymore.*

Fannie turned when she heard the back door open and click shut. Mary Ann and Nancy rushed into the room, their faces aglow.

"Guess what, Mama Fannie?" Mary Ann said breathlessly.

Fannie smiled. She liked how easily Abraham's youngest children had taken to her. "What's got you two lookin' so excited this evening?"

"There's a new batch of kittens in the barn," Nancy announced before Mary Ann could open her mouth.

"How many are there?" Fannie questioned.

Mary Ann held up five fingers.

"They're all white this time. Not a dark one in sight," Nancy said.

"Is that so?" Fannie got a kick out of the girls' exuberance. She'd always liked animals and could remember her own excitement over the birth of new arrivals on the farm when she was a young girl.

"When Papa comes in from feedin' the horses, I'm gonna ask if I can keep one of those cute little *busslin,*" Nancy added. "Naomi has her own cat, so I think it's only fair I should have one, too."

Fannie chuckled. "We'll have to wait and see what your daed has to say about that. In the meantime, I'd like you girls to run upstairs and wash your dirty hands. I'll be needin' help with supper soon."

"What are we havin'?" Mary Ann asked.

"*Buhnesupp*—one of your daed's favorites."

Mary Ann wrinkled her nose. "Bean soup? I'd much rather have chicken noodle."

Nancy grabbed her younger sister's hand. "Aw, quit your gripin' and come with me."

The girls' footsteps resounded on the stairs as Fannie gave the soup a couple more stirs. When she heard a horse and buggy come prancing into the yard, she glanced out the window and saw it was Naomi. She'd no more than climbed down from the buggy, when Abraham stepped out of the barn and unhitched the horse. He led him away, and Naomi headed for the house, shoulders drooping and head down.

Fannie moaned. *It doesn't look like things went well for my stepdaughter this afternoon.*

A few minutes later, Naomi entered the kitchen through the back door. She hung her black bonnet on a wall peg and without a word went to the sink to wash her hands.

"You okay?" Fannie asked.

Naomi shook her head but made no verbal reply.

"Did you get to see Caleb this time?"

Naomi's shoulders trembled as she nodded.

Fannie turned down the gas burner and rushed to her stepdaughter's side. "What's wrong? What happened that's got you so upset?"

When Naomi reached for a hand towel, Fannie noticed how red the young woman's eyes were. She'd been crying—probably all the way home, from the looks of it. "Caleb called off the wedding," she said with a catch in her voice. "He doesn't want to marry me anymore."

"Come over to the table and have a seat," Fannie suggested. "Then you can tell me what happened, if you like."

Naomi shuffled across the room as though she was in a daze and sank into a chair. Fannie took the seat beside her, placing one hand on Naomi's shoulder.

"The doctors told Caleb his left hand will never be the same, and it means he can no longer work on buggies." Naomi sniffed and blinked a couple of times. "He said if he can't make buggies, he won't be able to support a wife, so there will be no wedding for us in two months."

Fannie's heart went out to Naomi. She looked so downcast and discouraged. If there was only something Fannie could say or do to make things better.

"Caleb thinks it must not be the Lord's will for us to be together, or else God wouldn't have allowed the accident to happen."

Heavenly Father, give me the right words, Fannie prayed. *Show me how to help Naomi through this ordeal.* She gently squeezed Naomi's shoulder. "I know things look bleak right now, but God has a plan for your life, and you need to wait and see what it is."

A muffled sob erupted from Naomi's throat. "I think maybe God's still punishing me for leavin' Zach on the picnic table last summer."

"No, no, you mustn't think that way," Fannie was quick to say. "You didn't do it on purpose. God knows that, Naomi."

Tears rolled down Naomi's cheeks. "I—I don't believe I can take much more."

Fannie reached out to wipe away the tears. "Sweet girl, the Bible says God won't give us more than we can handle. And Isaiah chapter twenty-six, verse four, says, 'Trust ye in the Lord for ever: for in the Lord Jehovah is everlasting strength.'"

Naomi pushed her chair back and stood. "I'm goin' upstairs awhile. Is that okay?"

"Jah, sure. Take as long as you like. Nancy and Mary Ann can help me get supper on."

Fannie watched helplessly as Naomi trudged out of the room. *Why, Lord? Why'd You have to let this happen now?* She swallowed against the burning at the back of her throat. It didn't seem fair for her to be so happy being married to Abraham when his oldest daughter was suffering so.

Fannie had just started mixing biscuit dough when Abraham stepped into the kitchen. At the same time, Mary Ann and Nancy entered the room.

"Would you two girls mind going back upstairs awhile?" Fannie asked. "I need to speak to your daed a few minutes."

The children didn't have to be asked twice. They raced for the stairs, giggling all the way.

Abraham kissed Fannie on the cheek. "You're lookin' awful somber for a new bride."

Fannie slapped him lightly on the arm. "Go on with ya now. We've been married over three months already, so I'm no longer a new bride."

He snickered and chucked her under the chin. "Our love will always be new to me, dear wife."

She set her mixing bowl aside and hugged him tight. "The Lord God was surely smiling on me the day you walked into my life."

"That goes double for me," he murmured.

"Sure wish things would go better for Naomi."

"What's wrong? She went to see Caleb today, didn't she?"

Fannie nodded. "She didn't share with you what happened when you were both outside?"

He shook his head.

"Then I'd best fill you in."

Abraham leaned against the cupboard with his arms folded. "Jah, please do."

Fannie quickly related all Naomi had told her and ended by saying she wished something could be done to get Caleb and Naomi's relationship back on track.

Her husband's bushy brows drew together as he squinted. "I'm goin' over there to have a talk with that boy."

"Now?"

He nodded. "No time like the present."

"But what about supper? I've made your favorite buhnesupp."

He kissed the tip of her nose. "Keep it warm for me, will ya, fraa?"

"Jah, and I'll be prayin' the whole time you're gone."

Naomi pulled another box of books over to the shelf she was stocking. She hadn't slept well last night and could barely function here at the store this morning, so it was good she wasn't waiting on customers. She probably wouldn't be able to think clear enough to make change, much less carry on a pleasant conversation with anyone today. In her gloomy mood, Naomi would more than likely drive customers away.

She tipped her head and listened as her father whistled a merry tune. *Papa's sure actin' peculiar today,* she noted. *Whistling and kissin' on Fannie whenever no one but us three are around.*

Naomi didn't resent her daed and Fannie's happiness, but it sure was a reminder of her own miserable circumstances. It seemed like every time things were beginning to look up, something else went wrong. It was enough to make her give up hoping anything would ever be right again.

After Naomi emptied the first box, she grabbed another. *I know I shouldn't be wallowing in self-pity. At least I'm able to keep workin' at the store and don't have to give up a job I enjoy. Poor Caleb has lost the one thing he likes so much, and now he has nothing to look forward to.* She squeezed her eyes shut in an effort to keep the tears at bay. Giving in to her grief wouldn't change the situation.

"You doin' okay?" Papa asked as he stepped up beside her. "You gonna make it through this day, Daughter?"

She nodded, feeling a sense of comfort knowing her father cared. "It took me some time, but I finally came to grips with losin' Mama and then Zach. So, with God's help, I'll try to accept that Caleb and I can never be together."

Papa patted Naomi's arm. "What God doeth is well done."

She swallowed hard. "You really think so?"

He nodded.

"You believe I'd be better off without Caleb? Is that what you're sayin', Papa?"

Her father opened his mouth, but the bell above the front door tinkled, and he motioned toward the front of the store. "Why don't you go see what that customer wants, Naomi?"

She pointed to the box of books. "I still have these to set out."

"I'll do 'em."

"But, Papa, I—"

"Please. I'm tired of dealin' with customers this morning."

She sighed but nodded. "All right."

Naomi made her way up front, but she halted when she saw Caleb standing near the door. *What's he doing here? I can't deal with seeing him just now.* She started to turn around but was stopped by Papa's deep voice.

Naomi looked up at him and was surprised when she noticed the serious expression on her father's face. Only moments ago, he'd been whistling. "Caleb came by to sign some important papers," Papa said.

She looked back at Caleb, and he nodded. "You got 'em ready for me, Abraham?"

Papa stepped around the counter, reached underneath, and withdrew a manila envelope.

Naomi took a tentative step forward but couldn't find her voice. What kind of important papers would Caleb be coming to the store to sign? It didn't make sense at all.

Papa laid the paperwork on the counter and handed Caleb a pen. "You'll need to put your signature here on this line."

Caleb gripped the pen with his good hand and wrote his name, then he turned to Naomi and smiled. "Naomi Fisher, will you marry me?"

She stood frozen to the spot, feeling like her brain was full of cotton.

Papa cleared his throat real loud. "I believe the young man asked you a question, Naomi."

She tried to speak, but her throat might as well have been glued shut.

Caleb set the pen aside and reached out to take Naomi's hand. "Your daed came over to our place last night and offered to sell me his store. I've decided to take him up on the offer."

Naomi's mouth dropped open. "What?" She looked at Papa. "Why would you want to sell this place when you've worked here so many years?"

Papa glanced into the next room, where Fannie was busy sewing a quilt. "I've never been truly happy running the store," he said. "I took it over when your mamm's folks died and left her the place." He gave his beard a couple of tugs. "Sarah loved this business, and I think she passed that love on to you, Naomi, but I only agreed to work here because I didn't want to see Sarah run the place alone. It's too much for one person to handle." He smiled, and there was a faraway look in his eyes. "To tell ya the truth, I'd much rather be farmin' my land with the boys."

Naomi could hardly believe her ears. In all the years they'd been running the store, she'd never heard Papa admit he would have preferred to be farming.

"And since Caleb needs a job he can do with mostly one hand, I thought he'd be the perfect person to ask about buyin' the store," Papa continued.

Naomi chanced another peek at Caleb and noticed there were tears in his eyes. "You–you're really wantin' this?" she stammered.

He nodded. "More than anything I want to be your husband. If it means sellin' my buggy shop and takin' over here, then so be it." He made a sweeping gesture with his bandaged hand. "I know how much you love this place, and if your daed could run it for twenty-some years because he loved your mamm, I'll find pleasure in doin' the same for you and our future kinner." He smiled and squeezed Naomi's hand. "What's your answer? Will you marry me come November?"

Tears rolled down Naomi's cheeks, and she nodded. "Yes, Caleb. I'll marry you."

Papa cleared his throat again. "What God doeth is well done."

Naomi smiled. She didn't know what the future held for her missing brother, and she had no idea what might lie ahead for her, Caleb, or the general store, but the storekeeper's daughter knew one thing for sure— what God had done, He'd done well.

Center Point Publishing
600 Brooks Road ● PO Box 1
Thorndike ME 04986-0001 USA

(207) 568-3717

US & Canada:
1 800 929-9108